THIS IS A FANTASY...

Thank you for buying this book. For more content and info on new releases, please visit MichaelBreenBooks.com.

EVER THE NIGHT ROAD

For Denise.

THE CITY.

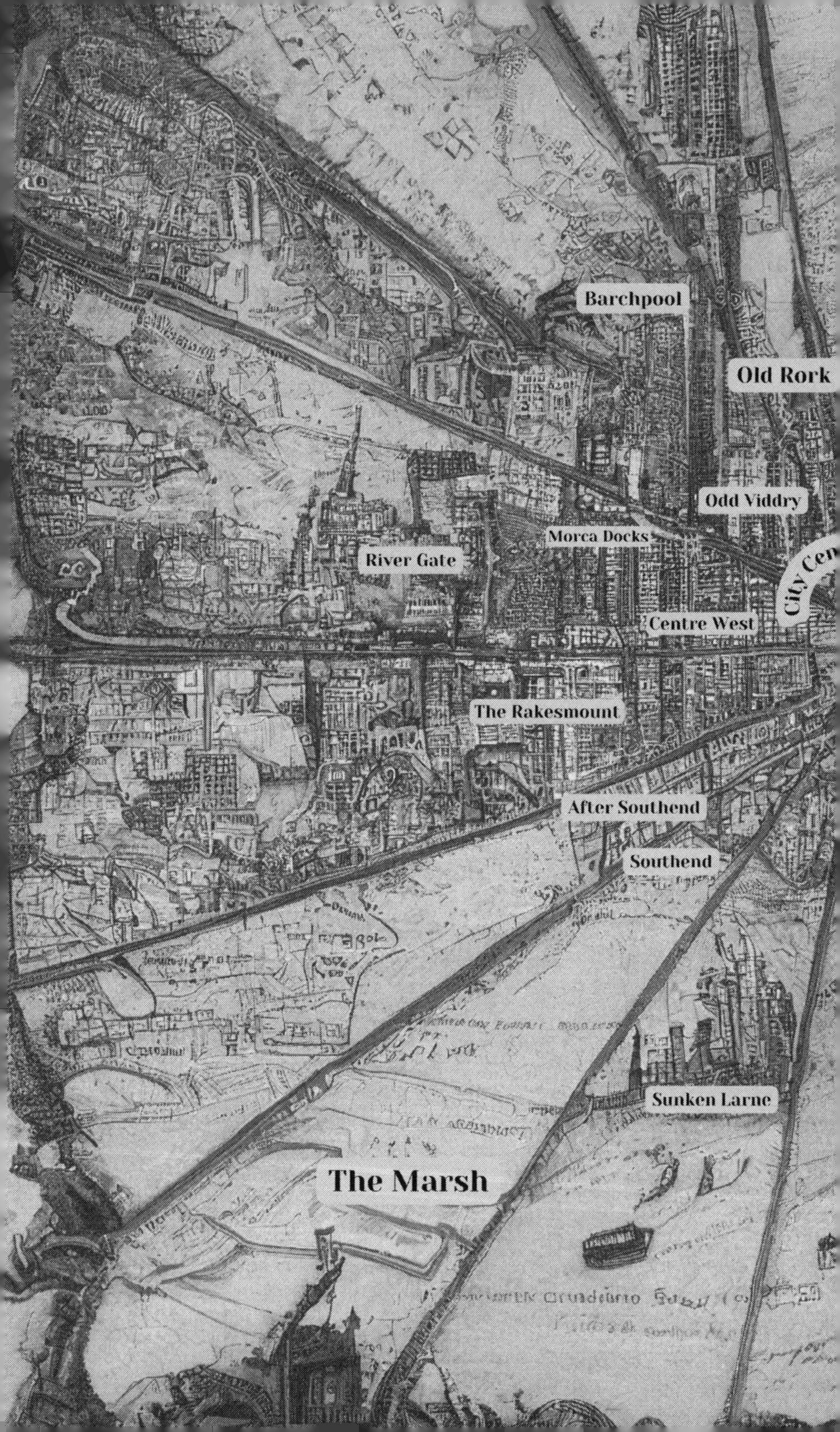
Barchpool
Old Rork
Odd Viddry
Morca Docks
River Gate
City Cen
Centre West
The Rakesmount
After Southend
Southend
Sunken Larne
The Marsh

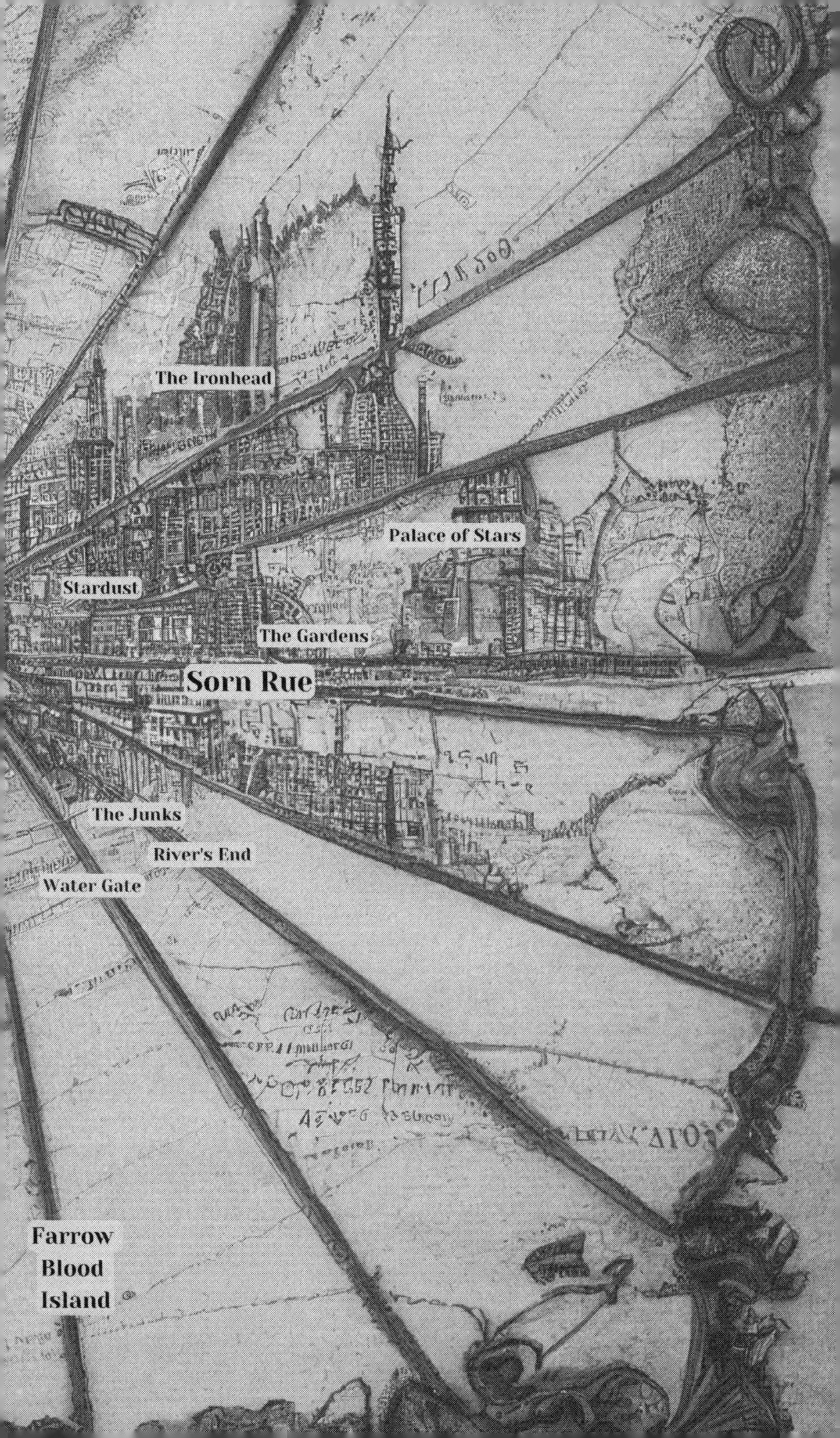

The Ironhead
Palace of Stars
Stardust
The Gardens
Sorn Rue
The Junks
River's End
Water Gate
Farrow
Blood
Island

Part I:

Deadgirl & the Naverung

Cherish the lonely places.

-Borgello; *Letters to Clespin*

Yield to me, Dreams Adventurous!

I am Griff Majestic and I have come for them all!

-Griff Majestic; *One Night at Stardust*

1

DAGNY HAD ONLY ONE thing on her mind as she raced down the stairs: finding a place to hide.

She'd forgotten how dark it was in the basement. Faint light from the garden outside streamed in through dirt-caked windows, but did little to illuminate the steps. So she ran her hand along the stone wall for guidance, trying not to stumble.

It had been years since she was down here last. Passages, crowded with stacks of crates and furniture, branched off in all directions. Dagny stopped only for a moment before deciding on a path. She needed to move away from the stairs, or she'd be seen as soon as someone opened the doors.

The girl knew they would come for her. The Hunters. There seemed to be dozens of them this time. Swarming the gardens above; stomping through the flower beds. She hoped they would search the house first, or the yard out back. She hoped she had fooled them, at least for the moment.

Only hours before, Dagny had sat quietly in the Rork library trying to study the works of dead men. She found it impossible to focus on those things, however, and soon enough her mind began to wander until she just couldn't sit anymore. If she'd been a normal girl, dedicated to her schooling, she'd still be there, secure in the library's reading room. But the afternoon had called, drawing her into the open air. And now...

Dagny ducked underneath a gauntlet of crisscrossing chair legs, and brushed alongside rough wooden boxes, navigating the labyrinth of storage containers. They were marked with cryptic descriptions such as *Mortiers '82* and *The Vahnland - Black Spring*. Likely references made by Alex of prior campaigns, but she couldn't be certain.

The basement really was enormous. Much too big for the house above. Stepping over fallen trinkets and pushing through cobwebs, Dagny finally reached the far wall and scanned the shadows. A thick layer of dust coated everything. No one had been this way for a long time. She was glad of that. It felt comfortable in the darkness, and there were plenty of hiding spots where she could wait for the sun to set. She just needed to find the right one.

Moving onward, Dagny came upon a large painting, turned on its side and leaning against the back wall. It was lit by a single beam of sunlight, specks of dust dancing in the glow. A large accidental tear split the middle, and the paint had begun to fade even before it was placed here, but Dagny could still make out the regal, peaceful lion postured in front of his jungle court. Two monkeys, dressed as knights, flanked the lion king as an assortment of beasts came to pay him tribute. The animals looked comical and self-conscious in their clothes. The armor was too big for the monkeys and the crown hung loose on the lion's head.

Dagny smiled at the king like an old friend. She'd forgotten he was here. Growing up, when Alex would leave for weeks on end, Dagny would stay with his grandfather and she would pass this painting several times a day from its place in the old man's great room. As a little girl, she used to hope the Lion's Court was a real place she could visit someday.

Dagny sat quietly on the floor, in the shadows near the painting, and waited. The sweat that had soaked her orange dress was already beginning to dry. She'd been running hard in the afternoon heat, a mix of nerves and excitement brought on by the hunt. But it was cool down here, among the pale stone, even in the summertime.

It should be easy enough to vanish for a while. The place was practically built for it. Dagny had heard that generations ago, elegant tunnels connected the neighborhood to an underground road leading to City Centre, so that residents could move around in secret. She wondered if this had all been part of those lost tunnels, sealed off a long time ago.

Suddenly, the doors above creaked open, breaking the silence, and a strained voice echoed across the chamber.

"Oh, ghoulie... You're down there, aren't you?"

Dagny tried to slow her breathing and sit perfectly still. Someone must've seen her running toward the basement. They'd be listening now and if they heard her moving about, one of them would block the entrance while the others tried to flush her out. She'd wait and hope to draw the whole group down. And once they started clomping around, bumping into chairs and boxes, she'd be free to move again.

Other voices whispered near the top of the stairs, but she couldn't tell what they were saying. After a moment, a different one called out, "Ghoulie... We're coming for you!"

To stay calm, Dagny focused on the painted lion. *What did I call you back then? I had names for your entire court, didn't I?* She'd even come up with her own stories for the king's animal heroes. Adventure stories, like the ones her brother told.

The coat...

It was down here, too. Wasn't it? Hidden inside a weathered chest with cracked leather straps, but she couldn't remember where. The coat itself she saw clearly. Handsome and long; made of waxed canvas; green and black; well-worn and reinforced at the elbows. In her mind, the collar stood tall to block out the wind, and was lined with soft brushed cloth.

At one time, the coat had been Dagny's most treasured possession. She would sleep in it every night as a child, covering her head to shut out the world. The coat fit well on her brother, Morgan, but hung so loose on Dagny's small frame back then that the hem would drag on the floor like a cape, and she would have to roll the sleeves over several times just to get her hands free.

Her brother wore it on his travels, and she pictured him in it now. Commanding and mysterious. Romantic and roguish. Smiling, with friendly sea-green eyes.

After Alex married Caternya and they moved into the house above, with the pruned garden and quiet cobblestone street, the coat eventually found its way into the chest along with what was left of Morgan's memory, and vanished in the basement.

Something toppled over in the passage to her left. There was a panicked cry, and the quick shuffling of feet.

"She didn't come this way," a young girl said.

"You don't know her like I do. She's tricky. Probably listening to us right now," a boy replied.

Dagny slowly got on her hands and knees and crawled further along the outer wall, away from the voices.

A boat. I'm sure the chest is under an old riverboat, she thought.

"Dag!" a boy cried in frustration. "Are you down here or not?!" The voice was distinct. *Lucas.* Alex and Cate's oldest child was leading this group.

Dagny crawled over a toppled crate and a pile of mold-specked books. A worn copy of Vittendorf's travelogue *All These Places* caught her eye, and she picked it up and stuffed it down her dress.

"*Shh...* I heard something," Lucas said from somewhere nearby. "Over there. Spread out." A dozen little feet answered his order, pattering out in all directions.

There was probably at least an hour until sunset, but Dagny still had every intention of winning the game. She just needed to avoid being caught until dark. It was one she'd played many times growing up, *Hunters and the Hunted.* At seventeen, she could've easily told herself she was too old to be playing such things, but what else was she going to do today? Study? Her schooling would be over in a few short weeks. What did any of it really matter? Besides, if she won the game, then the neighborhood children would crown her Queen Huntress. A title she'd hold until she lost a hunt. And if she was caught, she'd become one of the captured. Dagny wasn't quite sure what that meant these days. She didn't plan on finding out.

Except... her mind was becoming more focused on the coat. What if she couldn't find it? *Could the coat be lost?* The panic came on so sudden and strong it frightened her. Without another thought, Dagny stood up and ran down the passage.

A younger boy screamed with excitement. "It's her! *Get her!*"

It didn't make any sense. Dagny hadn't seen the coat for years. But she knew right then that she'd never forgive herself if it was gone.

Someone tripped over the books behind her, tumbled, and started to cry.

"He'll be fine! Keep going!" Another one shouted.

A dart board, covered in webs, came into view. It looked familiar. She'd come this way before, a long, long time ago. Her pace quickened. She was close.

Dagny cut down a passage of high shelves that stretched almost to the ceiling. Children ran on the other side of it, peeking at her through the narrow spaces between boxes. They called to her, but she didn't answer. Then she saw it. Against the far wall was the chest, tucked underneath a small river skiff that hung from two heavy chains in the ceiling.

She ran forward, ignoring the children approaching from multiple directions, and lifted the lid.

Lucas was the first one to reach her. He stopped several feet away and stared wide-eyed.

"Wow, where'd you get that?" he asked. He was dressed like a dapper little prince, but his face was dirty with dried sweat.

"Do you like it?" Dagny asked, pulling her arm through the coat sleeve. "It was my brother's. He used to wear it on his adventures with your father."

Lucas nodded his head excitedly. "You look like a pirate king."

Dagny reached down and ruffled his hair. "I know you never met my brother, but he would have loved you."

The other children had caught up to them now. Behind Lucas was his younger sister, Abrielle. She wore an expensively tailored blue and yellow skirt, and her honey-brown hair was braided with ribbons. Half a dozen other children from Old Rork approached cautiously from both sides.

"You lost!" A scrawny, blond-haired boy yelled.

"Did I?" With a flourish, Dagny spun around and leapt onto a nearby shelf, scrambling over the top before any of the children could react.

"Hey! That's not fair!" one of them screeched.

"—Get her!" cried a girl.

"—We caught you! You lost!"

"No one touched me," Dagny shouted back. She dropped onto the floor and sprinted to the basement stairs. There was a murmur behind her.

"Is that true?"

"—No one got her?"

Dagny leapt up the stairs, slammed the basement doors and ran into the sun. She skirted around the large, white-plastered house and past two small children sitting in the mud by the garden pond. They pointed at her, mouths wide open. Dagny was laughing hysterically by the time she entered through the kitchen door.

She had lived with Alex Benzara since she was a little girl. The better part of eight years. In the beginning, it had been just the two of them, but now the house was full and would be getting even more crowded in a few short months. The thought made her anxious, and Dagny pushed it out of her mind.

The door slammed closed behind her. Caternya stood by the stove, tasting soup from a large kettle, and shot her a quick glance, while the Benzara's cook furiously chopped onions and carrots nearby.

Alex's wife was one of the most beautiful women Dagny had ever seen. Slim with dark eyes. She took to wearing tailored skirts and stylish jackets, even around the house. Even now, pregnant with their third child. Alex had met Cate shortly after discovering the Prize at Oulen, a sunken treasure ship that rested in the shallow delta of that river.

Caternya looked like she was descended from the same aristocratic folk who would've owned the drowned ship. Dagny was wild-haired and weedy, pale with an overbite.

"That's a nice coat," Cate said casually, barely looking up at her.

"Thanks," Dagny replied, sucking down air. "I hadn't worn it for a long time, I'm surprised it fits like this—"

"Lucas! Abrielle!" Cate called out from the open kitchen window. "Where are they? Weren't they with you?"

"Yes. Don't worry. *They're coming,*" Dagny said dramatically.

Cate focused on the simmering pot. "Please tell them that dinner will be ready soon, and make sure they're clean."

"Sure," Dagny said. But instead of walking back outside to deliver the message, she stepped through the kitchen, into the adjacent hallway, and tiptoed toward the study.

Alex sat at his desk smoking a pipe, as Dagny slipped in and ducked behind the doorway.

"Hiding from the children?" he joked.

"Kind of."

"I thought you were studying at the library."

"No."

Alex smiled and gestured at her. "Well, look at that, Morgan's old coat."

Dagny smiled back. She enjoyed being around Alex, even if they didn't talk much anymore. He was always busy, it seemed, and although still a relatively young man, Alex appeared more haggard these days. Especially when sitting at a desk.

"That coat suits you now," Alex continued. "What made you look for it?"

Dagny shrugged. "I'm not sure. We were playing down in the basement, and I just remembered it. I don't know why."

"Sometimes things just happen like that. It's strange how the mind works." Alex glanced down at an open ledger.

Dagny heard the kitchen door open and Caternya shout something. Lucas came thundering down the hallway and burst into the study. He exchanged glances with Alex before turning around and spotting Dagny against the wall.

"There you are! You're caught!" he said, a look of smug satisfaction on his face.

"Really Lucas? You're gonna turn me over to the hunters?" Dagny asked him, smiling sweetly.

The boy hesitated. "It's just a game."

"But still, don't you want me to be the Queen Huntress?"

"Hmm, let me think about it." Lucas plopped down in a heavy, cushioned seat.

"You can be my champion."

"Okay."

"Ha. There's some negotiating for you," Alex said, still looking through his papers.

"So, what kind of adventures did they have?" Lucas asked her.

"Who?"

"Dad and your brother. You said they had adventures together."

"Oh... right... all kinds. When I was your age, Morgan would come home and tell us all about the latest one. Sometimes we'd stay up until the sun rose. He would wear this very coat and act out the stories for us."

"Like what? Tell me."

Dagny thought about it for a moment. There were so many stories, hundreds of them. She'd probably forgotten more than she remembered. "Well, let me think."

Lucas just looked at her with his wide, innocent eyes.

"Okay. I'll tell you one of my favorites." She leaned closer to him and lowered her voice. "This one time, they were sailing across the Ilvar..."

Lucas had a confused look on his face. "What's that?"

"The Ilvar is a sea far to the west. They had gone there chasing rumors of Avilys, a fabled glass castle that only appeared once every hundred years. Everyone doubted it existed. The ship's crew had taken the same route many times before, and swore there was nothing. Only on this particular day, as the sun began to set, they came upon an island covered in mist, and as they sailed closer, the mist began to clear... there on the cliffs was the great castle of glass..."

"Is that true?" Lucas asked his father.

"It's true, alright. But I like the way Dag here tells it." As soon as Lucas looked away, Alex gave her a wink.

Abrielle had snuck into the study while they talked and sat on a chair in the corner. She wore only one shoe and kicked her bare foot, now covered in mud, while grinning at Dagny. Abrielle was clearly baiting her to ask about the missing shoe, and when Dagny didn't take the bait, the girl started humming loudly.

Lucas glared at his sister. "Can you be quiet, please? I'd like to hear the story, thank you very much."

Abrielle snarled, but stopped humming.

"Good. Please proceed," Lucas said, acting very formal and dignified.

Before Dagny could continue, however, Caternya came into the room, sighing heavily. "No one thought to invite me to the gathering?"

"Sorry, it wasn't planned," Lucas said.

"Go on and clean yourself up, please."

"But mother, Dagny is telling me about the glass castle," Lucas said.

"I'm sure it will still be there when you get back."

Lucas pouted and stepped off into the nearby hallway.

"Thank you, dear," she called after him, dropping into Lucas' seat. "I'm absolutely exhausted. I really wish I wasn't the only one who had to chase the children around and make sure everything is in order."

"I'm almost finished here," Alex said, motioning to the stacks on his desk.

"It sounded like you were very busy," Cate said.

"Sorry, it's my fault," Dagny said. "We were playing in the basement and—"

"Abrielle! Where is your shoe?! You're absolutely filthy." Caternya sprung up with renewed energy, lifted the girl and carried her into the hall. Abrielle squealed and flailed her limbs the whole way out. "This is too much, really! I can't handle everything," Cate continued, her voice trailing off down the hallway. Alex chased after them, leaving Dagny alone in the study.

She didn't feel like eating dinner tonight. Instead, Dagny climbed the main staircase leading to her bedroom, thinking about Morgan's story of Avilys. She remembered huddling with her younger sister, Gretchen, in their old tenement building, as Morgan recounted the castle and his escape from the black-eyed princess of glass.

Dagny's bedroom here at the Benzara house was massive and elegantly furnished. A large feather-stuffed bed with embroidered silk sheets rested in the middle of the room, and a glass-paned door opened onto a balcony, which overlooked a private courtyard. Far beyond the peaked rooftops of Old Rork, Dagny could see the spires and domes of the City Centre.

She walked over to a gilded mirror in the corner and admired herself in Morgan's old adventuring coat. *I do look like a pirate king*, she thought. Much better than the delicate dresses and skirts that filled her closet. She felt like an imposter wearing those. A misfit in fine clothes. Perfumed with dirty fingernails. She was from the Rakesmount Tenements. And in some ways, it seemed like she never truly left.

Eight years had passed since she lived there, before running off forever. The building that she was born into was narrow and wild, crowded with an assortment of cousins and half-siblings. Their mother, distant and cold, was like a ghost in her memory, and the man who ran the tenement, the one they called Uncle Finkel, was an ogre.

If there was one thing that stood out in Dagny's mind about the Rakesmount, it was the wetness of the place. The moisture, mud and rot crept into everything. When she came to live with Alex across the river, it seemed as if the perpetual rains of her early childhood just stopped. The streets on this side were paved and clean, the gardens well-kept, the brass and iron gates polished. She knew there was much to be grateful for. Alex and Cate had provided her with everything she needed, really. The best tutors and wonderful meals. She had shared events and celebrations with plenty of other children. Yet somehow, she always felt alone.

Standing in front of the mirror, Dagny caught herself biting her fingernails. It was a habit she was keenly aware of and had tried to break, but when she became distracted, it was instinctive and there was no helping it. When Dagny was a little girl, she'd always be playing in the garden or climbing up trees, and her nails were always dirty. Caternya would be absolutely horrified whenever she caught Dagny chewing on them. Dagny would act ashamed, but inside she'd find Cate's reaction hilarious. It would take all the willpower she had not to burst out laughing. For the longest time, she'd chew them right in front of Cate just to see her expression. After all, Alex didn't care what she did, and certainly no one cared when she lived at the Rakesmount.

Thoughts of Morgan entered her mind again. Dagny tried to picture his face, but it was too hazy, like trying to see through fog. So she imagined how his body felt when he hugged her, and his dyed-blue hair. Stuck with sweat to his face when he became sick.

Dagny stepped onto her balcony and took in the evening air. She could hear people laughing from the street beyond. A drum and tin whistle cut through the wind as musicians started playing from a nearby plaza. After some time had passed, she reached for the trellis that stretched from the garden all the way to the roof and climbed up it, like she had done so many times before. The neighborhood children had all returned to their homes, forgetting about the game of *Hunters and the Hunted*, and allowing the garden to drift into the relaxed solitude of the moonlit night. Down below, Dagny could see the vague outline of the road from a streetlamp as she carefully moved across the pitched roof. The height didn't bother her; she found it exhilarating and knew no one else would dare climb up. Maybe that's why she liked it so much.

Dagny lay down on a flat part of roof near the chimney and gazed up at the stars. High above shone the brightest one this time of year: the Herald's Star. It was the adventurers' compass, Morgan had told her, and it would always guide him home should he become lost. She fell asleep there, under the night sky. Wearing her brother's coat.

2

Maris. Dashing and charming Maris Troipel. He lounged in a heavy armchair in the middle of the study. Over the years, Dagny had heard the man tell people he was a veteran from the Vahnland, a master-dancer, a Prince of Oulen. He could tell you one of a hundred different stories any given night. Who knew if any were true. He had a swashbuckler's swagger.

When Dagny woke this morning, Maris and Alex had already been talking for hours. Maris only came by when he had something interesting to discuss. So Dagny poured herself a cup of tea, sat quietly on the study's plush rug, and listened to the two men.

"There's no question it's unique," Alex said, as he inspected an odd heap of metal, the size of a man's fist. The thing appeared to be made of iron, layered upon itself, and fastened with small hinges and tiny latches.

"It's a Star Prism," Maris said, matter-of-factly. "And it's *very* old. There's no doubt in my mind." Maris was handsome with sleepy but cunning grey eyes. If Dagny did not already know him, she would not have trusted the man.

"Look, see this here?" Maris continued, taking the metal object from Alex. "If you open the bottom latches, the piece unfolds." Carefully, Maris started to pry the thing apart. For a moment, Dagny thought it might break; the Prism looked rusted and worn, but Maris worked it with delicate fingers and opened it without issue. "If light hits it, reflective glass inside will show you the stars."

He walked over to the window and held the object in the sunlight. Instantly, colored spots spread over everything in the room. The walls, the couch and floor, Alex's desk... everything was cast in various shades of blue and green, red and gold. It was like the study had a sudden outbreak of rainbow pox.

Alex leaned back in his chair and glanced around. "I don't know how you can make sense of this. I can't tell what these are."

Maris left the prism by the window and walked over to the opposite wall, pointing out a cluster of spots. It was like he'd been anticipating Alex's skepticism. "This is the constellation Endahl, the Great Bull."

"No. I don't think so," Alex said, rising. "The Endahl has three horns. Your cluster here has four."

"That's how I know it's *old*. This is the Endahl, *before* it was corrupted."

Maris hurried over to another section of the wall before Alex could respond. "And these are the Twin Firehunters. They haven't been seen in the sky for a long, long time."

Alex studied the shapes more closely. After a moment, he spoke. "It's interesting, I'll give you that."

"I thought you'd be more excited," Maris said with a laugh.

"I just want to know if it's worth getting excited about first," Alex replied. "What do *you* think its purpose is?"

"...I don't know yet," Maris admitted, laughing harder than before. "There are myths about paths in the sky. Connecting us to ancient places. I never fully understood what those stories were getting at. Whether they were symbolic or literal... I don't think anyone really does. Maybe it has something to do with that."

Alex walked over to the Prism. "Whoever made this put a lot of time into it. Where'd you say you found it again?"

Maris had been traveling the Shallow Sea for several months. He told Alex that he saved a sailor's life, and the man had given it to him as thanks. Dagny wasn't sure if Alex fully believed his story.

Her mind began to drift as the two men talked. It was the end of summer, and although the days were still mostly dry and hot, on this particular morning a breeze blew through the house and brought with it a touch of autumn, hinting at changes to come.

She thought of those first years with Alex. When adventurers of all types would come by the Benzara house. Strongmen and rogues. Caped figures with slouch hats and long pipes. Dignitaries, merchants, and storytellers. Soldiers who smelled of sweet liquor and gunpowder. She remembered a hunched old woman, with marbled eyes like those sheep dogs in the hills beyond the city, who read Dagny her fortune and predicted that she would have a short life, dying alone in an empty room. Dagny ran away and cried, and Alex came to her and said the woman was just a miserable old thing who liked to scare children. He promised Dagny that she would have a fulfilling life, full of happiness and excitement. She took it to mean that Alex would soon be taking her along on future journeys, but it never happened.

Lucas entered the study and sat next to Dagny without making a sound. She didn't notice him until he began to tug at her dress. The boy held a wooden checkered board, folded in half and secured by metal clasps. He looked up at her hopefully. Dagny couldn't help but smile at his expectant, innocent face.

"Can we play?" he asked.

"Okay," she mouthed silently. It was almost impossible to turn him down sometimes. She hated the idea of making him sad.

Dagny's tutors had finished with her a few weeks ago, and she wondered what her life would be like now. She spent every day playing games with the children or wandering into the City Centre, and every day Cate would ask if she had any plans or if she'd been invited to anything. But Dagny didn't have any interest in attending Rork social events and didn't know what else to do with herself. For now, she'd spend her time with the sweet boy who still watched her with fascination.

They set the Talvarind board on the soft rug. Dagny lay down with her head propped up, while Lucas sat cross-legged on the opposite side. Lucas played a set of Night Princes, elegantly carved figurines representing the rulers and constellations of the night sky. She found it fitting, surrounded by Maris' star pox. Lucas had also brought down Dagny's pieces. The Wild Court. It was one of the original sets and had belonged to her brother. But while Lucas' set was professionally made by a local artisan, Morgan had carved the animal figures himself. The only exceptions were several pieces that Dagny tried to sculpt, but they were still just ugly blocks. When she had found Morgan's Wild Court, it was incomplete. The great bear guardian was missing.

Lucas had just begun to take an interest in the game, and like everything else that drew his attention, he tackled it with the obsessed passion of a seven-year-old. Dagny thought she was a pretty good player. At least with the Wild Court. There were so many advanced theories and strategies of the game, and with all the different sets, each one having its own subtle advantages and slight tweaks in the moves its pieces could play or exploit, it was almost impossible to master. She didn't mind spending her time showing Lucas the basics. She was glad he wanted to be around her so badly.

Alex collected Talvarind pieces from all over and kept them displayed in an ancient curio cabinet set against the study wall. Dagny could see it from her place on the rug. Its shelves were filled with delicately crafted, finely painted figures of animals, heroes and kings, and creatures of myth. There was a rearing lioness with its claws raised to attack; a slim, robed guardian clutching his sword close to the chest; a wispy queen of the shadow woods; giant owls; a child holding a crescent moon over her head. Each one standing roughly four inches tall. As Lucas adjusted his opening position, Dagny glanced around the room at the bookshelves reaching to the ceiling, at trophies and artifacts, maps and paintings decorating the space. She felt a sense of comfort and calm, breathing in the scent of aged wood and old books, and relaxed into the warmth of the sun as it spread over her and across the floor.

Dagny started a simple advance, moving her twin foxes closest to the river that cut down the middle of the board, separating the two sides. Lucas carefully considered her opening and played the standard defensive line she had taught him the day before, bringing his chariot over to reinforce his magi.

The men continued to talk, as Dagny and Lucas exchanged moves. She half listened as Maris joked and recounted an adventure they had on the island of Caltra across the lagoon. Alex changed the subject back to the Star Prism and asked what Maris planned to do next. It was the mention of Magu Ogden that grabbed Dagny's complete and undivided attention.

"...That's what I figured," Alex said. "He's probably one of the few who could point you in the right direction. It's beyond me, but it's certainly worth discussing with him."

"*Ah,* Magu Ogden... did you ever read his book on the floating city?" Maris asked. "You should hear him go on about that one."

"Read it? I traveled with him, *searching* for it. But I'm convinced that place sank into the sea before any of us were born."

It was Dagny's move, and Lucas stared at her from across the board with growing impatience.

"He's some character," Maris said. "I haven't been by his shop since, well, I can't even recall. He's still set up over in River's End, right?"

"*Dag,*" the boy whispered.

"I believe so. It's been years since I've been as well. I was meaning to stop by but haven't gotten around to it. Was going to drop off the compass from the old boat."

"Not the *Courteous Fiend*?" Maris asked. "Tell me you aren't getting rid of it."

"No. Just finishing some repairs I've been neglecting. Ogden gave me that compass a while ago. Thought I'd return it. Let him know I was still thinking about him, and it would give me a chance to make sure he was doing alright out there in the Junks. But time's gotten away from me."

"Dag! It's your move," Lucas blurted out.

The two men looked over and laughed.

"I think you stumped her, boy," Maris said.

"No. She's not paying attention," Lucas said. "She's listening to you all."

"I'm paying attention," Dagny lied. "Trying to figure something out. Okay... here we go." She made a triple advance with her Meerkat Advisor, placing it across the river on Lucas' right flank. The boy focused intently on the board, confused as to what he should do next.

Maris came over and studied the positions. "Watch your Wizard," he said.

"I can do it," Lucas said sharply, without breaking his gaze.

Maris raised his hands up defensively and chuckled to himself. "I suppose I'd better be off," he said to Alex. "I'm not going to be able to rest until I solve this mystery."

"Good luck, friend. I hope Ogden can set your mind at ease," Alex said, as he started to walk Maris out of the study.

"Wait!" Dagny called. She surprised herself with the urgency of her voice. "Are you going to Magu Ogden's now?"

"—I *told you* she wasn't paying attention," Lucas said.

"Can I come?" Dagny asked. "I mean, if it'd be alright?"

"Well..." Maris began, glancing at Alex, who shrugged. "I was planning to head there now, and it looks like you've got quite the match going."

Dagny turned to Lucas. "Do you mind if we finish this up later? I'll take you down to City Centre tomorrow and you can pick out a new Night Prince for your set."

Lucas glared at her. "Fine."

"Thank you." She leaned over and kissed Lucas on the head. "Ready?" Dagny asked Maris, trying to smooth the wrinkles out of her dress.

Maris gestured at her bare feet. "Are you?"

"Oh. Right. Just a second." Dagny ran into the hallway and pulled on a pair of worn brown boots while the men talked at the entrance. She couldn't hear what they were saying, but when Maris started to shake his head, Alex laughed and patted him on the back.

Dagny walked just behind Maris as they made their way down Rork's main boulevard and toward the Central Bridge. Her neighborhood was one of the oldest parts of the city, where some of the most affluent residents lived. Ages ago, the scholar towers stood here, but most had toppled at some point in the distant past and were replaced by the grand buildings that lined the road now. A single tower remained, crooked with sand-colored brick, teetering out over a canal that eventually found its way to the lagoon. It looked like the tower could fall at any moment and sink into the water, but it had been that way for years.

The broad cobblestone street was busy today. Neighbors talked under the canopy of great oaks that lined the road, and children ran between the side streets and alleys that split the tall, regal homes. When they reached the plaza that marked the end of Rork, Maris turned and spoke to her for the first time since leaving the house.

"You can walk next to me, you know. You don't have to be weird, hiding in the back."

"Okay," Dagny muttered. She had wanted to tell him that *he* was the one being awkward. Marching in silence; ignoring her until now. Maybe Maris had something on his mind. Thoughts of the Prism, most likely. Still, she only wanted to tag along to Magu Ogden's place. He didn't have to act like she was such a burden.

"So, do you keep yourself busy back there?" Maris asked half-heartedly.

"No, not really. It can be pretty boring."

Maris nodded along, watching the road. "Sure. I can see that. Everyone in Rork probably sits around all day gossiping, concerning themselves with the latest fashion or who's taking so-and-so to the winter's ball. It sounds miserable to me."

"Yeah." When she first came to Rork, Dagny found herself feeling like an outcast among the children of wealthy, prominent families. Her friends, she told herself, were the adventurers who came around to see Alex. To trade stories, or pick his brain, or prepare themselves for the next expedition. Most were nice enough, but of course, they were never there to see her.

"I didn't get along too well, either," Maris said. "Sitting still doesn't suit me, and sooner or later I think I rub everyone the wrong way."

Dagny didn't respond. She was surprised by his sudden vulnerability.

"I don't know why Alex is so uninterested in everything these days," Maris continued. "He wasn't always like that, you know. He used to be the first one out the door the second opportunity presented itself. Things change, I suppose." Maris gently pulled her off the road as a large carriage rolled past. "So, what are you now? Fifteen?"

"Seventeen. My birthday was last winter." She had celebrated it in a grand hall near the center of Rork. Most of the families Alex and Cate knew were there. The hall was so crowded, with musicians and dancing, and the banquet felt like it was planned for a princess. It had been one of the strangest events Dagny'd ever been a part of.

Maris eyed her skeptically. "Seventeen, huh? You sure?"

"Of course I'm sure. What's that supposed to mean?" she asked, a bit perturbed.

"Eh. You just look younger. Don't get offended. I can't tell how old people are anymore. All you children kind of blend together. Anyway, aren't you tired of hanging around the Benzara estate yet? I left home when I was thirteen. Set sail the very next day. Didn't look back."

"No, I'm fine with it. Besides, I left home when I was nine. So I have you beat there," Dagny said.

"You mean when Alex took you in? That doesn't count. Isn't there anything you want to be doing with your life?"

Dagny slouched and stared at the road in front of her as they walked. "I don't know. Haven't really thought about it too much." That was a bit of a lie, though. The truth was more complicated. She couldn't figure out what she wanted, although Dagny was desperate for *something.* She used to think that she wanted to travel the world like Alex had... and her brother. Exploring drowned cities and the Land of Dead Kings, and seeing the Stilted Men of Ostrotha. But she'd been dismissed so many times before that she'd stopped talking to Alex about it a long time ago.

As if he was reading her mind, Maris said, "You realize Alex was only looking out for you, right? I mean, the circumstances there were awful. He wanted to keep you safe and do right by your brother. He had to honor that. But *you* didn't promise anything. You know what I'm trying to say?"

Dagny watched the ground.

"If there's something you really want, do yourself a favor and get at it," he said.

The pair approached the Central Bridge spanning over the river Morca. There were fourteen bridges that crossed the river, but the Central Bridge was the longest and most grand. Dagny hesitated, ever so slightly, before stepping onto it. Like the Talvarind board, this river divided the city in two, separating her world from that other time. Far south, where the city began to taper off into the marshland, was the

Rakesmount. But they would be following the river east, toward the lagoon, and River's End.

"Have you ever been to Ogden's place before?" asked Maris.

"A few times, with Alex, but it's been a while," she said.

"Been awhile for me, too. He's an odd one. It used to be that everyone would make it a ritual to stop by Ogden's. Especially the ones who came up with me and Alex. That was the place, and he seemed to know everything. Different time though. He's old now. Hell, he was old back then."

The Junks at River's End was a crowded shanty town of mismatched tin sheds, wood shacks, and busted concrete dwellings. Yet it was colorful. Brilliantly painted roofs and doors, and flowery overgrown gardens littered the district. Ogden's shop faced the water. It was an urban treehouse, a rickety metal stack fastened together with rivets. A large sheet of burnt copper covered the doorway, and it shimmered in waves when Maris pushed it aside.

Inside was altogether different. Dense with trinkets and oddities acquired over a lifetime, maybe several. Dust blanketed glass shapes and golden frames that were stuck in far corners. Hanging over the entrance was a large stuffed serpent; its fangs exposed, a malevolent hungry glare in its eye. The first time Dagny had been here, the shock of the giant snake froze her with fear. Even after she realized it was no longer alive, Magu Ogden told her to watch out, that its poison still dripped and would sizzle a hole through her skull. It probably wasn't the best environment for Alex to bring a ten-year-old, but, after that, the place fascinated Dagny to no end. And while Alex spent afternoons in Ogden's observatory up top, Dagny would comb through the various relics, her mind hitched to a greater world.

Magu Ogden stood across the room, rearranging items on a shelf, when they entered. Although bent and bald, his body was hefty and powerful, shaped by shadows from lamps overhead. Maris approached the man with his arms open, as if greeting an old friend.

Dagny began to follow when a pair of black studded bracelets hanging from a nearby hook grabbed her attention. She ran her finger over their metal clasps, wondering what they had been used for and heard Maris mutter several words to Ogden. Then the two men wandered up a circular staircase near the back of the room and disappeared, leaving Dagny alone in the shop.

She roamed the aisles of the ground floor for a time, making a mental inventory of the random treasures she might want to purchase, all while thumbing a fold of treasury notes in her pocket. Dagny identified a glass globe with a miniature bronze palace inside; an illustrated map of the nearby islands; patchwork charm dolls; a jade mask with a gold tongue and a handwritten note saying it belonged to *Gwern, Speaker of Fish*.

What about books, though? Where were all of Ogden's books? Dagny vaguely recalled a small room overflowing with them, a hidden library somewhere up above. She walked to the staircase and was halfway to the second floor when she heard voices. Not the voices of Maris or the old man, but younger ones. Brash and animated.

Dagny reached the landing, stepped through a beaded curtain and entered a glass-walled room with a clean view of the river. Three boys sat on and around a worn-out leather couch. They stopped talking and stared at her.

"Help you with something?" asked a dark-haired boy. He lounged in the center of the couch, arms crossed. A long cord of hair, half-braided like the end of a frayed rope, hung over his face.

"No. Looking around is all," Dagny said, trying to be polite.

"Alright... well, we're pretty busy here," he said.

"—Yeah, we're discussing important things!" the youngest one shouted, likely louder than he intended. He was small and wearing a faded yellow vest.

"Oh. Okay," Dagny said. "I was trying to find the library."

"See any books here?" the youngest one asked.

"No."

"Okay then."

"Wow. That's rude," she said, startled by the confrontation.

"He didn't mean anything by it," the black-haired boy said. "But you did just barge in."

"I did not just barge in."

"You didn't?" he asked. "What would you call it, then?"

Dagny thought for a moment. "Exploring."

He nodded. "Got it."

Dagny could have left. Part of her wanted to. The room was uncomfortably hot and stale, but there was something interesting here she couldn't quite place. The three boys had formed the space into a makeshift study, surrounded by broken furniture and random junk. By the look of it, the room was just a spot for Ogden to store rubbish rather than tossing it out.

"I don't know of any library here," the black-haired boy continued. He pushed the braid away from his face and spoke quickly. "Maybe there's one on the upper levels, but Ogden doesn't let anyone go there, so don't get your hopes up."

"That's disappointing," Dagny said.

"Right. So..." All three boys watched her, a look of impatience on each of their faces. Dagny glanced down at a small table by the couch, on which a map was placed. It seemed to depict the lagoon and nearby islands.

"What are you all doing in here?" she asked, her shyness starting to fade away.

"Ha! Wouldn't you like to know?" the youngest one said. "It's secret stuff."

Dagny shrugged. "Fine then. Don't let me stop you." She tried to give the appearance of calm, but the whole interaction was upsetting. They clearly wanted her to leave, but she had just as much right to be here, maybe even more so. She was friends with Maris and Alex. These three were just boys, and rude ones at that. So instead of leaving, Dagny walked casually to the window and looked out over the water. In the distance, she could barely make out the Central Bridge that she crossed more than an hour ago.

"Forget it," one of them muttered.

Dagny turned from the window and caught the dark-haired boy studying her.

"What?" she asked him, somewhat sharply.

But it was the third boy who spoke. He was broad-shouldered and dressed in black, and there was an intensity to his voice. "Why are you even here? This is a private place. Did Ogden let you up? You can't just wander in off the street, you know."

"I didn't just wander in, okay? I've been coming here for years," Dagny said.

"I've never seen you."

"So?" she responded.

"What's your name?" the dark-haired boy asked.

"Why?"

"I'm just trying to be nice."

"Really?" she asked, eyeing him suspiciously.

"Yeah."

"It's Dag. Dagny Losh."

"Alright Dag. I'm Max, the youngster is Kimberly, and that's Rodolph," he said, pointing to the boy with broad shoulders. Max and Rodolph looked to be about her age. Kimberly was considerably younger. "Nice to meet you, okay?"

Dagny laughed. "Yeah, real nice."

"—Now you can leave," Kimberly said.

"Alright, don't be mean," Max said to him.

"Me?" Kimberly said. "Max! We can't just let *strangers* in here."

"I'm not a *stranger.* Just because *you* don't know me," Dagny said. "I'm allowed to be here, too."

Rodolph shook his head. "This is really important, girl. A life is at stake. Can you just go already?"

"A life, huh? Really?" Dagny looked at each of them, trying to figure out if this was a lie.

"Yeah," Max said, softly. He had an honest face.

"Oh. Well, I didn't know that." Dagny felt embarrassed now. "You coulda just told me that from the start... Whose life is it?"

"Sorry girl," Rodolph said. "It's a secret."

"That's fine. Don't worry about it. I'll leave." Dagny forced a smile and walked back through the curtains. At the same time, Maris came down from above, and caught her on the landing.

"I'm going to be a while longer," Maris said. "Ogden's searching for a book on primordial astrology. Your face is flush, you doing alright?"

"Yes, just making friends," she said sarcastically, motioning to the curtain behind her.

Maris opened the curtain and peered in. "You boys behave yourself here. This one is a good friend of mine, got it?" Then he walked back up the stairs and out of sight.

Dagny heard the boys murmuring from the room behind her as she went down to the first floor. She tried to put the encounter out of her mind and wandered for a bit. She found a ragged black shawl that looked like it could've belonged to an ancient witch, and tried on several brass crowns of various sizes. *This is a look*, Dagny thought, while gazing at herself in a tarnished mirror. She imagined that she was a dead queen, reincarnated, from one of the drowned cities. A dead queen like Tilda or Ilsadun, who had ruled from gilded palaces, but drowned all the same as the Rakesmount poor. Just then, something nudged against her leg and softly purred.

"Oh, hello there," Dagny said, reaching down to scratch the snow-white cat with green eyes. "You're a handsome one, aren't you?"

Dagny heard footsteps coming down the stairs and turned to see Max, the dark braid tucked behind his ear. He stopped when he spotted her and smiled. "I see you found Twixel."

"Twixel, huh?" Dagny said, "Hello, Mister Twixel."

"That one is quite the evil genius," Max said.

"No," Dagny said. "Not evil." She continued petting the cat, then glanced at Max. "Did you want something?"

"Didn't wanna kick you out back there, but there wasn't much of an option."

"It's fine."

"Anyway, we were wondering... was that Maris Troipel you were with?"

"Yes."

"No kidding." Max cocked his head. "Who *are* you?"

"I told you. My name is Dagny Losh. There's nothing else. Maris is more of an acquaintance. He's really friends with Alex."

"Alex?"

"Yes. Alexander Benzara. We're family, sorta."

Max raised an eyebrow. "Alexander Benzara? You're related?"

"Do you know him?"

"I know *of* him. We all do... I mean, of course we do. He's famous. He should have a statue here. Nice outfit, by the way, reminds me of a witch-queen. Looks good."

Dagny shrugged her shoulders. "Thanks. So now you're talking to me 'cause I know Maris and Alex, huh?"

"Well, *yeah.*" Max continued to look at her for a moment. "We didn't mean any harm earlier. It really is important."

"What's going on?" she asked.

"It's kinda hard to explain. You wanna come back up?"

3

"So, what's your background?" Rodolph asked, as Dagny sat cross-legged on the floor.

"My background?" She didn't know how to respond to that.

"Yeah. If we're gonna let you in on our plans, we gotta know something about you."

"Okay. Well, umm, I live in Old Rork..."

"Old Rork? Ugh!" Kimberly said, dramatically. "Those people all think they're better than everyone else."

"No they don't," Dagny responded. "There's lots of nice people there. And anyway, I'm not like that. I was born in the Rakesmount."

"The slum?" Rodolph blurted out. "Sorry. I mean, how long did you live there?"

"Til I was about ten."

"Didn't the Morca flood that place a while back?" Max asked.

"Yes," she said.

"Oh right. I heard about that," Rodolph said. "That river is a monster. Good thing you made it out. I heard a lot of people didn't."

"Yeah. My family got washed away," Dagny said. It felt strange, hearing herself say it.

"You mean they died?" Kimberly asked, wide-eyed.

"Yes."

"That's awful."

An awkward silence overtook the boys. "Anyway... that's me," Dagny said. She could feel the mood of the room change into something heavy. "Someone can talk. It's okay. Really."

"What are you doing with Maris?" Max asked, after a moment.

"I'm just following along. I used to come here when I was younger, but it's been years. I remember it being a lot more crowded."

"It's slowed down a lot," Max said. "Almost no one comes here anymore."

"That's weird," she said.

"I guess. That's why we were so surprised to see you." All three boys were watching her.

Dagny gestured at the table. "So what are you planning?" she asked. "Something to do with that map there? Are you adventurers?"

"Something like that," Max said.

"My brother, Morgan, he was an adventurer of sorts. He went all over with Alex."

"—Alex... that's Alex Benzara," Max said to the others.

"Did your brother get lost in the flood, too?" Kim asked. The young boy was trying to be gentle. It was sweet.

"No. He died before then. Caught sick. But our sister, Gretchen, she drowned when the river broke. That's when I came to live with Alex. He brought me up after the flood."

"'Cause you didn't have anyone," Kim said.

"—Kimberly, stop," Max whispered.

"What'd I say?"

"It's alright," Dagny said. "Yeah. I didn't have anyone, I guess. Alex and Morgan were best friends when they were young." She pointed to the map. "What's this all about?"

Rodolph stretched his arms. "Get comfortable."

Dagny listened as the boys told her about Jorgie, a child of the Marsh Rats. It was two days ago that he disappeared. The boys heard that he had crossed over to Farrow Blood Island in search of the Oracle Tower. The island was sinking into the lagoon and rumored to be cursed.

"Jorgie's sister is a friend of Rodolph," Max said.

"We used to fish together. The Marsh Rats are mostly fishers, and thieves," Rodolph said, grinning.

"I've never heard of them," Dagny said.

"They live in those stilt-houses south of the city," Rodolph explained. "They're fairly harmless, but hated on by South Enders. I know what you're thinking... the South Enders... who are *they* to hate on anyone? Everyone's gotta feel better than someone else, I guess."

Jorgie had left for the island with two friends, slipping past the Authority's patrol boats under the cover of night. Jorgie's friends watched as he entered the tower through something called the *Orphan Gate*.

"We don't know what that is, exactly," Rodolph continued. "But we'll find out."

"Why would he go there?" Dagny asked.

"I really don't know," Rodolph said. "There's all sorts of myths about the island and the tower."

"So that's it? He just went inside and never came out?"

"Kinda. Except right after Jorgie went inside, his friends heard a terrible scream and ran away."

"Really? What do you think happened?"

Rodolph shook his head. "No idea."

"Why don't the Marsh Rats go search it?" she asked.

Rodolph pulled the laces tight on his boots. "The place is forbidden. There's dark stories about the tower, and the Marsh Rats are very superstitious about the curse. The Authority doesn't allow anyone on the Island, which is why Jorgie's friends only told his sister, and which is why we're leaving at night."

Dagny considered this. "Even so, his sister should've told the other Marsh Rats, don't you think?"

"You don't get it," Rodolph said. "That woulda done nothing except bring trouble down on them. The Marsh Rats won't go in there, no matter what."

"I understand," Dagny said.

"Jorgie's sister is terrified," Rodolph continued. "Their mom died last spring, and she can't lose him, too. I told her we'd take care of it, and if he's inside, we'd find him. But we need to keep this a secret, alright? Don't wanna bring any attention on us."

"Okay. So, what about this curse?"

Max spoke now. "It's got something to do with the Oracle. They say she died years ago, but hunts the Island... and if anyone trespasses, she'll follow them home and devour them. Anyway, you in?"

"You want me to come?" Dagny asked.

"I think so," Max looked at Rodolph, who nodded. "I mean, you got the background for it, growing up with Alex. Do you have experience with stuff like this?"

Dagny thought about it for a moment. If she told them the truth—that her only experience was dreaming about such things on the roof of the Benzara house—they were likely to realize the mistake they made and rescind the invite.

"Dag?" Max asked again. "Do you think you could help?"

"Yes. Absolutely."

"Alright, it's settled then," he said with a smile.

Dagny agreed to meet them that night, an hour after sunset, behind the last Scholar's Tower in Old Rork. Soon after they finalized their plans, however, Maris burst into the makeshift study, grabbed Dagny by the arm and rushed her out of the building. She was in such a shock that it wasn't until they were crossing the street outside that she yanked her arm away and spoke.

"What's the matter with you?" Dagny demanded.

"That place isn't right anymore. I don't want you going there again," Maris said. He reached toward Dagny's wrist.

"No! Stop it. What's this about?"

"The old man's mind has turned to rot, okay? He soaked all his books in vinegar. That book on the stars? It was nothing but a ruined children's book on some rabbit... there were other things too... I don't wanna talk about it. He's gone." The sudden shift in Maris' tone scared her. "Don't go back," he ordered.

"What about those boys? Are they going to be alright?" she asked.

"They're not my responsibility. You are. I can't be responsible for the rest of the world."

"I don't need you to look after me," Dagny said. But the event had shaken her, and truthfully, she was glad Maris was there.

"You became my responsibility when you left Alex Benzara's house with me. You think I like looking after some girl?"

Some girl? That last part stung.

Dagny once again fell quietly behind Maris as they continued the walk in silence. He said a brief goodbye at the Rork library, and apologized for frightening her. Then he was gone.

The house was empty when Dagny arrived, and she tried to forget about the way Maris made her feel during the walk home. Tonight there were more important things to consider. Tonight she would be heading onto the lagoon and out to Farrow Blood.

Dagny wandered into the kitchen, grabbed half a loaf of hard bread and some cheese from the ice chest, and hurried up to her room. There were preparations to make, and she couldn't go trotting around Farrow Blood Island in a summer dress embroidered with white flowers.

Part of her wished Alex was home. She imagined discussing the journey with him. Sitting in his study with pipe smoke and lamp light, like so many of his friends had done in the past. Plotting her strategy and finding out what he knew of the place. Surely Alex would be familiar with the Oracle, what was real and what was just a rumor. But she also knew that Alex wouldn't let her go, not now anyway. Maris was right about that much. Alex had been trying to protect her from the world.

The irony wasn't lost on her. Here she was, living under the same roof as one of the greatest adventurers in the city, and she'd have to go it alone, with no advice whatsoever. It was fine, she told herself. She'd seen enough of Alex's preparations to figure out the basics.

Dagny started laying out a new outfit on her feathered bed. She found a rough black work-shirt in the corner of her closet, and dark suede pants she used to wear for riding lessons. There was a pair of dirt-stained gardener's gloves. And from Alex's bedroom closet she took a leather cap and a broad belt. Finally, she retrieved her brother's coat and placed it on the bed. *That'll do. That'll do just fine,* she thought.

After packing a small waterproof satchel with some candles, matches, and a few other items lying around the house, Dagny snuck into Alex's study and unlocked the armoire with the key hidden under his desk. This was where Alex's more deadly treasures were kept: a pair of curved sabres; a polished, silver-plated rifle; finger-knives and a ceremonial hatchet. She gently cracked open an interior drawer and removed a more simple item: a small, bone-hilted dagger, sheathed in old leather, and placed it in her waistband because... *you never know.*

When she finished with her preparations, Dagny sat on her balcony, watching the street below, and tried to rest. But her mind was racing, and she felt manic with excitement. The closest she ever got to sailing the lagoon before was watching ships depart from the quayside. Of all the adventures Alex had taken, he never invited her on a single one. Yet Dagny was well aware that it was her connection to Alex that opened the door for the journey tonight.

She wondered about Magu Ogden. What else had Maris seen? Was it really something so shocking, he couldn't even mention it? And if it was, would the boys be alright? *I should've said something to them, shouldn't have left them*, Dagny thought.

Caternya and the children came home shortly before twilight. Dagny told her she was tired from the trek to Ogden's and had already eaten dinner. Cate didn't ask any questions. When she got back to her bedroom, Dagny changed outfits and lay on her bed, waiting.

It was an odd feeling. Some of her earliest memories were watching Morgan fill his backpack and wax his coat, readying himself for another journey. He always said he loved her before he left. Always. Now it was Dagny's turn, but she was alone, and there was no one here to say goodbye to. She couldn't risk telling Lucas or Abrielle of her plans. They'd almost certainly tell Cate, and then she'd be stuck.

Even if Grete was still alive, she wouldn't have approved, either. Grete would've hated the idea of actually going to some haunted place. Her sister's favorite stories were the ones of magical places, with grand castles and kind queens, simple stories without violence or sadness. There had been too much of that in the Mount as it was.

After the sun had fallen behind the western hills, and Old Rork was cloaked in darkness, Dagny carefully climbed down the trellis and crept through the garden toward the main street. She pulled the leather cap low on her face, in case anyone recognized her, and made her way to the Scholar's Tower.

The sand-brick spire shone like a beacon, even in the night. It was the best landmark Dagny could think of in her neighborhood. The boys said it wouldn't be a problem, still she was surprised they agreed to come pick her up in Rork. Dagny scouted out the tower, and seeing no one around, sat down at the edge of the canal, dangling her feet over the water, watching for Rodolph's boat. Just when she was beginning to think they weren't coming, Dagny saw a small light swaying and bobbing on the water.

Max sat near the bow of a rugged flat-bottom skiff, and Rodolph stood near the stern operating a single long oar. An iron lantern rocked from a curved pole, giving it the look of some alien yellow-eyed creature.

"Where's Kimberly?" Dagny asked, as the boys approached.

"Changed his mind," Max said. "For all his talk, Kim's still a child, and a bit afraid when it comes to the idea of actually wandering Farrow Blood at night." His dark hair was unbraided and tucked behind his ears. Both boys wore tight black jackets.

Rodolph carefully guided the boat up to the edge of the canal.

"You sure you're ready?" Max asked. "Once we hit the lagoon, we're not coming back until we search the tower."

"Just hold still," Dagny said, and dropped into the boat. "This is gonna make it to Farrow Blood, right? I don't feel like swimming back."

Max nodded. "Definitely. She might not look like much, but she'll do just fine. Besides, the Island isn't too far."

Before she could respond, Rodolph kicked off of the canal wall and they were off. He took them through the twisted canals of the old district, eventually connecting to one of the broad main waterways that criss-crossed the city. Dagny felt a rush of excitement when they passed underneath the Water Gate and into the open lagoon.

The stars glittered overhead and reflected in the dark water like a thousand shards of broken glass. When the lights of the city were nothing but a distant thought, Dagny spoke. "This is the first time I've been out on the lagoon."

"That's surprising," Max said. "I woulda thought you'd been all over the place, having someone like Alex Benzara around."

Dagny felt a slight panic in her chest before saying, "Just never been on the lagoon." She sensed the boys were on the verge of discovering how inexperienced she truly was. But if they were, Max didn't let on.

"Well, during the day, once you get away from the city, the lagoon is so clear you can see straight to the bottom," he said.

"Sounds pretty," she replied. The wind felt cold and exhilarating on her face. She was unsure of what more to say, and her delay turned into a long silence.

"...You grew up in Rork, right? After the Rakesmount?" Max asked, after some time.

"Yes." It wasn't something she talked about much. She'd already revealed more about herself to these boys than she'd ever told anyone, and they'd only just met.

"It seems nice. Rork." Max was scanning the water, probably looking for any sign of the Authority's patrol boats, but it seemed to Dagny that they were alone out here.

"It is," she said. "Rork can get boring sometimes, but yes, it's nice. Have you two ever gone anywhere dangerous before? Other than Farrow Blood tonight?" Her teeth chattered in the chill of the night.

"We went into the caves of the Glimmer Ghost, but it was more exhausting than anything else," Max said. "Usually we just stay around the city and lagoon. There's plenty of interesting stuff around here. Take Southend, there's all sorts of forgotten things buried in that place."

"How come you have so much free time?" Dagny asked. "Are you both finished up with school?"

Max gave her an odd look. "Neither of us have had real schooling for years. Only you North Enders get to go for longer." Dagny felt a bit foolish. She should've remembered that. There were differences here. These boys were from a world that was caught in the middle of her two lives. Up until recently, she spent most of her time in classrooms. She had private tutors and studied the maths, philosophy and art. But she was also from the Mount, and no one there ever went to a school. Ever.

Max continued, "My dad runs a river boat and hauls supplies up the Morca. I help out every week or so. It leaves me with a lot of time. And Rodolph... well..."

"—Alright, quiet now," Rodolph said. "She's coming up soon."

The boat weaved between two smaller islets, and as they turned the corner, Farrow Blood Island appeared. A hulking black mess snuffing out the starlit sky in front of them. Dagny sat in silence, listening to the gentle lapping of the lagoon against the skiff.

They entered the shallows and passed the hump of a broken wall at the edge of the lantern light. It hinted at an ancient time when the island was inhabited. Rodolph piloted them through sludge and water toward the Island's core.

Max adjusted his position behind her and rested his hand on the iron lantern pole attached to the stern. "There used to be lots of buildings here," he whispered in her ear. "An entire complex. The tower's the only thing remaining now."

"What happened?" Dagny asked.

"It all sunk into the swamp." Max was leaning slightly over her shoulder. She turned and looked at his smooth face, silhouetted in the yellow light. "Keep your eyes sharp for any movement," he said. His gaze was intense and focused on the shadows surrounding the boat.

Dagny leaned closer into him and spoke softly. "Do you believe she's still around?"

"The Oracle? No... but this whole place doesn't feel right. There could be something else," Max said. She could feel his breath on her ear, and the weight of his body next to hers.

They moved slowly under gnarled trees that stretched to the sky. Even during the day it would've been dark here, but at night it was suffocating. Dagny could see how stories were told of a ghoulish hunter stalking the Island.

She wondered why Jorgie felt compelled to take such a risk, coming here and entering the abandoned tower. The swamp was certain to be filled with very real dangers, like serpents and worse. Dagny imagined the young boy terrified and alone inside the black rooms of the Oracle

Tower, and wondered if he was alive. *If anyone trespasses,* Max had said, *the Oracle will follow them home and devour them.* Dagny pulled Morgan's coat tight around her body.

They entered a small lake within the Island's interior, illuminated by moonlight overhead. It was a desolate place. A dank smell of rot wafted over from across the water, and as Dagny scanned the opposite bank for its source, she saw the tower.

It was a sad, crumbling thing. Huge stone parapets jutted up from the lake's surface like mangled teeth, having toppled into the water at some point in the past. As they approached, the massiveness of the tower grew. Heavy and enormous. Dagny wondered how it hadn't completely sunk into the marsh from the weight.

Rodolph rested the boat against a section of ruined wall that stood along the lake's edge and gazed up. "Does anyone see a way inside?"

Dagny scanned the curved stone for doors, but there was no entrance that she could see. *The original gate must be underwater... far below*, she thought.

Finally Max spoke, in a hushed whisper, "*There.*" He pointed to a bent chimney that sprung like a branch from the tower's trunk about halfway up. Dagny almost didn't notice it, as thick vines had taken over that side of the structure, suffocating the tower in a tangled heap. "Think *that* could be the Orphan Gate?"

"Maybe," Rodolph replied. "I don't see any other openings."

"Can we get closer?" Max asked him.

"I don't think so. Don't wanna risk getting stuck in the bog."

"Okay... I should be able to make it. It's awfully cold out here now, isn't it?" Max took a deep breath. "Good enough time as any..." he said, but didn't move.

Rodolph nudged his shoulder. "Hey, Max… if you don't wanna go, it's alright. This looks worse than we thought. Besides, I don't see how Jorgie could've gotten through that. Maybe his friends lied."

It took a moment before Max answered. "No. He went inside. It's just that… it looks really tight from down here. Think that's why they called it the Orphan Gate? Cause only little orphan kids can fit through?"

"You don't have to go," Rodolph repeated.

"Don't know if I could fit is all," Max said, softly.

"…Maybe I could do it," Dagny said. Her voice sounded awkward, almost muffled in the bog air, like she was listening to someone else speak.

"No way, I'll go. Just give me a second," Max said.

Dagny stood up, took her coat off and handed it to him. "Don't leave without me, okay?"

"You sure?" Max asked.

"If you keep asking, you're gonna make me change my mind. And there could be a child trapped in there."

"Okay, but if it looks too dangerous…"

"Then, I'll come back. But seriously, do not leave without me."

Max looked at her and nodded. "We won't."

Dagny picked up a bundle of braided rope from the boat deck, climbed onto the broken wall, and made her way across a mound of wet earth on the opposite side, slushing into the muck as she went. The soft hill was covered with knotted roots that tripped her up and grabbed at her boots like the knuckled fingers of some greedy witch.

She reached the vine wall and surveyed her surroundings. The vines were thick and looked like they stretched all the way to the top of the tower. Thankfully, they weren't thorned. Dagny grasped one and yanked hard. It barely flinched. *This could work*, she thought.

The tower was surprisingly easy to climb. It leaned gently to one side and the vines led straight to the chimney, almost as if they were guiding her there. The trellis back home was more difficult than this, and she had climbed that hundreds of times. Still, Dagny proceeded cautiously, taking her time, placing one hand over the other and making sure her footing was secure before shifting her weight. Part of her felt like one wrong step would send the entire tower crashing into the lake.

When she reached the chimney, Dagny stopped for a moment to catch her breath. She could see the boat below, a small bead of light from the lantern outlining Max and Rodolph. Further into the sinking forest, on the opposite side of the tower, it was pitch black. Dagny leaned over the uncovered chimney, listening, trying to catch the slightest sound of someone or something below. She heard nothing but trees rustling overhead.

A section of rope was already tied around the chimney and lowered into the shaft. A sure sign that Jorgie, or someone, must've come this way. Even so, Dagny wondered, could a boy younger than her really have crossed the lagoon and climbed into this place? She pulled the rope up and found it frayed and broken. Pressing her face to the opening, Dagny whispered, "Jorgie... Jorgie, are you down there?"

There was no answer. She reached into her satchel and pulled out a candle, struck a match, and dropped it down the shaft. The flame bounced off and down the chimney and then snuffed out when it hit the bottom, but Dagny saw enough. It would be a tight fit. Even for her. A nervous chill spread across her body.

What did she get herself into? Maybe she should just go back. The boys wouldn't fault her for it. After all, Max had been too afraid to go. Maybe Rodolph was right and Jorgie went somewhere else entirely. Maybe the young boy's friends really were liars and made up the whole story. But she knew deep inside that wasn't true...

It felt as though she was on the precipice of a great choice. She could return to Rodolph's boat and go back to her life in Rork, or she could go down this chimney. Somehow she knew that the decision would change things forever, and determine the type of person she'd become from now until the end. It wasn't dramatic of her to think that. It was the truth. But... she could also die down there, and the place terrified her.

Dagny stared into the black hole, thinking, and the more time that passed, the more inclined she was to return to the boat. She thought of herself trapped in that dark chimney. Her body wedged between the sides of the narrow shaft, unable to free herself. Would anyone be able to rescue her? Would Max and Rodolph leave and promise never to talk about it again? Could she trust them? No. Not really. She barely knew them. Alex and Cate, Lucas and Abrielle... none of them would know what happened to her.

She was almost ready to climb back down the muddy hill, when she started to feel... *angry*... It started small. A tiny bead of anger forming in the pit of her stomach, and as strange as it was, she found the feeling oddly comforting. The more she thought about retreating, the more it began to grow. Until she was no longer afraid. Just mad. At herself. At her hesitation. She thought of the child, Jorgie, alone and hurt... or worse... inside whatever black room this chimney led to. She thought of herself as a coward, wanting to be like Morgan, yet unable to take the smallest risk. Suddenly, her mind switched off, and she thought no more about it.

Dagny took off her mud-caked boots and wedged them between the chimney and the tower. It would be tough enough to slide down as it was. The passage was so narrow she didn't want anything getting in the way. She tied her own rope around the chimney, tested it, swung her leg over the edge, and descended.

The darkness engulfed her immediately. The rough stone pulled at her clothes and scraped against her feet. But she was doing it. Placing her free hand on the wall and squirming her way down, she moved like some kind of centipede working its way into the earth. It actually wasn't so bad. The chimney was tight, but she was scrawny and as long as she kept a level head...

...Dagny's ankle caught an odd piece of stone jutting out from the shaft. She traced it with her bare foot, feeling around for an opening, and found a space between the jagged edge and the chimney wall. Bending her knees awkwardly and rolling to her side, Dagny slowed her movements and squeezed her way through. The passage felt very tight, constricting both of her legs.

She attempted to control her breathing, taking slow, deep breaths, but a sense of alarm twisted her stomach. Maybe this wasn't a good idea. She needed more time to think. Maybe she could try again in the morning with the daylight. Yes, that would be better. Dagny tried to pull herself back up, bracing her feet against the shaft, when she slipped.

The rope dragged against her skin, burning her hands, but somehow she held on. Her heart pounded hard in her chest. She'd almost fallen into the narrow space. This was too much. She needed to get out. *Now.* Dagny pressed her feet into the wall again and pulled hard on the rope.

Suddenly, the shaft rumbled. She dropped, felt a quick jerk, and lost her grip. Scrambling in the dark, Dagny saw the stars overhead disappear, watching in horror as the chimney above slowly collapsed. She hung there for a moment, floating in space, almost like she was weightless, caught in some weird dream. And then she fell. Into the blackness.

She bounced against the chimney wall, and felt that jagged stone edge cut across her thighs and stomach. She sucked in air, fumbling for a grip on the stone, but kept sliding further down until the hard edge pinched her shoulders and jammed her into the crevice.

Dagny reached out, searching for the rope again, but found nothing. She tried to scream for help, but her voice was lost. It was like she was drowning. Gasping for breath that she couldn't catch. Helplessly blind in the dark. Bits of crumbling rock fell onto her face, threatening to bury her. She started to suffocate, and kicked her legs wildly, flailing her body, clawing her fingers into rock. Swallowing spit and dirt. She pressed her burning hands into the wall and tried to pull herself up, but it was hopeless.

No... no, no, no, she thought, scrambling, scratching at the stone. A nail on her finger bent and came off. *Not like this. Please! Please get me out!* The hard edge was squeezing her chest. The rough wall flattened her cheek. Her mind raced, trying to come up with a solution. She couldn't die like this. Dagny started to *push* now, as if she could force the chimney open. Desperate for air. She was driving herself further into the narrow space, and risked becoming wedged in there forever, but she didn't know what to do. She couldn't climb out. She couldn't do *anything*. Little by little, her shoulders scraped painfully along the stone, and then, just as she forced one shoulder free, the shaft sucked her down.

She hit the bottom hard. A jolt shot through her ankles and knocked the remaining air out of her lungs. But she was free.

Dagny collapsed onto the ground and stayed there for a long while, wiping snot and spit from her face. Her whole body pulsated with an aching pain. Where was she? Nothing made sense. She checked her eyelids, rubbing them with raw fingers to make sure they were open.

Candles... find the light.

Her hands moved to the satchel, but it was gone, lost during the fall. Dagny tried to gather herself and began to crawl, slowly, across the floor, searching blindly for her belongings.

Here.

Her hand caught something. Then another. She gathered them close to her. She tried to strike the match. Dropped it. Again. It was gone.

Calm down, she told herself. *You can do this. It's okay.* She steadied her hand. She was safe.

Then. A soft swish. Light.

She was in an old bedroom. A rusted bed frame rested nearby, partially collapsed. Leaves and debris littered the area, blown in over time from the chimney. Heavy dressers and a wardrobe were pushed against the wall at the edge of her candle light, likely having shifted across the tilted floor as the tower slowly sunk. And there, in the far corner, was a staircase connecting the levels.

The smell of mud and earth permeated the room. Nothing else. She was grateful for that. If the boy had died in here, it would've been noticeable. Dagny scanned the floor and found a long trail through the leaves leading to the staircase. Like something had been dragged across the room.

She looked up the shaft, hoping to see the rope, but it must have caught somewhere high above. And the chimney had collapsed. There was no way she'd be able to make it back now.

After filling her pockets with all the matches and candles she could find, Dagny cautiously approached the stairs. The trail blended into the stone steps and disappeared. There was no indication whether it led up or down. Dagny needed to make a decision. The tower was enormous. It could take a full day or more to properly explore. The bottom floors were probably flooded, but that would be the most likely place to find a gate. Perhaps she could make it onto the roof if she climbed high enough, but then how would she get down? One way or another, she'd need to locate an exit.

She decided to search the upper levels first. The thought of swimming through the pitch-black, flooded rooms below frightened her. If she had to, she would, but only if there was no other choice. What creatures could be lurking in the darkness down there? She felt the bone-hilted dagger, still tucked in her waistband, and relaxed ever so slightly.

The candlelight flickered along the staircase as Dagny ascended higher and higher. From somewhere above, she heard a faint thumping. *Probably just branches knocking against the outer wall...* but she couldn't be sure. There had been lamps here at one time, contained in small alcoves set into the wall; they were all gone. Hers was the only light here now.

The first hallway she came to contained several doors and ended at a small window. Dagny stepped off of the staircase and approached. Hopeful that the window could offer a way out, she was quickly disappointed. The glass was thick and its iron frame was secured to the wall with rusted bolts. She pressed her face to the window, trying to look outside, but found only blackness.

Each of the doors opened into small bedrooms that contained short bed frames, built for children. There was a set of ruined storybooks in one, and a game of *Rattle-stacks* in another. She found a pair of rotting leather shoes, sized for a toddler, and wooden blocks shaped like horses pushed under one of the old beds. None of the rooms contained windows. There was a sadness here, and Dagny wondered why there would be any accommodations for children at all? What was the Oracle planning to do with them? Were they the Oracle's own children? And if not, whose children were they?

Dagny left the row of bedrooms and continued her ascent. The stairs took her to a wide, curved hallway that wrapped itself along the interior ring of the tower. Smaller passages branched off toward the building's core, like the spokes of a wagon wheel. All led to stale, silent rooms.

She was beginning to think she'd never make it out. That the tower was nothing but a tomb. And where was this child? Maybe the trail she saw in the first bedroom was from something else, not Jorgie, or maybe the Oracle was real and had found him first. Dragging the boy into her lair.

Suddenly, the hallway ended. Dagny found herself standing in front of a heavy, iron-bound door with etchings carved into the wood. Pushing it open, Dagny looked into a vast chamber with high ceilings. It reminded her of a throne room from some fairytale of ancient knights and queens. Stained-glass plates, depicting scenes of giant beasts under stars, hung from the rafters and seemed to gently sway. Then she felt it... *a breeze.* The wind caught the candle. It flickered and faded for a brief instant, threatening to leave her abandoned in the darkness. The thought of her light going out terrified her more than anything. Dagny quickly tried to shield the flame with her body.

The breeze had to be coming from somewhere, she thought, scanning the room for an opening. Rotten tapestries had collapsed onto the floor and the remains of a dilapidated, old rug stretched into the darkness.

Dagny stepped further into the chamber. Part of her felt like calling out for Jorgie. She was afraid that if she found an opening in the wall, she'd leave and never come back. She should at least try to call for the boy before that happened, but she stopped herself. Something else appeared at the edge of her candlelight.

A tiered, raised platform came into view. And there, sitting behind a thin curtain, was a figure.

The Oracle.

Dagny froze. Not knowing how to proceed. It didn't make any sense, but there she was, sitting in the darkness. Waiting. Dagny wanted to turn and run. But to where? The Oracle was facing her. Staring at her through the curtain.

"Hello?" Dagny said, her voice echoing oddly across the room.

The breeze swayed over her hand and flicked the candle flame again. Dagny moved closer. There was no response. The figure sat cross-legged, wearing a crimson dress and a tiara that glittered in the light.

Then Dagny noticed. The Oracle was pale. Too pale. A translucent bone face and empty eye sockets stared out. A jeweled corpse.

There was no question about it, this place *was* a tomb. Dagny took a step back. She needed to find a way out.

In the shadows behind her, something moved.

4

DAGNY SPUN AROUND. "HELLO? Is someone there?"

She heard a strange noise, like something being dragged across the floor.

"Who is that? Look, I'm sorry to intrude... I really am. I'm looking for a boy." Her candle flickered and faded for a brief instant. She hoped it was the wind.

A faint voice spoke. "Are you here to help me?"

"*Jorgie?*" Dagny asked. "Is that you?" She stepped forward, allowing her candlelight to break up the darkness.

Standing in the shadows was a boy. Rail-thin with long, greasy hair.

"Jorgie?" she repeated. Almost instantly, tears began to well in the boy's eyes, and his face scrunched and quivered. Pitiful and traumatized, he looked no older than nine or ten. She walked over and touched him. "It's okay now. I'm Dagny, and I'm here to get you out."

The boy threw his arms around her waist and sobbed into her chest. "It's been so dark," he cried.

"Are you alright? Are you hurt?" she asked.

Jorgie nodded and pointed to his leg.

"I hurt myself, too," Dagny said gently. "Let me see." She knelt down and examined him. The boy's ankle and knee had swollen to twice their normal size, each developing a sick, purplish bruise.

"It hurts real bad," Jorgie said.

"It'll be okay. Have you had anything to eat or drink?" she asked. It'd been two days since Jorgie disappeared, Max had told her.

"I did, but it's all gone now."

"We'll get you more soon. We need to get out of here. Do you know where that breeze is coming from?"

"You can't get out that way..."

"Why not? Can you show me?"

Jorgie looked up at her and nodded. He limped forward, but then stopped and gasped when he tried to put weight on his injured leg.

"Why don't you wait here? I'll check it out by myself," she said.

A look of fear washed over his face. "No... don't leave me, *please.*" He grabbed onto her shirt. "I can do it."

"Okay. Don't worry. I won't..." Jorgie loosened his grip, but didn't let go. They moved slowly, with Dagny doing her best to support the boy. "How did you find your way up here, from the chimney?" she asked.

"I had a candle, but it's all burnt out. When the sun comes, it shines in from the hole. It's the only place with light."

"You must be very brave, coming here."

Jorgie paused before responding. "I just wanna go home now."

"We'll get you back. I promise. Can I ask what you're doing in this place?"

"The Oracle was supposed to be here," Jorgie said. "Do you think that was her? The skeleton?"

Dagny scanned the darkness as she spoke. "It could be. I don't really know."

"It's weird how she was sitting like that. Think she was resting when she died?"

"I have no idea." *It would've been a deep rest indeed,* Dagny thought, *resting herself into oblivion.* "You weren't afraid of her?"

"No. Mom said she helped people. And then she was in my dream."

"The Oracle? That's nice," Dagny said. She remembered what Rodolph said about the boy's mother passing away last spring, and tried to keep his spirits up as they walked across the chamber. "I don't know much about the Oracle. She's friendly, then?"

"Yeah. In my dream, she wanted me to come to the tower. But she's all gone now, isn't she?"

"Yes. I'm afraid she is."

They were approaching the end of the great hall, and Dagny could feel the chill of the night air, when Jorgie pulled her sleeve.

"It's over there. Watch out, or you'll fall."

"Fall?" Dagny slowed her pace. "Is it a hole?"

"Yeah... in the wall..."

Just then a gush of wind came, blowing back Dagny's hair and blowing out the candle. But she wasn't in complete darkness. Instead, a thousand tiny lights appeared in front of her. She could smell the decaying stink of the swamp and the salty lagoon beyond. They were staring out across the sunken forest and into the night sky.

Dagny inched closer to the collapsed wall and peered over the edge.

"Be careful," the boy whispered.

Dagny had hoped there would be a way to climb down. That maybe the vines had reached this place. But they had no such luck. They were far from the vine-covered side of the tower, and it was a sheer, straight drop to the forest below. Slowly, she began to back away.

"That's disappointing," she said.

"I told you."

"Is there no other exit? Have you explored anywhere else?" The starlight illuminated Jorgie's face. He glanced at the ground and twisted his lips.

"Not really," he said, avoiding her gaze.

"You saw something. What it is, Jorgie? C'mon, you need to tell me."

"It's... a creature... an awful, awful creature..."

"What kind of creature?"

"A monster. I only saw it real quick."

"Where?"

"Up *there...*" Jorgie said, pointing at the ceiling.

A creature made of shadows, Jorgie told her. Huge. Bigger than anything he'd ever seen. It lived in the highest part of the tower. Jorgie had gone up there the day before, trying to find the Oracle, and the creature went wild. Flailing and screeching. Beating the ground and shaking the walls. Its eyes were glossy black and the size of barrels. Jorgie escaped, hurting his ankle even worse. He hadn't gone anywhere near it since.

"You say it was at the top of the tower? Like the attic?" Dagny asked.

"I think so. I didn't see much, but there were lots of boxes and things. The room was really big."

"We need to find a way out of here. I wonder if we could make it onto the roof." If so, she could try calling down to Max and Rodolph. The hole in the wall was on the opposite side of the lake, far from their boat. There was no way they'd be able to hear her from there.

The boy, however, was having none of it. "No. I won't show you."

She knelt down and held his face, gentle but firm. "Jorgie. You need to trust me, okay? I'm not going to do anything dangerous. I just wanna take a quick look. I'll be really careful."

"It's gonna get you. Don't do it."

"Either you can show me, or I'll find it on my own. We need to get out of here."

"What about the rooms downstairs?" he pleaded.

"They're flooded, I'm sure."

"We could swim them, couldn't we?" Jorgie asked.

Dagny would rather take her chances with the monster in the attic. "Let me do this first, and if it's too dangerous, we'll explore the flooded rooms, okay?"

"I don't know..."

"Come on now. I'll be careful," she said, flashing her best smile. "I made it into the tower and found you, didn't I?"

"Yes."

"Trust me." Dagny surprised herself with how confident she sounded. In another world, the one of Rork gardens and games of *Hunters and the Hunted*, children seemed to gravitate toward her. She couldn't really explain it. If it was a skill, she hoped she could put it to use now. Dagny leaned closer to Jorgie's face and stared into his eyes. "You need to tell me."

The boy hesitated. "Fine... I'll show you... but you're not gonna like it."

"Thank you." Dagny lit a pair of candles and handed one to Jorgie. Then they made their way back across the great chamber.

"There's another staircase in the middle of the tower," Jorgie said, limping along. "You just go all the way up."

The tower really was massive. It seemed even larger inside. It probably could've housed over a hundred people at one time, but Dagny had a hard time imagining it filled with much life. Instead, she thought of the Oracle wandering these gloomy halls alone until the day she rested on her pedestal in the great chamber and passed.

"You didn't see anything else, did you?" Dagny asked. "Like other creatures, or people, or bodies?"

"No..." Jorgie's eyes grew larger, like he was considering the possibility of other things lurking nearby.

"Sorry. I was just asking. I'm sure there's nothing else," Dagny said, but she didn't fully believe it.

Jorgie led her down one of the side passages, into the middle of the tower, and to a circular staircase rising up from the floor.

"Do you wanna stay here this time?" Dagny asked.

"No. I'll come."

She had to hand it to the boy. He'd just spent two days alone in the darkness, wondering if he'd ever be rescued. And here he was, following her into the most threatening part of the tower.

They were getting close to the attic. Dagny could feel the boy shaking as he held onto her. She turned around and pressed her finger to her lips, then slowly tiptoed the rest of the way up.

There was no trapdoor or landing. The stairs simply wound straight into the chamber. Jorgie had finally let go of her shirt and stood several steps below, watching. Dagny winked at him and crawled into the attic above.

...Or what she had thought was an attic. Almost immediately Dagny knew this was no ordinary storage room. Even though she could barely see beyond the candle flame, she felt the enormity of the space. This so-called attic likely stretched the entire width of the tower, bigger than even the great hall below. Above her was a sprawling glass ceiling. It was murky, but Dagny could still make out the stars and moon shining through.

She scanned the room, searching for movement, but had a hard time seeing anything. Despite her better judgment, Dagny blew out her candle and crawled over to a nearby crate, hiding behind it. The glass ceiling was dissected by metal edging, like dozens of window panes, and each pane contained a set of metal gears. The ceiling could be opened to the sky.

Crouching in the shadows, Dagny considered her options. They could try exploring the flooded floors below, but that would likely mean swimming through underwater hallways and rooms in the dark, hoping to find an exit and hoping they didn't get lost and drown. Sure, she told Jorgie she'd think about it, but that wasn't really an option. On the other hand, they could go back to the hole in the wall and wait until morning. Eventually, Max and Rodolph would come looking for her. It seemed like they would do that much. They might even be doing that now, having heard or seen the chimney collapse. But then what? It was way too high for anyone to climb or throw a rope. Besides, they didn't have any food or water... how long could they really last here?

With the candle extinguished, her eyes were becoming more adjusted to the darkness and starlight above. She peeked around the crate, looking for the creature. The enormous room was stuffed with all manner of junk, from crates and boxes to weirdly shaped objects and old furniture jutting out from the shadows. It was impossible to see across the entire room. Anything could be hiding in here.

Dagny decided that she wouldn't just wait to be rescued while they slowly withered away. That was a false hope. No one would be able to break them out, and she'd soon burn through her candles. Dagny needed to explore this room. There could be other passages, or something useful in one of the crates, or something she hadn't even thought of yet. But first, she needed to deal with the creature Jorgie had seen. If she could find a way to open the ceiling... well, maybe the thing would just leave.

Dagny slowly pressed herself onto the floor and began to crawl further into the space. She was dressed in black, in near-total darkness, and figured herself to be naturally sneaky. It was possible that she could explore the area without the creature ever knowing she was here.

As she slithered across the floor, Dagny kept her eyes on the ceiling, looking for any indication as to how it could be opened. Perhaps there was a winch or lever somewhere... but the more she considered it, the more disheartened she became. Any chains or gears would've rusted a long time ago.

Then, just as the far wall came into view, she saw that the entire glass ceiling on this side of the tower was already raised up, revealing the night sky. Dagny felt a twitch of excitement. *A way out.*

And she had seen no sign of this *creature* yet. Could it have already left through the open ceiling? It certainly could have entered that way. The thought made Dagny feel a little more at ease. Assuming Jorgie *did* see something, it could've been any animal flying in from the lagoon. Not necessarily some vengeful spirit of the tower. The boy had been lost in the darkness of this place; even a swamp owl or hawk would've seemed monstrous to him.

The glass ceiling was high. She would need to stack some of these crates to reach it, or else find a ladder. Dagny stood, dusted herself off, and tiptoed ahead, more relaxed than before. It was colder here. But it was the cold of the fresh, nighttime air, and that felt just fine to her.

Two steps later, a thundering crash shattered the silence and sent Dagny reeling. Crates erupted from behind, tumbling across the floor. She stumbled, almost tripping over her feet, and turned to see a giant, fluttering shape rushing toward her. A massive shadow so black that it seemed to suck the moonlight into it. Features and form were lost to her.

She was a lucky person. She'd survived life in the Rakesmount and the floods that came later, only to find herself being raised in the richest part of the city. She'd survived the chimney collapse tonight and found the boy Jorgie. Only now...

Something sharp caught the light, and flashed and scraped over the floor sending sparks into the air. A monstrous tooth or talon, perhaps. Dagny gasped and ran, diving into a narrow space between two rows of stacked boxes. On the other side, claws raked stone and she could hear the *thumping*. Actually, she could *feel it*. Deep in her chest. As if the shadow beast had reached down her throat and was pounding her lungs.

Suddenly, everything stopped. Dagny believed she'd been screaming, but when her mind finally slowed down enough to process what was happening, she realized she was only panting in harsh, quick bursts. She crawled to the end of the row and prepared to dash over to the stairs and Jorgie. But as she peeked around the edge of the last box, she saw the thing looming nearby, blocking her escape. Fear had rooted itself so deep that Dagny couldn't bring herself to leave her hiding place. There was nowhere else to go. She was trapped. Dagny retreated behind the wooden boxes, curled into a ball, and waited for the thing to get her.

Except nothing happened. There was no more thumping. No more scraping of claw on stone. No sound but her own staggered breathing. More and more time passed, and still, nothing. Slowly, Dagny lifted her head and looked around the corner. She half-expected the creature to be waiting there, inches from her face, ready to snatch her into the air. But the beast hadn't moved. She studied it from the edge of her hiding place. It was definitely watching her. She saw a slight movement. A blinking eye. Its shape became clearer. Round and glistening, black and sleek. And the light from the night sky outlined something else. A beak. This wasn't a creature of shadow. Dagny was staring at a giant bird.

There were legends of enormous birds from the distant past, the size of dragons, that would drag off lions and elephants. The sailor Dreel of Bluestone described such a bird destroying his ship somewhere across the Shallow Sea. The stories were thought to be no more than exaggerated accounts... and this bird, in front of her now, was not big enough to be destroying any ships or dragging off elephants... but a lion? Possibly.

There were other stories too, of crows and ravens that would help the lonely traveler, or bring food to the girl lost in the woods. Or seek vengeance against the cruel-hearted woodsman who destroyed their nest.

Is that what you are? A giant crow? Dagny thought. She knew those birds to be smart. How long had it been here? She leaned forward and whispered, "What do you want?" Almost as if answering her, the animal fluttered its wings and hopped, revealing something tangled around its leg.

"What is that?" Dagny said to herself, crawling further out from her hiding spot, but it was too dark to see.

"If I come closer, I don't want you trying to eat me, alright?!" The creature just cocked its head in the moonlight and watched her.

"Okay... here I come... easy now." She stood up, ready to jump back behind the crates at the slightest sign of aggression, and cautiously approached. Wrapped around the bird's legs and feet was a thick mess of knots and braids. *A net.*

"What happened to you?" It looked like one of those giant nets the fishermen used when harvesting the lagoon. *Did you get tangled in an abandoned line? Or was someone trying to capture you?*

Parts of the cord were frayed, as if the bird had been trying in vain to free itself, but the net was so densely weaved around the poor thing, it had been a hopeless undertaking. And it didn't end there. The net had trapped a horde of boxes and other random objects from the room. There was no way this bird would be able to flee the tower. Had it come to see the Oracle? Hoping she could help?

Dagny's mind turned to the bone-hilted dagger on her waist. It would take some time to cut through the cord, and she didn't like the idea of getting so close. Besides, the stairs were nearby now. She could probably make it if she ran. Still, the bird, only moments ago a terrifying creature, looked so lonely and helpless. There was no way she could leave it here.

"I'm gonna help you, okay? Will you let me do that? But I gotta get close... real close... don't be scared." The bird turned slightly and faced away from her. As if beckoning Dagny closer.

She didn't draw her blade until she was right underneath its breast, and quickly got to work. The sooner she could cut the net, the sooner she could find a way out for her and Jorgie. The bird just waited patiently, and with every knot and braid Dagny worked through, she felt her anxiety increase. Sweat beaded on her forehead and ran down her arms, making her hands slick. She was still afraid of the thing. Its beak, thick as an axe, perched inches from her face, and its talons would've made short work of her. But the bird *was* smart. It had trusted her so far.

As the net fell apart and Dagny pulled her dagger through the last piece of cord, wrapped tight around a leathery ankle, Jorgie popped his head up from the stairwell and called, "*Dagny!* Where are you?!"

The bird screeched, unveiling huge dark wings, and flapped, the force sending Dagny to the ground. Its wicked claws, now freed of the net, hit the stone by her head.

Sucking in cold air, Dagny gazed in awe at the creature. It was deadly and magnificent. A beast from another age. Ancient. Primordial. It studied her one last time, before fluttering into the air and out through the opening in the ceiling, vanishing into the night sky.

Jorgie came limping over to her. "Are you okay?! It was a *bird!*"

She rolled over, pushed herself up, and ran to the opening, hoping for one last look at the creature, but it was gone.

"Dagny!" Jorgie called from behind her. "It was a bird!"

"Yeah... something like that," she said with surprising calm. "We need to find a way onto the roof."

They found it on the opposite side of the chamber. Another set of stairs and an old metal door. Dagny pushed it open and stepped outside onto a wide stone walkway that framed the entire edge of the leaning tower. It felt like walking into a storm. The wind whipped her hair and sucked her clothes tight around her skinny frame. She pushed forward and found the lake side, identifying Rodolph's boat by a dim glimmer of light. It seemed so tiny from up here. Jorgie held onto the end of her shirt and watched her face.

"I'm not sure they'll be able to hear me, even if I yell," she said.

"Don't do it," Jorgie warned. "It won't matter anyway, and something else might hear you."

"You think there's other things? Other than that bird?" she asked.

"I know there are... darker monsters, in the swamp..."

"So what do we do?" she asked, although the question was more to herself than to Jorgie.

Dagny glanced around. The walkway was shaped by staggered parapets, and a short distance beneath them, on the inside, was the glass ceiling. There were no other stairs or doors. But something did creep over a portion of the outer wall and onto the walkway floor. *Vines.*

The same vines she'd seen from the lake. The same vines she'd climbed to reach the chimney. Dagny glanced over the edge of the wall and into the darkness. The vines were thick and easy to climb the first time around. But she had Jorgie now, and he had an injured leg.

"...I don't think I can do it," he said.

Dagny stretched her arms. Her shoulder still twinged, and her ribs hurt from the fall in the chimney.

"Try climbing onto my back," Dagny said, kneeling down.

"No way."

"Just try it. I wanna see something. I'm not gonna do anything."

Jorgie eyed her with suspicion, but came over and placed his arms around her neck.

Dagny groaned and stood up. Thankfully, the boy was light. He'd probably been half-starved his whole life.

"Okay, get off now... I think we can do this."

"No. We're gonna fall and die. It's way too high."

"Look," Dagny said. "You don't need to do anything but hold on. Just shut your eyes. I've been climbing my whole life. You trusted me before, and everything worked out. Can you hold tight?"

Jorgie nodded.

"Okay then. Don't think about it." Dagny pulled herself onto the battlement and secured her hands on the vine. Once she was in place, Jorgie climbed onto her back and wrapped his arms and legs around her body.

Dagny followed her own advice and emptied her mind. She moved slowly. Securing her hands and feet before each steady movement. The tower leaned in their favor, and she was able to rest herself against it at regular intervals. Neither of them dared to speak, and when they moved below the sunken forest's canopy, the wind eased. She didn't look down, and was unsure of how far off they were from Rodolph's boat. She could worry about that soon enough.

It was pitch dark now, in the shadow of the swamp trees. But even before they reached the bottom, Dagny knew they'd made it.

She landed in thick mud and pried Jorgie's arms off of her neck. "It's alright. We're safe now." She reached into her pocket for a match.

The flame illuminated a mass of brambles and twisted trees. They circled the tower until they found water. Jorgie tried his best to limp through the muck, whimpering with each step.

After a short time, the boy wheezed, "...I need to rest... no more."

Dagny, herself, was on the verge of collapsing, but they were so close. She lifted him onto her back again. Struggling with the weight, her ankles sinking deeper and deeper into the ground. She called out into the night, "Max! Rodolph! Here, help me!" Her voice echoed across the bog. And then something sounded in the distance.

A boat appeared in the water. Light illuminated the shapes of Max and Rodolph. Their faces turned toward her, scanning the darkness.

"I found him! Here, follow my voice!" she cried. "Hurry!"

Max jumped into the shallows and moved to her, slogging through as best he could, while Rodolph operated the skiff.

"Dagny! Dagny!" Max yelled with excitement. "Hold on, we're coming!"

Max reached them first. He hoisted Jorgie and embraced Dagny with his free arm. "I can't believe you! You did it! This is incredible."

Rodolph came around with the boat, and they loaded into it. She could no longer speak, gasping for breath.

"Well done, Dag. Well done," said Rodolph with a grin.

After setting Jorgie onto the deck, Max turned to Dagny and pulled her close. "You are *incredible*," he said, hugging her tightly and lifting her into the air. Pain from her shoulders shot through her body, forcing out a hiss.

Max set her down gently. A look of concern spread across his face. "Are you okay?"

She spoke through heaved breaths. "...We need... to leave..."

"Okay, we're going... you're safe," he said.

Dagny looked down at her hands now in the lantern light, raw and bloody. Her body still throbbed from her fall in the chimney and the climb down the tower; her bare feet were sore and numb; her clothes were covered in black filth. But the whole thing had left her strangely thrilled.

Rodolph steered the skiff out of the lake, away from the ruins. Dagny retrieved her brother's coat from Max, and draped it over herself and Jorgie.

Once the Island was behind them, Dagny told them about the giant crow, and how she entered the tower and found Jorgie in the great hall. For his part, Jorgie had fallen asleep and snored next to her, loudly. Rodolph kept glancing over his shoulder as he steered.

"Where are we going now?" Dagny asked after some time had passed.

"We're heading to Rodolph's house by the docks," Max said. "We told Jorgie's sister we'd meet her nearby, regardless of what we found. I can't imagine how thrilled she'll be... I didn't wanna say anything, but I was afraid of what could've happened to him."

Dagny lay down and stared up at the sky. She could see so many more stars here, on the black lagoon, than she could from the rooftop back home. It was comforting and took her mind away from the tower. She tried to trace the star lines that she knew. There was Azathur the Glitter Rat, and she found the belt of Gylathrik... There was the outline of an entire kingdom up there. The Night Kingdom.

She pulled her hands into the sleeves of Morgan's old coat, ran her fingers along the velvet-smooth lining, and tried to imagine how he must've felt on that first adventure of his. Dagny couldn't recall which story it was, so she made one up, picturing her brother at the edge of a great enchanted forest with a ruined tower in the distance. Random images flooded her mind. A feast in a moonlit clearing; silver monkey knights guarding the drawbridge of a white castle covered in rose thorns; a boy riding a crimson horse from out of the mist. She didn't think of Morgan sick with fever. Only as a young man, full of life and excitement. Staring not at the end of the world, but at the beginning.

5

THEY DOCKED THE SKIFF near Rodolph's place. It was more of a fisherman's shack than a proper home, with rigid tin walls and a flat wood roof. After mooring the boat, Rodolph gathered Jorgie from the deck and stepped off.

"I shouldn't be too long. Wait for me," Rodolph said and walked out of sight.

Dagny joined Max on a simple bench just outside of the shack. "Does he live here by himself?" she asked.

"Mostly. His father is usually out on the water. Sometimes for weeks at a time."

"Must get lonely then," Dagny said. Although she knew loneliness wasn't always the result of being alone. She often felt lonely, and the Benzara house was almost always crowded.

"I don't think he minds it... You sure you're doing alright? Your face..." Max said, grimacing.

Dagny turned away. "I'm fine."

"No... I mean... it's all scratched up... it's still a pretty face. I'm just asking... does it hurt?"

"What do you think?" she said.

"Right... I bet..."

They sat for a moment, in silence. Dagny could tell that Max was searching for the right thing to say.

"Do you live around here, too?" she asked.

"No. I'm close to the western wall. Like *real* close. You can actually reach out and touch it from my bedroom window," Max said.

"Do you have a big family?"

"Oh yeah. I'm the youngest of eight. Most of my brothers are masons. I suppose I'm a bit of an outsider, but it's fine. I don't wanna spend my life fixing walls," Max looked down at her muddy feet. "What happened to your boots?"

"I left them on the tower when I climbed down the chimney."

"Why?" he asked, studying her face again.

"Well, the shaft was so narrow I didn't want them causing me to get stuck, but I got stuck anyway." Dagny tried to act nonchalant about the whole experience, but even as she spoke, she realized she was still in a state of shock.

"There's a barrel around back for collecting rainwater, hold on." Max ran off around the shack, and returned shortly with a metal bucket. "Here ya go."

"Thanks." Dagny started to wash her hands and face, and poured water over her feet, watching the mud run down the cobbled road.

"All better," Max said with a smile.

"Yep..."

"What you did was really brave," he said. "I don't think I could've done it. If you weren't with us, Jorgie might've been lost forever. You're basically a hero."

Dagny shook her head. "Don't say that, it's embarrassing. I don't know what came over me. I never did anything like that before in my life, not even close."

"Still, it was incredible. You should be proud. If anyone should be embarrassed it's me, just sitting in the boat, watching you go."

Dagny felt awkward listening to Max talk like that, and wanted to change the subject. "Hey, how well do you know Magu Ogden?" she asked.

"Umm, pretty well, I suppose. We've been hanging around his place for a few years now. Why?"

"I was just thinking, remember when Maris came and pulled me out? It was because he saw something upstairs with Ogden. Maris was really disturbed by it. I was worried about you all after we left. It was so strange."

"Oh. What was it?"

"Maris didn't tell me everything, but said Ogden soaked all his books in vinegar."

Max tightened his face. "Really? Huh."

"You don't think it's concerning?" she asked.

"I guess. Ogden's always been kind of odd. Ever since I've known him, anyway."

"It was surprising to Maris. He didn't know anything about that, and he's known Ogden for a long time."

Max looked down at his own feet now. "Well, Maris doesn't really know him. Not anymore, anyway. No one really does, because no one comes around anymore."

"That's sad," Dagny said.

"In the beginning, Rodo and I would go to the shop every day. I'm not exaggerating. Every single day, listening to him tell stories. Then he invited us to use that storage room whenever we needed to, sorta like our base of operations. Only now, he barely acknowledges us when we come by. Sometimes it seems he doesn't recognize us at all."

"I'm sorry to hear that," she said.

"There's nothing to be done about it. Just have to accept things like that, I suppose." Max gave her a smile to soften the mood.

"Is that where you first heard about Alex? At Ogden's?"

"I don't know. It could have been anywhere. Do you realize how popular he is?"

Dagny shrugged. "I have an idea." She tried to steal looks at Max when she could. He had a nice face and innocent eyes. She liked that he was sitting so close to her. He felt different from the boys she knew in Rork. It was comforting and peaceful here on the bench, and Dagny was disappointed when Rodolph came marching around the corner of the nearby shed.

"That's done," he said. "First time I've seen her cry. Jorgie's sister was quite thrilled with us."

"That's good. It's not a bad thing to be friends with the Marsh Rats," Max said.

"How you feeling, Dagny?" Rodolph asked.

"Alright. A little sore." It was late. The streets quiet and empty. "How far off until dawn?" she asked.

"I think we have a few hours still. Where to now?" Max said, standing up. "I'm not gonna be able to sleep anytime soon."

Rodolph looked at him with a wide grin. "Stardust?"

"Yes! To Stardust!" said Max.

∾

The old building sat in the shadows of the original city wall, near some canal Dagny had never traveled down. A rusted metal gate and gravel path led to a squat structure with white plastered walls and large, dark windows. A plume of smoke rose from a brick chimney. The front door, imposing and solid, was propped open, and a faded sign hung above. *Of Stardust and Light*, it announced.

Despite the late hour, Stardust was loud with music and laughter. Thick, earthy-smelling smoke enveloped Dagny as they walked inside, and stung her eyes. From across the room, drums mixed with a melody of strings. Rodolph shouted something inaudible to Max and walked off.

Dagny was thankful for the dim light, looking the way she did, bruised and scratched. Max led her to an empty booth set in an alcove near the fireplace and they sat, watching the room. The heat was stifling. Almost immediately, Dagny started sweating through her clothes. Still, she was glad to be here. She wanted to ask Max more questions and listen to any stories he had, but it was so loud.

The song ended and Rodolph returned with three glazed mugs and a large, dented pitcher. "Here, drink this, it'll cool you off," he said to Dagny. Max clinked her mug and gulped it. The drink was sweet and warm, with a mild bitterness underneath. It did not cool her off.

"I saw Sarna and her sister near the back," Rodolph said to Max.

"Are they playing?" Max responded.

"Didn't ask."

Dagny leaned into the conversation. "Who are they?"

"Musicians," Rodolph told her. "They're pretty good. Max and them go way back."

She caught Max rolling his eyes, as Rodolph chuckled to himself.

"Is this where you usually celebrate your adventures?" Dagny asked. She felt out of place in the crowded room.

"Our *adventures*?" Rodolph laughed. "Yeah, we don't have too many of those."

"That's not true," Max said.

"Exploring caves and walking around the city aren't really adventures," Rodolph said. "We come here just for something to do. I'm surprised you've never been."

"I didn't even know this place existed," Dagny said. "Do you have anything else planned? Now that Jorgie is back."

"Not really," Rodolph said, tapping the table to the rhythm of the fiddle players.

"I'm just enjoying what we accomplished tonight, saving Jorgie," Max said.

"True... but it was all Dagny. She saved him. We didn't do anything." Rodolph raised his mug and gave her a nod.

A pair of girls moved through the crowd, approaching their booth. The taller of the two, skinny with a freckled nose, carried a mandolin. The other was a fuller, sweet-faced girl, with braided purple hair. Both had similar, deep-set eyes.

Max glanced down at the table and picked at a piece of splintered wood.

"Hey there, Moongoose," the freckled girl said, almost smiling. *Moongoose?* Dagny wondered. It must be a nickname of sorts.

Max looked up at them. "Hi Hanette. How is everything?"

"—Let us in," she said to Max, who scooted down. The girls joined them at the table. Dagny, squished between the boys, finished her drink and poured another from the dented pitcher. It tasted like apples and berry. Despite what she'd just been through in the tower, only a couple of hours ago, she still felt nervous at the table.

"We missed your crew at the festival last week," said the freckled girl.

"Sorry 'bout that, something came up," Max replied, looking embarrassed.

Rodolph, perhaps recognizing Dagny's discomfort, began to introduce them. "Sarna... Hanette... this is Dagny Losh."

"Nice to meet you," said Sarna, the girl with purple hair.

"A new member?" Hanette asked. "How'd you get involved with this bunch?"

"She's related to Alex Benzara," Max said. "We just got back from Farrow Blood. Dag helped us out with something in the tower." For the first time in her life, Dagny was getting tired of hearing about Alex Benzara.

Hanette looked skeptical. "You don't say." Then she let out a long sigh before speaking again. "So, Moongoose, I have a question for you..."

"—Hold on a second, alright," Max said, his face sweating. "I gotta get some air real quick." He was sandwiched between Dagny and Sarna with no easy escape. Before Dagny could let him out, Max slipped under the table and crawled on the floor.

Sarna muttered "Stop it" to her sister, and nervously twisted her purple braids. Rodolph leaned over and whispered in Dagny's ear, "I'll be back," and left as well, leaving her at the mercy of the two stranger girls.

"I'm just having a little fun with him," Hanette said. She set her mandolin on the table and drank from Max's mug. "Careful with this stuff, it's stronger than you'd think."

"Farrow Blood Island, huh? Is that true?" Sarna asked.

"Yes," Dagny said, somewhat guarded.

"What'd you go out there for?" Hanette asked, finishing what was left in the mug.

"You should probably ask Max that question," Dagny said.

Hanette gave her a long, curious look, then leaned in closer, inspecting her face. "What happened to you?"

Dagny instinctively touched her forehead. "...I fell down a chimney, getting into the Oracle Tower—"

"Ouch, look at your finger!" Sarna said.

Dagny covered her hand, where her nail had torn off during the fall.

"Are you alright?" Sarna asked. "What happened in there?"

"Not a lot, really. I'm fine." She didn't want to reveal too much. The boys had told her they were keeping the mission a secret. She was surprised Max had mentioned it at all.

The two sisters exchanged glances before Hanette spoke again. "How come we've never seen you around? Where you from?"

Dagny almost said 'Rork,' but she stopped herself. It didn't feel right. "The Rakesmount." She gulped down what remained of her drink and poured another.

Dagny could feel the mood shift, and as the drums began to beat again, they sat quietly, trading awkward looks at each other from across the table. In another part of the room, a gruff male voice began to sing about the Golden Leper from Solevay. When the third verse started, Hanette casually picked up her mandolin and started to pluck along, her fingers drifting skillfully along the neck. She was scrunching her freckled nose, a distant look on her face, as though thinking about something else entirely.

"They're good people... Max and Rodolph," Sarna said, sliding closer to Dagny. Sarna's eyes were honest, sensitive.

"Seems like it. I only met them this morning, though." Had it only been a single day? Time felt surreal. Dagny glanced around the room, wondering about all the different lives here, each existing and flourishing in their own unique way. Suddenly she became detached from everything, a wave of odd euphoria washing over her.

"You alright?" Sarna asked. The concern seemed genuine.

Dagny tried to smile and nod. Her head started to spin. The noise and smoke. The heat. When was the last time she ate? She stared down at her empty mug. What was it? Something in the drink? She was going to be sick.

The song of the Golden Leper ended, and the place erupted in cheers. Someone in the crowd called for Hanette and Sarna, and a group of people turned and looked at the booth. In the dizzying smoke, Dagny couldn't focus on any of their faces. Hanette left the table and pulled her sister along behind her. Dagny lost sight of them in the crowd.

She had to get out of here. Dagny stood up. The floor became an uneven whirling mess, and she rushed outside just as the mandolin started to chop through the chords of the first song. She threw up in the rose bushes.

After wiping her mouth on her shirtsleeve, Dagny walked around the building to a small, vacant yard growing between the tavern and ruins of the old city wall. The night wind blew in from somewhere beyond, cooling her skin.

She lay down, staring at the stars, feeling unmoored, as if she could let go and drift toward the sky. She could still hear the music from inside, filtering out through the windows and the open doorway. It was a stormy sound. A brooding, descending melody, droning on and on and on...

A voice spoke out. "Dag? You back here?"

"Yes. I'm here, *Moongoose*." She began to laugh.

"What you doing?"

"Laying down, looking at the sky." She heard Max walk along the gravel and grass, and lay down next to her.

"Sorry about that back there. I wasn't planning on running into them," he said.

"They seem nice..." Dagny said.

"Yeah..."

"Do you know the Night Princes?" she asked. The sky was brilliant.

"Some of them... there's Gylathrik," he said pointing at a line of stars. "And see that bright one there, to the left of his belt?"

"I see it."

"That's the Black Star, Gylathrik's eye, after it was torn out..."

"That sounds pleasant," Dagny said, laughing again. This time, Max laughed too.

"Actually, when the star's bright, it brings good luck. You're in a giddy mood. I like it."

"I thought I was going to die in that chimney," Dagny said with an unexpected seriousness.

The statement caught Max off guard. "That's... awful... I shouldn't have let you go."

"You didn't let me do anything. And it's fine. We found the boy."

"Yeah."

She paused for a moment. "Is there something going on between you and those sisters?"

"What do you mean?" he asked.

"I think you know what I mean."

There was another moment before Max answered. "No. There's not."

"Okay."

They lay there for a while in silence, before Dagny fell asleep from exhaustion.

~

Dagny awoke shortly after dawn. The sun slipped in through the building's shuttered windows and washed over the room, the dark wood tables and floors glittering like polished amber. Only embers burned in the fireplace now, but the place still smelled heavily of smoke and ash.

She was lying in a sticky, cushion-lined booth that reeked of spilled drink, and had flattened to such an extent over the years that Dagny felt nothing but the hard surface underneath. Her entire body hurt; her hands and forehead throbbed with a constant pulse.

Someone must've carried her in here after she fell asleep. A musty blanket covered her, and a mug of water had been placed on the table. She slowly sat up and scanned the room.

Sitting nearby, and speaking in a hushed whisper, were Hanette, Sarna and an older man who was hunching over. A guitar was on the floor next to him. Sarna was the first to notice Dagny and gave her a friendly smile and wave.

"Hello there," she said. "Sleep well?"

"No," Dagny said, rubbing her eyes. "How did I get here?" Her mind was a blur.

Hanette glanced over her shoulder. "Max carried you in. He asked if we could watch over you 'til you woke."

"Oh... did he leave?" Dagny asked.

"Yes." Hanette turned back to the table.

"He lives across town," Sarna said. "Had to get back before the sun rose."

Dagny rubbed her face and drank some water from the mug, while the group went back to whatever it was they'd been discussing. She realized she didn't even know what part of the city she was in, and needed to get back home before any more time had passed. "Hey, umm... could someone give me directions to Rork?"

"Rork?" Hanette said. "What are you going there for?"

"I live there." She didn't feel well and wasn't in the mood for a long-winded discussion.

"I thought you were from the Rakesmount."

The Rakesmount? Right. Last night. It was coming back to her in pieces.

"I'm from the Rakesmount, originally. I live in Rork now." Dagny explained, in as few words as she could manage.

Hanette shook her head. "That's dishonest."

Dagny shrugged. "Anyway, could someone help me? I need to get home."

Hanette started to say something else, when Sarna cut her off. "I can show you. It's a little too complicated to explain."

"Great. Can we leave now?"

They stepped outside. Dagny's eyes ached from the sunlight and she shielded them with her hand, until they made it across the main road and into an alleyway shaded by high buildings and balconies.

"...Thanks for walking with me," Dagny said as they crossed over a narrow canal.

"Sure. Don't want you getting lost," Sarna said.

"I got the sense that you and your sister didn't like me very much."

Sarna looked hurt. "Why would you think that?"

"I don't know. Maybe because I was with Max?" It was true, wasn't it? There *was* something there. Dagny could see it on Sarna's face last night.

"The thing with Max is... complicated. But that's his fault more than anything. And to answer your question, we don't dislike you, and it certainly wouldn't be over something as silly as that. Would we have watched over you all night if that was the case?"

"I doubt it."

"So there you go."

They cut through a small park, with white- and pink-blossomed trees in full bloom. Two old men sat at a stone table playing Talvarind. Dagny tried to peek at what sets they were playing as she passed.

"Did you really sneak into the Oracle Tower?" Sarna asked.

"Yeah."

"Did Max and Rodolph go inside?"

"No, but the only entrance was very tight. They wouldn't've fit."

"So it was just you then?"

Dagny nodded. Her head a constant, dull ache.

"That's impressive... Hey, if I'm asking too many questions, let me know. Don't wanna be annoying," Sarna said, stopping to pick a purple wildflower off of a nearby bush.

"No, it's fine."

"How long have you lived in Rork?" Sarna asked.

"Seven years or so."

"That's a dramatic change. From the Rakesmount to there..."

"It is..."

"Probably don't go back much, huh?" Sarna said.

"No. Not really." She'd only been back once. With Alex, the day after the flood receded. It was not something she ever tried to think about, but sometimes the images just appeared: wooden frames sticking sharp and awkward from the drowned earth; the mound of debris, like a giant splintered ship, littering the place where her family had lived.

Sarna led Dagny across an open plaza, as the city was coming alive. Merchants set up booths around a marbled fountain and statue of some proud soldier whose name was unknown to Dagny. The soldier had a stern face, but looked friendly enough, standing at the top of a heap of skulls.

They bought some biscuits and boiled eggs from a vendor, and crested a small hill. Dagny could see the Odd Viddry Bell Tower in the distance, signaling the border of City Centre.

"It sounds like you're officially in with Moongoose and company," Sarna said, as they walked next to each other. Dagny could find her way back home from here, but she enjoyed Sarna's company. The purple-haired girl had a calming presence, and didn't seem to mind walking through town with Dagny, barefoot and disheveled.

"I don't know. We only went on that one trip together last night," Dagny said.

"Yes, but they don't invite anyone on their little expeditions," Sarna explained.

"It's because I live with Alex Benzara. I know that's the reason."

Sarna gave her a blank look. "Moongoose mentioned him last night. I don't know who that is."

Dagny smiled. *That's refreshing,* she thought. "Why do you call him Moongoose anyway?"

"It's from that children's book, *Flight of the Moongoose...* about the goose who tried to fly to the moon."

"I'm afraid I'm not familiar with it. I didn't have any children's books when I was younger."

"Ah. Well, the goose fell to his death from exhaustion, only to come back as a spirit who would take good-natured children on trips across the stars... A few years back, a group of us was watching the Spring Renewal parade from the rooftop of Stardust, and Max fell right off, hurt his leg pretty bad. Someone called him Moongoose and it stuck. It's silly how nicknames get started sometimes."

The Bell Tower chimed eight o'clock. Dagny would have some explaining to do if she were found crawling into her room now, especially looking the way she did. Dagny was trying to come up with a believable explanation... but nothing came to mind. She would just have to deal with it.

They skirted the outer edge of City Centre and reached the main plaza marking the entrance to Rork. A troupe of performers was setting up a small stage, as many were apt to do this time of year in celebration of Summer's End. Dagny didn't recognize any of the actors here, though. Probably one of the traveling groups from up river. The traveling companies were usually quite awful.

The shift was noticeable when they crossed into Rork and passed underneath the thick canopy of ancient oaks spread over the main road.

"This place is just... *gorgeous...* I love it here. Can I come live with you?" Sarna asked, with a laugh.

It really was grand. So much attention was paid to the way the gardens and grounds were kept, compared to most of the city. Dagny thanked Sarna again when they reached the Benzara house. "I'd ask you to come in, except I need to sneak back inside."

"That's okay. I need to head back myself and get some sleep. Me and Hanette... we sleep at odd hours, if you couldn't tell."

Dagny smiled at her and climbed up an old, gnarled walnut tree that worked its way over the garden wall.

"Dagny!" Sarna called out, stopping her before she disappeared. "I'm glad we met."

6

Dagny climbed up the trellis and entered her bedroom from the balcony. Upon seeing the door closed and room undisturbed, she quickly stripped off her filthy clothes and collapsed onto the bed. No sooner had she started to drift asleep, however, when she heard a quiet knocking at the door. Dagny tried to ignore it at first, but the knocking only grew louder and more determined. She crawled out of bed, covered herself with a blanket, and peeked into the hallway. Standing in front of her were Lucas and Abrielle, handsomely dressed with fresh smiling faces. *Ugh... City Centre...* she suddenly remembered her promise to take the boy there today.

"Are you ready Dag?" Lucas asked hopefully. "Mom said we could eat brunch at the park."

Her exhaustion was borderline painful, but Dagny found a way to shove it deep inside. "Sure... give me a moment to wash up."

She had her own private bath just off the bedroom, and after filling the tub, Dagny lowered herself in, watching as the mud on her legs turned the water black. She tried to scrub the swamp from her body and out of her hair, yet, despite her efforts, Dagny still felt dirty. When she'd finished, she glanced at her face in the gold-framed mirror above the tub. The left side of her forehead was scraped and starting to scab, and Dagny did her best to cover it with her hair. Then, she slipped into a breezy orange dress, covered her bruised arms with a light shawl, forced a smile, and stepped out to greet the day.

Dagny Losh walked with her two young wards, Lucas and Abrielle, holding their hands as they made their way down Old Rork's main boulevard and toward the City Centre. They were on their way to Ettrick's, a master craftsman of Talvarind boards and figure pieces.

"I would like to go to the sweet bread place," Abrielle said. Her mother had braided her hair that morning, and she wore a crisp cotton dress that complemented the outfit Lucas had on.

"No. The game shop first... please Dagny..." Lucas begged.

"I'm sure we can do both." Dagny enjoyed their company and the time they spent together lately. When they left the house, Dagny did her best to avoid Cate and any potential questions about her injured body. The children were too excited about the trip today to notice.

They reached the plaza that marked the end of Rork where a large crowd had gathered around the group of entertainers that Dagny had seen setting up earlier. A crudely painted backdrop of a forest scene now stretched behind them, between two poles. The crowd laughed, and a bearded actor in a patched, multi-colored robe gave a speech from a small stage. From this distance, Dagny couldn't hear what he was saying.

"Ooh, performers! Can we go see?" Lucas asked.

Before Dagny could respond, the boy broke free from her grasp and ran into the crowd, slipping between a hefty man wearing a sleeveless vest, and a bent old woman.

"Lucas!" Dagny cried, picking up Abrielle and chasing after him. The boy weaved between more bodies, squeezing his way to the front of the audience. Dagny tried to press through, but the heavy-set man bumped her with his hip and stared coldly at her with small, beady eyes. He had the face of an ugly woman with a sweaty, thin mustache.

"Back girl. No cutting," he said.

"Please, I need to get through. My... brother slipped past," Dagny said.

"You little liar," the old crone answered. "You're just trying to get a better view. Well you shoulda gotten here sooner. You spoiled Rorkers, think the world exists to serve you. Well, not today! Now piss off or Bershom here will have to thump you good."

Dagny scowled at them. "You two are awful."

"Get! Scatter!" the woman said, shooing her away.

Dagny thought of arguing the point further when Abrielle began to cry. She did her best to comfort the girl, while circling the crowd looking for another angle to reach the front. It was no use; there was no way through, and the only place where the audience hadn't swelled thick was behind the curtain. But Dagny could see the front of the crowd from there, and felt a sense of relief when she spotted Lucas, sitting crosslegged near the stage.

Dagny waved her free hand at Lucas, trying to get his attention. It worked, briefly. Lucas glanced at her just as a bald strongman flung a gold-painted child high into the air. The crowd gasped and Lucas forgot all about her.

"Your brother's safe, and I guess we're here until the show's over," Dagny said to Abrielle.

She had a hard time following along with whatever story the performers were trying to tell, something about a misfit prince courting a set of sisters while avoiding a black-clad executioner who spun thick-bladed knives around his body. The acrobats were good, but the actors were terrible. Dagny didn't recognize a single one. None of them could have played at any of the lesser theatre troupes throughout the city, let alone the Barchpool Players where Dagny had seen *The Winter's Comet* last season.

It was during the final scene and climax of the show, when the prince professed his love while dressed in a rooster costume, that Dagny first noticed a pack of dirt-stained youths milling about.

One rough-and-tumble girl eyed Dagny from across the crowd, and Dagny's hand instinctively covered her satchel. The girl just stood there, staring. Dagny felt a sense of uneasiness creep up. *Alright, time to leave.* She lifted Abrielle, marched right in front of the stage, and grabbed Lucas' arm, pulling him to his feet. The crowd began to boo her, and one of the actors held his hand out, shouting, "How 'bout a little something before you go, beautiful?" His beard was splotchy and his teeth were black.

Lucas began to protest, until she reminded him that they better make it to Ettrick's before it closed. As they left the crowd and production behind, Dagny heard the distinct voice of the old crone screaming that her purse had been snatched.

They made their way to market street and skirted the edge of the domed governmental palace, stopping briefly for a brunch of noodles and smoked fish at one of the many cafes that bordered the park. As they ate, a group of fiddle players practiced underneath an enormous topiary bush clipped to resemble a rhinoceros. Lucas did his best to remain patient, but he was practically sprinting by the time they reached the paved lane leading to the shop. A carved wooden sign hung out front, spelling *Ettrick's* with a flourish, and a large window display contained life-sized animal statues gathered around a game of Talvarind.

Inside, the proprietor, Ettrick, talked with a friendly couple about a birthday present for the man's father. "He's played the Red Guard since I was a young child... I'm so happy to replace his main figures with something so grand. *Exquisite really.*"

Ettrick had a long, greying mustache, and he greeted Dagny with a nod. She was about to ask where the Night Princes were kept when Lucas pulled her by the wrist deeper into the shop.

The boy scanned the rows at the rear of the store, searching for the figurines, while Abrielle stood silently watching, holding Dagny's hand. Tucked in a corner nearby, a small workshop had been set up, where a young man focused on painting a new set of playing pieces. Beyond him, the back door stood open, leading into the alley.

"They're not here... Dagny, they're not here!" said Lucas in a panic.

"Hmm, which ones are you looking for? What do they look like?" Dagny asked, trying to peer over the top shelf.

"Like... like *Night Princes*... but they're gone. They're all gone."

"Is there something I can help you with," said a voice from behind them. It was the young man from the workshop.

"Oh yes... hello," Dagny said. "We were wondering if—"

"You don't have any more Night Princes," Lucas cried.

"We don't? Let me see here." The young man reached into the back of the top shelf. "Oh yes, here we go." He brought down two figures. One was an old man painted shades of blue, and the other a gold-colored house cat.

"Those are Night Princes?" Lucas asked doubtfully.

"They sure are. This is the Wizard of Luxdar, named after the constellation, and this is his companion, the cat Marvert."

"I've never heard of them," Lucas said.

"They are probably the most unique pieces in the whole set. Which is why, I suppose, they are still here, and lucky for you. Most people aren't familiar with them. But the Wizard can move two extra spaces when threatened with capture, just like the Queen in the original Red Guard. And Marvert... well, I think he just may be my favorite. He reminds me of my cat back home."

Lucas was intrigued, staring at the figures. "Is the Wizard a real person?"

"Yep. He actually lived around here a long time ago but now wanders the space between stars, keeping the darkness of the Universe at bay."

"Dagny, can we get both of them, please? I want the Wizard, and the Marvert cat. He needs him so he won't be lonely out there."

Dagny smiled, "Yes, we can get both of them."

"I hope it pays off for many games to come," the man said.

They walked to the front counter, where Ettrick had just finished boxing the gifts purchased by the couple.

"Ah, I see you've found the last of the Night Princes," he said, winking at Dagny. "Congratulations my boy, these are some fine pieces, indeed. I know an expert Talvarind player when I see one."

"I'm finishing my first set. Dag is teaching me how to play," Lucas said.

"You have a discerning eye, which is very important to be successful at the game," said Ettrick.

Dagny reached into the purse from Caternya to pay the man. And as she did, she looked up and saw the dirty-faced girl from earlier, staring from across the street through the display window. It took Dagny a moment to realize that the girl was looking straight at her. A chill ran down her spine. The girl had followed them here.

"I... think we're going to look around some more, but we'll take these... here," Dagny said, quickly handing the man a fistful of treasury notes.

"Oh, of course, maybe something for the little girl, then? I'll wrap these up for you."

"No, that's okay." She grabbed the figurines and shoved them in her satchel.

"Well, if I can be of any further assistance..."

"Let's go," Dagny said to the children, hurrying them through the store and out the rear door into the alley. To her left, the path led back around to the storefront and the dirty-faced girl, so they headed the opposite direction, down the shaded alleyway.

"What's going on? Why are we going this way?" Lucas said.

Something about the street girl vaguely reminded her of Gretchen. She couldn't say what it was exactly. The two couldn't have looked more different. For one, the girl around the corner had pink skin, where Grete's had been a dark brown. It was something in the eyes, the expression on the girl's face: blank but not empty. Almost mournful.

Dagny could have easily pitied the girl, but she'd heard stories of aristocrats wandering too far from home, only to be found floating down river after a run-in with rogues from the lower side. Dagny thought about what easy targets they must look like. Her, the scrawny girl in the lace orange dress, and Caternya's two sweet-faced children, primped and styled by their mother in the latest fashion. Maybe it'd be different if she were alone, but right now her only concern was Lucas and Abrielle and getting them to safety as quickly as possible.

Dagny realized she was pulling the children hard.

"You're scaring me," said Abrielle.

"I'm sorry. I didn't mean to, I just realized that this is the quickest way to the sweet bread place. You still wanted to go there, right Abrie?"

The girl nodded, but watched Dagny with distrustful eyes.

This girl is too smart, Dagny thought as she took the children further down the twisting alley. She hoped the path would wind its way back to the posh cafes and ornate window fronts of the market district.

"Does this have something to do with the girl that's following us?" Lucas asked.

Dagny looked back and saw the street girl peering around a bend.

"Quick, quick. Faster." Her heart pounded and she picked up Abrielle and ran as best she could. The path twisted and weaved among the back ends of tall buildings. Dagny almost slipped when they descended a narrow staircase that appeared suddenly in the alley, and her dress tore when they skirted past a rusting gate. They kept moving further and further down and yet no pathway opened up that would lead them back to the main roads. It felt as though they were descending into the bowels of the city. Finally the alley forked, with one branch leading into shaded darkness and the other opening up into a sunlit plaza.

Dagny was gasping for air when they entered the vacant courtyard and almost dropped Abrielle on the ground. There was a dried-up fountain in the center, and shuttered windows looked down on them from brick buildings on all sides. They squeezed through a tight, open space that connected to a side street and eventually made their way back to Rork's main boulevard, losing the rough-cut girl somewhere in the alleyways of City Centre.

7

It was windy and warm in the garden outside the Benzara house. Dagny sat with her legs stretched in the sun, while Lucas lay on a blanket nearby reading a book from Alex's library. Across the yard, Abrielle giggled with some friends from the neighborhood, as they searched for other children hiding throughout the gardens, screaming, "Ghoulie! Ghoulie!"

It had been almost a week since her adventure in the Oracle Tower, and with each passing day, Dagny waited expectantly for Max or Rodolph to show up at her door. The boys knew she lived in Rork, and Alex's house would've been easy enough to find. But they never came.

Dagny wished she didn't feel like this, but she couldn't stop thinking about them. Max in particular... They shared something together under the sky that night after Farrow Blood. Dagny was certain of it. Since then, whenever she was alone, Dagny would imagine wandering the city with him, or sailing across the lagoon. She'd think about what to bring on her next expedition. The tower had been dangerous, but was also thrilling. It was so boring here at home. She was sick of feeling lonely.

She did have one visitor, though. Yesterday, Sarna had come by after lunch. Caternya was practically beaming with excitement when she made the announcement that Dagny had a guest. It was as if Cate had given up all hope that anyone would ever stop by to see her. At first, Dagny thought that Max and Rodolph must've finally gotten around to it, but then Caternya said, "She seems like a very polite young woman," as they walked toward the front door.

Sarna was funnier than Dagny would've guessed. It was a quiet funny that seemed to only come out once the purple-haired girl was comfortable. They'd spent the afternoon talking in the Benzara parlor. Sarna told Dagny about her favorite musicians in the city. At the top of the list was Marfisi and the Mirage. They would be playing at the Ironhead, along with Hanette and Sarna, and Dagny was invited to come. They didn't talk about Max. When Sarna left, she gave Dagny a hug and kiss on the cheek. "See you tomorrow. It's going to be great."

That night, Dagny asked Alex about the Oracle of Farrow Blood.

"Huh. I haven't heard that one mentioned for quite some time," Alex had said, sitting at the desk in his study. "What makes you ask about her?"

"No reason. I just heard some people talking. Why doesn't the Authority allow anyone out there?"

"Oh, I'm not sure they really care much. The place was forbidden during the Regime of Man. The penalties for even mentioning it back then were severe. So much so, that people still fear it. Anyway, the island is best to be avoided. It's a dangerous place. Anything still standing out there is likely to collapse, soon enough."

"Why did the Regime of Man forbid it?"

"The Regime was nervous about everything. They sought to control everyone's thoughts. The Farrow Blood tower, and the estate it was attached to, were some of the oldest structures on the lagoon. All sorts of stories and legends came from it. There were some about the Oracle being connected to a lost queen – an ancient guardian who guided suffering children. During the time of the Regime they were popular stories, but brought a lot of attention to all the misery the Regime was responsible for."

"So they outlawed it? Over a story? Why?"

"They were weak."

"Do you know anything about the Oracle, herself?" Dagny asked.

"A bit. People said she could see the future and speak to the past, and those who made the trip across the lagoon spoke of other encounters. But who really knows."

"What kind of encounters?"

Alex glanced down at the stacks on his desk. "Oh, all kinds of mystical stuff."

"You don't know where she came from? The Oracle?"

Alex started to thumb through one of his ledgers. "Tell you what, tomorrow when I'm not so busy, we'll sit down again and we can talk about it some more. How's that?"

Dagny agreed. And as the next day slowly slipped away, she waited for Alex to find some time and tell her about the Oracle of Farrow Blood. She had walked by his study a dozen or so times, until finally giving up and settling down in the garden outside.

Stretching out on the grass, Dagny watched the clouds as multi-colored finches darted overhead. She could hear Abrielle and another child running along the edge of the small pond, kicking up water and mud and laughing hysterically. It made Dagny think of playing with Grete, in the muddy path that connected the Rakesmount with the stewhouse at the top of the hill. She had friends back then, didn't she? Other children of the Mount... what kinds of games had they played? Dagny tried to remember, but she'd blocked so much of it out. Gretchen was a sweet girl. Kind. Feeding strays in the wet alley behind the row house. Gretchen didn't deserve that sad place, or the ogre Finkel, or the flood that came later. What their life could have been like together, if only things had been different. Dagny started to cry, and rolled over, putting her face in the ground, so Lucas wouldn't see.

By the time supper was ready, Dagny was anxious and ready to get over to the Ironhead. It was still early when she finished her meal of buttery shellfish and roasted potatoes, and the sun had just begun to dip behind the Old Rork rooftops when she stepped out the door. Dagny knew she'd be getting there well before the musicians started, but she just had to get moving.

The Ironhead was located at the top of a rocky overlook that jutted out into the lagoon. When Dagny arrived, the main room was almost empty. An older woman wiped down heavy oak tables and gave her a smile as she entered. Opposite the front doors was a raised stage, and off to the side a staircase led down.

Dagny was hoping that Sarna and Hanette would be here already, but she had no such luck. She paced about for a bit, feeling awkward and out of place. As she headed toward the bar to order some food – even though her stomach was full – a young man carrying a Talvarind board came stomping up the stairs with a deep scowl on his face. He marched straight through the room and out the front doors. The woman wiping the tables called out, "Better luck next time."

Dagny, curious, approached the stairs and peered down. She was greeted by a rush of cool air and could hear the slush of water breaking below. She followed the staircase underneath the Ironhead, to a hidden cove where the fading sunlight still crept across a rocky beach. Lanterns illuminated stone tables where a handful of players focused on dueling games of Talvarind. At the middle table, a stooped and skinny man played the Jade Horsemen against a sly-looking younger boy with blood-red hair. It was the boy's set that grabbed Dagny's attention. His queen-piece was abnormally tall and sleek, almost stick-like, its outstretched hand gesturing to a mismatched band of unique figurines. There was a lady flanked by two lions, one red and one white. Several knights made out of glass. And an angelic minister with delicate wings, protecting the center. Slowly, his set came into focus. It was the old Court of Jud. Dagny had never seen it before, but she recognized several of the boy's pieces from one of Alex's books back home. She wondered how he came to possess such an unusual set.

The boy looked slightly older than Dagny, and wore chunky rings on every one of his fingers. He moved his pieces with a graceful easiness, and had the skinny man playing defense the entire game. After crossing the river with his glass knights, the boy systematically separated and captured the man's Horsemen, suffocating any hope of a counter-attack. When the match was over, the man sulked in his chair and passed the boy a leather pouch. They packed up their pieces in silence, with the boy only checking the contents of the pouch after the man had left.

Dagny watched the other games for a while longer, until the sun faded away, and the only light was from the brass table lamps. The remaining players were all amateurs using the traditional, popular sets, like the Red Guard or the Diviner's Set, but it was still interesting to watch them. Suddenly, Dagny heard drums beating from above. She broke away from the games and rushed up the stairs.

The Ironhead had filled quickly while she was below. Transformed into something utterly different from the room she had walked into less than an hour before. Dagny felt tension creeping into her core, and looked around for Sarna and Hanette, but before she could find them, the music erupted, the crowd swelled, and Dagny found herself trapped between tall, thick bodies. She caught sight of the musicians on stage: dark-eyed men with coarse faces, dressed in splashes of bright color dusted by travel. People next to her shouted along with a song about Freshing's Kiss. The booming drums, strings and pipes built into an inescapable beating riot.

Someone grabbed her from behind. Dagny spun her head around to see Sarna's smiling face, and immediately felt comforted. The girl hugged her and danced along until the song was over. Sarna had just enough time to shout, "Over here," before the drums pounded once again.

Dagny followed her to a table where Hanette sat with another young woman who barely acknowledged them when they approached. She had close-cropped hair and wore a purple jacket and ruffled skirt. Her skin was sun-kissed brown and smooth.

"This is Telga," Sarna shouted in Dagny's ear. "She's more Hanette's friend, than mine."

After the music ended, Hanette glanced at Dagny and asked, "So how are your adventures going with Max and company?"

"They're not. Haven't seen them since that night at Stardust," Dagny replied.

"You don't say..." Hanette said with a smirk.

"—We're going to play a new song tonight," Sarna said to the group. "Last Call of Kilkeken, about a fabled ship that left Larne before it sank."

Hanette scrunched her freckled nose. "Sarna wrote it. I hope it works. We haven't practiced it as much as I would've liked."

"Oh, don't worry, it's good," Sarna said, winking at Dagny.

"You know who I saw earlier," Telga said, speaking for the first time. "Tash."

Hanette snorted. "Goodness no..."

"He winked at me, like some sort of charmer."

"Who's Tash?" Dagny asked.

"Some blowhard," Hanette replied, "who thinks he's much fancier than he is."

"How do you know him?" Dagny said.

"What are you, writing a book?" Telga said with a chuckle.

"What do you mean?"

"Just that you ask a lot of questions."

"Be nice," Sarna said. "Dagny is one of my friends, and I don't recall asking you to come, Telga."

"I'm the nicest person you'll ever meet," Telga said, grinning. Suddenly her eyes flashed over to the crowd and she put her face down. "Oh no..."

"What?" Sarna asked.

"Jauson Tasher..."

Dagny looked at the approaching figure. It was the boy with the blood-red hair.

"Hey there, Telga," Jauson said as he sauntered over, ignoring the other girls. He had a tan bag, patched with rough stitching, slung across his chest. "I saw you earlier, but you didn't see me."

"No. I saw you," Telga said.

Jauson Tasher gave her a smile and nodded his head as if receiving a compliment. "You staying for the whole show tonight?"

Telga rolled her eyes dismissively and shrugged her shoulders.

"You want someone to keep you company?" he asked.

This time, Telga stared right at him. "Gross..."

Hanette snorted and started to laugh.

"Oh real nice," he said. "You know, I just won the Talvarind contest down below, and I'm perfectly okay with finding someone else to celebrate with. It'll be a good night for romance."

Hanette made a gagging sound, pretending to vomit onto her lap, and Sarna put her head on the table and started to laugh uncontrollably.

"*Real nice...* real nice company you're keeping these days," Tash said, turning away.

"That one cannot take a hint," said Hanette. "I don't know what charm you put on him, but it seems to be unbreakable."

"Lucky me," Telga said.

"Oh, there are worse ones around than Tash," said Sarna. "He's obnoxious, but harmless, and kinda cute." Telga gave her a cold stare, which caused the sisters to laugh even harder.

Another group of troubadours took to the stage and rattled off a series of drinking songs. Sarna brought over a pitcher of sour-tasting cider and the girls drank along with the rest of the crowd. By the time the sisters left to play, Dagny's head was foggy and Telga's eyes were dazed and glassy.

Dagny had assumed Hanette was the singer of the pair, but it was Sarna who sung out the verses of The Long Way Home. She was one of the most talented singers Dagny had ever heard. Strong and passionate. Off stage, she was a little shy and deferential to Hanette. Yet, on stage, there was a magnificent confidence to the soft girl with purple braids. The sisters switched instruments on several songs, cycling through fiddles and drums, a flute and guitar.

Telga scooted closer to Dagny. "Sarna is one of the sweetest people I know. Don't make her sad, alright?"

The statement caught Dagny off guard. "I'm not sure what you mean..."

"I meant just what I said."

Over a rhythmic beating, Sarna sang about being adrift in a dream.

The sisters finished their set, and Dagny and Telga made their way to the back of the crowd that had gathered in front of the stage. Sarna joined them, her face wide and excited. "*Marfisi,*" she whispered.

An odd strain of melody began to rise from somewhere beyond the empty stage. It was unlike anything Dagny had heard before. The sounds were, at once, both energetic and haunting. They echoed and amplified across the crowded room. The lamps in the ceiling went dark, and when they lit again a multi-colored glow spread over four figures on the stage. Dagny felt like she was at the edge of something unfamiliar and grand. Standing in the center of the musicians was a young female, dressed in a long, white cloak. She seemed liberated and dignified, like a queen in disguise.

For a moment, the rising melody stopped. An energized silence buzzed through the crowd, and when the first drum snapped, the space electrified. In an instant, the room turned manic with excitement. Sarna danced and spun, grabbed Dagny's hand and pulled her along, almost crashing into a throng of people. It was playful and wild. Ethereal and hypnotic. Dagny laughed and lost herself...

When she was child, she had gone to a celebration in a great hall, but like everything from that time, the memory was almost gone. There was dancing and music, and a scratchy green dress that fit like a tent. She was there to honor a cousin she never met, and everyone seemed happy for once. Grete was small, dark and shy, sitting by the wall, wearing her bracelet. A cheap tin thing, engraved with flower petals. Of no value to anyone else. It was the most important thing Grete owned. A gift from her father, before he disappeared. Dagny sat with her, until Grete felt comfortable, and the two of them danced in the corner.

Later, the ogre Finkel snatched the bracelet off of Grete's wrist, saying ugly girls don't get pretty things. Her sister howled something awful, sobbing hysterically in the bedroom they shared. Finkel forced Dagny to sell it at the market; her mother sitting voiceless nearby, hardened and cold. The ogre welted Dagny's face until she left in tears. But Dagny didn't go to the market. She hid it somewhere under rotten floorboards. She couldn't remember if she ever told Grete.

When the last of the songs had ended, Dagny stood in the darkness. A low hum buzzed through the room, as lamps were slowly lit and the crowd began to disperse. Dagny stepped out into the cool night air, blowing in strong from across the lagoon.

"I told you! Wasn't that fabulous?" Sarna yelled over the chatter.

"I never heard anything like it," Dagny said.

They walked with the mass of people streaming down the steps away from the Ironhead. On the other side of the plaza, Dagny saw the boy Tash sitting by himself on a bench, overlooking the lagoon.

"Hey, I know it's late, but did you want to come over?" Sarna asked. "If you get tired, we can pull out a cot for you."

"I should probably head back home," Dagny said. "But thanks again. Will you stop by soon?"

"Of course I will." The girls hugged and Dagny watched the sisters and Telga depart.

Instead of walking home, however, Dagny went over to the boy on the bench.

"That's an interesting set you play with," she said.

Jauson Tasher spun around, clearly surprised. "Oh. You're that stranger girl, the one with Telga."

"Yeah. I don't know her though... Your Talvarind set, it's the old Court of Jud, right?"

"It is..." Tash replied, a hint of suspicion on his face.

"I recognized it from one of the books back home."

"The original *Talvarind Compendium*? You have it?"

Dagny nodded. "We have one at the house anyway. It's not really mine."

The smile he gave her was genuine. There was no flirtatious charlatan behind it. "What were you doing with Telga and them?" he asked.

"Sarna invited me to come watch them play. *Marfisi and The Mirage* were great, weren't they?"

"I couldn't really hear," Tash said.

"I saw your match in the cellar. You were really good."

"Yeah. I'll be the first to admit I'm a bit obsessed with the game." His demeanor was different out here. Tash was not the cocky boy she encountered inside with Telga.

"Your queen figure, it's Odestinas, isn't it?"

"You know about her, huh?"

"I know it from the compendium. Is there something more?"

"She was the first Queen of Jud," Tash said.

"Jud? You're talking like it's a real place."

"It is. Or was. It was one of the ancient lands that got lost when the world changed. Jud's all gone now."

"That's interesting. Where was it?"

"The location is lost." Tash said, playing with his rings. "Not much is known about it anymore, only small parts of a big story, like random pages torn from a book. There was a city there, with shimmering dark walls erupting like a mountain of glass from the earth. And there's another story about the Imposter, who came to Jud in its final days, and turned all the city's daughters to metal, doomed to watch the world pass as they slowly set to rust."

"That's dark," Dagny said.

"You don't like dark stories?" he asked with a smirk.

"I don't mind them. How did you come across that set?"

"I'm going to keep it a mystery." His eyes suddenly lit up. "Do you want to see my other pieces? The ones I didn't play?"

"Alright," Dagny said, and sat down next to Tash on the bench overlooking the lagoon.

Jauson Tasher opened his stitched tan bag and pulled out two figurines. One was a small boy dressed like a wolf, and the other was a bent figure with no face who appeared to be covered in thorns.

"I don't play these," Tash said. "There's no rules for them that I can tell... not sure where they would fit. Do you recognize them? From your book, maybe?"

"I'm sorry. They're not familiar to me."

"That's okay. I think they were added later. The original pieces were all glass, like the knights here. Now the knights are the only glass ones left."

"Really unique. Beautiful," Dagny said.

"Thanks. What set do you play?" Tash asked her.

"Why do you think I play?"

"I can tell."

"...The Wild Court," she answered after a moment.

Tash considered it. "That's a good choice. More balanced than some give it credit for. It should beat the Red Guard every time. You ever play down at Sorn Rue?"

"No."

"That's where most players spend their time," Tash said. "I'm there occasionally. If you ever wanna stop by."

"Really? Thanks."

"Sure. Say, do you wanna play a game?"

8

"ALRIGHT, FROM HERE ON out, everything we discuss is secret," Rodolph told her, his face dimly lit from the lamp above. "I mean it, if you're joining us, none of this can be discussed outside the group, okay?"

Dagny nodded in agreement. Max opened a large canvas sack that he had carried down into the basement and emptied its contents on the dusty work bench near the stairs. The boys arrived this morning, picking up right where they left off that night at Stardust. There was no explanation or apology for their absence over the course of the last few weeks, but Dagny was so excited when she saw them outside her front door that all was forgiven in an instant.

"This is everything we acquired so far," Max said, stacking a dozen or so books on a variety of topics such as *History of the Hundred Isles and the Shallow Sea*, *Herbology*, *A Novice's Primer of Star Maps*, *The Drowned Lands*, a pamphlet on sailor's knots, and a collection of Ostrothian Legends. Next came the shiny metal sculptures—characters from fairy tales and constellations that the boys had "rescued" from a collapsed factory on a nearby island.

They set four chairs around the makeshift table. The older boys wore their black jackets, and Kimberly once again dressed all in yellow:

faded and cracked pale-yellow leather pants and vest; a bright lemon undershirt; a dull mustard bandana tied across his shaggy blond head.

More mundane items were pulled from the second bag: adventuring gear, climbing hooks and rope, theatrical costumes and makeup, hair dye. ("Disguises," Kimberly told her). A jar of marbles. A spyglass.

Max tucked his dark braid behind his ear and watched Dagny. "So, we gotta know if you're ready to join the group... *officially*. We thought about it, and you risked your life going into the tower. There's no better test than that. What do you say? You ready?"

"I am," she said without hesitation.

Max nodded to Rodolph, who removed a sleek, silvery drinking horn slung underneath his jacket and filled it with a thick, black substance from a jar that he pulled out of the canvas sack. Once it was filled to the brim, Max took a deep breath, held his nose, gulped and grimaced. Then he wiped his mouth and choked out the words, "Across the dusted road is you and me."

He handed the horn to Kimberly, who drank the slightest of sips, and had tears welling in his eyes before saying, "Amongst the drowned ruin of prophecy."

Broad-shouldered Rodolph was next. He didn't flinch, but his lips and teeth were black when he smiled. "No more we ponder the tales once sung."

The horn made its way to Dagny. The drink smelled like burnt licorice.

"What is it?" she asked.

Just before Kimberly spoke, Rodolph cut him off. "—Nah. No cheating. You just have to trust us and drink it."

She raised the horn to her lips and felt a glob of sludge enter her mouth. She slurped it down like a massive, runny egg. The taste was horrible. Something of a cross between thick, rotten milk and sugary metal. It expanded inside her, coating her throat and warming her chest. She felt for a moment that she might vomit but held it down.

When she was finished, the boys all announced, "Into the void, the Naverung."

"Welcome, Dagny," Max said, smiling broadly. "Welcome to the Naverung."

The Naverung? she thought. Before she could ask about it, Rodolph clapped his hands together, saying, "Alright! Now that's done, we can let you in on something."

Dagny's nose was running, and she discreetly wiped it on the sleeve of her dress. "...And what's that?"

"We didn't wanna say anything before, but the reason why we hadn't stopped by yet was because of Magu Ogden," Rodolph said. Max eyed the table, and Kimberly stared at Dagny with a curious look on his youthful face.

"What happened?" she asked.

"Max mentioned that you were concerned about him; that Maris saw some things when he was there with you."

"What'd you do? Break into the upper floors?" Dagny asked.

"Not really *break in*," Rodolph continued. "When Ogden was down below rearranging shelves, we snuck above. There were piles and piles of books turned to mush. The mirror in the bath had been shattered. All the objects that Ogden hid up there, the ones he thought were too valuable to keep downstairs, had been destroyed. It was really weird... and sad. We tried to make it up to the very top, but the door was locked."

"What? Why? Why would he do that?" Dagny asked. Rodolph just shook his head. "What happened next?"

"We got back to the second floor study before Ogden caught us. We were planning to try again, but before we could do it, Ogden disappeared."

"He disappeared?" Dagny asked.

"Yep. We showed up to the shop one day, and everything was locked and shuttered. We sat outside that entire morning and into the afternoon, and came back the next day and the day after that. But nothing... I wanted to break in through the back window, but Max—"

"I figured we'd done enough breaking in," Max said.

Dagny chewed on her fingernail, processing what she'd just heard. "What's the plan then? With Ogden?"

"The plan?" Rodolph replied. "I don't think there is a plan. He's gone."

Max nodded. "Yeah. I mean, we'll keep an ear out... in case we hear anything. That might be a mystery that never gets solved."

"It's just so strange..." Dagny said.

"Yeah..." Max said, still nodding his head. "In the meantime, there's the Marsh Rats. They want to thank us all, and you in particular. Throw a celebration tonight."

"Really? Are we going?" Dagny asked.

"Unless you have something more important to do," Rodolph said. Kim watched her intently.

"More important than an adventure to the Marsh?" Dagny said with a laugh. "No... I don't think so."

"Great. There's one last thing," Max said. "I was thinking... remember outside of Stardust?" *Of course she did.* "When we looked up at

Gylathrik? There was the Black Star, signaling good luck." With that, Max handed her a fist-sized orb of polished, blueish-green stone. She had no idea what it was, but it seemed to her one of the most beautiful things she'd ever seen.

"What is it?"

"I don't know," Max replied. "Last year, Rodo and me were walking around the junk piles outside the city and came across it. Just lying there on top of a pile of slag. There had been a star shower the night before, and I like to think it fell from the sky. It felt special and lucky, and just reminded me of the Black Star. It looked like it could be Gylathrik's eye, don't you think?"

Dagny twisted it around, catching the light. "It's really, pretty."

"It's yours," Max said.

"We're glad you're here," said Kimberly.

Rodolph crossed his arms, and looked at her from across the table. "Welcome to the group, Dag."

∞

Dagny stood in her closet changing clothes, while the Naverung boys traipsed about her bedroom. She watched them through the narrow slats of the closet door as she removed the rough-hewn gardening dress she'd been wearing when they arrived this morning. Either none of them had been inside a girl's bedroom before or none as grand as hers. They stood there marveling at the masterwork furniture, rich decorations and high ceiling painted with a mural of the afternoon sky. Kimberly collapsed in the middle of her feathered bed and stretched his arms out to see if he could reach the sides. "I'm just going to sleep here forever," he said before Rodolph told him to get off, that he was dirtying the sheets. For her journey to the Marsh, Dagny chose a sleeveless grey undershirt and the same suede pants she wore to Farrow Blood. She pulled on a pair of soft, fringed boots and tied a black bandana around her neck. And, of course, to cap it off she took her brother's coat.

Dagny had been living alone for the last week. Alex and Cate decided it would be best to stay with Caternya's family on their estate north of the city until the baby was born. Dagny was invited to come, but it felt to her like a formality, and no one pressed her when she said she'd stay at the house. Dagny wondered if she should send a message to Alex and tell him about Ogden's disappearance, but it was probably best not to bother him with such things right now. She would've told Maris but hadn't seen him since that day at River's End. She heard from Alex that Maris left the city not long after.

When she finished dressing, Dagny joined Max on the balcony. He sat at a small metal table off to the side, with his feet propped up on the railing.

"I swear, you can almost see Southend from here," Max said.

"No. It's too far," Dagny said. "Maybe from the roof, and *maybe* if you had a spyglass."

"Oh, I bet you could." Max continued gazing out over the skyline. "Hey, I think I can see the western wall over there. Is that the River Gate where the Morca enters?"

Dagny couldn't see what Max was referring to, but nodded anyway and said, "Probably. I think so."

"Okay. So my place would be about... *there*," he said moving his hand to the left. "It's a blocky green and white house. I knew it was far, but it seems infinite from up here. Glad the canals are much easier than walking."

"I think I can figure out those directions," Dagny said with a laugh. "Careful, now that I know where you live, I may randomly stop by when I'm bored."

Max smiled. His black hair tucked behind his ears. "I'm counting on it, and it's only fair since we've been to your home."

"You know, you could've come by sooner. I'd sorta been waiting."

"I thought you'd be upset... I wanted to come here days ago, but didn't know how to bring up what happened at Ogden's."

"I don't know why you'd think I'd be upset. You could've just come over and told me. I'm not mad about it."

"Well, you're one of us now. No more secrets."

"Yeah. There is one thing I wanna tell you, though," she said, hesitating.

"What is it?"

"I misled you before. When we first met. About adventuring with Alex. He actually never took me anywhere. I just wanted to come with you that night. I'm sorry."

"You know, I kinda figured that when we were on the lagoon. I thought it was weird you'd never been on the water before, but I didn't wanna say anything. And then, the way you marched up to that tower, I thought *this girl has definitely gone adventuring with Alex...* Anyway, it's alright. It all worked out. I'm glad you misled me."

Dagny laughed. "Me too." She sat next to him and they stared out across the city for a bit before Dagny spoke again. "What's the Naverung? Where'd that come from?"

It was a story told to Max by his father when he was very young. One of the few memories to survive the fog of early youth. The Naverung was a companionship, Max said, that began on the back of a giant titan who crossed the forested plains of what now lies beneath the Shallow Sea. The companionship was formed from life-giving clay that grew on the titan's back and molded the companions into the shapes of all great animals except for that of Man. And as they journeyed with the titan, the companions began to dream... and dreamed of an ending to the world. A great sadness came over the Naverung and they agreed to bid farewell to their titan and travel the land, gathering and safeguarding its memories before the ending snuffed them out forever.

"I don't remember all the details," Max said. "There was a story about a cauldron deep beneath a city, and an underground kingdom ruled by a giant soaked in blood."

"I've never heard of it. I'm sorry, it seems like something I should know. I feel like I'm not adding much," Dagny said.

"I doubt you would've heard it. I spent so much time searching the libraries and booksellers of City Centre looking for any hint that the Naverung – or at least parts of the story – were real, but found nothing. When I got older, I asked my dad about it. He couldn't recall ever telling it to me... said it was probably something he just made up since I liked stories so much when I was young... so there you go," Max shrugged. "The Naverung. The name just stuck with me."

"No kidding, do you think that's true? He just made it all up?" Dagny asked.

"My dad didn't remember anything about it. I almost second-guessed myself that he ever told it to me. But I have these vague memories of sitting with him on the floor of our house, listening..."

"I bet it's true. The whole thing," Dagny said.

She glanced into her room and saw Rodolph staring at himself in front of the gilded mirror, and Kimberly sitting at the vanity trying on her jewelry.

"Hey, how come you never wear any of this?" Kim called to her. He was wearing a thick jeweled necklace and had piled about a dozen rings on his fingers.

"—Put that back, it ain't yours," Rodolph ordered him.

"I'm not doin' nothin' wrong. I can look fancy, too," the young boy answered, but took the jewelry off.

They went downstairs where Dagny made red-root tea, and filled up on salted meat, biscuits and honey. Max figured no matter what time they departed, they wouldn't get back to the city until well after nightfall, so it made sense to eat beforehand.

They left through the kitchen, out the back door, and crossed the garden to a sunken dirt and gravel path that ran behind a stretch of Rork houses. The pathway used to serve as a shortcut between the road at one end and the canal docks at the other. But over the years, the path was blocked off. First, a high, brick wall was constructed at the road entrance, and later an iron fence was put up near the canal. Now, the pathway served as a sort of alley to nowhere between the gardens.

In the few weeks since her journey to Farrow Blood, autumn had descended on Old Rork, and the cooler air ushered the party along on their journey. Dagny marched in front, underneath rustling branches and past shrubs and hedges that screened adjacent homes. From somewhere nearby, she could smell someone cooking with ginger and garlic.

When they reached the iron fence at the end of the path, the four of them climbed over, then descended a small hill to the canal dock where Rodolph had tethered the boat. No one else was around as they boarded and kicked off toward the canals of the city proper.

"What kind of celebration do you think Jorgie's folk will give us?" Kimberly asked as they crossed under the Oyster Street Bridge.

"I'd wager some kind of spiced fishgut," Rodolph said, steering the boat. "Maybe a diviner song or two—"

"Or a fire show?" Kim asked. "Ya think? That'd be quite grand."

"Maybe..."

The southern marshland jutted out and away from the city like a curved knife, and the Marsh Rats lived at the tip. Once they were through the Water Gate, Rodolph cut a straight path toward the marsh, taking the boat into the open waters of the lagoon. As they departed, Dagny watched the city's jumbled outline of jagged rooftops, spires, turrets and domes shrink into the horizon. Out here, the lagoon was clear turquoise, just as Max had told her it'd be, and Dagny could see straight to the bottom.

Leaning over the edge of the boat, she saw a school of yellow striped fish swimming over and through the barnacle-covered ramparts of a tower and wall, still standing at the edge of an underwater plaza. Seagrass grew up from between the stones and gently swayed, as if waving to them as they crossed.

"This is the edge of Larne," Max said to her. "I'm always fascinated, every time we pass over it. One night a few years back, I was out here with my brothers, and I heard the lost bell tower chime."

"What? No you didn't," said Kimberly.

"What would you know? You weren't there," Max said.

"I know because it's not true. There's no bell tower down there."

"I'm telling you, I heard it... signaling to the ghosts of the town that the waves were coming. It scared us all half to death. You can ask my brothers if you want."

Kimberly said nothing else but eyed Max skeptically.

Even though she'd never been here before, Dagny knew about the sunken land. There were competing theories about what happened to Larne. Some said it had once been part of the outer-city and broke off, sinking into the lagoon. But Vittendorf wrote that Larne didn't sink. Rather, the sea itself rose and engulfed the lowlands. At one time, the entire region had been a single, enormous connected country. She thought about the Naverung titan from Max's tale, and imagined it crossing the underwater world below.

Several hours later, they arrived at the marshland. Protruding above gnarled swamp trees was a litter of shambling stilt houses connected by rope bridges and a suggestion of fire and smoke from somewhere beyond. Children wandered the mudbank scouring for clams, and narrow streams criss-crossed the marsh. The whole scene blended into the lagoon and shimmered against the cloudless blue sky.

Rodolph guided them along one of the shadow-covered streams and toward the stilts. There were people here. Watching them from platforms high above in the trees. Dagny caught glimpses of half-sunken vessels and the occasional mud-caked face peeking through tangled roots.

The stream converged with several others and opened into a sprawling, edgeless wetland blanketed with reeds that brushed along the side of their boat. It was here that a great number of stilt houses rose above the marsh and surrounded a circular dock. Swaying nearby was a rag-tag fleet of small skiffs, rafts and the occasional fishing ship.

One large, colorful vessel stood out among them, tied to the dock. A makeshift tent had been tacked to its deck and a laundry line was strung up between the mast and the hull. The yellow paint was peeling, and dull, pinkish-red curtains covered windows on the lower level. It looked like something from a vagabond caravan.

Rodolph moored their craft next to this peculiar ship, and an old woman dressed in tight, black leather appeared on the deck and waved.

"*Rodolphie!*" she called to him, exposing a toothless grin. Her skin was tanned and cracked from the sun. "Our strong, handsome friend, so gracious to us... come and be welcomed."

Rodolph hopped onto the deck and was immediately embraced by the woman. A pair of gulls sat on top of the ship's cabin, eyeing him lazily, clearly unimpressed.

"Hello, Seanmare," Rodolph said. Dagny wasn't sure if *Seanmare* was the woman's name or a title. A sort of clannish grandmother.

The old woman pointed a bent finger at Dagny. "Is this her?"

Rodolph nodded. "Yes, she's the one who saved Jorgie."

"Please, come to me," Seanmare said.

Dagny made her way onto the vagabond ship. As she walked past the cabin, she could smell something nutty and sour boiling on the stove. Sitting inside was a young, pregnant woman dyeing the hands of two children blue.

"Here, please. Dagny, is it?" The old woman beckoned her closer.

"Yes," Dagny said, lowering her head. She felt embarrassed by the attention.

"You've done a great thing for us. Rescuing our dearest Jorgie."

"Is he here?" Dagny asked. "I was hoping to see him today."

"He's on the water with his uncle. The young one was clearly scarred by the blood island and that haunted tower. He has barely spoken of it."

"He told you about the tower? I'm surprised. I thought the island was forbidden." She looked at Rodolph, who seemed just as shocked as she was.

"It is forbidden, and don't you agree it should remain that way, dear? But what did you think would become of Jorgie? That we'd exile one of our own to some foreign corner of the lagoon? His heart was in the right."

Max and Kim joined them. There would be a feast and songs tonight. And a fire show, to Kimberly's delight. Seanmare and the young, expectant mother walked them down a connecting boardwalk to the base of the largest stilt house. They stepped onto a platform and Seanmare rang a bell signaling to the operators high above. In an instant, the platform jerked and tilted, and the group was slowly raised up.

"Will you tell us, about the tower and what you saw?" Seanmare asked.

"I didn't really see that much. Just found Jorgie in a dark room."

"You don't say..." Seanmare said. "Maybe there's something you'll think of. I'm curious how you made it out. Based on the little that Jorgie told us, it sounds like you encountered something special there. Not much is known about the *true* history of that island. The Oracles were always secret about their dealings with our world."

"Our world?"

"Yes. They operated in a separate reality than the one we exist in... you and I... the dwellers of the marsh and the children of the city."

"Oh. I see," Dagny said, but she was more confused than anything.

"The Oracles came from the Eternal Forest," Seanmare continued, as they slowly rose above the water, "that ancient wood that once stretched from the edge of the world to the mist of the Rhyming Sea. They dwell in places forgotten by us, but connected to that earlier age."

Dagny was high above the marsh now, and could see for miles in all directions. The city was etched in grey to the north. Down below, where the lake of reeds met drier land, Dagny could see thatch-roofed buildings lining a serpentine road that curved and weaved through the wetlands toward the city.

There was a man here, sleeping in a chair next to the stilt house entryway. He was bare-chested and wearing baggy blue leggings, tapered at the ankles. He looked like a performer, a roguish acrobat. Seanmare patted the man on one of his calloused feet, waking him. "Tell the others that Rodolphie and his friends have arrived." Then the man walked off, groggy, and the old woman took them into the building.

It was one enormous chamber with a high, wood-beamed ceiling; dominated by a long table surrounded by mismatched chairs. Seanmare told the boys and the pregnant woman to wait outside. When they were alone, she instructed Dagny to sit, and motioned to a cushioned bench that looked like it was pulled straight from a carriage.

"The others will be joining us soon, but for now..." The woman took Dagny's hands and pressed into her palms. "Tell me who you are."

Dagny was surprised by Seanmare's sudden forcefulness. The woman's thumbs pushed along the fortune lines of her hands, and she smiled at Dagny with the same toothless grin she'd flashed Rodo.

"That's a broad question," Dagny responded. "What do you want to know?"

"Rodolphie mentioned that a Rorker girl rescued Jorgie, but you don't seem like the Rork type to me."

"I'm not. I was taken to live there by a friend, after my brother passed."

"You're from somewhere closer to our own. I can sense it."

"Before then, I lived near Southend. At the Rakesmount."

"Ah. *Spit-born!* Your hands are soft. Maybe the hands of a girl who'd play in the gardens. Not one who labored much, and your fortune lines... are ordinary. You should be glad. There will be no expectations of you."

The word felt like an insult. *Ordinary*. Like she had disappointed the old woman.

"Under which of the night rulers were you born?" Seanmare continued.

"The Herald," Dagny replied.

"Ah. The Doom Angel."

"I never heard of that one."

"It's another name for the Herald. It represents change, and change brings doom for some. Who were your parents, dear?"

"My mother is dead. I never knew my father."

"I see. What was your mother's name?"

"I don't want to say. I don't like to think of her."

Seanmare continued without missing a beat, as if reading from a list of questions. "Who do you love most in this world?"

"I don't know. My brother and sister are both gone." The questions made Dagny uncomfortable. It was a strange intrusion.

"What do you *want* most in this world?"

"I... I'm not sure..." That wasn't true, though. She knew what she wanted. But it was impossible. She wanted her brother and sister back. She wanted to belong to something and be loved. An unexplained wave of melancholy washed over her.

"I can tell you are a sweet child... tell me, what do you want *most*?" It seemed like the woman was staring straight into her. Could sense her every vulnerability. There was an odd twinkle in her eye.

"I don't know. I'm not sure it matters."

Seanmare leaned close and whispered. "Tell me what you saw in the tower and I'll grant it to you."

"I don't know... it was mostly empty..."

"*Tell me.*" Her voice was fierce and frightening.

"I mean it. It was too dark. Maybe Jorgie saw something, but I didn't. Now let go." Dagny yanked her hands away.

"Jorgie said there was a giant bird. Dark as a shadow. And that you freed it."

"Yes... I did..." Dagny didn't feel guilty about being caught in a lie. She didn't owe anything to this woman.

"Where it is now? Where did it go?"

"I didn't see."

The woman leaned closer, and stared into Dagny's eyes. "Did it tell you its name?" she whispered.

"What are you talking about?"

Just then, the young, pregnant woman entered the room. "Seanmare, some of the others have arrived."

"Ah. Thank you, Runa. Fetch our guest some drink from the pot." Seanmare acted like nothing happened. She reached over and touched Dagny's cheek. "You've got quite a spirit, young one."

As the old woman rose and walked to the entryway, Dagny wondered why they were so interested in the bird? And then it dawned on her... the fisher's net... did these people have something to do with trapping it?

Seanmare beckoned the Naverung boys and a dozen others into the chamber, and each of them bowed their head to her before taking places at the table. Runa came over with a mug of something dark and warm, and sat next to Dagny on the bench.

Finally, a bronzed, rough-looking man with big hands cleared his throat and spoke. "I *suppose* thanks are in order. Had we known that Jorgie was trapped on that cursed island, we'd've gone ourselves... broken through the door and smashed anything that stood in our way. But of course, we weren't told. The boy was afraid of what his punishment would be." The man wore a blue greatcoat, almost dark as night, and his thinning hair was greased and combed back from his forehead.

"There was no door," Dagny said under hushed breath.

"Huh? What's that?" the man said.

"There was no door to break down."

"How'd you get in then?" he asked.

"I climbed down a chimney, but none of you would've fit."

"Then we'd break through the wall!" He glared at Dagny.

"—We heard the rumors of the Oracle and Farrow Blood," Max interrupted. "Glad it worked out for the best."

"...Mmhmm... Jorgie said there were other things inside... What did you see?"

"I just told Seanmare everything I know, which isn't much. I'm sorry. Maybe Jorgie was imagining things," Dagny said.

"Our boys don't imagine things."

"Sorry then. I don't have anything else to say about it."

Dagny noticed that the room had been quietly filling up while she was talking. There was a group standing in the shadows behind her, and another set off to the side behind Seanmare. The people there were both young and old but dressed in simpler clothing, rags. Some of their faces were sunken and yellow, all were dirty.

"Enough about this," Seanmare said. "It is time for us to celebrate you all, and the blessing you've brought back to us."

Seanmare's voice was friendly and positive, but Dagny was worried about what this bunch might do after she left... They seemed more concerned about what was in the tower than about thanking her.

A man stepped from the shadows and started to sing. His voice was harsh and he struggled with the melody, straining to reach certain notes. Dagny couldn't tell what the words were, and wondered if it was in a different language altogether. There were no instruments to cover his faults, and Dagny felt awkward and embarrassed for the man. Over at the far wall, Seanmare had huddled with the man in the great coat. The two were talking, close to each other's ear. Whatever their topic of conversation, Dagny didn't feel good about it. Once the singer was finished, the mood in the room relaxed. People started chatting. A couple of women chuckled. Naked children ran in circles around the table, chasing one another.

An enormous wooden bowl was brought to the table, and Runa stood and filled a small bowl for each of them, piling in heaps of meaty stew. Max glanced at Dagny from across the table. *He's concerned about something as well*. But it would have to wait; they couldn't talk about it now.

Runa sat back down next to Dagny and patted her hand. "Go ahead and eat. The lads started cooking this morning for your arrival." Dagny tasted the stew. It was spicy and bitter.

"Thanks. Do you live on the boat, with Seanmare?" Dagny asked, between sips of the stew.

"I do," Runa said, resting her hand on her pregnant belly. "She's my grandmother. And after she is gone, the task will fall to me. Until then, I serve our people in other ways."

"Do you ever come to the city?"

"Some of us do, from time to time." Runa had a sly look on her face. "I've never been there, myself." She was quite pretty. Under different circumstances, Dagny thought, she could've fit right in at Rork.

"Who was that man talking? The one in the blue coat," Dagny asked.

"That was Ferko. He's kind of a leader around here," Runa said.

"Why is he and Seanmare so interested in what I saw?"

"The giant bird, you mean. We all know you saw it. Maybe they wanna know if you saw something more. Did you see the Oracle?"

Dagny thought of the jeweled bones and paused briefly before responding. She didn't want to tell these people anything else. "No, I didn't. What do they want with that bird?"

"Ferko is a great hunter, and Seanmare seeks to harvest its properties."

"Harvest? You mean like take its bones and feathers?"

"And other things. Eyes and heart, its beak. Properties from the ancient beasts will help to heal our people and bring back the strength we lost long ago."

Dagny felt ill at the thought. "That's disturbing. You should just leave that poor creature alone."

Runa's face tightened. "It's not your place to judge us."

Two women in billowy orange and yellow outfits entered the room. They were carrying torches and had flasks hanging from wide belts. "The fire weavers," Runa whispered. "You should just enjoy this. We have lots to offer to those who befriend us."

A hush fell over the room as the weavers began to flip and twist their torches about. One of the women took a swig from her flask and blew into the flame, igniting an enormous fireball.

While the group was distracted, Dagny quietly slipped out of her chair and snuck onto the boardwalk. It was peaceful out here, above the marsh. She looked toward the city. What was she doing? These people didn't care to thank her for saving Jorgie; they wanted to use her to kill something special. Dagny didn't belong here.

The wooden deck creaked as someone stepped toward her, from the direction of the stilt house. Dagny turned and stumbled backward, almost tripping over her feet. Approaching her was the dirty-faced street girl from City Centre.

"Dagny Losh... I thought it was you," she said.

"You... you're the one who was following us that day in the city..."

"Didn't mean to scare you."

"Who are you? How do you know me?"

The girl just stood there. Waiting for a moment. Not sure what to say.

An image started to take shape in Dagny's mind. The Rakesmount. And a small, shy girl who rarely spoke, and would watch them from the neighboring row house across the street.

The girl's name was...

"*Corlie?*" Dagny asked.

The girl smiled, exposing a prominent gap between her front teeth. "You *do* remember me."

The apprehension left Dagny instantly, and she ran over to the girl and hugged her tightly.

"Why was you running from me that day?" Corlie asked.

"Really? You're surprised? You'd been stalking us for hours!" Dagny said.

"Well. I didn't want you to get away!"

"What are you doing here?! It's been so long. Are you one of the Marsh Rats?" Dagny asked.

"Kinda. We came here years ago. After the Mount collapsed."

The flood. Her building would've been caught up in it, too. Dagny nodded her head.

"I'm glad you're alive," Corlie continued. "Never knew what happened to you."

"I got out." Guilt and emotion welled up in her. Dagny sat down on the wooden planks.

"Sorry," Corlie said, sitting next to her. "Didn't mean to make you get like this."

"It's okay. You didn't do nothing wrong."

"Your brother... Morgan... he was always so nice to us. I'll never forget it."

"I came back to the Rakesmount once. The day after the flood. I didn't think anyone survived."

"It was really terrible," Corlie said. "I still dream of it."

"I'm glad you got out." Dagny placed her hand on top of Corlie's. "You remind me a little of Grete, my sister. Do you remember her?"

"Of course."

"I miss her so much." Dagny felt tears in her eyes.

"Yeah..." Corlie nodded. "So, you haven't seen her since, then?"

"Seen what? What do you mean?"

"Gretchen. You haven't seen her at all?"

"Corlie, what do you mean? How would I have seen her?"

"Don't you know? She's been living in Limer's Town."

9

DAGNY'S HEAD STARTED TO swim. *Limer's Town*. It was clear on the opposite side of the lagoon. Too far to see, even from the top of the Central Spire. She had never known anyone who'd been there before. It was a lawless place, abandoned by any sort of proper authority, and worse off than even the Rakesmount or Southend.

"How do you know this?" Dagny asked.

"I seen her a couple years back, down at the grotto-market by River's End. We was... uh... putting on another show. It's seeming like that's the best way to run into you all," Corlie said with a grin.

"She survived..."

"I'm not sure how. Yours was the first building to fall. I watched it from across the road. Everyone else died, you know."

Dagny stood up and began to run her fingers nervously through her hair. Corlie sat on the planks, watching her.

"I'm sorry... I'm just... this is a lot for me," said Dagny. She tried to keep control of her thoughts, but felt her focus slipping away in a swirl of emotion. "Grete told you she was living there? In Limer's Town?"

"Yeah. Say, you wanna go talk somewhere else, quieter? I live just across the lake, by the old south road."

Dagny looked into the great stilt house and hall. Flames spun back and forth between the fire weavers. She should wait for the boys.

"They gonna be a while in there. Supposed to last far into the night," Corlie said.

"I should stay here."

"Okay. My mom'd be thrilled to see someone from the Mount, though."

Several naked children ran past, their hands dyed blue, and crossed a rope bridge connecting the next stilt over.

"Have you seen Grete since?" Dagny asked.

"No. Just the one time. She'd been runnin' with Sliver Farn. You know of him?"

Dagny shook her head. She'd never heard that name before. "Sliver?"

Two men came out onto the deck. They were both barrel-chested and draped in dark shawls.

"Hey, it's the girl. The one who was fussing with Ferko," one man said to the other, pointing at Dagny. "She's a storyteller, this one."

"You got any other tales, little girl?" the other man asked her. There was something antagonizing about his tone.

Dagny looked at Corlie. "You know, why don't we head down to your place after all."

They left while the two men jeered at them, "Hey! Don't be a brat, come here now and tell us a good one!"

Corlie led her down a rope ladder to the base of the stilt house. "Don't be minding those men," she said. "Not everyone here is as well-behaved as me." Corlie guided her to a small raft, and Dagny tried to manage her growing excitement as they paddled across the lake to drier land.

"...*Grete*... you can't believe what this means to me," Dagny said.

"Sure I do. That's your blood and all."

Corlie lived in one of the thatched-roof buildings Dagny had seen from above. Inside, the dwelling was not much more than a wooden shack, with dirty floorboards and a small, unlit hearth.

"Mom," Corlie called out toward a curtain separating the only bedchamber from the main room. "You never guess who I got with me."

Dagny took a seat at a table near the window. On top of the table was a brown purse with metal clasps, several rings, a gold-framed eyeglass and an odd copper tube.

Someone rustled behind the curtain.

"Hey, you know what this is?" Corlie asked Dagny, picking up the copper tube.

"No," she said. It looked like a piece of mechanical equipment.

"Eh. Me neither. I picked it off some fancy man, up by the River Gate. Figured it'd be worth something... but no one knows what it is... You want it?"

"No. That's alright." Dagny examined it closer. "Looks like it's from some kind of gear set. Probably holds the River Gate together and now the whole thing is gonna collapse."

Corlie stared at her, wide-eyed.

Dagny giggled and shook her head. "I'm just kidding... who knows."

"Stop it!" The girls both laughed, and Corlie joined her at the table.

"You steal all of this from the city?" Dagny asked.

Corlie shrugged. "Mostly." She was playing with the clasp on the purse, avoiding eye contact with Dagny.

"I don't really care, you know. I'm just asking."

"Yeah..." Corlie said, pushing her tongue through the gap between her teeth.

"So, do you know whereabout Gretchen lives? You ever been to Limer's Town? Know anything about this Sliver person?" Dagny tried to talk calmly, but her voice came out high and quick.

"I never been there. But I know enough. Sliver and his crew run a lot of bad stuff over there—"

"Don't you talk about Limer's Town!" A strained voice shouted from behind the curtain. "Don't be gettin' all excited about it!"

"No one's gettin' excited 'bout it, Mom!" Corlie yelled back.

The curtain flung open and a large, veined woman waddled out. She was covering herself with a stained sheet, and pointed sharply at Corlie.

"Don't you talk 'bout it. People don't come back from there."

Corlie looked at Dagny and rolled her eyes. "That ain't true. Hey look, Mom, this is Dag Losh from the Rakesmount."

The woman studied her for a moment. "The Rakesmount, huh? That place is trash."

"C'mon, now," Corlie said. "Look around you. Think this is the palace gardens we're living in?"

"I got my freedom here. It's good."

"You got your freedom to starve to death, if I'm not bringing back stuff from the city."

"Pfft..." the woman swatted at the air and moved over to a rusting stove in the fireplace.

"Dagny lived across the street from us, remember?" Corlie continued.

The woman was trying to light the cold stove with a piece of tinder and match. "Was you related to that Finkel one?"

"No," Dagny said. "Not related."

"Good. He was a mean bastard. Glad he's dead."

Dagny turned to Corlie and whispered, "Any idea what part of Limer's Town Grete might live in now?"

"Nah. The place is a mess. I seen it once from the water. It's all twisted and dark. Like wet wood. Takes up the entire shore."

"How could I find her?"

"Oh. Dag... don't be doin' that. Look, I know you wanna see your sister, but that's not a good idea."

"Why? I can handle myself."

"C'mon, now. Looking like you do? You're too pretty and soft. You can't be goin' over there."

"Pretty and soft, huh? That's a first. Grete was smaller than me, and she's over there."

"Yeah, but I only saw her that one time, remember? And... I didn't wanna say it... but she didn't look great."

In an instant, everything changed. Dagny felt her heart race and a dread sweep over her. "What do you mean?"

"There was something... like dead in her eyes. You know? Like she was bruised on the inside. And when she saw me she smiled, but it was kinda... crazed."

Dagny stood up. She couldn't hear this. *Crazed*? *Dead eyes*? She had to get out of here. What had she done? She'd lost her sister. All this time, spent living safe and comfortable in Rork, while her sister was alive, but dying over in Limer's Town. She couldn't stand herself. She had to go.

"What's going on? Dag, you alright?"

"No. I'm not. I gotta go."

"Huh? Where?" Corlie asked. Dagny didn't answer. She headed out the front door, but stopped in the autumn sun.

Where *was* she headed? Dagny looked across the lake and up at the stilt houses where Max and the others were celebrating with the Marsh Rats. The Naverung boys were nice enough, but... these weren't her people. This wasn't her blood. No, her blood had all been taken from her, washed away in sickness or water, or snuffed out... in Limer's Town.

She was in a daze. Corlie called to her from the entryway. Dagny didn't hear what she said. She just hurried away, up the Old South Road, toward the city.

~

The road was dilapidated and worn down to the earth. Weeds sprung from holes, and the ground was busted with jagged shards of concrete and stone. It had once been wide, smooth and proper. A feat of civil engineering back in some forgotten time. Dagny didn't know what its original purpose had been, but she was sure it wasn't built for the Marsh Rats.

What was she going to do? She needed to clear her head. Plodding along, Dagny let her mind wander and thought of the road. The men whose lives were spent constructing it, and the countless hours, months, years they must've toiled here. Only to have it fade off into nothing, and sink into the swamp.

Eventually the dampness of the wetlands gave way to a higher, rockier ground, and when Dagny crested a small hill, the city slowly began to rise up in the distance. Like a ship coming into harbor. First, its mast-like spires and ramparts, then the hull of its wall breaking the horizon. Dagny saw no one else on the road until she passed the junk piles off to the east. It was where Max found the polished stone. He said it felt lucky. Far away, several figures stood on a great mound of debris and scrap, caught bright in the late afternoon sun.

She pulled the collar up on her brother's coat and tied the dark bandana around her head. Anyone watching her from a distance would probably assume she was just another wayfarer drifting across the wasted South. That was the hope anyway.

She reached the South Gate at twilight. A number of people had gathered outside the abandoned watchtower, now turned into a drinking house. These were workers, no doubt, from one of the shanty-towns that sprouted along the outer wall of Southend. Dagny put her head down and walked through the crowd. There was no laughter here. The men drank and spoke in short, terse statements or stood in total silence, and no one paid her any mind whatsoever.

She crossed the Southend Plaza. The market stalls were all closed, and a couple of rough-looking youths lounged underneath the overhang of a boarded-up inn. They eyed her suspiciously when she passed. One of them opened his mouth as if to call to her, but — for whatever reason — thought better of it at the last moment. She tried to recall the map of the city mounted in Alex's study back home. She wasn't familiar with Southend. However, if she stuck to the main road, it would take her all the way up to the Central Bridge.

Dagny left the youths and plaza behind, and began to smell the scent of decay and death wafting over from a tannery on the nearby Grand South Canal... or was it from the rendering pits? The scent brought with it the gnats and flies of dusk, and they swarmed her head. The rendering pits... she'd heard about all the children who died there, being pulled out lifeless and blue. Whenever Dagny misbehaved, Finkel and her mother would threaten to hand her over to work the narrow vents, clearing shafts clogged with refuse. Dagny wasn't sure about her mother, but Finkel sure meant it. The trauma had seared itself into her deepest subconscious. Dagny tucked her head below the collar even further and quickened her pace, trying to put the place out of her mind.

She kept thinking about what Corlie said. About Grete's dead eyes and crazed smile. *My sweet, sweet sister. How bad were you hurt?* It was a couple years ago, Corlie told her. How far gone would she be now? Living in Limer's Town, running with that Sliver Farn... Dagny couldn't think about that. She'd just found out Gretchen survived the flood. She wouldn't let her thoughts go somewhere darker. Not now. As long as Grete was alive, there was a chance.

The road passed beneath an enormous stone arch, elaborately engraved with the images of mystical creatures. A hydra and manticore gazed down at Dagny menacingly, taunting her as weak and insignificant. She glared back — W*hat do you know? The carvings of dead men* — and walked through the arch, away from Southend.

Limer's Town... Grete, are you still there? How could I find you? A message to Alex, maybe. Yes. He'd help... but... the baby would be born soon. Would he really rush away from his family to help her find her own? Besides, Dagny wasn't even sure if Alex would know where to look.

She was at a crossroads. To the north, the main road continued on, weaving itself toward the river Morca. To the west was the Rakesmount. She stopped. Her feet hurt. Sore and exhausted, she sat just off the road and put her head in her hands. There was no one else around. She was on the border here, between memories.

For a moment, Dagny considered going back to the Mount. Just to see if it still meant something. To see what, if anything, remained from her youth. After the flood, Dagny had harbored fantasies that Grete was alive and well. Playing them out in her mind. They would live together and she could share the world with someone. The guilt and shame of losing Gretchen suffocated her, like the vent shafts of the rendering pit. A tightness rose in her chest, constricting her heart. She had to get Grete back. Dagny grabbed her hair, pulled, and screamed.

Someone heard her. There were voices from an alleyway to her left. Dagny's instincts kicked in. She jumped to her feet and ran. Away from the strangers, away from the Rakesmount, away from her feelings. It was dark now, the main road lit only by the moon above and the occasional lantern from a nearby dwelling. Dagny knew better than to navigate the alleys here at night. The blackness hid shallow pits, sharp things, and worse. Even as tired as she was, as much as her feet ached, she was fast...

Sprinting down the road, kicking up gravel and sand, Dagny knew she was going to Limer's Town. As soon as she admitted it to herself, she began to feel better. In control. And, really, her mind had been made up the moment Corlie mentioned it. She just hadn't realized it yet.

∾

She came to the ferry station. A long, open-air, flat-roofed building that sat at the convergence of several canals. Dagny stopped just before the service counter. Behind it, a man was reading a pamphlet next to an old-fashioned oil lamp. He looked up as she approached.

Dagny was apprehensive. Her grip tightened around a wad of treasury notes inside her pocket. *What am I doing?*

"Need a ride, do you?" the man called out, cheerfully.

Dagny nodded and walked up to the counter.

"Great, where you headed?"

"Limer's Town. Do you go there?"

The man leaned back and crossed his arms. "Now, what you wanna head there for?"

"I got my own reasons. It's personal."

He shook his head. "Fine with me... but no. We don't."

"Oh..." She loosened her grip on the notes.

The Central Bridge was still a considerable distance away. The blisters on her feet were sharp and raw. She thought for a second before asking...

"Do you know Stardust? Of Stardust and Light?"

~

The canal boat dropped her off several blocks from the tavern. Dagny's plan was to ask someone for directions to Sarna's house, but as soon as she entered, Dagny saw her there, standing amongst a small group of people.

Sarna's eyes lit up when she caught sight of Dagny. She scrunched her face into a silly smile and wandered over.

"Hey you. Here by yourself?" Sarna asked.

"Yes. I was actually hoping to run into you."

"Oh? Everything alright?"

"No... not really."

A worried look spread over Sarna's face. "What's going on?"

Dagny wasn't expecting Sarna to be here. She hadn't thought out what to say. Her mind was a swirling mess. "It's hard for me to talk about."

"That's okay. Wanna sit down?" Sarna led her over to the same booth where Dagny slept the first night she was here. The old tavern was fairly quiet tonight. A fire burned and the smell of spiced meat and carrots enveloped the main room. Nearby, several young musician-types sat on the stage and talked.

There was no easing into it. As soon as Sarna sat down, Dagny said, "My sister's alive. I thought she was swept up in the flood and drowned like my mother and cousins. But she's alive and over in Limer's Town."

"What? Oh Dagny... I don't know what to say... that's... a lot."

"I know. I'm gonna go... over to Limer's Town."

"Right. Of course."

"Do you know anything about it?" Dagny asked, hopefully.

"Umm..." Sarna started to say something, and then stopped herself. "It's a dangerous place, but part of me feels like you already know that. And if it was my sister, I'd find a way to get to her." Sarna thought for a moment. "Telga. She'll know. She's from there."

"Telga? But—" She seemed so delicate and smooth. If anyone was too soft and pretty for Limer's Town, wouldn't it be her? "—I'm surprised is all," Dagny said.

"Her family goes back there generations. If you knew her better, you'd see it. Anyway, I'll take you." Sarna reached over and held Dagny's hand. "We'll find your sister, okay?"

"Okay."

"Are you hungry, or do you wanna leave now?"

~

By the time the girls stepped out of Stardust, Dagny was calmer and starting to grasp what happened. What a strange, bizarre day it'd been. Max and Rodo brought her into the Naverung only this morning. She had imagined scouting around the lagoon with them, searching old ruins, discovering lost artifacts. Now she was heading toward another kind of adventure. One that was all too real and absent the trappings of some childish fantasy. Across the lagoon was a different world altogether, and she could be heading there tonight.

Two figures emerged from a side street and entered the moonlight. A broad-shouldered one and a smaller boy dressed in yellow.

"Dagny!" Kimberly yelled, running toward her. "You're safe! What happened?"

"Of course she's safe," Rodolph said, as he walked up.

Dagny couldn't help but smile. "I'm sorry. I shoulda came and found you."

"That swamp girl got us. Told us about you just storming off to the South Road," Rodolph said. "—Hey Sarna."

"Hi."

"She told us about your sister, too. She thought it's what set you off."

"Yeah... it was." Dagny was physically and emotionally exhausted, and didn't want to go into it again. "Where's Max?"

"He's not here yet?" Rodolph looked past her at the building's front doors.

"No," Dagny said. "Why isn't he with you?"

"He went up the South Road, trying to follow you. Me and Kim took the boat to Rork and then walked down... planned to meet here. Figuring one of us would run into you along the way."

"Think we should head south and look for him?" Kim asked.

"Umm..." Rodolph glanced off into the distance, at nothing in particular. "Nah. He'll be good. Max knows his way around."

Dagny wasn't so sure. There were too many traps around the Rakesmount and the southern neighborhoods, and if you were unacquainted, it could turn out bad.

"What do you wanna do?" Sarna asked Dagny.

"We should go look for him."

Sarna nodded, and walked with Dagny to the rusted gate by the street. "Telga will still be around tomorrow."

"Ugh. Wait. I'm coming," Rodolph said. "Kim, you stay here in case we miss him on the way."

Dagny was comfortable walking with the pair. There was a sense of belonging here she hadn't felt in very long time. It was a mistake leaving the Naverung boys at the stilt house, not trusting them. They'd come looking for *her.* Maybe she didn't have to go it alone.

"I thought my sister was dead for most of my life."

It was like a valve had been released. Dagny told them the entire story. About her life in the Rakesmount, and Morgan's adventures with Alex Benzara. How she'd cuddle with Grete in the row house attic. Morgan wearing the very coat she had on, performing stories for them. About his death, and the flood, and coming to live with Alex. Growing up with Rorker children and the Winter festivals. Sitting in the walnut tree by the garden wall. Feeling alone... And then Corlie and Limer's Town.

Rodolph and Sarna let her talk, offering nothing more than the occasional nod or smile or solemn glance.

"It might not feel like it now, but I'd say you're a lucky one," Rodolph said, once she'd finished. "It's turned pretty tragic for everyone else."

"You think?" Dagny asked.

"I think."

They ran into Max on the Central Bridge. He looked haggard but had the widest grin on his face when he saw her. "I don't know how you walked the whole road. My feet are probably bleeding through my boots," he said.

Dagny ran over and kissed him on the cheek. "Thanks for doing that... looking for me. It means a lot."

"Hey, of course... it's what we do," he said nervously.

"Oh man, you're blushing," Rodolph said, approaching them. "I guess you're gonna have to walk across the city every time you want one of those."

"No... no you don't," Dagny said, smiling.

"Okay, okay," Max said. "I'm really glad to see you all... So, did I miss anything?"

"Yeah," Rodolph said. "We're going to Limer's Town."

10

In the morning, they went to Telga's house by the Morca quayside. Dagny had spent the night with Sarna and Hanette, at their parents' place. Sarna didn't mention Limer's Town to her sister, only that she would be spending the day with Dag.

"I love my sister, but I don't want her gettin' in the way of things," Sarna said, as they walked along the busy morning canal streets. "I'm sure she'll find out what we're up to after we speak with Telga... I'll just get the lecture from her when we get back."

It was a gloomy, overcast autumn day, and the girls met Max and Rodolph in the Gardens at Sorn Rue, the largest park in the city. They ate a quick breakfast of sugary bread and eggs, washed it down with fragrant brown coffee from a copper pot, and then crossed the park to the river.

"How we gonna get all the way across the lagoon?" Rodolph asked. "I wouldn't risk the trip in Max's skiff."

"I wouldn't either," Max agreed.

"Let's see what happens with Telga," Sarna said. "Just be nice. I think you two can manage it."

"Don't know her," Rodolph shrugged. "But how's she gonna help with that?"

"She's got her own ship. A good one."

The yard in front of Telga's home was overflowing with children. A handful of elderly men and women, draped in wool shawls and grey coats, sat around a table and talked. Telga's was a small brick house, next to a three-story one where several generations of her family lived. The entire yard became quiet as soon as Sarna opened the gate. The children stopped playing, and the old ones stopped chatting.

Sarna spoke politely. "Hi, we're here to see Telga. Do you know if she's inside?"

One of the men said something in a foreign tongue and pointed at the house. The whole clan stared at them blankly.

"Thanks... Okay, let's go," Sarna whispered. Dagny followed, while Max and Rodolph shuffled along behind them.

The front door was iron-bound, weathered wood, like something from the hull of an old boat. Sarna knocked and then gently pushed it open. There was whistling from further inside.

"*Hello*... Telga?" Sarna called.

"Yes," came a voice from across the room. "Sarna? What a surprise."

She was even prettier than Dagny remembered, dressed in short cut-off pants, gold boots, and a black cable-knit sweater. Her cropped hair was now blonde. Dagny couldn't recall what color it had been at the Ironhead.

Telga looked at Dagny. "Oh... it's you... what's-your-name."

"Dag... Dagny."

"Hanette's not with you?" Telga asked Sarna.

"No. Not today. We wanted to ask you something, if that'd be fine."

"Okay," Telga said, eyeing the group. "Well, come inside."

Her house was a treasure trove of curious objects. Oil paintings of someone's regal ancestors, and another of a ship caught in the storm. Wood carvings and brass navigational tools. A giant flute from a hollowed-out animal bone. Curved swords above the fireplace. The curtains were drawn tight, and several lamps illuminated the space. It looked like the interior of a pirate ship.

Telga sunk into a large armchair and kicked her feet up on a stack of books.

"So..." she gestured outlandishly. "Ask away."

Sarna glanced at Dagny, then spoke. "It's about Limer's Town."

Dagny told Telga about Corlie and Gretchen, and how her sister'd been running with someone named Sliver Farn. They were heading over there to get her back and hoped that Telga could help.

"I'm guessing Sarna mentioned I was from there, huh?" Telga asked when Dagny had finished.

"Pretty much."

"Well, not only am I from there, there's probably no better guide in the city... But it also begs the question... why would I help you?"

The question stumped Dagny. "...Because you're nice?" she asked. "Didn't you say at the Ironhead that you were the nicest person around?"

"I don't think so."

Sarna spoke up. "—Because if you don't, then Dagny and me will have to find another way there, and then hope we don't disappear forever in Limer's Town and you can deal with my sister afterward."

"Ugh. Don't go there, Sarna," Telga said. "The place has changed since my family left. I mean, it was always bad, but now it's *bad* bad."

"We're going. I hope you will help us," Sarna said.

"Alright, look. Finding her sister, that's important. I get it. Family's important. And I don't want you to die."

"So you'll help?" Sarna asked.

"I guess."

"Oh, that's great!" Sarna said. "I told you Telga was a good one!"

"Sliver Farn, though... he's someone to avoid. That whole outfit is dangerous. It'll be tricky." Despite her warning, Telga seemed to be getting visibly excited at the prospect.

"You know him?" Dagny asked.

"I know enough. They spend a lot of time at the Crescent Lounge. In the shadow of the old refinery."

Dagny and the Naverung boys nodded along, like they understood.

"We'll want to get there after nightfall," Telga continued. "Easier to sneak around if we need to. And no one would be at the Lounge during the day."

"Thanks. Umm... any thoughts on how we can get there?" Dagny asked.

"We'll take my ship," Telga said. "*The Mangled Misfit.*"

~

The ship was past a locked gate, tucked away at the dead end of a nearby canal. Telga stepped on board the glossy black, single-mast sloop, and began to set the sculling oar in place.

"This is *impressive*," Rodolph said, looking around the ship in awe.

"Don't stare to hard. I don't want you falling in love," Telga said.

"Too late. How'd you get this?"

"—Hand me that lanyard," Telga said, pointing to its place on a hook by the cabin.

"Oh sure," Rodolph said. "You should really keep it by the oar, though."

"...Ugh... just hand it to me."

"I'm just saying..."

"Yeah. Well, I have my reasons, and if I need to explain everything, this is going to be a very long trip."

Dagny sat off to the side as Telga operated the single oar, taking the ship gently through the canal. There were no other boats moored on the waterway, and they passed through the shadows of tall buildings stained green and black that blocked out the sun. An old woman rocked along, watching them cross from her place on an iron balcony. Dagny smiled and waved, but got no response. *Probably one of Telga's great-grandmothers*, she thought.

Eventually, the canal emptied them into the lagoon, with Max observing that this particular exit was like a secret passage out of the city. Once they hit the open air, Telga raised the sail, allowing the wind to push them toward the far-off coast of Limer's Town.

It was cold out on the water, and a light drizzle began as they sailed along the grey-pebbled shoreline. Dagny pulled her coat tight, watching the city fade into the gloom, before heading below deck.

A small stove dominated the space, along with water jugs and a milking bucket for a sink. Charts of the lagoon and the hundred isles were displayed in foggy glass frames; a shallow bed was set against the opposite wall; and a Talvarind board was on the table. Two factions played against each other: the Caltra Teamen and the Wild Court. The pieces stopped mid-game. Telga's Wild Court figures were different from the wooden ones Dagny had back home. This set was polished onyx with small pieces of amber inlaid for eyes. Some years back, Caternya had offered to replace Dagny's pieces with "fine ones." She imagined Cate meant something like this.

Sarna and Max came down from above.

"The weather's turning awful out there," Sarna said, her purple hair wet against her face.

"Any idea how long until we get to Limer's Town?" Dagny asked.

Max shrugged. "No clue. Probably a few hours at least… Hey, Talvarind, do you play?" he asked Dagny.

"Sometimes."

"Telga's really good," Sarna said.

"Is that how she knows Tash?"

"Ha. Good guess. Yep. He's sharp as salt. I think she hates on him because she could never figure out a way to beat him… jealousy and whatnot… but for whatever reason, it just made him crush on her more. People are weird."

"Do you play?" Dagny asked Max.

"—No. He doesn't have the patience for it," Sarna said with a thin smile. It was an odd interjection.

Max walked over to the porthole and looked out at the coast. "What's the plan when we get to this Lounge?"

"I… don't know," Dagny said.

"We should probably come up with something, don't you think? Gonna walk in there and start asking for Sliver Farn?"

"Telga will have an idea," Sarna said.

"I doubt it," Max replied.

"Why are you acting like this?" Sarna asked.

"Like what?"

"You know what I'm talking about. Being so negative. Shooting everything down like you do."

Max shook his head. "I just think we should know what we're doing if we're gonna walk into some cutthroat's hangout."

Sarna scoffed. "No one said we weren't gonna come up with a plan."

"Fine." Max headed toward the stairs. "I'm going up top because I'm starting to feel seasick with all this lurching, not 'cause of you," he said to Sarna.

"...Okay."

Sarna gave Dagny an awkward smile, like she was trying to keep the situation light. But her eyes were furious. Dagny didn't want any distractions from her goal today. They could talk about it later, if it came up.

"Thanks again for coming... helping me out," Dagny said, trying to change the subject.

Sarna's face softened. "Max and me... we used to be together... but it didn't work. I don't want you worrying about that. Sometimes I can't stand him is all." Apparently, they would talk about it now.

"I figured as much. How long ago was that?"

"Last spring. Do you like him? Like that?" Sarna asked.

"I'm not sure," Dagny whispered.

"If you do, don't let me keep you from it, alright? I don't care."

"I've never been that close to a boy before."

"It's overrated," Sarna said. "Just kidding. Have fun, see what happens."

"I don't even know if he feels the same way."

"Who knows. He's a tough one to figure out."

Dagny felt guilty talking about this now, with her sister over in Limer's Town. What would she even say to her? She needed to think.

"This is all too much. I gotta focus on Grete." Max was right, they needed a plan.

"Yeah. I'm sorry," Sarna said. "Telga will know what to do. I meant that."

The ship swayed along. Dagny could no longer see the coast through the porthole, as the mist and spray from the waves blocked it out. She headed over to the stairs and looked up at Max and the others. Telga now wore a long, waxed jacket and hood, her tan-brown legs and gold boots sticking out from underneath.

"You feeling any better?" Dagny asked Max.

"I'm good."

"You can come back down if you want, get out of the rain."

"I'm good."

"Okay. Hey Telga, any thoughts on what we should do once we get to the lounge?" Dagny asked.

"I've been thinking about that... I think we should play it easy. Watch from outside at first, from a distance. See if we notice anyone who looks like your sister."

"And if we don't?"

"Just see how it goes," Telga said, eyeing the horizon. "I don't think we should push too hard."

"Alright." But that didn't sit well with Dagny. She had a strong feeling she would be going in there tonight. She wasn't going to just watch and leave. She was going to find Grete one way or the other.

They passed under and between enormous spindly metal structures that towered over the ship, rising from the lagoon's basin. The forms cast twisted shadows onto the deck as they went by. Dagny thought they looked like haphazard black steel buildings, set at odd angles, but instead of windows, huge rivets marked the facades. The water here was murky with rust.

"What are they?" Max asked.

"You want the truth or fantasy?" Telga said.

"The truth?"

"No one has a clue. And don't let 'em tell you otherwise. This is the only spot in the lagoon where you can't see the bottom on a clear day... The fantasy is that this is where the floating city crashed into the water."

"Well, that's not true," Dagny said. "Alex and Ogden went all over the lagoon and Shallow Sea searching for it. Didn't find anything."

"I know it's not true," Telga said. "There's no such thing as a floating city."

Rodolph was sitting near Telga, staring wistfully at her legs and gold boots. "We gotta find out what happened to Ogden when we get back," he mumbled, almost to himself. Telga caught him looking at her, took his chin in her hand and raised his face up.

"That's enough," she said. He gave an embarrassed smile.

Dagny stayed below deck with Sarna for the rest of the journey. None of the others joined them. Dagny drank some tea, and the girls ate salted fish and pickled fruit that Telga had stored in a container. The cold penetrated the hold, so Dagny and Sarna sat together on the bed, under a thick wool blanket.

"What's the furthest you've ever traveled from the city?" Dagny asked.

"Let's see... When I was real young, me and Hanette went with Dad to the Winter's Palace at the edge of the world. We stayed in this walled country estate in the green hills of the Vahnland."

"How'd that happen?"

"Dad was a painter, commissioned by one of the Grandmasters there. He was really great. We stayed for an entire season."

"I bet that was amazing... did your Dad stop painting?"

"Yeah. His hands don't work anymore. Haven't for a while."

"Oh..." Dagny glanced at her. "Are you still cold?"

"Yes. Here, feel my fingers." Sarna placed them on Dagny's face. They were like ice.

"You're freezing!" Dagny took her hands and tried to warm them with her breath.

"Ha, thanks. Much better... Are you scared?" Sarna asked.

"No. Just nervous."

"I bet you probably don't get scared. Something about you."

"I get scared." She thought of the black chimney on Farrow Blood, and the room with the giant crow.

"You're different than other people I know," Sarna said. "I could feel it the instant we met."

"Different how?"

"Like you could do anything."

There was an intimacy here, tucked in the corner of the ship's hold. It felt like a dream, where they could share secrets with each other that no one would ever know.

"I think my heart has hurt my entire life," Dagny said.

"That's... so sad. You don't deserve that. I think you're really special."

"Why?"

"I just do. Okay?"

They huddled together for a while longer in silence, rocking with the sway of the boat. When they reached the coast of Limer's Town, in the late afternoon, Telga lowered the sails, still a ways offshore. Waiting for night to fall.

"Want to go up top? I'd like to see the coast," Dagny said.

Sarna grabbed her arm. "Don't go. Don't leave me just yet." Dagny didn't know if she was kidding or not, until Sarna started laughing.

The girls both walked onto the deck and Telga pointed out the old refinery. It sat at the water's edge. A giant splotch of bruised purplish-grey in the middle of the twisted black knot that was Limer's Town. A smudge of foggy wet mountains rose above it, far beyond the urban landscape.

"Dagny, Max and me will head to the lounge. Sarna will stay here with this one," Telga said, pointing at Rodolph.

"No. I'm gonna go, too," Sarna said.

"Nope. No way. Hanette will likely claw my eyes out for taking you this far. You stay here with big boy... make sure he doesn't run off with the *Misfit* and strand us there."

Rodolph looked genuinely hurt. "I'd never do such a thing."

"Okay, fine. Sarna, you stay here and help keep watch while Rodolph defends the ship with his honor. Seriously, I'm not leaving it unattended on the bank of Limer's Town. I'd stay with it, but you all would get lost."

There would be no arguing with Telga. Not on her ship, anyway. Dagny had a hard time picturing anyone arguing with her on land either, for that matter. Dagny had hoped Rodolph was coming with them, but she was glad he'd be staying with Sarna to keep her friend out of harm's way. As twilight approached, Telga gave the shoreline one last look with her spyglass, then started to bring the ship toward the refinery.

"What do you think?" Dagny asked Max. "Are you up for this?"

He nodded and winked at her. "That's what I came here for. You feeling alright?"

"Yes. Just ready to get going." Dagny's voice was shaky with nerves.

"It'll be alright," Max said. He was trying his best to look confident and calm, but his hands were jittery.

No one else said a word as they approached the great cement walls of the refinery. The sun's last ray of light illuminating the scene in front of them. Dagny didn't know what to expect when they reached Limer's Town, but it wasn't this. The place seemed empty. Almost sad in a way. In the distance, she could see a gravel path leading away from the massive structure into a nest of rickety, dark buildings. They loomed over the road, along with empty laundry lines, rusting ladders, and criss-crossing planks that connected the buildings where the trail disappeared. It was a teetering canopy of neglect.

Telga guided the sloop to the refinery's concrete edge, where remnants of a pier could still be seen protruding out of the water. When they got close, Rodolph jumped off and tied the ship to a piece of the old dock.

"Alright, from here on out, it'll be us three," Telga said, turning to Rodolph. "If you run into any trouble, kick off and head east along the coast... You'll come across a light-tower. If you're not here when we get back, we'll meet you there. But it's quite a haul. So don't go unless it's necessary."

Rodolph nodded. "Understood. Be safe."

Telga walked in front, leading them down the concrete dock and around the perimeter of the refinery's outer wall. The pathway turned into crumbling pavement marked by deep fissures on either side, like some great bladed machine had rolled over the street long ago. They passed a roofless structure on the outskirts of the refinery, derelict and empty, an abandoned guard tower. It was plastered with posters depicting the face of some regal-looking man of importance, but the eyes had been cut out. Underneath was scrawled *Watching You.*

"Who's that?" Dagny whispered.

"The last official Governor of Limer's Town. He's been missing since before I was born. Now shush," Telga said, putting her finger to her lips.

The wind pushed the clouded sky and revealed a bright moon. Dagny could see that they were heading toward the gravel path and the rickety buildings of black wood. There was no light coming from inside. A cold, lifeless abyss. *This can't be the right place,* Dagny thought. She couldn't possibly imagine her sister living here. No matter how bad things had gotten. And Telga was taking them straight to it.

Dagny thought she heard something. A whisper from the blackness ahead.

"Wait, wait..." she said quietly, grabbing Telga's sweater as they approached.

"What did I tell you—" Telga snapped back. And that's when Dagny saw it.

A pale, bloated face appeared from the dark pit where the road disappeared. It seemed to float there for an instant, and then a body slowly took shape as well, dressed in rags. Telga stopped talking and took a few steps back.

"What the—" Max started to say.

The figure stopped at the edge of the moonlit road and smiled something strange. Like it could sense their fear.

"Go, go... back... back," Telga instructed, and the three of them turned and ran toward the refinery wall. They didn't slow down until they reached the old guard tower. Dagny couldn't tell if the thing had been chasing them, but when she turned around, there was nothing.

"What was that?" Max panted.

"That route is supposed to be clear... It was the last time I came," Telga said.

"The last time you came? What are you talking about?" Max said.

"I still have old friends here. Courtesans for the Young Governors. You know what those are?"

"The Young Governors?" Max asked.

"No. Courtesans."

"...I have an idea..."

"Good, then we don't need to talk about it."

"But... that thing," Dagny said. "I don't wanna go in there."

"We won't. We'll just have to take the long way 'round."

This time they walked along the opposite side of the refinery's shell, where a wide, smooth-surfaced roadway led them north, in the direction of the mountains. There were no trees or plant life, other than the prickle-weeds that grew from the pavement itself and stuck to Dagny's boots and pants. Seeing no sign of anyone else around, Dagny felt free to speak.

"You know Sliver Farn," Dagny said to Telga. It wasn't a question.

"Yes. He's awful." There was an edginess to her voice.

"Does he know you? Would he recognize you, I mean?"

"Not my face, he doesn't."

"What'd he do?" Dagny was trying to keep pace with her, while Max walked behind.

"He's got no morality. Just a selfish liar. Anything he wants, he'll take. Objects, people, anything. So if there's an opportunity to take something away from him, it gets me excited." Telga had a venomous look in her eye. Dagny glanced back at Max, but he was watching the sides of the street.

They reached an intersection and climbed down to the cross road, which was sunk deep into the earth.

"This is Burrow Street. It'll take us to the Lounge." The ground here was soft. Pieces of metal and rubbish were pushed off to the side. It had the feeling of an open-air sewer. "See why I wanted to take the shortcut?" Telga laughed.

They crept along for a time, passing small crowds gathered around fires on the land above them. There was the occasional shout or scream. Something breaking. A coughing, guttural laugh. The symphony song of the slum. This was much more familiar to Dagny than the refinery's surroundings, and she felt oddly comfortable here on the edge of violence. At least there was life.

They walked underneath a metal railing, and the ground flattened out into a wide concrete field, circled by buildings. Telga snuck over to a loose pile of rocks.

"Okay, the field in front of us is a sort-of no man's land between the border of Sliver's crew and Cradle Creek. See that fence over there? That's where we're headed. The Lounge is just beyond it. Follow me, keep your head down, and we should be fine."

Dagny smelled toxic smoke, like the burning of lacquered wood mixed with straw and excrement. It spewed out of crooked chimneys that pierced the neighborhood ahead of them.

"...What about the black place?" Max asked. "Your shortcut... where is that?"

"There." Telga pointed off to a large, pitched-roof building with a belfry, densely buttressed on both sides by the slum. "...It's through there..."

"Got it," Max said.

"Alright. Let's go."

~

The Lounge was a stout, three-story structure at the corner of intersecting alleyways. It looked formidable. Like a fortified keep in the middle of the wild night city. Heavy, half-shuttered windows framed the single entrance, and colorful shades of crimson and yellow spilled out from within. Above the doorway, spelled in vivid, brightly glowing lamps of reddish orange and blazing pink was *The Crescent Lounge*. There was a sort of buzzing electricity in the air. It was dangerously attractive.

From their spot in the shadows of the alley, Dagny could see figures moving about inside. Telga had told them to "just watch," so they crouched there, in the dark, and did just that.

The door opened and a man came stumbling out. He braced himself on the edge of the wall for a moment and then bobbled over to a side street and disappeared from Dagny's view. The man was either drunk or dying. Maybe both. She tried to see through the haze, looking for any girls or women. There were shapes of people, but she couldn't make out any distinct features. The door closed, and Dagny sat on the ground, waiting for it to open again.

But it didn't. They stayed there for what felt like hours, listening to the mumbled sounds and chatter that came from inside the building. Dagny tapped Telga on the shoulder and leaned close to her ear.

"What are we gonna do? Should we get closer? Go inside?" Dagny whispered.

Telga just looked at her and shook her head. Dagny was getting more and more antsy. Her nervousness turning to frustration. *Well, what* are *you going to do? You've come this far. You can't stay here all night.* Dagny told herself she would be okay if her sister was inside, despite what Telga believed. Grete was part of Sliver's group. She'd watch out for her, wouldn't she? *Just go in there and say you're looking for Grete. These are her people.*

Dagny took a deep breath, stood up and walked out of the shadows toward the lounge. It must've come as such a shock to Max and Telga, because neither one of them had time to reach up and stop her. Dagny stepped quickly. There was a sharp whisper from Max, "Dag, don't!"

She'd never been this nervous in her life. Even in the Oracle Tower. That was instinct. This was a slow build. Dagny's stomach tightened, and underneath her brother's coat, she shook uncontrollably. *Stop it,* she commanded... and reached for the door.

At first, no one noticed her as she slipped inside. Figures, bathed in shadowy tones of orange and blue, drank flame-colored liquid from clear glasses. The stone floor was partially covered with ornate rugs, and smoke filled the space, casting a colorful haze over everything. Dagny stood by the door while she tried to orient herself to her surroundings. It was loud with voices. Men and half-clothed women sat in corners, sucking on curved pipes. She scanned the room, looking for anyone who could be her sister. Gretchen was a small child the last time they saw each other, but Dagny hoped she'd recognize her nonetheless. She moved further inside, toward a circular bar where several shirtless and tattooed bodies stood gathered around. Behind it, a tall woman with a shaved head served drinks.

Dagny approached the bar and sat on an empty stool, doing her best not to draw attention.

The tall woman noticed her first. "Are you... wait... what are you doing here?" A splotchy rash covered most of her face.

"...I'm looking for my sister..." Dagny said, her voice almost catching in her throat. "Her name is Grete... Gretchen, from the Rakesmount across the water."

The woman glared at her. "Are you stupid? There's no one here... hold on..." A look of recognition spread across her face. "Dead girl? No way. I don't believe it... hold on right there. Don't move." The woman turned and walked away, through a curtain behind the bar.

Dead girl? Dagny was more confused than concerned. It didn't sound like she was saying Grete was dead. After a moment, a woman with red hair peeked out from behind the curtain, then disappeared.

The tattooed men were watching her now. Dagny glanced over quickly, and in the multi-colored light, she saw a rough man with wilted ears nudging one of his companions.

The red-haired woman stepped out. She had a pretty face, but hard eyes, and was almost spilling out of a short skirt and tight vest.

"Oooh, you have such nice hands, let me see..." The woman took Dagny's hands in her own and examined them. It was strange. A flashback to Seanmare's study of her fortune lines. "Oh, so nice. Quite beautiful." The woman turned and walked back through the curtain.

Dagny opened her palm. Inside was a note: *Run Now. Wig Maker Water Street.*

"—What you got there?" a voice asked.

Instinctively, Dagny crumpled the note in her hand and looked up. Two men were standing over her. The scary one with curdled ears, and another who now spoke. This man was more handsome, but the look on his face seemed, somehow, more dangerous. His eyes reminded Dagny of a wolf she'd seen at the Viddry Park Zoo, and he had a long mustache, lit orange by the lamp overhead.

"...It's nothing," Dagny said. She was trying to judge the distance to the door. The men were too close for her to run. Neither of the women were within sight.

"Oh no? Don't lie to me. Who are you?" He had a thick accent that Dagny couldn't place.

"I'm no one. Just lost. Looking for my sister." Did she say too much?

"That's not what I asked, is it?"

Her heart raced with panic. Other men appeared and started to surround her. Dagny didn't know what to say. She blurted out the first thing that came to mind. "My name's Sorrow Bird." It was what the children at the Mount called a vagabond woman who lived on the street. She'd forgotten all about it until just now.

"I see. Do you bite, Sorrow Bird?" The man moved to touch her face, while the other men watched. One of them, fat-bellied and toothless, laughed. His head was covered in a tattoo of an open-mouthed beast.

"Don't touch me," Dagny said, pulling her face back.

The woman with the shaved head came out, grinning. "Hey Jago, that's Dead Girl's sister."

The man's eyes narrowed. The others were no longer looking at Dagny. They were watching their comrade with the wolf-eyes and orange mustache.

"True? You are her sister?" he asked. Before she could respond, he spoke again. "She has done some very bad things, little girl... *some very bad things...*" The man was inches from her face, and she could smell pipe smoke and spice on his breath.

"I didn't know that. I can just go. I'm sorry, I thought she was here," Dagny said.

"Maybe we just keep *you* until she comes back, huh? You can take her place."

"What are you talking about?" She tried to keep calm, but started to tremble under her coat. Suddenly the wolf-eyed man reached out, grabbing her tightly around the waist.

Dagny sucked in air and stared in shock at the man. His fingers dug into her skin. "You're hurting me..." she gasped, fumbling at his grip, trying to pry it from her body. He looked straight into her eyes and grinned. The others were smiling behind him. She heard someone laugh. Then the man squeezed. Crushing painfully hard into her hip. Dagny reached for his face and pushed, falling off of the stool and onto the floor. The impact knocking the breath out of her lungs.

All the men howled with laughter. A sharp, stabbing pain radiated from her side, like the man had crushed her bone. There was a gleeful look on his face. He enjoyed this, hurting her. The man grabbed her again with powerful hands, and lifted her off the ground.

But his hands were grasped around Morgan's coat, and as he held Dagny in the air, she twisted and slipped out, falling back down. In an instant she was on her feet, sprinting toward the door.

There were shouts behind her. Dagny could feel and hear the pursuit. She hit the front door hard and flung it open. Running out into the night. For a moment she almost ran forward, to Telga and Max, but she stopped herself and cut to the right. She couldn't lead these men to them. She'd take her pursuers into the alley further away.

The flight was a blur. She seemed to glide over the pavement, cutting down a side street. But the men were fast, too. She could hear their feet thudding across the ground. They wouldn't stop. She'd lost her brother's coat, but there was no time to think about that now.

Another twisted alley. She jigsawed her way around crooked buildings on crooked angles. Things moved in the shadows. Dagny saw eyes and hands. A drunkard's bulbous nose. Everything was distorted. She could still feel the man with the orange mustache. *Jago*. He was so strong. She didn't know that *anyone* could be so strong. She didn't dare look back but imagined him right behind her, gaining ground. Grabbing her hair this time. With the same hand that had hurt her. Pulling her down into the ditch. What would happen to her then? What would they do after dumping her in the gutter?

The path widened. A murder of crows erupted from an enormous tree nearby. Dagny hopped a fence and landed on rocky earth. She gasped for breath and took off again, her hip throbbing painfully. Nearby, across a short field, was an enormous pitched-roof building with a belfry. Its entrance wide open, like a gaping maw.

The men were almost at the fence.

With no time to think, Dagny ran into the building, and toward the black nest beyond.

11

Into the darkness.

She slowed down, ever so slightly. It didn't sound like the men were chasing her anymore... yet, she couldn't be certain. She could hear nothing but her own footsteps and strained breathing.

It was complete blackness except for a point of light at the far end. Had Telga really come this way before? It seemed frighteningly dangerous.

Dagny stopped for a moment, trying to catch her breath. She tried to think. The men would be waiting for her back there. Watching, for who knows how long. She couldn't stay here, but going forward meant heading toward that pale-faced thing they'd seen earlier.

She needed to get back to the others. The note had mentioned a wigmaker on Water Street. It was her only chance to find something out about Gretchen. For some reason her sister had fled Sliver Farn and his gang. Dagny was glad of that. She hoped Grete was far away from this awful place.

Dead girl...

Dagny pressed on, through the pain in her hip. Rows of disheveled pews took shape in the dim light near the exit ahead. A house of worship in different times. She hurt even worse now. The pain pulsated from her stomach to her thigh. What had that man done to her?

The smell of mold and rot was overpowering, as if nothing existed but decay. Dagny pulled her bandana over her nose and limped outside, into the moonlight. The air, damp and cold, engulfed her, and she wished for her brother's coat. The coat... *It was gone now. Likely forever.*

She listened for the slightest sound. Any indication that there was something on the road ahead. Was that footsteps behind her? Dagny forced herself to move again. Onto a single path. It slid between warped, bloated buildings that buckled outward from the wetness they'd sucked up over the years. It was a mystery how any of them were still standing. Yet, standing they were. Tall, monstrous things. Reaching to pluck the stars from the sky. There were ghosts here. Dagny could feel them. Watching her move with milky, hollow faces gaping from inside black rooms where families once lived.

She wasn't sure if she could do this. The place had turned into a nightmare a long time ago. The road slithered in front of her, like the trail of a giant snake. Dagny leaned against one of the buildings and grimaced in pain. She thought of the boat ride with Sarna, *I bet you probably don't get scared,* she had said. *Something about you*. But she was scared now. Sarna didn't know her. No one really did.

It reached for her.

A gnarled, grasping hand. A foul smell. Damp, rotten and sweet. Dagny flinched and jerked her head to the side, away from hulking shoulders and shredded rags. It was here. The bloated man. Looming in the shadow by her face, in the terrible darkness between the water-logged buildings. Dagny screamed, stumbled and fell.

Again it moved and stepped into the moonlight, a dark shape towering over her. She sat in the mud, unable to react, struggling to breathe. It felt like she was drowning, a sensation of waves sweeping over her, pulling her down.

Did it say something? A squeak? It's voice chirped like a high-pitched animal, a squirrel or a rabbit. But, it wasn't talking. No, it was *slurping* the air. Sucking it through tight lips.

She was shocked, confused. Almost in awe at the magnificent horror of the thing. Everything happened so slowly. It was beautifully odd. Like she had all the time in the world. The long moment before everything ended. She looked down on herself as the scene unfolded. Her feet kicked, her hands stretched backward, trying to drag herself away from the man-thing, but she was moving so slowly. She just slid in the mud. *So slowly. You'll never make it. You'll never get away.* She screamed again, yelled, in agonizing anger.

For a brief moment, the thing stopped. She heard something else. Her name. *Dagny... Dagny!* It was a boy's voice. Suddenly the bloated man lurched forward and tumbled into the shadow.

Max almost fell on top of her in the darkness, but pivoted and rolled to his side. He was panting. "Dagny!" He reached out. "Are you okay?" He repeated it before she could answer. "Are you okay?"

Max found her arm and yanked her up. "Go!" he yelled, and they scrambled away, running blindly down the road. Max grasped her hand hard, as if he never planned to let go. The clouds had cleared and it would've been bright with starlight in an open field, but the decaying canopy above blocked out so much. When the road weaved away from the moon, it was almost impossible to see.

Dagny had no breath left to talk. She would've asked where they were going. How he made it to her. But she just struggled to keep up.

"C'mon, you're slowing down. C'mon!" he cried. Her side was on fire.

"...I can't... I'm hurt," Dagny muttered.

"Okay, okay, but we gotta go. We have to." Max slowed some, but was still in front, pulling her along.

"Max, please. I can't." She was gasping hard now, and leaned over, pressing on her knees.

"Dag..." He touched her back. "What's wrong?"

"My... hip..." she said through strained breaths. "They hurt me."

"Can you climb on my back?"

"I... can... try."

The sharpness cut across her belly, but she held on, as Max carried her. He continued forward as best he could. "We're getting out of here," he said.

Dagny closed her eyes. She could feel Max breathing heavy, but he was stronger than she thought, plodding through the mud.

Her mind began to catch up. What kind of things could live here in the wet blackness? She'd heard childhood fairy tales, ghost stories really, of dead things that came out of the drowned cities when the world first sank. No one really believed stories like that, but it's what she thought of. Dead things, come up from the water's edge.

...And the red-haired lady. Who was she? A friend of Grete's maybe. The woman had tried to warn her, but it was too late. *The wigmaker.*

"Max... we need to go to the wigmaker on Water Street."

"Huh? Sure thing. We need to get out of here first, though." He stopped and Dagny opened her eyes. Narrow passages cut between buildings. She tried to glance down them, to see if another pale-face was here, watching. It was just so dark.

"Please don't stop," she said.

"Right." He continued on, to a split in the road. In front of them was a towering building. Taller than all the rest. And there was a light coming from its upper window.

"I don't like the look of that," Dagny said.

"Yeah, me neither... look, someone's up there."

Dagny stretched her neck over his shoulder. It was a woman with long wild hair, her naked body illuminated from behind. She was staring at them.

"Go Max... go..."

"Which way?"

"I'm not sure," she said. Both directions looked the same. "Let me think... we need to head southeast. Can you see the Adventurer's Compass?"

Max stepped back, into the starlight. "Yeah, there it is... okay... this way I think," he said and headed to the left. "How you feeling?"

"It hurts," she said. "But I finally caught my breath."

"Just hang on. It shouldn't be far. Telga said it was a shortcut, remember?" They were in darkness again. Shades of damp brown, fading into nothing.

"You came after me..." she whispered.

"Of course I did. Please don't do that again, though," he said with a laugh. For a brief moment, it broke the spell of wickedness surrounding her.

"Who do you think that naked woman was?" Dagny asked.

"Someone we probably don't wanna meet. It takes a special kind of person to live in a place like this." Max struggled to adjust her position on his back. He was getting tired. Dagny knew they should keep quiet here in the darkness. But even though she clung to him, she needed to hear his voice, to make sure Max was still there. She would just whisper. It'd be alright.

"How did you get past those men?" she asked.

"They were so focused on the church, I ran right past them. It wasn't hard. They weren't expecting me. Right into the church you went, even after seeing that thing earlier. You are the bravest, most foolish person I know."

"You're a close second..."

"Did you see your sister?"

"No. She's not here anymore. Sliver's men are after her for something."

"Oh. Why? Do you think she double-crossed them?" Max asked.

Dagny couldn't imagine Grete betraying anyone, but she had a hard time picturing her here at all.

"I don't know. It sounded like it from the way they were talking."

"Those men were serious. Total brutes. I woulda come into the Lounge too, but it seemed like you knew what you were doing."

"Well, you were wrong about that... What do I know?" Dagny said.

"You must've found something out. What's this about a wigmaker?"

"There was a woman inside. She tried to warn me. I think she wants to meet me at the wigmaker's shop. Maybe she knows about Gretchen."

"Got it. We need to check it out, then."

"...I lost my coat back there, in the Lounge."

"I noticed."

"It belonged to my brother. He got sick on a journey with Alex. I was the only one with him when he died. I saw him slip away. Saw the life just leave his face. I went crazy when it happened. I still remember them taking him from our room... and then, that was it. He was gone."

Max spoke softly, "I'm sorry."

"I think it saved me. The coat."

"Your brother... he's still watching out for you."

"Yeah." Dagny rested her head on his shoulder. The pain was a dull throbbing now, becoming slightly more bearable. "Do you know the story of the Night Road, Max?"

"There's a story? I mean, I know what it is... a path between the stars."

"A flight from the dark. There was a nameless wanderer in the land of endless night. He'd been chased there by the Basilisk who'd turned his home into metal and ash."

"The Basilisk?" Max asked.

Dagny gave him a gentle shush, and continued, "...The land he was chased into was desolate. No one ever lived there. There were no buildings, no cities. No man-built pathway to guide him. It was a primordial land, and it was full of traps and pitfalls. The Basilisk assumed the wanderer would perish there alone. It's what all such creatures desire. Feeding off others' misery and fear. But Skarlap, the she-wolf, had been following the wanderer and pitied him. She knew the secret pathways. Those lit in the sky. The wanderer's destiny was not predetermined to end there. For the Night Road connected all things. If one only knew where to look. There was no destiny for the wanderer except that which he chose. Skarlap found him, looking out mournfully across a deep chasm, and showed him the Night Road. And the long way back."

"Are you my Skarlap, Dag?" Max asked with a laugh. "Showing me the way out of the darkland."

"Ha. *Grrrowl.*" She sighed into him.

"—Look! There!" Max called out suddenly.

The street led out into the moonlit grounds in front of the old refinery. In the distance, Dagny could see its grey concrete walls. Shimmering like a castle from a dream. It was the most exciting thing she'd ever seen.

Max set her down by the posters of the eyeless governor.

"Thanks," she said. "I think I can make it on my own. Let's just take it slow."

"Sure. We should be good now. Sliver's men are probably still watching the churchyard."

"They knew better than to go inside, huh?"

"Sure did," he said.

"When we get back to the others, don't act... different, alright? Even if I'm with Sarna. Don't stand off from me. We've been through too much now."

"I won't..."

She almost didn't see the ship, black as it was against the sky. Rodolph jumped onto the concrete pier and ran to them, while Sarna stood on the deck and waved.

"You made it. Hey, where's Telga?" Rodolph asked, looking over Max's shoulder.

"We took a different route," Max said. "Dag's hurt. We need to get her onboard."

"What? What's wrong?"

Dagny pulled up her shirt. Even in the night, she could see the dark red skin stretched across her abdomen, and the sickly yellowing bruise taking shape.

"What happened?" Rodolph asked, as he helped her on deck.

"Sliver's men hurt her," Max said.

Sarna came over with a jug of water. "Wash it off to be safe. I think Telga had some salve down below."

"Anything happen here?" Max asked Rodolph.

"Nope. Quiet all night until you showed up. It's been pretty boring, actually."

"Lucky you," Max said.

"I'm comin' next time," Rodolph said. "Don't care what Telga wants."

Sarna came over with the salve and spread it on Dagny's hip, rubbing it gingerly across her bone and stomach. It felt cold, like frozen mint, and numbed her side.

"I don't think anything's broken," Sarna said. "Does this hurt?"

"Ow. Yes. The whole thing hurts. Don't push."

"Okay. Sorry. Just needed to check."

"We'll get someone who knows something about wounds to look it over when we get back," Rodolph said. "Honestly, I can't wait. This place is creeping me out."

"We're not going back. Not yet," Dagny said.

"Yeah, get used to the creeps," Max told him. "We're going to Water Street. Wherever that is."

"What? Why?" Rodolph asked.

"–Glad to see everyone's alive and gettin' on good," Telga called from the dock. She was sweating.

"Some shortcut – that didn't take you much longer than us," Max said.

"Well, I ran all the way here. Thanks for leaving me."

"Leaving you? You're something else, you know that?" Max said. "Dagny got hurt back there."

"Hmm... she looks alright to me."

"Thanks for your concern," Max said.

"You're alive. What do you want me to do? Anyway, I'm ready to go. I assume you didn't find your sister?" Telga asked.

"Not yet, no. But there was this note." Dagny gave the crumpled thing to Telga. "A woman handed it to me. She must've overheard me ask about Gretchen."

Telga read it to herself and nodded. "Alright. Fine. It's not too far. The Water Street district is down the coast a bit. Rodolph, unmoor us, would ya?" She began to raise the sail as she continued to talk. "Water Street is the only place with some kinda order here. You'll like it better."

"Any clue where the wigmaker shop is?" Dagny asked.

"I have an idea."

They pulled away from the broken dock. Dagny gazed over the ruined, vacant landscape and thought again of the Oracle Tower. How she'd conquered the choking darkness there as well, and escaped for the better of it, having rescued Jorgie. It's what led her to Corlie and now to Gretchen. All these things were connected, like the Night Road, set in the stars far above.

Just as they were passing closest to the refinery's forgotten guard tower, Dagny saw two figures standing on the gravel path. One taller than the other. She couldn't make out any features, but there was no doubt in her mind that they were watching the ship depart and that they had come from the dark mass of buildings. A chill ran through her.

"Telga..." she whispered, motioning to the silhouetted forms. "Look, over there."

Telga grabbed her spyglass, but by the time she scanned the area, the figures were gone.

"What was it? What did you see?" Max asked.

"Something followed us out of there," Dagny said.

"Was it the pale-faced thing?"

"No. It was two of them, smaller. Wispy, like ghosts." Dagny turned and looked at him. "Do you think they were watching us, or... listening to us talk?"

"Don't worry about that. It's alright now," Max said, putting his arm around her. "We're safe. You don't have to think about that place ever again."

But Dagny wasn't so sure.

12

THE WATER STREET DISTRICT glittered on the coastline, or as close to glittered as one could get in Limer's Town. Torches and lamps dotted the area with orbs of amber and yellow. They bobbed and flickered inside deep pockets of night, like the torsos of glow-flies that lit up the city parks in summertime.

Telga steered the *Mangled Misfit* toward a proper-looking dock that split off in multiple directions. The place was busy. Drab-cloaked bodies milled about the tethered boats. It didn't seem like a safe place, but Telga reassured them. "There's protectors here from the Young Governors. Just pay 'em and you'll be good." Still, Telga seemed a bit nervous when she paid the grizzled man with broken teeth, armed with a banded club, at the entrance to the dockyard.

They'd all go to the wigmaker's shop this time. Telga walked in front with a small lantern, and Rodolph took up the rear.

"Now, I'd say let me do the talking," Telga said, looking over her shoulder at Dagny, "but for some reason, I think you'll just do what you want anyway, so why bother."

"Is this really the shop of a wigmaker that we're headed to?" Dagny asked.

"Sure, why wouldn't it be?" Telga said.

"Just seems a bit weird."

"You don't think the people in Limer's Town can appreciate a good wig?" Telga asked, chuckling.

"If I'm being honest? I didn't think it'd be on the list of necessities."

"Well, they might sell other things, too, if you're in the mood for some shopping."

"No. That's alright."

The streets and narrow lanes were crowded. They weaved through groups of shady people, and passed the entrances of drinking holes like *The Snake Pit* and *Margot's Shed.* The signs weren't emblazoned in lights like the Crescent Lounge, but scribbled in paint or scratched into the wood.

"I'm surprised people in Limer's Town can read," Rodolph said, pointing to one of the signs.

"I'm surprised you can read," Telga shot back.

"I didn't mean anything by it."

"No matter, Water Street isn't really here for them, you know," Telga said. "It's more like a stopping point for those traveling the lagoon, or headed into the hinterlands. There's a market for everything."

"The hinterlands? Like into the mountains?" Max asked her.

"Ha. No. People don't go into the mountains."

The wigmaker's place was up a hill and nestled between two vacant buildings. A gated alley ran beside it, covered in knee-high weeds. As they approached, Dagny noticed a light from inside, spilling out from under the battered front door. Otherwise, the path was dark except for the lantern Telga carried.

"Here we go," Telga said, and knocked.

There was a long moment before anything happened. Dagny felt like they were being watched, but couldn't tell from where. Finally a voice spoke from the alley beside them.

"Whatcha want?" It was a gruff voice, and came from a massive figure in the shadows.

"Are they open?" Telga asked, pointing at the door.

"No. We're closed... Looking to buy a wig, huh? The five of you?" It sounded like a woman's voice.

"We were told to come here," Dagny said. "I was handed a note in the Crescent Lounge. By a lady with long red hair."

"Alice?" the woman asked.

"I don't know her name," Dagny replied. She could see the woman's eyes now. Beady yellow things. "Can we come inside?"

"Hmm... Alice ain't here," the woman growled. "But she might be later, does so from time to time."

Dagny glanced at Telga before speaking again. "Can we wait for her inside the shop?"

The gruff woman was sizing them up. Shifting her gaze between the five of them. She didn't say anything, but unlatched the gate and waved them into the alley.

Dagny gave a curt nod, but just before stepping into the alleyway, she saw movement on the rooftop above and Telga grabbed her shoulder.

"Who you got up there?" Telga asked.

"What's that now?" the woman said.

"Up. *There,*" Telga pointed sharply at the roof.

Suddenly the front door of the shop opened and a stout, short man came marching out.

"You leave them be! Ain't no meat for you here, Elda!" the man shouted. Dagny noticed he was missing his left hand.

The woman hissed and ran off into the alley.

"A trap..." Sarna said quietly from behind.

Dagny couldn't believe that she'd almost walked right into it, after everything that happened earlier. Her mind was so focused on Gretchen, she had ignored the danger.

"Come on, inside, all of you," the man spit out. "I was listenin' to you talk... If Alice sent you, she'll be here tonight."

Another trap? Dagny looked past the man and into the building. Inside were dozens and dozens of wigs covering wooden heads.

"Well... you comin'?" the man asked.

Dagny took a breath and entered the shop.

After they had all stepped inside, the man closed, barred and triple-locked the door.

"Not from here, I take it," he said.

"No. We're from the city," Dagny said. Telga huffed disapprovingly.

"Ah... come for one of my glorious wigs, have you?"

"No, not really."

"I'm just joking you. Although yours would make a fine one," he said, touching Dagny's mess of hair. "Name's Grutter."

"Who was that woman outside?" Max asked.

"A beast." Grutter spit on the floor. "You need to be more careful in this place. It ain't the city."

"Good advice," Max said. "Did she... uh... take your hand for meat?"

"Oh, this thing?" Grutter said, raising his stump up to Max's face. "Nah... I lost this one fair and square."

"How come you helped us out?" Telga asked, arms crossed.

"I wasn't plannin' on it, but if Alice sent you here, she's got good reasons. You can wait in the back, if you want." Grutter motioned to a faded blue door.

The blue door led to a blue room. A blue cushioned sofa took up the center, and a giant wardrobe rested against the far wall.

Rodolph plopped onto the sofa. "That was fun. What you think that beast lady would've done with us, if she had her way?"

"Meat. Probably have started with you," Telga said.

"—Stop it," Sarna said. "That's horrible. This is all very horrible."

"Yeah. I'm getting tired of this place," Max said. "What a nightmare. I thought Water Street was supposed to be better."

It would be over an hour before Alice appeared. By then, Sarna had fallen asleep on Rodolph's shoulder. Telga, Max and Dagny sat on the floor, waiting, until at last they heard the front door open.

"Up... up... someone's here," Max said, jumping to his feet.

The blue door opened while Sarna was still rubbing her eyes. In walked the red-haired woman from the Crescent Lounge.

"This is quite a group," she said. The woman wore a cream-colored cloak, and underneath, the same tight, red clothing from before. "I'm Alice, and you are Gretchen's sister."

"Yes! I am," Dagny cried. "You know her! They called her Dead Girl at the Lounge."

"That's her name around here. I'm pleased to see you got away from the men. I thought Jago would have you for sure. It was quite fortunate you escaped like you did."

"I was fortunate Jago grabbed my coat... you didn't see it back there, did you?"

"The men took it."

Dagny nodded, and tried to push her sadness away. She didn't want to waste any more time. "My sister. Do you know where she's at?"

"Far away from here. She ran off a couple weeks ago, with some musicians that played for Sliver's birthday celebration."

"A couple *weeks?* That's all?" Dagny said.

"Seems like your timing was bad," Alice said.

"What kind of musicians? I mean, what did they look like? Did they have a name?" Dagny's mind was spinning out of control.

"No name that I heard. They dressed in colors of orange and brown."

"Sarna, does that sound familiar?" Dagny asked.

"No. I'm sorry."

Dagny turned back to Alice. "Do you know where they were going?"

"Only that they went across the Shallow Sea. Nothing else." *The Shallow Sea*. It was beyond the lagoon, and connected to the rest of the world. Grete could be headed anywhere. "I wish I could tell you more... I know what it's like to lose someone close."

"You have no idea where she was trying to go?" Dagny asked.

Alice shook her head. "I don't."

And with that, any hope Dagny had of seeing Grete again, evaporated. It felt like a weight had been dropped on her.

Dagny sat on the couch, as tears began to well in her eyes. "Thanks… for telling me." Sarna came over and held her. Gone. Her sister was truly gone.

"Your name is Dagny," Alice said.

"Did Grete tell you that?"

"Yes." Alice smiled, gentle and kind. "She reminded me of a daughter I lost. We were close, your sister and me."

"We were close too, at one time," Dagny said. "It seems like time is always against me."

"Gretchen. She's a fighter, you know. She'll be alright, so long as she stays far away from here."

A fighter was not what Dagny remembered. "Why are they after her, those men? Why did she need to leave?"

"She didn't have a choice."

"Why? What did she do?"

"Oh, my sweet girl, she stole Sliver's heart."

Grete came to Limer's Town some years ago with an unnamed scavenger from Caltra. She rarely spoke of the time in between, after leaving the Rakesmount, but she did tell Alice about Dagny: her sister who disappeared the night of the flood. And there was an angry fire in her eye when Alice first asked about the Mount. After that, she dropped the topic altogether. Gretchen had a pureness, but also an edge. "That's one of the things Sliver liked so much in her… she was sweet but could be furious, too." The Caltran scavenger had planned to head into the hinterlands, taking Grete with him, but he fell to poison before they could make the trek.

"I won't tell you everything Gretchen had done. You shouldn't worry about those things. There's a different way of life here."

Grete came up in Sliver's gang as it expanded from a small operation, robbing ships and drunken travelers around Water Street, to large-scale plots, the details of which Alice would also not discuss.

"I tried my best to watch out for her, but there's only so much a person like me can do. I wanted her to leave, but this place is a swamp, and once you're here, it takes all you have just to reach some air."

It had been on one of Sliver's "scavenging expeditions" on the bank of the lagoon that he came across the box. An elaborate thing. A work of art, really. An artifact from an older time, made of white bone and steel. Intricately carved with sliding pieces and joints. It was a puzzle box, and try as he might, Sliver could never open it. *There's a beating inside*, Sliver had said. A living heart, powerful and calling to him. He showed it to his closest companions. Vile men like the murderous Jago and Rotterbrag. But no one else heard the beating except for Sliver.

He called it his heart of fortune, and was convinced that something powerful had been placed inside the box. He started to convince others of the same thing. Rumors began to circulate that it was from the spirit realm, and contained all the blessings and hopes of Mankind. Sliver's men became fanatical about it, thinking the box had the power to transform their lives.

On the nights that Grete slept close to Sliver – and the box – she would dream. Of a magnificent shifting city, where the walls and buildings constantly changed; and of the deep, dark underground beneath a cauldron of black iron. At first, the dreams were minor things, a vague recollection of trivial events. A rose garden, or the sunrise from a terrace. But as time passed, the dreams became more vivid, and pressing. Near the end, Grete dreamt she was a woman there, wandering the shifting city's ever-changing landscape.

"The girl told me everything. I feel like I lost a part of myself when she fled."

"What happened?" Dagny asked. "She stole the box then and left?"

"It was during the week of Sliver's birthday celebrations," Alice told her. "Grete took up with one of those musicians, and saw her chance to escape. She's a charmer, your sister is."

A charmer of brutes and performers. Dagny tried to imagine her little sister becoming such a person.

"She didn't have much time, though," Alice continued, "and had to leave everything else behind. Sliver told everyone the box was gone, and that it was Dead Girl who took it..."

"Why would she steal it?"

"Maybe she thought it could change her life too, but I don't know."

"What would Sliver do, if Grete was found?" Dagny asked.

"Don't ask me that question. She can't be found, alright?" Alice leaned forward, her face serious. "And now that they know Dead Girl has a sister, I'm afraid they'll be looking for you, too." The thought had crossed Dagny's mind on the boat ride to Water Street. The way Jago and those men had pursued her from the lounge... they weren't planning to let her go, ever, if they had their way. And all she did was *ask* about Grete. Dagny was lucky the men's fear of the dark place was greater than their fear of Sliver.

"But they don't know who Dagny is, or where we live," Sarna said. "Will we be safe?"

"I hope so," Alice replied. "If you care about your friend, go back to the city, and tell no one you came here."

"Why don't you leave too, Alice?" Dagny asked. "You seem too kind for Limer's Town."

"You think so?" A slight grin formed on her hard but pretty face. "You shouldn't let your guard down so carelessly. Gretchen got away before she could be changed forever. And I'm glad of that. Me? I'm a part of Limer's Town as much as Sliver and the rest."

"Is there anything else you can tell us?"

"Your sister had a hiding place, where she could get away from the world and be safe for a moment. She left things there. I doubt Sliver would find it, but... her belongings should go to you, her family."

Dagny nodded. "Where's it at?"

Alice pointed at the wardrobe. "Through there."

Dagny stepped into the piece. A false back slid open, revealing a passage leading down narrow stairs. Alice and Grutter had provided and guarded the secret room for Gretchen, and at their own risk, no doubt. At least her sister hadn't been alone here.

When she reached the end of the stairs, Dagny paused for a moment before moving into the hidden space. It was a tight fit, and Dagny had to crawl to get inside. But once she wormed her way through, the room opened up somewhat, and she could stand tall.

On the floor was a blanket and a rough sack stuffed with straw for a pillow. Stacks of parchment and books were pushed against the opposite wall, and clothing and other objects poured out of wooden boxes that had been shoved in the corner.

Dagny wandered over to the pile, picked up a thick, canvas-bound book and opened it. The first page was a detailed sketch of a princess with black eyes and a castle overlooking the sea. *Avilys... and the Princess of Glass.* Gretchen had been drawing pictures of stories told by Morgan. There were others. The talking hyena-men who guarded the desert plains near Solevay; a wandering oyster knight who Morgan traded stories with on several occasions. And near the end, pictures that Dagny didn't recognize: giant, long-eared cats sitting in a garden; and a chamber filled with toads.

She emptied straw out of the pillow-sack, and stuffed the book inside. She grabbed a worn, discolored sweater from the floor, and pulled it to her face. It smelled vaguely of something sweet. She would take this as well.

"Hey Dag, everything good down there?" Max called from above.

"Yes. Just give me a moment." Dagny took one last look at Grete's hiding place and clutched her sister's things close to her chest, taking a slow, deep breath before turning away.

⁂

They left the Water Street district behind, its yellow lights vanishing in the gloomy, autumn fog. Alice looked sad when they departed. Dagny said she hoped to see her again, but Alice simply replied, "You won't."

It was even colder on deck now, so Dagny stayed below, wrapped in the wool blanket. Max and Sarna joined her, and they huddled around the cabin's table.

"You seem like you're handling this all very well," Sarna said. "How are you feeling?"

"I'm not sure. It's strange," Dagny said. "I'm more at peace with it than I would've thought."

"Sometimes, I suppose, it's good just to know what happened," Sarna said.

"Yeah. And she's gone from there. Even if I can't see her again, at least I know that... Alice said she got out before it was too late. There must've been enough spirit left in her."

"Oh definitely, *definitely*," Sarna said. "She sounds like a strong person, your sister."

"I just wish I could've seen her again."

Sarna nodded sympathetically. "I know."

"...What do you make of those dreams?" Max asked. "The ones Grete had?"

"I don't know what to think," Dagny said.

"Adventurers talk about powerful artifacts from the world before. Things we can't understand. I wonder if the puzzle box is something like that."

"Maybe," Dagny said. "I believe everything Alice told us, don't you? I mean, Grete could have just ran off without angering Sliver, right? If she just wanted to leave... She risked her life stealing the box."

"I believe Alice, too," Max said. "It was interesting, those dreams. Remember when Alice mentioned the one about the deep underground beneath a cauldron?"

"Yes..."

"Do you remember my Naverung story? There was one part about a giant king soaked in blood."

"Right. You mentioned that," Dagny said.

"My memory is real hazy, but it was something like he ruled an underground kingdom, went mad I think. Maybe it's a coincidence, but..." Max shrugged, "...it's interesting."

"You know what would be great," Sarna said. "Not talking about blood, or horrible things, or death for a while."

That made Dagny smile and laugh. "You're right. We can stop."

"I wasn't trying to be morbid," Max said. "I just found it worth mentioning. I didn't make up the story."

"...It's okay. I know," Sarna said. "Let's just go home."

~

Dagny arrived in Rork at dawn.

When she stepped off of Telga's ship, at the canal docks near the alley behind her home, she hugged each one of them in turn. Max was last. He pulled her close, carefully, conscious of her injury. "Goodbye Moongoose," she said. "Thanks again."

"You want me to check on you tomorrow?" he asked.

"I think I need a few days to myself... It's been a lot..."

"Alright. You just find me when you're ready. Hope to see you soon."

Dagny walked the long pathway home. She went in through the kitchen door, climbed the stairs to her room, and emptied Grete's belongings onto her bed. It would be alright, she told herself. Gretchen was alive, after all. It was more than she had two days ago. Dagny stepped onto her balcony and took in the early morning air. Across the street, and over a garden wall, a neighbor stood with her children and gathered flowers. A dog barked from somewhere further beyond. The crooked scholar's tower peeked above a rooftop. It was peaceful here, and, for the first time ever maybe, Dagny felt at ease in the Old Rork Benzara house.

She took Grete's sketchbook and placed it on her ornate dresser. Above, on a shelf, was Morgan's Wild Court set. The meerkat advisor, twin foxes, jackal scouts, and other pieces placed neatly in a row. She would finish carving the missing great bear guardian soon. She owed that much to her brother.

Dagny lay down, embracing Grete's worn, discolored sweater. She felt like a chapter was closing. She could move on now, toward what the rest of life had to offer. Yes. There was a sense of closure here. Grete was out there, somewhere, living the adventures Morgan had told them about. Like the ones Grete drew in her sketchbook. She'd be traveling the world. Dagny could be happy about that.

She dreamed that morning. About Gretchen lost in a tower. Dark and ominous. But it wasn't the Oracle Tower or any other that Dagny had seen before. This one was bigger. The size of a palace, with walls made of living wood. And Grete was dressed like a queen. She was running toward or away from something. Around her were animal companions. A great bear knight, and a lion crying mournfully. Grete was trying to escape but couldn't find her way out. There was no gate. Or maybe it was hidden somewhere. Inside a riddle. Grete was calling to her. She was afraid. *Dagny, help me. Please.*

I'm trying, where are you?! Dagny screamed. But there was no answer. Her sister was lost in a dream.

Part II:

The Under Road

A City of Water and Glass.

The scavenger or sailor, approaching from the lagoon, first discovers the border islands in mist. To the unacquainted, they are a hallucination, shambling and trancelike. Strange and distorted. The islands never fully emerge. They only hint at the promise of land. Eventually the coastline appears, still wavering and blurred. Suggesting, like a mirage, the southern marsh and the rag-tag armada of flat-bottom ships littering its shallows. The mist will vanish, and the bumps and spires of the city proper will come next. The twin river-towers, framing the Morca, survey the incoming vessel. They are as much a contradiction as the city itself. Welcoming and distrustful. Open and protective. There is no mistaking the sense of former greatness here. The city has stood at the convergence of empires for two thousand years, and believes it will last forever. It has produced more than its share of artistic genius and storied conflict. It is a treasure trove one cannot ever fully grasp. Gilded and tarnished. Hazy and pure.

The scavenger or sailor will recognize its melody, although they cannot recall from where. And when they leave, their memory of the place will blur. There are distinct landmarks here. The Odd Viddry Bell Tower. The Palace of Stars. But the city overwhelms the stranger. So dense are its offerings that once the stranger leaves, they will recall almost nothing at all.

The scavenger will know that it was in the city that the Regime of Man fell, and it is to the city that the exile escapes and finds redemption. But there is also much the scavenger will never know. This place is built on an even older history. Of forgotten, ancient things. From a time before the forests were ravaged. From before the legendary firestorms, the floods and the withering. It is a history that runs deep. Deeper than anyone will ever go.

-Preja Vittendorf; *All These Places*

13

"Do you see it yet?" Jauson Tasher asked. He ran his fingers through blood-red hair, sweeping it back from his face.

Dagny stared at the checkered board in front of her. She had crossed the river with two of her monkey sentinels, and her bear guardian protected the center.

"Do you need me to show you?" Tash asked again. They'd been sitting outside for hours. Dagny drank so much tea from the nearby cafe that her hands shook.

"No. Just give me a moment," she said. "Stop rushing me." This must've been how Lucas felt when she first taught him the basics in Alex's study.

Tash leaned back and crossed his arms, a slight grin on his face. "I'll wait."

Dagny would've loved to wash that cocky smirk away, but she knew she was unlikely to beat him. Ever. The boy really was a master. She had spent every morning the last few weeks playing Talvarind at Sorn Rue, and she still felt like her game hadn't improved.

As she reached for her guardian, Dagny looked up at Tash, who let out a groan and shook his head. She pulled her hand back and studied the positions further.

"You make me feel like a novice," she said with a heavy sigh. "It's frustrating."

Tash shrugged. "You *are* a novice."

"Thanks." Dagny rested her chin on her hands. Whatever he was planning, she didn't see it. "Okay, maybe just a hint. Has it got something to do with your stone knight on the third column?" she asked.

"Kind of. That's the feint. Soon I'll use it to put your king in jeopardy. But the real trap is *here.*" Tash picked up one of his Caltra Teamen and moved it up a single square. A seemingly innocuous position. "Now, my cannon is protected and there's nothing you'll be able to do to stop *my* sentinels." He made a rapid succession of plays, and at the end had Dagny's guardian trapped and her forces eliminated from his side of the river.

Dagny sighed again. "Okay. I understand... I think." But there was no way she would've figured that out on her own, no matter how long she stared at the board.

"It's only useful if you move across the river piecemeal, like you do sometimes. Remember, if you're playing against the Teamen, you need to attack their side in force. Especially if you're playing someone like Telga. I swear, it's the only way she knows how to win... counting on her opponent to just step into the trap."

"Is Telga playing in the tournament?" Dagny asked. She hadn't seen her since leaving Limer's Town, almost a month ago.

"I don't know," Tash said. "She sort of hates me, if you hadn't noticed."

"Hate? I'm not sure about that, but definitely a strong dislike," Dagny said, teasingly.

"Same difference."

"I don't get it. Why are you so infatuated with her? And more importantly, why do you put yourself in that situation? I mean, if someone didn't like me, I don't think I'd go out of my way to talk to them. Is it really because she's pretty? Tell me it's not that."

"First of all. She's beyond pretty, it's unreal, but no. I'm not sure what it is. I know she's gonna reject me," he shrugged. "Maybe a part of me likes it. The challenge, you know."

"You don't do yourself any favors. The way you approach her, it's *way* too much," Dagny said.

"You're right," Tash replied.

"Telga isn't bad. She can be a little harsh. But it's understandable, when you talk to her like that."

"Do you want to call this one?" Tash asked, directing her back to the board.

"No. Let's play it through. I know I've lost, but I wanna see how you finish it."

Tash winked at her, and advanced his cannon to her king's weak side. There was no doubt that Tash knew exactly what he would do, but he made a game of it, pursing his lips and rolling his chunky rings over and over, as he pretended to think about his next move.

Dagny's mind drifted as she thought over the past few weeks of playing games with Tash. She had needed a change, after everything she'd been through with her sister and Limer's Town. Dagny found him playing matches at the heavy stone tables in the Gardens at Sorn Rue. She pretended it was an innocent coincidence: *Hey, Tash right? We met at the Ironhead... want to play a game?* But she knew that somewhere, deep down inside, she'd been seeking him out.

Maybe she was just looking for a friend who was disconnected from everything else. Dagny felt a sense of peacefulness when she played Talvarind. It reminded her of pleasant times with Morgan, before everything fell apart. And there was something about Tash, behind the cocky facade, that felt comforting too, in an oddly familiar way. So she spent her mornings here, under the thick shaded canopy and amongst the thorned yellow flowers, playing matches with the blood-haired boy. And she spent her nights at Stardust, listening to Sarna and Hanette try out new songs, drinking with Max and Rodolph, telling stories and wasting time. Hanette was still furious with her for taking Sarna to Limer's Town. It made Dagny feel horrible. Sarna said not to worry, that Hanette would forgive her in time, but Hanette had not even looked at her in weeks.

Dagny almost didn't make it today. Last night she drank so much that she almost fell off the Stardust roof. What kind of nickname would they give her then? Was there a children's story about a drunk girl who broke her neck? But Max grabbed her at the edge and carried her down. They sat outside, just like that first night together, staring up at the stars. She thought he might kiss her, or hold her hand, but nothing happened.

She awoke with an aching head and dry throat. Still, Dagny managed to pull herself out of bed and meet Tash. Gretchen... Limer's Town... it all ate at her. She didn't like spending too much time alone with her thoughts inside the empty Benzara house. She needed to take her mind off of such things. And Talvarind usually did the trick... usually.

"You seem distracted," Tash said, as he picked off her king.

"My head kinda hurts today."

"Oh." Tash put his hand out. "Nice match."

"Yeah. Thanks again for showing me." Dagny slowly started to gather her figures and place them in her case.

"Did you wanna go over the Red Guard again? It's the most popular set in the city. You're likely to face it more often than anything else. But like I said, the Wild Court *should* beat it every time."

Dagny rubbed her eyes. "No, that's alright. I think I've taken all I can handle."

"Alright," Tash said. He seemed disappointed.

"I don't need to go home though. Just can't do this anymore. You want to walk over to City Centre? The booksellers are out today."

"Sure, why not. I got some time." He picked up her bear guardian. "You did a good job carving this."

"Thanks. I cared about it. I'm glad it's turning out alright."

"It's the most important piece of the set. The great bear is a protector, but also destined to sacrifice itself for the survival of the Court."

"It was missing from my brother's set. That's why I had to carve it myself."

"What's that?"

"My Wild Court set," Dagny explained. "It belonged to my brother, but the bear was missing."

"What happened to it?" Tash asked, as he began to place his own figures in his case. Spread across the table were random pieces from the Red Guard, the Teamen, and the Court of Jud.

"He must've lost it or something."

"That's strange. Any master knows how important it is. Without the bear, the Court is doomed to fail. Occasionally I'll see players who forego it, just so they can field an extra lion. It never works."

They finished packing their Talvarind figures and board. Tash picked up the Jud queen, Odestinas, and placed it in his pocket, like he always did.

“How come you don’t put that one away with the rest?” Dagny asked, stretching her back.

“It’s an old master’s habit. You carry your most important piece with you, to remind you that the game never ends.”

"I wonder if that's what happened to the bear guardian," Dagny said.

"Maybe."

They left the park and walked along the Morca riverside, toward City Centre. A light wind stirred the water, and the occasional ship’s bell rung and gull squawked.

“When you gonna tell me where you got your set?” Dagny asked, playfully nudging his arm. The cold air seemed to energize her.

“Ha, give it a rest, will you? You’ll never know.”

“I won’t tell... *you steal it?*” she whispered.

“No way. I don’t need to steal. You’ve seen my game. I can get anything I want when I’m playing for Gambles. You’re going to watch tomorrow, right?” Tash asked. He was playing in a small tournament at the Rork library.

“Of course. It’s close to my house. You should come to Stardust with me after. Hopefully to celebrate, and if not, to drown your sorrows,” Dagny said with a laugh.

“I don’t know, maybe.”

“Why don’t you ever come there with me? You seriously can’t think about Talvarind all the time. It’s not good for you.”

“None of those people like me.”

"Why do you think that? You just need to give them a chance. You gave me a chance and look at us now."

"That's different. I know that group. We don't get along."

"Suit yourself. I won't push it... Hey, I hear Vittendorf has a new compendium out. Think they'll have it at the booksellers?" she asked, switching topics.

Tash shot her a glance. "Vittendorf, huh? You read that?"

"Are you kidding? Of course I do. He's probably the best author of compendiums for adventurers."

"He's alright. He's not entirely accurate, though. He embellishes too much, but I guess that's why people like him."

"Embellishes? How would you know?" she asked, challenging him.

"I just know."

Smoke billowed out of the chimney of the thick, squat building, and Dagny pushed her way through a small crowd that had gathered outside. All of them were here to see Marfisi and the Mirage.

Dagny would've rather gone home tonight. She needed a rest. Yet, it was only the second time Sarna and Hanette would be playing with Marfisi, and Dagny couldn't let her friend down by missing it.

The sisters were on stage already when Dagny entered *Of Stardust and Light*. Sarna sang about the *Last Call of Kilkeken*, but had introduced a new verse. Her voice carried mournful and pure across the room.

With the final light cast off from the dead girl's face
She's dispersed like a dream in the time it takes
For the living boys to move on away

Back to their homes and safest place

Will you recall the truth when she returns to sing

The lonely sound of yesterday

When the verse ended, the sisters chopped into one of their instrumental songs, and the volume and chatter of the great room rose, almost eclipsing them. Most of the faces here tonight were new, and the crowd didn't seem to care much about the two girls.

Dagny found Max standing by himself against the wall, casually drinking from a tin mug.

"Where's Rodo?" she asked, leaning into Max's ear.

"Don't know... probably with Telga."

"Those two have been getting along well, huh?"

"I'd say so. More than just getting along, if you ask me," Max said, with a touch of bitterness. "Marfisi... pfft... I don't even like that music. Don't know why I'm here."

"To support Sarna, like me?" Dagny said with a smile.

"Eh. She doesn't care." He was looking away, across the room.

"Is something wrong? You're acting kind of odd."

"Nah. I'm fine." He took a sip from his mug and glanced past her, as if searching for someone more important to talk to.

"You looking for someone else? Don't want my company tonight?" she asked, jokingly.

"No."

"No?"

"No... I mean, I'm not looking for someone else. Just looking around, okay? You can stay if you want. I don't care."

"Really? You're gonna treat me like that? Are you serious?"

He shrugged. "I don't know what to tell you."

"Okay then. I'm leaving." Dagny marched off toward the exit out back. Max caught her when she was halfway there.

"Dag! Wait. I'm sorry... I'm just... I don't know... feeling kind of stupid."

"Stupid about what? I didn't do anything," she said.

"I know. I'm just feeling down. I don't mean to take it out on you."

"Well, get it together then," she said. "What's bothering you?"

"It's just... Rodolph's gone now, Sarna and Hanette could care less about me, you're spending all that time with Jauson Tasher."

Wait. How did Max know about Tash? She'd mentioned she had been playing Talvarind at Sorn Rue, but she purposely kept Tash a secret... unless...

"You were spying on me?" she asked. Dagny could feel her blood beginning to rise.

"What? No. I just thought I'd come by today and see how you were doing. See if you wanted to go to the booksellers after your games. And then I saw you making nice with *that* one... Jauson Tasher... what an arrogant fake. I mean, c'mon Dag... Jauson *Tasher*?"

"Wow. What's wrong with you? First of all, you have no right to call him names. And second, what's it to you who I spend my time with?"

Max was on the defensive. "...It's nothing. I don't care. I was surprised it was *him* is all... I just thought... forget it."

"Thought what? No. Don't answer. You *should* hope I forget it. He's a friend of mine, okay?"

"Oh sure. Is he playing his famous Court of Jud set?" Max asked, mockingly.

"How'd you know about that?" Dagny asked.

"Did he tell you how he got it? Probably not. Didn't want to shatter your hero worship of him."

"You are being a real ass tonight. Why are you acting like this?" People were watching them. Even in the crowded, noisy room, their voices carried.

"He took it from Ogden," Max said.

"Huh? What do you mean?"

"What do you think I mean? Tash basically stole it."

Dagny stared at him in disbelief. "How do you know that?"

"We all know it. He says he 'won' it, fair. But he knew Ogden's mind isn't what it once was... and Tash being Tash, took advantage and challenged him to a Gamble when no one was around to stop him. That set was one of Ogden's most important possessions. I wouldn't be surprised if that's why he disappeared. To go looking for it."

Dagny opened her mouth to respond, but didn't know what to say.

"Jauson Tasher doesn't care about anyone," Max continued. "And it just makes me sick, absolutely sick, thinking about you falling for him."

"I'm not *falling* for him... and even if I was... never mind. I don't want to be here anymore." Dagny turned around, without another word, and ran outside into the dusty field behind Stardust. This time Max didn't chase her. She was crying by the time she reached the rubble of the old city wall.

The tournament was played in the basement of the Rork Library, just a short walk from the Benzara house. Dagny wrapped herself in a thick scarf and took one of her simpler jackets — a brown one, tailored and fit with a shawl collar. It was nothing like Morgan's coat, completely unsuitable for adventuring, but it was the only one in her closet that was somewhat muted. She didn't feel like wearing anything colorful.

Dagny tried to stay in the sunlight as she walked into the crisp morning air, down the main Rork boulevard to the library. Her breath puffing out faint white clouds that enveloped her like swamp fog. It seemed like any other day outside the grand, marble-columned building. Several children, bundled in feathered coats, screeched cheerfully and ran up the steps away from a young mother. An elderly couple huddled nearby, sharing a drink of something hot between them. You'd never know there was a master Talvarind tournament being played inside.

She found Tash sitting alone, staring at the floor, while other players crowded the main chamber. He had sweet eyes and a nice face, but Dagny was not attracted to him. Not like the way Max suggested. *I can't believe you're falling for him*, Max had said. The way he spoke to her last night still made her furious. She tried to put it out of her mind as she approached Tash.

"Hey you," she said.

Immediately, the far-off look on his face vanished and he smiled at her.

"Oh, hi."

"You look intense."

"Just thinking through a couple things."

"There's quite a crowd here. Hope I'll be able to watch you play."

A tall man with a salt-and-pepper beard came over and pointed to one of the wooden tables near the back.

"Jauson Tasher... you're on table three... first opponent is Laurence Overman, playing Night Princes."

Tash glanced over at Laurence. A young man with a thin, blond mustache, dressed in black.

"You know him?" Dagny asked.

"Nah."

"Looks like he's taking the Night Prince thing a bit too seriously."

"—Hey, did Lana Dusk show up?" Tash asked the tall man.

"No. Not yet, anyway," the man said and turned away.

Tash began to quickly tap his fingers on his knees.

"No need to be nervous," Dagny said. "You got this guy."

"It's not *him* I'm worried about." Tash stood up and walked toward wooden table number three. "Oh, and thanks for coming. I appreciate it," he said over his shoulder.

Their match was the first one to finish. The young man, Laurence, played with an overaggressive posture, and placed his figures with quick, decisive movements. Tash countered each one of his positions almost instantly and captured the Night Prince king without losing a single piece. When it was over, the young man stood and bowed his head. "It was an honor. I think you're the best in the city."

"Thanks." Tash said softly, without looking up. Then he scanned the room, watching the other players.

The next two games were more difficult than the first, but Tash never found himself in any real danger. He bested each of the challengers, losing only a glass knight and several watchers in the first game, and sacrificing both cannons in the second. Tash had placed in the championship round by early afternoon.

"So how long until the final match?" Dagny asked, after the players had finished packing their figures.

"We have three hours for dinner," Tash replied.

"Is there anything you need to do? Any championship rituals?"

"No. Not really. Get some food, I suppose. I don't want to sit around here waiting. Don't you live nearby?"

"Yes. Want to come over?"

∞

The Benzara house had been so quiet with Alex and Cate and the children gone that Dagny appreciated having some company. If Jauson Tasher was impressed by the grand house, he certainly didn't show it. He looked like he could care less about rich furnishings and gold-framed paintings. The only thing he did seem to care about was quickly eating as much sausage and bread as he could.

"You live here by yourself?" he asked, while stuffing his mouth.

"No. I thought I told you. I live with Alex Benzara and his family."

"Oh. I don't think you mentioned that." Tash gulped down some water, before turning his attention back to the plate in front of him. "You're not eating?"

"I'm not very hungry."

"So how come you live with the Benzaras? What happened to your own family?"

"They're gone."

"Yeah. Mine, too," Tash said, matter-of-factly. This was new information to Dagny, and she wondered how she missed it. She assumed that Tash always returned to a house filled with life. "I lived with my grandfather until two years ago," Tash continued. "That's when he went. What about you?"

"Everyone's dead except my sister. She's somewhere across the Shallow Sea now." Dagny hadn't planned to talk about Grete so soon. "I have no idea where."

Tash gave her a nod, as he finished his meal. "Maybe she'll come back someday. You never know."

Dagny grabbed his empty plate and turned to the sink. "Sorry. I shouldn't be distracting you like this. You've got a big match to focus on."

"Don't worry about that. I appreciate the distraction. What's she like? Your sister?"

"I don't really know anymore. As a child, she was very shy and sweet."

"You don't know what she's like now?" Tash asked.

"No. It's been years since I've seen her."

"Really? How come I'm only hearing about this? We've practically seen each other every day for the last month." Tash smiled. "You're keeping secrets."

"I just didn't wanna talk about it."

"That's fine. I understand."

They looked at each other for a moment, in an uncomfortable silence, before Dagny blurted out, "She's a good artist. I know that much."

Tash cocked his head. "Huh?"

"Yeah. I have her sketchbook. I haven't shown anyone."

Tash studied her face. "You wanna show me?"

"Umm. Sure, I guess that'd be alright. Hold on." Dagny ran to her bedroom and returned a short while later with Grete's sketchbook. She sat next to Tash, thumbing through the pages.

"Your sister drew these?" he asked. "I mean, it's obvious she had no real training, but they're still pretty good."

"I thought so. These are pictures of stories our brother told us, as children. Well, most of them are anyway." She flipped to the black-eyed princess. "This is from the story of Avilys... have you heard of it?"

"No."

Dagny turned the page. "What about Jesper the Oyster Knight. Do you know him?"

"Nope."

"Maybe our brother made them up. I kind of suspected he did that." She stood and walked over to the counter, then poured herself a cup of tea. "I'm glad I found the sketchbook. Not just to remind me of Grete, but to remember my brother as well. I was starting to forget his stories. I'd kept them close to me for so long, but just like everything, they began to slip away. Now I have her drawings, and a piece of them both." Dagny turned around and noticed Tash staring intently at one of the pages. "What is it?"

Tash lowered his face, closer to the book, without speaking.

"See something you recognize?" Dagny asked with a laugh.

"I think so."

"Really?" She walked behind him to look at the page. It was opened to a drawing of the giant, long-eared felines. "Do you recognize those cats? I don't know that story."

"Not a story," Tash said. "And I don't think these are cats. I think these are *statues* of cats. Drey Garders."

"Drey what?"

"...*Garders*. Great hunting cats. I think this is a drawing of the old palace garden." Tash pointed to details on the page. "See these columns and the fountain? This is all old palace stuff."

"How do you know?"

"My grandfather was the grand archivist for the Authority. I was kind of raised on this."

"Have you ever been there? To the old palace?"

"No, but I always wanted to go."

"Where is it?"

"On an island, off the coast of Deep Lake, across from Lomenthal Station." Tash flipped the page.

"Is that close to the city?"

"It's about a day or two, depending." Tash directed his attention back to the sketchbook. "Do these look like shadows to you?" He was pointing at a number of black streaks, roughly smeared across the page. Dagny presumed they had been mistakes, like Grete was trying to wipe something off, or wet marks from being left in the rain.

"Just look like smudge marks to me," she said.

"Look closer. That doesn't look like a face to you?" he asked.

As if she were studying clouds in the sky, a shape took hold, and Dagny saw the image that Tash was talking about. One of the smears seemed to have a face like a bearded man. And another... was he wearing a crown?

"Okay. So you know Jud, right?" Tash began. "Well, a long time ago, before the Imposter, but after Odestinas, it was ruled by seven Kings of Amber. They were only called that later though, after their heads were sealed in blocks of resin. It looks like there are seven shadows of old men here." Tash handed her the sketchbook. "Anyway, your sister seems like a *very* interesting person. I don't know anyone who's been to the old palace before."

"I didn't say she'd been there," Dagny said. "Grete lived over in Limer's Town. She didn't have opportunities to leave."

"Hmm. I don't know..." Tash said. "I think she must have been there. Either that, or someone gave her a detailed description of the place. You sure she never went?"

"Maybe she just imagined it," Dagny suggested.

"The columns she drew have lotus-shaped bases. That's very specific to old palace architecture. And the cats, with the long floppy ears, fangs, and spots. I doubt a lot of people know that anymore. She couldn't have just *imagined* it all on her own."

Dagny started to chew on her thumbnail. "If I tell you something, can you keep it a secret? Can I trust you?"

"Yes," Tash answered without hesitation.

"It's going to sound very weird."

"That's alright. A lot of what you say is weird."

"For the longest time, I thought my sister had died. Drowned in a flood when the Rakesmount washed away. I went looking for her in Limer's Town, and although I couldn't find her, I did find a friend of hers. She told me about *dreams* Grete was having. Real vivid dreams."

"Okay..."

"I don't know... I'm thinking... maybe..."

"—Maybe your sister dreamed those drawings?"

"Yeah."

"Hmm," Tash said, then shook his head. "No. I don't think so."

14

THE WIND WHIPPED HARSH and wet against the heavy windows of Lomenthal Station. From the great dining hall, Dagny had watched the storm take shape on the far side of the lake, cross the water, and bare down on the rocky coast.

They arrived this morning, taking one of the river boats out of the city. It was an expensive trip, but comfortable. They had planned to rest only briefly before heading across the lake to the island and the old palace. Now Dagny found herself restlessly watching the storm, wondering when it would pass.

Lomenthal Station was enormous and grand. A former palace itself during the Regime of Man, Tash had told her. *The New Palace.* When the Authority took control, a generation ago, they gave the sprawling complex over to the People. The idea was that everyone should be allowed to make use of the grounds. The reality, however, was much different. Lomenthal was simply too far removed from the neighboring towns, and *the People* were simply too busy trying to survive to allow for lazy vacations on the banks of Deep Lake. So the Station, especially during autumn and winter, went mostly unused.

There were only two other occupants of the Station today: the Authority's steward, and a fresh-faced soldier of the Vahnland. They seemed pleasant enough, but had both consumed enough wine to be throughly drunk by noon. The soldier was presently passed out at the far end of the dining hall, next to a grand double staircase that led to the Station's ballroom. Dagny could faintly hear his snoring over the downpour.

Before leaving Rork, Dagny had told Tash he didn't have to come. If he could just tell her what he knew of the old palace, she'd find it on her own, but Tash wouldn't hear of it. "No way," he said. "This is too interesting, with your sister having drawn those pictures and everything. Besides, this is my chance to see the place for myself."

They made their plans on the floor of Alex's study. Tash had gathered his grandfather's maps and spread them over the rug, pointing out the various chambers and locations of the old palace grounds. "This used to be the hunting preserve," he said, gesturing to a massive area on the west end of the island, then moving his hand over. "And this is where the gardens are."

"That's where I want to go," Dagny said. "The gardens. I wanna know why Grete drew them." Maybe there was something there, a clue to where her sister had gone. Dagny knew it was unlikely, but still...

Lightning crashed in front of the Station's high, arched windows, briefly illuminating the empty dining hall. It was mid-afternoon now, but it might as well have been late evening, as dark as it was inside.

Just before the storm arrived, Dagny could see the old ruins from her place at the window, almost shimmering on the distant shore of the island. Now she couldn't even see the rocky beach on the other side of the glass. The wind and sleet had churned Deep Lake into a blinding mess. She glanced around the hall, looking for Tash, but he hadn't returned yet from the kitchens.

"Have you always been a loner?" Dagny asked him as they left the city, their river boat gently making its way through the canals that spread across the heartland.

"Pretty much," he replied. "There weren't many people around, growing up. It was a bit lonely, I suppose."

"Your grandfather. Did he teach you Talvarind? Is that how you got so good?"

"Good guess," Tash said. "Yeah. He coulda been a master himself. We played pretty much every night until I got good enough to start going into the city and playing Gambles."

"...Can I ask you another question?" she asked with sudden seriousness.

"Maybe," Tash replied, watching the river bank from their cabin window.

"I was trying not to mention it, but the more I think about it, the more I need to know."

Tash sighed. "Go on."

"Well, it's about your set, the Court of Jud..."

"Yes..."

"Did you get it from Magu Ogden?"

Tash turned from the window and stared at her. "Who told you that?" In that moment, the way he spoke and the expression on his face, Dagny knew it was true.

"Tash... Did you know his mind was slipping away?"

"Who told you? Was it Max? I don't know why he needs to be talking about me. It's none of his concern."

"It doesn't matter. Max was just upset about Ogden losing it. They're friends."

"I doubt it. Max and them, they just used Ogden like everyone else."

"That's not true," she said, and when Tash didn't respond, Dagny repeated, "Did you know his mind was slipping away?"

"How am I supposed to know something like that? Look, I won it fair, okay? We played for it. Do you know what Ogden wanted? If he won?"

"No."

"My grandfather's books. All of them. And he would've taken them, too. So no. I don't feel bad about winning the set."

"His books? Why would he want those?"

"I don't know. I didn't even know that they knew each other. But Ogden must've known my grandfather was the archivist. And he was dead, so I couldn't really ask, could I?"

"I'm not trying to get you upset," Dagny said. "I just felt like I needed to know what happened. I'm not judging the situation?"

"You're not, huh? Sort of sounds like it."

"No," Dagny decided. "I'm not." She didn't know Ogden that well, and she wasn't going to jeopardize their new friendship, or Tash's help getting to the palace, over this. "Forget I asked, okay?"

Another crash of thunder and lighting shook the roof, but did nothing to wake the Vahnland soldier from his slumber. Dagny stretched and left the dining chamber, wondering if Tash had gotten lost. She passed the double staircase and walked through an inner atrium, where rain pummeled the glass ceiling high above. *Where was he?* Dagny was on the verge of getting lost herself, when Tash appeared from around the corner, carrying two bowls of steaming noodles.

"That steward is pretty friendly," he said upon noticing her. "Operates this whole place himself, kitchens and all. Did you know he was a general for the Authority during the war?" Dagny shook her head, as Tash handed her a bowl. "Yeah. He says the Station is haunted, but not in a scary way. People have seen ghosts, and things just vanish in the night. Just a couple weeks ago, a boat disappeared. I said maybe it was a thief, but the steward said no one was here at the time."

Dagny took a mouthful of noodles before speaking, "Did you ask him if we can get a ride out to the island once the storm passes?"

Tash looked at the ground, and Dagny knew immediately the answer wasn't good. "Turns out, people don't go to the island," he said. "It's not necessarily *off-limits,* but there's a pack of bone crushers out there."

"Dogs?"

"Barely. Thick, massive beasts with enormous skulls. The steward thinks they probably swam over to get at the old hunting preserve. They're real dangerous, so nobody goes close to the island anymore. Sorry, I'm disappointed, too."

Dagny sat with him at a small table, considering their next move. "It's a long way to come, just to turn back."

"I know," he said. "I didn't think it'd be so difficult."

"...I'm not surprised."

"Why's that?"

"No reason. So, what do you want to do?" she asked.

"I don't think there's anything we *can* do."

Dagny shrugged. "We could pretend we're ghosts and steal a boat."

Tash laughed at that one. "Are you serious?"

"Would you still go? I mean, knowing there are bone crushers over there?"

"Sure. Why not."

Dagny smiled at him and took another bite of noodles. They were spicy with a hint of lime. "First things first, we gotta wait for this storm to pass. If it ever does."

"Yeah," Tash agreed, pulling his coat tight around his body. It was chilly in the vacant Station, away from the fire. Despite the storm, and despite the bone crushers, Dagny didn't feel hopeless. Somehow she knew she'd make it to the island. She listened for a while to the rain tapping on glass from the nearby atrium.

"What happened to your parents," she said, "if you don't mind me asking?"

"They died when I was young. A fire tore through the academy where they taught. My grandfather said they shouldn't have even been there at the time. It was real late when it happened, and they were helping a group of students. Just unlucky, I guess. What were yours like?"

"I never had a memory of my father. He was gone before I was born, and my mother never mentioned him."

"Never?" Tash asked.

"No."

"Does that make you sad?"

"It's hard to be sad about something you've never known," Dagny said.

"That's true. And your mother..."

"She's dead. Still under the Rakesmount, most likely."

"I'm sorry," Tash said.

"Don't worry about it." Dagny hadn't felt anything for her mother for a long time. Although it was strange now. For some reason, she felt like she was about to cry.

"Your sister then, that's all you have?" Tash asked.

"Kind of..."

"What's she look like? In case I ever come across her. Does she look like you?"

"I don't know," Dagny said. "I don't know what she looks like now."

⁂

They rented two rooms from the steward, far on the other side of the Station.

The storm continued into the night, chilling her bedroom so much that it was impossible to sleep. Dagny huddled under the sheets, shivering for a long while, until it simply became too much and she headed off to find a fire.

The Station wasn't pitch black, but it was close. Dagny took one of the small globed lamps that the steward had placed near her bedroom, and wandered down the darkened halls. The only active fireplace she found was the one smoldering back in the dining room. There was no sign of the Vahnland soldier. The wind and rain continued to pound the windows, but she felt safe under the mighty roof of the Station. She sank into a large, weathered armchair by the fire, and watched the last of the dying embers peel off and float away until she drifted off, herself.

⁂

Some time later, Dagny awoke to footsteps. Craning her neck around the armchair, she thought that maybe Tash or the soldier was approaching, but Dagny couldn't see anything beyond her lamplight. She tried to focus on which direction the steps were coming from. They sounded odd... hollow... like maybe the person was walking down the grand staircase. Then, suddenly, there was only silence.

Ghosts.

Dagny slowed her breathing and tried to remain as still as possible, straining her eyes and scanning the darkness. Trying to will herself to see.

...And something appeared. Floating at the far end of her vision. A pinprick of light dancing in the darkness. At first she assumed it to be nothing more than a floating ember, kicked off from the fireplace. But it was too far away for that, and as more time passed, the light continued to swim through the air... and sparkled.

Then she saw another one, near the stairs, and another floating down the steps from the second floor. Dagny rose from the armchair, grabbed her lamp, and crept toward the tiny orbs of light. They were like luminescent snowflakes drifting in a breeze, emanating a soft-bluish glow.

As she approached the closest one, the lights gently floated away, high toward the ceiling, then crested over the rails and balcony of the floor above, leaving trace specks of illuminated dust behind.

Dagny's apprehension was gone in an instant. She raced up the stairs and rounded the corner of a wide carpeted hallway, leading to the ballroom. The lights stayed just out of reach, like they were beckoning her forward, or playing a game. Dagny was vaguely aware of the passage becoming brighter, its cream-colored walls reflecting the glow. The lights drifted toward the doors of the ballroom, which stood ajar at the end of the hall.

"Wait..." Dagny whispered, extending her hand, but the lights weaved into the room beyond and disappeared.

She rushed to the doors and took a breath to steady herself. What was happening? Was she dreaming? Still asleep at the fireplace? Although Dagny knew she was very much awake, she still pressed her fingernails into her palms, just to feel something. Then, almost instinctively, Dagny placed her hands on the double doors of the ballroom. And pushed.

A brilliant blue light poured out. Powerful and dazzling. The ballroom in front of her blazed, lit by hundreds, if not thousands, of the sparkling lights. It was the most fascinating thing she'd ever seen. They zipped through the air like comets, and chased and played with each other like finches in her garden back home.

"What are you?" she said softly, slipping into the room and closing the doors behind her.

A flurry of lights rushed over, circling her head and swirling around her body. She felt no fear about it, though. Instead, a warm, electric sensation tingled down her back. It brought a sense of weightlessness, almost like she could float up and join them.

"Hello there..." she said, reaching into the flurry. A single, twinkling orb hovered over her hand before darting back to join the others.

Dagny glanced around to gather her surroundings. An elegant but dusty floor spread out and ended at a raised stage framed by purple curtains. The largest group of lights clustered together in the middle of it. And just like the lights in the hallway, this massive cluster seemed to beckon her closer.

Dagny crossed the room, in a sort of half-daze, and crawled onto the stage. Off in the wings, she could see tables littered with props and discarded costume pieces. She turned around and gazed over the chamber. It was like the entire night sky had come alive, chased inside by the storm. The mass of lights on the stage nearby swirled and fluttered.

A beautiful, twinkling flutter. They were calling to her. And then, just as she stepped closer, the ballroom doors opened.

Her heart raced. Someone was coming. Instinct took over and Dagny ducked off into the wing, sliding underneath a giant horse made of wire and parchment, and turned off her lamp.

The mass of lights dispersed, then swarmed into the opposite wing. The glow illuminated everything: old, discarded costume pieces, a feathered mask against the wall, scratches in the floor.

The lights made no noise, but Dagny heard something: the shuffle of feet and the creak of wood. Seconds later, a shadow spread over the floorboards of the stage. Dagny held her breath, certain that she'd be seen. Someone sighed and sniffled, and a small form appeared. A young girl... no, a boy. No older than nine or ten. He was dressed in dirty, white clothes and eating noodles out of a wooden bowl — stolen, no doubt, from the kitchen. For a brief moment, Dagny could see the side of his face, which appeared to be smeared with dark ash. She thought about calling out to him, but for some reason held her tongue. It was all so odd. Before Dagny could decide what to do, the boy marched off, toward a small door set in the opposite wall, opened it, and disappeared. Just then, the lights went out.

Dagny stumbled in the dark, knocking her head on something hard. She turned to face the ballroom, searching for any sign of the lights. But they were gone. Almost like they never existed at all.

She turned her lamp back on and slowly moved toward the opposite wing, where the boy had disappeared. She found the side door shut tight. Like it was sucked into the wall. Yanking hard, the door flew open and a gust of wind and rain smacked against her face. Lightning in the sky illuminated a single pathway that trailed off into the night. It wrapped around the Station, overlooking the lake. She was hoping to get another glimpse of the child, but like the lights, he had vanished as well. *Who are you?* she thought. Another orphan? Like Jorgie? Like her? Come to the Station for food? Perhaps. But the lights... who could explain that?

A crack of thunder rattled her nerves. Dagny put her head down and stepped outside.

She followed the walkway as it curved around the building. The Station looming large overhead. Although she tried to pull her collar tight to block the rain, it wasn't long before Dagny was thoroughly soaked and sloshing in her boots. She hated this weather. "Where *are* you?"

She was starting to sniffle, just about to give up and head back, when she spotted the wooden bowl tossed on the ground. Dagny ran to it. There were no noodles left, but thick sauce still coated its surface.

Dagny quickened her pace. As soon as she turned the next bend, she saw him. Standing in the distance, the young boy was pressed against the guardrail, staring out over the water.

"Hello there! Hello!" Dagny called into the wind, waving her arm. He threw her a quick glance, scowled, then hopped over the edge.

Dagny screamed, "Wait!" and ran over to where the boy had stood, thinking he had just thrown himself into the lake. But when she looked down, she saw a narrow ledge jutting out from the wall, and what appeared to be a passage under the stone. Dagny hesitated, questioning whether there really was a ghost here, intent on leading her to an early death. She called after him one final time, "Hello? Boy!" There was no answer. Just the splashing of waves on the rocks below.

Dagny shook her head. She knew what she was about to do was stupidly dangerous. If the fall onto the rocks didn't kill her, the storm would likely drag her underneath Deep Lake itself. It didn't matter. Dagny carefully crawled over the guardrail, and lowered herself onto the ledge, trying her best not to slip. A rough-hewn passage opened up in front of her, running underneath the Station, looking as if years of erosion had worn away part of the rocky wall. She crouched and crawled into it, out of the rain, the flame on her lamp casting black smoke over her face. The passage was so low that Dagny had to continue forward on her hands and knees. It was wet and dirty, and sharp bits of rubble dug into her skin, but she kept going, scanning the passage for any sign of the boy or the lights, until she finally emerged into a small chamber. Dagny saw a strange assortment of items scattered around the floor: pots and pans, a woman's slipper, a broken drum. Near the back of the chamber, where part of a wall had crumbled away, was an old stone well.

Dagny approached cautiously. A heavy chain hung from a rusted crankset and disappeared into the well-shaft below. Could the boy have disappeared down there, too? Dagny peered over the edge. The light from her lamp flickered across smooth walls decorated with gorgeous tile-work: delicately painted scenes of naked bathers by a lake, and monstrous fish swimming up from the depths. And further below, at the edge of her light, she saw something else. Something that excited her very core.

15

"It's a staircase!" Dagny told Tash, as he rubbed the sleep out of his eyes. "The well is a staircase! A secret passage. I'm not sure how far it goes down, but it looks deep."

"Hold on. You're throwing a lot at me. Who's the boy?" Tash asked.

"I don't know."

"But he went down the well?"

"I don't know. I think so." Dagny pulled the compass out of her adventuring pack and handed Tash the lantern. "But we need to hurry, before he gets too far."

She rushed down the hall, leading Tash to the ballroom, trying her best to describe the glowing lights. "I didn't imagine it, you know."

"I didn't say anything," he responded.

Dagny hopped onto the stage. "You didn't have to. I can tell you're skeptical."

"Who wouldn't be?"

"Fair enough. But I'm telling you, it was the most beautiful thing I've ever seen. *This way.*" She took Tash out the side door, into the night. "He's not a ghost either. He was stealing food from the kitchen."

"You sure it was a child, right?"

"Yeah," she said, then hesitated. "Why?"

"I just don't want to run into any wicked little fairy creatures that *look like children*."

"You don't really believe in things like that, do you?" she asked.

"I don't know."

Dagny stopped at the guardrail overlooking the lake. "Be careful." She thought Tash might be reluctant to follow her further, but he didn't complain. They crawled onto the ledge and into the tunnel, and when they arrived at the old stone well, Dagny reached over the edge with the lantern, illuminating the tiled walls and further down, a spiraling staircase.

"Now this is quite interesting," Tash said.

"What do you think it is? A secret escape tunnel or something?" Dagny asked.

"Probably. That makes the most sense." Tash reached over and pulled on the heavy chain, testing its strength. "So I guess we climb down this thing, huh?"

"Think it'll hold?"

"Only one way to find out." Tash took the lantern and looped it through the strap on his pack. "You ready?"

"You sure?" she asked.

"Yeah. Even if we fall, it won't kill us. It's not that far to the stairs."

He swung his leg over the edge, and descended the chain. Dagny watched as the lantern cast waves of amber and shadow over the painted well shaft. The forms of naked swimmers blissfully unaware of the jagged-toothed creatures below. When he reached the steps, Tash called up to her, "That wasn't so bad. Your turn. Just keep your eyes focused on the chain. You'll be fine."

"Don't worry about me. I know how to climb."

She reached the landing with ease, and let Tash take the lead. The staircase funneled them far down into the earth. Lower and lower they traveled. Minutes passed, and they encountered no doorways or passages or landings. Just the singular set of sharp, twisting stairs. A dull ache in her legs began to set in, and yet, they continued to descend. Trudging lower still.

After some time, they stopped to rest and sat on the steps. "Who built this?" Dagny asked. "It feels endless."

"We probably haven't gone as far as you think. We've been moving slow. But to answer your question, I'd say it's a leftover from the old palace... maybe even older, though."

"Older? You mean there was something here before?"

"Possibly. My grandfather seemed to think so, but he didn't tell me a whole lot. I wish he would've gotten to see this. He was obsessed about the palace, but never went anywhere. I think he both loved and feared the outside world." Tash stood and reached out his hand. "Let's see if these stairs really are endless."

Eventually, the staircase did end, and they found themselves standing in front of a flat stone tunnel, stretching into the dark. It smelled dank and musty, like a sunken ship that'd been pulled from the sea. Even though Dagny couldn't see any water, the air *felt* wet.

"Which way is it heading?" Tash asked.

Dagny pulled out her compass. "North."

"Into Deep Lake," Tash said.

"More like under it."

They walked for what seemed like an hour. Just like the staircase in the well, this passage was singular, leading straight north. *Straight to the old palace*, Dagny thought. "Still think this was an escape route?" she asked.

"I have no idea. There's nothing like this on any of the maps."

"You brought them with you, right?"

"Of course," Tash said, patting his bag. She was surprised by his seemingly fearless attitude. Dagny would've thought that, between the two of them, she'd be the courageous one. But here she was, nervously watching the ceiling for any sign that it might collapse, while Tash marched forward, all but oblivious to the lake above.

The passage finally opened into an enormous chamber that seemed to go on forever. It could've stretched across the entire underworld for all Dagny knew. Their path ended at a vast pool of water. *Another lake*, she thought. But this one was silent and still. Large columns rose from its basin, connecting to a vaulted ceiling. The column heads were carved into shapes of winged serpent-like creatures.

"This must be the cistern," Tash said. He set the lantern on the ground and opened one of the maps.

Dagny gazed across the dark water. "A cistern? This whole thing was a reservoir for the palace? It seems like it could supply a city."

"Yeah. Definitely excessive, I'd say."

"Do we have to cross the water?" Dagny whispered over Tash's shoulder, as he studied the map.

"I'm trying to figure that out."

"I hope we don't," she said.

Tash mumbled something under his breath, then walked over to the edge of the platform and scanned the underground lake.

"...Everything alright?" she asked.

"Doesn't look too deep... I can see the ground."

"You're saying we swim it?" She didn't like the idea of that. Not at all. Although it was slightly warmer in the underground, it was still cold, and she didn't like all the carvings of monstrous serpents and winged creatures covering the columns. It seemed like a warning, and an obvious one at that.

Tash considered her question. "I don't think we'd have to swim. That water might only be chest deep."

"Oh... that makes me feel much better."

"There's a landing just on the other side that will take us into the palace proper. From there we can find the gardens. Are you really scared?" he asked.

"Yes, I'm scared. This place is *scary,* and it feels like something could just swallow you up." The silent, dark water truly frightened her.

"We've come pretty far. You just wanna go back?"

Dagny didn't answer. She just stared at the water.

"You think there's some monster swimming around down here?" Tash asked with a wide grin on his face.

"...I don't know... I mean, look around at all the carvings. And why aren't you scared?"

"Eh. The palace builders were obsessed with covering any kind of stone or marble with dramatic images. There's nothing down here. What would it eat? Think about it. A creature's been lurking here for hundreds of years? It'd've starved to death long before you were even born. There's nothing alive in this water."

"Couldn't something have come in from somewhere else?"

"Nah. I don't think so," he said.

"You don't *think* so?"

"If you don't want to go, we don't have to. I just thought you wanted to see what your sister had been drawing."

"I do," Dagny said.

Tash put his hand on her shoulder. "Then focus on the old palace. Remember, there's a reason for all of this."

Dagny took a moment to listen and absorb the silence of the chamber. The water sat perfectly still. She thought of her sister. What if Grete *had actually* been here, just across the cistern? What could've compelled her to come? Or what if Grete really did have a dream? But one so vivid and important, she felt compelled to draw it in detail.

"You really think we can walk across?" Dagny asked.

"Yeah." Tash looked into the water again and smiled. "I think so."

"Okay then. Let's do it."

Tash sat on the ground and started to take his boots off. "Trust me, you're gonna want to be in dry clothes when we reach the other side."

"Is it far?" Dagny strained her eyes, but couldn't see anything beyond the glow of the lantern.

"Hard to know." Tash took off his shirt and pants and began to wrap everything into a tight bundle. "Just carry it over your head when you cross." Finally he pulled off his undergarments and kneeled by the edge of the platform.

"You're going across naked?" she asked.

"I'd recommend it, but do what you want." Tash dipped his feet into the water. "Wow, that's cold... Once I drop down, I'm going across as quick as possible."

"Alright. Hold on. Just wait a moment." Dagny turned away from Tash and nervously removed her shirt and pants. She'd never been nude in front of a boy before. "Don't look... seriously."

"Don't *you* look. I mean it," he shot back.

Dagny wrapped her jacket around her clothes and boots, and tied it as tight as she could with her scarf. She walked across the cold stone to where Tash was kneeling and began to shiver.

"If it's too bad, we'll come back, okay?" Tash said. "But you gotta let me know. I'll go first."

"Sure..."

He took a deep breath and jumped into the water. Dagny cringed as the sound of the splash shattered the silence and echoed across the chamber. When she glanced down, the water was only slightly above Tash's waist. He swung his arms around from the chill.

"Everything good?" she asked.

"...Yeah..." he wheezed in between short, sharp breaths. "...Gimme... the lantern and clothes."

As soon as Dagny handed him the bundle, Tash was off, quickly slogging through the water toward the opposite bank.

"Hey, you gonna wait for me?" she called.

"—Too cold, hurry up," he said over his shoulder.

Dagny moved her clothing to the edge of the platform, took a deep breath and jumped in. The shock that hit her was suffocating. She gasped, sucking in even more air, as the cold pinched at her bare skin. Without any time to think, Dagny grabbed her bundle of clothes, and started off after Tash.

The chamber felt even larger as she waded through the giant cistern. Tash's lantern light bobbed along in front, casting amber tones up the marble columns that faded onto the ceiling above. Dagny tried to remain focused on that light. It wouldn't do her any good to let fearful thoughts creep into her head. But the cold, black water rose high on her ribs, and on more than one occasion, she almost slipped on the slick stone beneath her feet. If something *was* here beneath the water, she'd be completely helpless against it.

Was that her greatest fear? Being pulled down and drowned. Like the flooded Morca, rushing over the Rakesmount. If she hadn't gotten out the night of the storm... hadn't run away during one of her *episodes*. She'd be drowned with them. There was something destructive hiding in the back of her mind... like she wasn't supposed to have gotten out of there. Just one random decision to run off was the only thing that separated her from life and death.

...But Grete had gotten out... and so had Corlie.

Her teeth chattered, and her arms ached from holding the bundle of clothes above the waterline. Tash's light moved further and further away.

Random images of death and water poured into her mind. She saw the pale, bloated face from Limer's Town, the image of something drowned and dragged up from the bottom of the sea.

Tash's light suddenly rose in the air, and stopped moving. There was the sound of sloshing and Tash's voice, "Dag.... Dag... you there?" It sounded faint.

"Yes... I'm here..." she wheezed out.

"Hurry. I reached the opposite side."

You're making too much noise, she thought. Dagny could see the outline of his body, crouched over the water, waiting to help pull her out. And then she saw something else. A mass in the water, just to the edge of the light, near the bank. *Something* was *in the lake.*

Dagny panicked, racing toward Tash and the platform.

"Slow down," Tash said. He hadn't seen it.

"Get me out of here! Something's in the water!"

"Huh? Quiet," Tash said, but he scanned the area, trying to find what Dagny saw.

It was impossible to see if the thing approached. She splashed toward the platform and tossed her clothes onto the ledge. She wouldn't allow herself to look at anything but Tash. She didn't want to know if the thing was almost upon her.

Tash reached out and grabbed her hand, but before he could strengthen his grip, Dagny pulled and slipped free, falling back into the lake. The cold water covered her face. She gasped under the waves, sucking it in.

There was a splash next to her, and another moment of fear, before Dagny realized Tash had grabbed her around the waist and boosted her up, onto the dry ledge.

She rolled onto her side, coughing and spitting up lake water. Tash climbed out and covered her with his coat.

"There... it's okay now. You're alright," he said awkwardly, patting her back.

"What... was it?" Dagny managed to say.

"Don't worry. Just catch your breath."

Dagny kneeled there for a while, doing just that. Tash untied the scarf holding her clothing together, and once she had regained herself somewhat, he turned away and dressed.

"I didn't see anything," Tash said. "You sure you didn't just imagine it?"

"There was something there. I know it," Dagny said as she tried to slide her pants up.

Tash took the lantern and slowly walked along the platform's edge, looking at the lake.

"Don't go far..." Dagny started to say, but Tash had stopped dead in his tracks.

"—What the..." he muttered to himself.

"What? What it is?" Dagny raced over to Tash and the light.

There, floating in the water, rested the giant corpse of a bone crusher... one of the terrifying wild dogs that hunted the island above. Its head tilted sideways, and a single massive eye gazed lifelessly at them from above the waterline.

Tash stood in stunned silence.

"Did something kill it?" Dagny asked. "Tash? Did something kill it?"

"Let's go," was all he said, turning and walking away from the water.

But she called after him. "*Tash!* Aren't you concerned? How did that thing get here, dead in the lake?"

"*Quiet!*" he hissed. "Something's gonna hear us with all your screaming."

Dagny lowered her voice. "Fine. But enough with the mystery. Can you talk to me?"

"I don't have an answer for you. But if something killed one of those beasts, we need to get away from it quick. Okay?"

Dagny nodded. He was right. They needed to move. Dagny thought about going back the way they came, but knew she couldn't get back in the water.

The passage on this side of the chamber was as broad as a city's main throughway. It had cobblestone pavers like a proper road, and was wide enough for multiple coaches to easily cross side by side. She followed behind Tash and he led her up a short flight of stairs that connected to a smaller passage with a curved brick ceiling.

"If we go right, it'll eventually lead to the old palace kitchens," Tash said, looking at his map again. "To the left... that's where we'll find the armory wing and the entrance to the palace proper. Just beyond that—"

Dagny put her finger to her lips. She heard something. A distant sound. Soft, but noticeable. Like the quick tapping of nails on stone.

"What is that?" Tash whispered. "Does that sound like..."

Dagny cut him off. "—Running." Someone or something was running. And it was getting louder.

Tash pointed to the right, away from the approaching sound, and the two of them sprinted into the dark.

They passed other hallways splitting from the main one. Dagny wondered if they should veer off and try to hide from whatever was coming. But, almost as if he sensed her thoughts, Tash huffed, "I don't know where these lead. We'll get lost."

More stairs.

They ran across an empty stone room with dozens of alcoves. Tash stopped when they reached the end. There were two tunnels in front of them. And the sound was getting closer.

"Which way?" Dagny whispered in Tash's ear.

"I don't know. Over here, quick." Tash took her hand and led her into a corner of the room, turning down the lantern.

As soon as the flame went out, the running behind them stopped. Were they seen? Dagny held her breath.

A white light entered the chamber, from the way they came. And another. Two small candles and two wispy shapes. One slightly larger than the other. Their movements were so delicate. They seemed to glide across the floor. In the white light, the figures looked pale as snow.

They stopped in front of the two tunnels. A boy and girl. Long grey hair flowed down across their bodies and over dark tunics. They wore an old style, like that of the Vahnland Courts during a royal ceremony.

The girl stepped forward and sniffed the air in front of the left passage, then the right.

Dagny felt a hand on her shoulder, and Tash gently pulled her backwards, away from the figures. He guided her slowly. Feeling his way along the stone wall. Dagny felt the floor sloping upward and after a while, Tash turned the lantern back on, as dim as possible. Neither one of them spoke as they continued their ascent.

The smooth, stone floor turned into rough, rocky ground, and they found themselves wandering into a natural cavern. Small beads of water dripped from the ceiling and a footpath continued forward.

When they were certain that no one was following, Tash finally spoke. "What do you make of our pursuers?"

Dagny shook her head. "Did you see the way the girl was sniffing the air? Like she was smelling us out. That's not natural."

"No," Tash said. "There was nothing natural about any of that."

Dagny looked around. "Know where we're at?"

"Not really."

Dagny followed behind him, as they made their way further into the cavern.

"Do you think those two, the boy and girl, could've killed that bone crusher?" Dagny asked.

"I been wondering about that," Tash said, but he didn't give an opinion.

"Think there's anyone else around?"

"I have no idea." Tash peered down an intersecting footpath. "Over here." He led her to a large archway. "Let's be quiet now. We don't wanna cross those two again. Don't say *anything*."

The path took them to a long room with two giant hearths and an enormous stone slab that ran the entire length of the chamber. Everything was covered in dust, including iron pots that hung above the slab and a pair of dark cauldrons that rested nearby. *The old palace kitchens.*

Now what? Dagny wanted to know what the map depicted, but didn't dare open her mouth to ask. The kitchens had an exit at each end, and rusted grates in the floor. Tash didn't seem confident about which way to go. He wandered over to one of the hearths and glanced around. Dagny stood at the edge of the lantern light and strained her eyes, trying to look down the passageway.

Just then, a tiny bead of light appeared, floating in the darkness. For a brief instant, Dagny panicked, thinking it could be the grey-haired boy and girl. But this wasn't a candle flame. Suddenly, the light spun through the air and vanished.

Dagny rushed back over to Tash and grabbed his sleeve, silently mouthing, "This way." He looked confused, but followed her without protest. She stepped into the dark passage and saw another one of the lights swimming through the air. And another, hovering just inches above the floor.

Dagny crept toward the closest one, but before she could reach it, the pair of lights spun themselves into a tight circle and darted away. Without looking back at Tash, Dagny raced after them. And just as before, the lights stayed just out of reach, playing the same game with her that they had played in the Station.

The passage became brighter, but Dagny remained too focused on the pair of lights to pay it much notice. She reached the end of the hall, marked by a rotting door, and as Dagny ran forward, the lights flew into a small crack in the wood, and disappeared.

Tash grabbed her shoulder. "Wait."

Dagny ignored him. She leaned into the heavy door and slowly pushed it open. This time shielding her eyes. Brilliant blue light flooded the hallway, and Dagny had to squint to look into the chamber beyond.

"What are you?" she heard Tash whisper from behind. His voice sounded like a child's. A mix of innocence and awe.

Dagny just turned and smiled.

16

"You believe me now?" Dagny asked him, quietly.

Tash nodded and watched the lights play. "It's like something out of a fantasy."

They stood in some kind of feasting hall. Stretching in front of them was the longest table Dagny had ever seen. Tarnished silverware and glass goblets were placed by each chair, and a pair of enormous chandeliers hung from rafters above, all cast in the dazzling blue glow. At one time, this palace must've been filled with a great deal of life, but then Dagny noticed the crumbling walls and thick layers of dust. It had been a long time indeed since this table was last used.

Several of the lights weaved around the statue of a faceless man near the back of the chamber. As Dagny wandered further into the room, she noticed something else. Behind the statue was a tear in the wall. A jagged crack, like a lightning bolt, stretching from ceiling to floor.

She moved closer. Something lay just beyond the crack, on the other side of the wall. Another passage perhaps. She knelt down and pushed her face into the opening. A metallic door glinted in the bluish light. The crack was extremely narrow at the top, only large enough to fit a hand inside, but at the bottom, it widened. Wide enough for a girl to crawl through.

"Tash. Come here, take a look at this," she said.

"There's lots of cracks all over this place. It's practically falling apart," he said, approaching her. "See something unique?"

"There's a door back there. It's very odd. Think you could fit, if we crawled over?"

"I don't know." Tash got down on his hands and knees, and peered inside. "It'd be tight."

All at once, the lights glowed even brighter, filling the room with a near-blinding glare. They swirled around Tash and Dagny, then flew straight into the crack. In an instant, they were gone. The only light left was that emanating from Tash's lantern.

"Aww, no... don't go!" Tash called after them. He stared back into the crack, trying to get one last look. "What do you think that was about? You think we spooked them by getting too close to it?"

"Who knows what spooks ghosts," Dagny said.

"Ghosts? You think?" Tash thought about it for a moment. "Nah. Something else... Should we follow them?"

"I'm not sure." Dagny stood and glanced back around the room. Far in the distance, down the same hallway they entered from, came another light. A pair of pale white ones. And they moved quickly.

A chill ran across her body. She reached for Tash and grabbed his shoulder hard.

"Hey. That hurts—"

"It's them... Tash, it's *them*!"

He didn't have to ask who. Tash scrambled onto his feet, just as the pale lights entered the room. Dagny saw the figures clearly this time, with skin the color of bone, and long grey hair that looked greasy, or wet. The girl came first. She had deep, traumatic scars that stretched across her face and a set of cold, frightening eyes, but there was also something unexplainably beautiful there, underneath the violence. The slender boy moved behind her with an elegant grace, like a dancer. He jumped onto the table and ran forward, crushing the ancient plates and glassware beneath his feet, staring straight at Dagny. His lips peeled back in a twisted contortion of rage.

The boy terrified her. Yet, it was the scarred girl who caused time to stop. Tash seemed to stand frozen in place, his mouth ajar. His eyes slowly growing in size. The slender boy stopped in midair. All at once, it was just Dagny and the girl. And the smell of something fishy and rotten. Of a dead place. A dead sea. Dagny envisioned buildings draped in slimy seaweed and waves eclipsing the sky, and when the water retreated, Dagny saw the remains of washed up bodies, piled high and baking under a red sun. These two, the scarred girl and the slender boy, meant to take her back to that ancient and corrupted place, far beneath the black waves. Dagny felt her body go cold.

The girl reached for her, slowly, her hand stretching out from across the room...

Tash's scream jolted Dagny out of her trance. There was no time to think. Dagny turned and dove into the crack, hoping Tash had enough sense to follow. She crawled quickly, scraping her knees and palms over the ruinous ground, and as she neared the end of the passage, it felt like the walls began to narrow, tightening around her shoulders. Was it her imagination, or was the crack squeezing her?

Dagny popped out and reached back, grabbing Tash and pulling him through. Then she saw the girl, skittering across the ground after him. Her long, slender fingers grasping at his legs. Dagny fell backwards, but her eyes remained fixed on the girl's face and twisted mouth.

The chamber rumbled. A loud, grinding sound. It rattled the ceiling, dropping rubble and dust. Dagny tensed, thinking the room was about to collapse. Thinking they were about to be buried alive. And the girl was almost upon them, stretching toward Tash with that long hand, ready to emerge from the hole in the wall. The chamber groaned one last time, and with a sudden shift of stone, the crack closed on the girl, leaving behind nothing but a thin line, barely wide enough for a finger to fit.

The rumbling stopped. Bringing an eerie silence to the room. Tash panted heavily beside her, his eyes wide. Dagny found herself unexpectedly calm, but balancing on the edge of terror. Perhaps in shock at the whole thing.

"What happened? What was that?!" Tash blurted out. "Did the lights do that?" Tash slowly crawled toward the thin line in the stone, where the opening had been, trying to look into it.

"Careful..." Dagny said.

Suddenly Tash jumped back. "She's there," he cried. "She's watching us..."

Dagny saw it, too. A single grey eye, the color of fish scales, watching through the small crack.

"Who are you?!" Tash yelled at the girl in the wall. "Why are you after us?!"

There was no answer. The eye just watched, unblinking.

Dagny tried to gather herself and stood up, dusting the dirt from her clothes. They were in a narrow room that held the musty, mothy smell of an old, neglected shed. She glanced around, picking out details in the light: cobwebbed shelves; a heavy block of nicked wood where ancient things had been chopped; metal hooks in the ceiling; and large, dark stains on the floor. There were other items here too: misplaced furnishings and artwork, a gilded mirror.

"Where are we?" she asked. In front of her was the metallic door she'd seen from the other side. It seemed to be made of copper, and it was etched with stars. Lots of them.

"We need to find a way out of here," Tash said. "In case that crack opens back up."

Dagny walked over and tried the copper door. It didn't budge.

Tash took his lantern into the shadows, kicking up more dust as he went. "I don't see any way out. Do you?"

Dagny pressed her ear to the door and knocked. Nothing. She glanced around the room. Hanging on the wall was a large painting, the kind that should've been in the entryway of some wealthy estate. It was a portrait. Of a young girl in a rich red dress that flowed elegantly from her shoulders and dripped onto the floor, spreading out like a wave of blood around her bare, dirty feet. And behind her, barely illuminated, were two muscular, long-eared cats. They watched, ready to emerge from the shadows; or perhaps they were the hallucination of the artist's subject, threatening to fade into obscurity.

"Aren't those cats the Drey Garders?" Dagny asked. "Like the ones Grete sketched?"

Tash turned and inspected it. "Yeah. The painting looks really old. Maybe a forgotten princess who lived at the palace... dead people gazing at us from across time."

"So the cats are real? Not just mythical?"

"Maybe. I don't know."

Dagny looked back at the thin line in the stone and the eye that still watched them.

"Enough of this," Tash said. He lifted the painting off the wall and placed it over the crack. "I can't have that thing staring at us anymore."

"Those lights must've gone somewhere," Dagny said, then shouted at the ceiling, "Hello!? Are you there?!"

Tash stepped close to her. "What are you doing?"

"What's it sound like? There's no sense in keeping quiet anymore, is there?"

"Right..."

"Maybe there's another secret passage or something," Dagny said, as she started to inspect the walls.

"*Sure,*" Tash whispered, almost to himself.

"Don't get hopeless on me. We need to stay positive."

"I'm not getting hopeless, just recognizing our situation. We're trapped."

"You don't know that yet. What do you think this place could be?"

"Your guess is as good as mine," he said.

"You're the expert."

Tash looked around and shrugged. "The pantry? The garbage room?"

"Those lights, they brought us here. Maybe they were trying to warn us about—" Dagny motioned to the painting on the floor and the crack behind it " —those two."

Tash nodded. "Yeah. You might be right."

"That wall closed right behind us. I don't think they'd bring us here to die. Is this place on your map?"

Tash opened his pack and pulled one out. Dagny wandered away and glanced at herself in a tarnished mirror leaning against a shelf. She could feel a prickle of fear in her chest, and tried to push it away. It wouldn't do any good to let that take hold now. She took a deep breath and tried to smooth out her messy hair. Still wet from the lake. Just then she caught the reflection of something else on the mirror's surface. She spun around, half expecting to see the pale girl, but instead, there stood the small boy from the Station, next to the copper door.

He was definitely a child, Dagny was certain of it. He wore the same long-sleeved, dirty white clothing, but had added a metallic headdress, with two coppery triangles that popped up like animal ears.

"*Delos itha shein,*" said the boy. "What are you doing here?"

Dagny and Tash stared at him, not sure what to do. The copper door stood ajar, the boy only feet away from it. One wrong move could send him diving back inside, never to be seen again.

"Hello..." Dagny managed to say, then forced a smile. "Sorry to intrude. I'm Dagny Losh, and this is Jauson Tasher. We're looking for a way out."

"Why are you here?" the boy asked.

"We got lost," Tash said, stepping forward.

"—Stop!" the boy commanded, inching closer to the door. "*Shey takka!* Stay there. You're not allowed this way."

Dagny put her hand on Tash's shoulder, gently pulling him back. "What's your name? I like your headdress."

"My name is for myself. Not for you."

"Do you think you can help us?" she asked. "We were chased here by two... people. One of them is trapped in the wall over there. We were just trying to get away."

"You brought them here!?" the boy cried. "No... No. No. No." Suddenly, he darted behind the door.

Tash lunged after him. "No! Don't leave us!" But it was too late. The boy was too quick. The door slammed closed before Tash could reach it.

"No!" Tash yelled again, banging on the door. "Come back!"

Dagny was right behind him. "Please! Let us come with you!" she shouted. "The lights brought us here! They're trying to help us!" There was no response. She collapsed onto the floor and leaned against the door. "Are you there?"

A small hidden panel opened. "You saw the lights?" the boy asked from the other side.

Dagny looked into the opening. She could see his green eyes and dirty cheeks. "Yes. Please, can you help us?"

The boy hesitated. "I don't know."

"I saw you in the Station. I know you saw me there, too. We're friendly. You can trust us."

The boy narrowed his eyes and began to pull his face away.

"Wait!" Dagny cried. "The lights helped us escape and sealed the wall behind us, trapping that girl on the other side. Those lights, they're friends of yours, aren't they?"

"Maybe..." he said from the shadows.

"Look, I *know* they're your friends," Dagny said, pleading with the boy. "They want you to help us. They brought you to us, didn't they? *Please help.*"

There was a long moment before the boy answered her. "Fine. I'll open the door. But if you're lying, I'll have to slay you."

"Okay, that's fair."

"Hold on."

Dagny stood up and stepped back, and the heavy copper door cracked open.

"*Tioula nog,*" the boy said. "Quickly now."

Dagny almost kissed him, but the boy had a feral seriousness to him, which made her keep a distance. They entered a long hallway with a low ceiling. The boy carried his own lantern, made out of colorful glass, and the smooth, glossy floor reflected the light, giving the appearance that they were traveling through a rainbow prism.

Their guide was a pretty child, but stunk like a wet animal. He resembled some kind of ashen beast with his metal ears and soft, filthy clothing. Dagny didn't speak, and every time Tash tried to ask a question, the boy just turned around and shushed him with a quick "*Tsst.*"

Other hallways branched off from their main path, vanishing into darkness. They must've been some distance from the old kitchens when the boy finally stopped. He opened a simple, nondescript door in the wall, and hurried them into a tight, square room that reminded Dagny of a storage closet. It contained a small cot, some rough sacks, and a pile of books. The air was stale, smelling of mildew and rot.

"You can live here now," the boy said, calmly.

"—What!? *Live here?*" Tash blurted out.

The boy suddenly howled with laughter. "No... No... I'm joking," he said, gasping for breath. "Your face... it's so funny."

"That's not nice," Tash replied.

The boy fell onto the floor, cackling wildly.

"Yes, yes. It's very funny," Dagny said. "Can we know your name now?"

"...Melwes..." the boy managed to wheeze out. He had tears welling in his eyes. "*Live here...* you should see yourself."

"Hello, Melwes. It's nice to meet you," she said over the laughter, trying to stay polite. "We've been through a lot tonight." She waited for the boy to calm down somewhat, before speaking again. "Thanks for helping us."

"Where are we?" Tash asked.

"Ahh," Melwes took a deep breath. "Under the red ruins, near the archives. It's safe to talk here. There's no one else around."

"Who were those two?" Tash continued. "The ones who chased us."

"That's Galwed the Collector, and her twin brother, Tewdred. I thought everyone knew them."

Dagny caught Tash's eye. "No. I don't think we've ever heard of them," she said.

"The Drowned Twins of Gort. They come from the darkest of dark places, and hear secret whisperings as though they were screams." The boy spoke with a nonchalant easiness to him.

"You said the girl one is called *the Collector*?" Dagny asked.

"Uh huh."

"What does she collect?" Dagny wasn't sure she wanted to know the answer.

"All sorts of things, but mostly people's desires. The more hidden a desire, the more it echos across the plane where they dream."

Tash spoke now. "Those two... they *dream*?"

"They dream of sunken Gort, a wytchland," Melwes said. "You know that, at least."

"No. I don't," Tash replied.

The boy looked disappointed. "*Anyway*, they showed up a few days ago, and have been trying to get inside, but I wouldn't let them."

"Do you know what they're after?" Dagny asked.

"Desires. I just told you that."

"And those lights..." Tash said. "What are they?"

"Spirits of the Under Road. The ones who came before me. Once my watch ends, I'll join them," Melwes said, beaming with pride.

"Join them?" Dagny asked.

"—The Under Road?" Tash interjected. "What's that?"

Melwes eyed him suspiciously. "You ask too many questions. Don't you know *anything?*"

"Umm, Melwes," Dagny said. She could sense the boy getting tense and wanted to take back control of the discussion. "Do you know how to get to the palace gardens from here?"

"What you wanna go there for?"

"I'm looking for something, you could say."

Melwes pursed his lips together, before speaking. "You're strange."

Dagny laughed. "Ha. Yes. I guess I kind of am. But this whole place is a little strange. Don't you think I fit right in?"

"No. Not really."

She laughed again. "You're blunt. I like that."

"Yep."

"Are the gardens far? Could you take us there?"

The boy sighed. "I suppose. We can go in the morning. It's very dark right now."

"Okay." Dagny looked around the room. There was barely enough space to sit. "Is this where you sleep?"

He nodded.

"Really? Below ground all the time? How do you eat?" This should've dawned on her sooner, but she'd been so wrapped up in the underworld that she assumed Melwes was just part of the magic of this place. As she watched him now, she realized he was just a child. A unique one, no question, but a child nonetheless.

"I find food here and there and everywhere," Melwes said.

"Like at the Station," she said.

"Sometimes..."

"You're very resourceful. That's a great skill."

"You're sure we're safe here, right?" Tash asked.

Melwes ignored him and looked at Dagny. "My turn to ask a question. Why did you come here? To the ruins?"

"I'm searching for my sister. She drew pictures of this place, and I want to know why. I guess I'm hoping that something could lead me to her."

"You lost her?" asked the boy.

"Yes. A long time ago." She felt emotion rise into her throat. "It's hard for me to talk about."

Melwes nodded, a serious expression on his face. "How long ago did your sister come here?"

"I don't know. I'm not sure she ever came. Part of me thinks she dreamed about the gardens, and drew those pictures from things she imagined. I just feel like I need to see it. I know that doesn't make sense." Dagny stopped, waiting for Melwes to respond, but the boy just listened. "Have you ever seen anyone else come this way?" she asked him.

"Yes. People used to come all the time. Actually —"

"Really? People like who?" Tash asked, interrupting.

"Travelers of the Under Road," Melwes said. "You don't listen real good, do you?"

"Where does the Under Road go, exactly?" Dagny asked, keeping her voice gentle and kind.

"Everywhere."

Dagny lay on the cot for a long while. Tash grunted and moaned uncomfortably on one of the sacks, while Melwes slept peacefully, curled up on the floor like a cat. There were no covers, and the cot was hard as stone, but Dagny felt grateful to be lying down, somewhere safe. She needed to get some sleep. Who knew what tomorrow would bring. Her body was exhausted. Yet, her mind threatened to keep her awake forever.

Her thoughts jumped randomly from the drowned twins to the Station to the spirit lights and the young boy. She still hadn't even seen the gardens. Dagny knew there was something special about that place. There just had to be.

Her mind turned to Max. Had she treated him fairly that night at Stardust? The whole interaction was so upsetting. *He was just trying to watch out for you.* "I don't need you to do that," she whispered aloud. She hated when Max became cold and distant. *Why can't you just act normal? I don't care how you act around other people, but just be normal around me.* She rolled over and pulled her knees into her chest. Despite everything, she missed him. Maybe she should've told him where she was going... *If he hadn't been watching out for you, you'd have fallen off of Stardust and broken your body or worse...*

She thought next of Grete. Picturing her in the secret room under the Wigmaker's shop, drawing Drey Garders and Oyster Knights. Dagny saw her playing in the Rakesmount, in the alley behind their tenement building. She tried to imagine what Grete looked like now, but her mind wouldn't allow it. The only shape Dagny could see was that of a child, smiling sweetly. Her face all but a blur.

"How long have you been living down here?" Dagny asked, as they moved through the Archives: a series of spacious, domed halls with multiple levels. It used to house an enormous library, but the shelves were all empty.

"I've always been down here," Melwes said. "I was born anew from the lights. *Telgotha benown.*"

"I see. Don't you ever get lonely?"

"No."

"That's good. The spirit lights probably keep great company."

"All the books were moved to the Great Below before I got born," Melwes said, pointing to the empty shelves. He guided them to a staircase tucked in a side wall. Dagny probably would've missed it entirely if Melwes wasn't with them.

"So how deep do those passages go?" Tash asked.

"Real deep," Melwes said. "You don't wanna get lost down there. You may never find your way back up. Stick with me, and don't go any deeper. It's real simple."

That sounded fine to her. Dagny was glad they weren't going deeper. Instead, they ascended the staircase and stepped into the outside world. The morning sun shone brightly in the cloudless sky. Dagny shielded her eyes and stumbled forward. She smelled flowers and wet grass on the wind. Heavy, naked statues stood in a row, lining the pathway ahead of them. The ones that weren't broken or toppled reached up toward the sky, their faces contorted in agony as if begging for deliverance.

"Where are we? What is this place?" Dagny asked.

"This is the Martyred Path," Tash said. He seemed happy to contribute. "The Gardens are close. I have this part memorized."

They crossed a field and approached a set of ruins. Dagny was grateful for the fresh air. She'd grown tired of the darkness and lantern light of the underground. Through a breach in the wall, Dagny could see a lush and wild area, with plants swelling and stretching toward the sun.

They followed Melwes through the breach, up and over crumbled stone; then down a long, sloping hill and into a garden that chattered and chirped with the life of birds and grasshoppers. Clusters of red and purple berries hung heavy from wild bushes, and apple trees dumped their harvest into sun-streaked grass.

Melwes stopped and began to gather some flowers, as if he was suddenly oblivious to their presence.

"Umm, Melwes?" Dagny asked. "Can you show us where the statues are? The ones of the long-eared cats?"

He just pointed down the path.

Tash gently pulled Dagny's sleeve. "C'mon, let's go ahead. Let him pick his flowers."

"No. Just you should go," Melwes said, pointing at Dagny.

"Huh? Why?" she asked.

"She's scared," Melwes answered. "I can tell."

"I'm not scared," Dagny said.

"Not *you.*" Melwes looked up at her. "The other girl."

All at once everything became very surreal. Dagny turned and stepped away, Tash and the boy vanishing behind her in the tall grass. Tash may have said something, but Dagny couldn't hear it. She walked forward, as if in a trance, onto a natural path between thick roots that cascaded over rocky edging and funneled her even further down. She wouldn't allow her sister's name to enter her mind. As if the simple thought of it could shatter the dreamland Dagny now wandered. She knew hope was fickle, and too much of it could turn against you.

A bend in the forested path brought her to a small pool of water surrounded by statues of mythical beasts, and on the other side stood a girl, reaching into an apple tree.

Her body was skinny and brown, with sleek black hair dripping down her shoulders. The girl glanced over. A sliver of sunlight spreading across her face.

A familiar face, shining with sweat. In the farthest recesses of Dagny's mind, at the beginning of youth, it was the giggling face of a girl who had once escaped from the confines of their crowded tenement building to play in the mud until she was black as soot.

Later, it was the face that stared out from their shared bedroom, hand on glass, watching as Dagny left the Rakesmount forever.

Dagny stood there, stunned. Not knowing how to proceed. She'd thought about this moment over and over again, even as a child, when she believed her sister drowned. Only now, she was frozen. Gretchen shimmered like a dream in the clearing, with Dagny slow to awaken.

17

THE RAIN FINALLY STOPPED that morning. It had rained for three days straight. So much that the road to the Rakesmount from the stewhouse above had turned to mud.

It was always wet here, but summer was the worst. And even after the last three days, the afternoon sky still looked gloomy. Dagny felt like it would pour again soon.

She trudged along the mushy ground, next to an older, scraggly boy named Duk who pushed a small cart loaded with pots. Dagny was trying to keep the mud off her skirt; Duk seemed to take delight in violently mashing his way through.

"I'm telling ya, Roach doesn't know what he's missing by keeping me down in that pit. I should be working the rending shaft. That old piss-ass Marco is *weak* and getting weaker every day. He can't crank like these can," Duk said, slapping his arms.

Dagny was focused on the ground, making sure she didn't sink into a pit of her own, as she struggled down the hill, falling further behind.

"You know this morning, the whole thing came to a stop because of that turd. They said it was a broke gear, but us pit-boys knew they were just excusin' and Marco needed to rest those old bones of his." Duk glanced back at her. "Keep up Dag, the stew's gonna be dead-cold by the time we make it back 'cause of you."

"I'm trying," she said under her breath. "You're going too fast." But either Duk didn't hear, or he ignored her, moving further away.

The road evened out, and most of the Rakesmount tenants were outside finishing their chores before the rain came again. Clyde Lodor, who was dumping something stinky onto the ground, winked at Dagny as they passed. "Tell your mother I said hi, will ya, then?" he said. Dagny smiled and nodded. Clyde looked like a witch with a bent back and stringy hair, but seemed friendly. Dagny felt like something was going on between him and her mother, but she didn't know what.

She caught up to Duk as they approached the row house where her family lived. He was in the middle of another boring story, and clearly thought she'd been listening the whole time.

"...Anyway the whole crew laughed. He was just dripping with filth... that'll teach him to get smart with me." He stopped the cart in front of her door, then turned to look at Dagny as it began to drizzle.

"Gotta go," Dagny said. "Thanks for helping with the stew."

Duk unloaded an iron pot from the cart and chuckled. "When your hair's catching rain you look like a wet rat."

"Thanks," she mumbled.

"It wasn't a compliment, stupid," Duk said, turning the cart back onto the road. "See you tomorrow."

Dagny watched him go and took a deep breath before pushing the front door open. The last thing she wanted to do was go inside right now, but there was no choice. Not yet, anyway. Across the main room, three of her cousins began to heat vats of water for the weekly bath that they'd all share. In the middle, several feet from the stove, rested a single wooden tub. Nobody paid her any attention.

"Stew's here," she said. "Can someone help?"

The oldest one, a boy named Alen, begrudgingly came over and lifted the pot. "This feels cold... and light. You better've brought enough."

Dagny didn't care whether she did or not. She ignored Alen and made her way up the broken stairs, dodging to the side as two more boys came tramping down.

The row house was narrow and crowded. Dagny's bedroom was on the top floor, the highest spot in the tenement. That meant they were always the last ones to eat and the last ones in the bath. No one had their own space here. She shared the room with her sister, Gretchen, and two of their cousins: young ones who always seemed to be outside, even in the rain. Her brother's bed sat empty, closest to the window.

She wandered over to it and watched the rain hit the glass. The drizzle had quickly turned into a storm, pounding the roof above. It made her nervous. Yesterday, there was so much water that it entered the building and pooled in the low spots. Uncle Finkle, always in a bad mood, had become particularly nasty about it.

Dervin Finkle wasn't her real uncle. He just lived on the ground floor and made everyone call him that. He was mean and sour-faced. Wherever he'd touch her, Dagny's skin would bruise, an awful reminder of where he'd been. And when he hit them, her mom just stared into the fireplace. He was sure to get really mad about the rain tonight.

Dagny sat on her brother's bed and ran her hand over the pillow. It had been two weeks since he got sick and left her forever. Gretchen hadn't spoken at all since then. She watched Dagny now, tucked in her own bed on the other side of the room.

Lightning crashed outside. A second later, thunder rolled across the house, shaking the walls. For a brief moment, Dagny wished the building would collapse, crushing her and everyone below. She glanced over at Grete, who had bundled herself under the covers, and immediately felt guilty about her thoughts. "It's okay, nothing's gonna happen. You're safe," she said. But Grete stayed hidden.

Dagny hated it here. Hated the people downstairs, filling themselves with stew. Laughing and yelling. Their voices booming through the house. Morgan died two weeks ago, and not one of them cared. Not her mom and not her cousins. No one even said his name anymore. He was just *gone* now.

Tonight she would leave again. Go even further this time. So far that she wouldn't return until her quest was done. Dagny had tried to keep her feelings hidden from everyone, but somehow Gretchen knew. She always knew. It seemed like Dagny couldn't hide anything from her sister. Gretchen had wanted to come, even going so far as to pack her own kit. It was just an old sheet tied with cord, but Grete had filled it with stuff: a pair of torn stockings, her straw doll, a cookie tin and several pieces of shiny glass. It was sweet. Even though they were only a year apart, Grete seemed so young. Too young to come with.

Dagny reached under her bed and pulled out her own knapsack. A proper, canvas pack that Morgan gave her during last year's holiday. *"One of these days, you'll come along with me... I'll take you through the Vahnland and into the Ilvar,"* he had told her. "*We'll chase adventure, find a treasure, and then you, me and Grete will leave the Rakesmount and never come back."*

Grete peeked out from under the blanket. "You'll be fine here. I'm the one that has to leave," Dagny said, rummaging through her supplies.

"You didn't hear them. They were gonna send me to the vents for causing trouble. But it's really 'cause I remind them of Morgan, and he reminded them of how worthless they all are."

Dagny checked her bag. Her adventuring stuff was still there: a small metal pot stolen from the kitchen; her other shirt and socks; Morgan's compass; a bundle of dried noodles; two potatoes; and a water-stained copy of Kofric's *Ruminations on the Wild Court.* She didn't understand the book, but it had been Morgan's, and she wasn't leaving it here.

"I'll come back for you, okay? It might be awhile, but I will." Dagny walked over to her sister, and sat next to her on the mattress. "Do you remember Morgan's last story? About the sunken treasure ship in the river?"

Grete nodded.

"He said there was so much gold that it probably washed up all along the shore. One just has to go pick it up. *You don't even have to get wet,*" Dagny whispered. Grete's eyes widened. Her sister *hated* getting wet. So much so, that she'd throw an enormous fuss... squealing and kicking... whenever they'd take her down for a bath. "The river's big, so it might take some searching. I'm gonna go there and get it. But you gotta keep it quiet, alright? You promise?"

Grete nodded again.

"I'm gonna do it. I'm gonna leave the Mount, and the city, and travel to the river and get it. Then I'm coming back for you. I love you, sister." Dagny leaned down and kissed Grete's head.

Grete just stared at her. She had such a sweet face. She didn't belong here, but Dagny couldn't do anything about it yet. At least Grete had food and a bed in the Mount. It would be okay.

Dagny waited for the storm to stop, but it didn't happen. So after some time, she pushed the window open and stepped out onto the wooden planks that ran along the building. Her heart raced and she quickly wiped the rain from her face, trying to balance herself as she made her way over to the long, rusting ladder leading down.

The climb was easy. She'd never been afraid of the height. But once she reached the ground, Dagny noticed that the road had already turned from mud into a flowing river of sludge. She had planned to cross the street and take the path from the stewhouse. That was impossible now. She'd have to take the longer way out of the Mount.

She wouldn't miss this. Everything about the Mount was miserable. She wondered why they even called it the Mount. Maybe as a joke. Or a lie. They should've called it the Trench, cause it was so low and dark.

When she reached the split in the path, Dagny took one last look at her building. The ground floor windows were bright, and she could see the shapes of her cousins. They would be loud in there. They were always loud, but the rain muffled the sound of their shouts for once. The rest of the house was dark. She glanced up at her bedroom and saw Gretchen standing at the window, watching. Her hand pressed against the glass.

Dagny turned away. It was too sad, so she moved off into the night without looking back.

After the tenement buildings came the Common Houses. Old warehouses where men without a space of their own could rent a bed. All the children knew to avoid it, especially near the evening hours. There were bad people in the dark that would do bad things to girls like her. Dagny hurried past, cresting another hill. The rain had drenched her clothes, but it also kept others off the streets.

An old sign for the Spitborne Market Gardens marked the exit onto the South Road. Before the Rakesmount was built, they used to grow food here. Carrots and cabbage and other things. New life springing up from the soft earth. A hard change from the hungry and starved who lived here now. When she hit the main road, a sense of urgency washed over her, like a prisoner escaped. Dagny started running as fast as she could, as if Finkle and the others were behind her, trying to catch and bring her back.

The rain seemed to be landing even harder. Dagny had hoped to make it across the Morca before stopping, but she was starting to shiver and could barely make out the buildings ahead. Even the cobbled South Road flowed like a stream.

Dagny ducked into an open stable off to the side. Half-a-dozen horses, anxious from the storm, snorted and watched her from their stalls. The other end was open as well, leading into a courtyard with an inn beyond.

Someone else was here. Whistling a tune from a small loft above. A stablehand, perhaps. Dagny wasn't stupid. At this time of night, everyone needed to be avoided. She dodged into the first vacant stall and huddled in the far corner, where it was darkest, quietly grabbing fistfuls of loose hay to blot her wet clothes as best she could.

Her teeth started to chatter. Her pack was soaked through as well. Everything would be wet. She didn't need to check. The Rakesmount was only a few blocks behind her, and already her escape had hit a wall. Dagny needed to get further away – and quickly. Her cousins would take a sick delight in hunting her down and issuing punishment for "making Finkel worry so much," especially after they'd discover the pot and food she'd taken. As soon as the storm broke and the rain slowed, she'd run out again. She just needed to warm up a bit first.

The whistling stopped and the floorboards above creaked. Dagny tensed, trying to remain quiet. She slipped off a ratty blanket that hung over the stall and covered herself, trying to muffle the noise of her chattering teeth.

The rain was so loud that she didn't hear the person again until they were right outside the stall. A man's voice, not a stableboy as she had hoped. But he was speaking to the horses. "Now what has you all riled up?" he asked softly. "It's alright. Storm's not going to bother us."

Dagny pressed her face deeper into the hay. It was too late to run. Her only option was to stay hidden. She heard feet shuffling and then, suddenly, silence.

"Is someone in there?" the man asked.

Dagny stayed silent. Maybe he'd just move on.

"Who is that? Show yourself... *Show yourself, I said!"* The man's voice turned scary and full of anger. "If I come in there, it'll be violent."

Dagny slowly moved the blanket off of her face. "I'm sorry. I didn't mean to scare the horses."

"A child..." the man said to himself. "What are you doing in here? Step into the light."

"I was just tryin' to get out of the rain," she stuttered.

"Goodness girl, you're shaking to death. We gotta warm you up, come on now." The man wandered over to the steps leading to the loft. Dagny glanced into the rain, and for a moment thought about running off. But she felt so cold. And the man had already left her. Maybe she didn't need to go just yet.

"I got some shirts here," he said from across the stable. "It'll be way too big for you, but it's important for you to get dry." He returned and tossed her the garment. "Go ahead and change. I'll grab a cleaner blanket than that rag," he turned and left her alone again.

Shaking fiercely, Dagny quickly put on the shirt. It came down to her knees and fit like a dress. She immediately felt better. Her old clothes were lying in a drenched mess on the floor.

The man came back with a proper, heavy blanket and wrapped it around her shoulders. "There you go, child. What are you doing out in this weather?"

Dagny looked at the ground and didn't answer.

"I see... you're not gonna cause me trouble if I let you stay, right? You're not a thief?"

Her eyes snapped up at him. "I'm not a thief!" But she was, wasn't she? She'd stolen more than just the small pot and food from the kitchen. She'd actually stolen quite a bit when the opportunity arose. But she wasn't going to steal anything here, and she didn't like being accused.

"Good. That's good, girl. I don't wanna send you off into this. Can you tell me your name?"

She watched him carefully before responding. "Dag..."

"Dag? What kinda name is that?"

"It's my name. Dagny," she said.

"Oh. Alright. I'm Simon. Are you hungry, Dag?"

She nodded quickly.

The man laughed. "I bet. You look it. Nothing but bones. You're probably the skinniest thing I've ever seen. Wait here." He stepped off, into the rain and toward the inn.

She wondered if he was tricking her, and meant to go get more men so she couldn't escape. But when Simon returned, he was alone and carrying a large wooden bowl and half a loaf of bread.

"Eat this, child. It'll warm you good."

She gulped down as much of the meaty stew as she could without choking, and stuffed her face with the soft, squishy bread.

"Easy there. Take your time. We can get more." Simon gestured to a bench against the wall. "Have a seat. Storm is going to be awhile, I think."

"Are you the stableman?" Dagny asked.

"Sometimes. I'm the proprietor of this inn. *The Pickled Pig of South Road.*"

"Okay."

"You don't like the name. I can tell."

"No. Who wants to eat a pig pickle?" Dagny said.

"True. You don't like the way it rolls off the tongue, though?"

"It's okay." She finished what stew she could get with the spoon, and began to trace her fingers across the bowl, sucking down the remaining bits.

"Ha. You don't need to do that. I'll get you some more," Simon said.

Dagny began to feel anxious again. "This rain's gonna last a long time. It's been raining four days," she said.

"You could be right. I'm not sure I've ever seen so much water come down. This is the kind of rain people remember."

"I need to go then. I have to go." Dagny stood up. "Thank you."

"Wait. Hold on. What's so important?" Simon asked, standing up as well.

Dagny began to back away. "I can't say. Don't try and stop me!"

"I'm not stopping you. Look, if it's so important, we have a coach. Where do you need to go?"

"I..." she thought about it for a second. A coach would be nice. It could take her across the city, maybe even to the River Gate. But, the thought of being confined and at the mercy of a stranger didn't sit well with her. "Thanks. I should just go. I'll be alright now."

Dagny started to walk back to the stall, to get her shoes and things, when the man grabbed her.

"Oh, no you don't," he said, spinning her around. "I was trying to be nice." His hand was grasped tightly around her shirt, inches from her face. He twisted her collar, almost choking her. "You're gonna do what I want now —" Dagny bit hard into his wrist. It was pure instinct. The man screamed something wild and horrific. She latched onto his arm, grinding her sharp teeth through his flesh.

Simon flung her to the ground. Her shoulder smacked painfully hard on the stone. She looked up and saw blood... *gushing*... from his wrist, streaming to his elbow. "*What did you do!?*" he screamed. "*What did you do!!?*"

Dagny was in shock. She scrambled away and ran into the rain, leaving everything behind. She had no boots, no food, nothing. And the storm was pelting her with what felt like hard pebbles. Water, as high as her knees, came flowing down the road, threatening to sweep her away. She glanced back toward the *Pickled Pig*, but no one pursued her.

Dagny panicked. What would she do now? Should she return to the Rakesmount? What would they say? Finkle was sure to send her to the vents after this. She'd taken his things again, and lost her clothes and shoes as well. Then something came to her. Something so obvious, she should've thought it from the beginning. Dagny reached the cross canal, and took a right, toward the home of Alex Benzara.

She'd only been there once before with Morgan, and even then, she didn't go inside. But she knew it was just off the main road, a little ways past the bell tower. It was a long walk, and Dagny's face was numb by the time she reached the house. Made of red brick, it stood two stories tall, with a single chimney puffing out smoke. Dagny's legs had given out on her an hour ago, but she pushed herself forward nonetheless, wheezing and snotting through the storm.

She pounded on the door, ready to collapse from exhaustion. A short while later, an older man came to the front window. "Who's there?" he asked.

Dagny tried to answer. She just couldn't get enough strength to do it. Another shape appeared by the old man, and there was muttering from inside. *Please, just let me in,* she thought. They had to see her out here. What were they doing? Dagny knelt and then sat on the ground. She couldn't do this anymore. There was nowhere else to go. "Please help me," she said into the door.

It opened a crack, and Dagny looked up at the face of Alex. He recognized her immediately and in an instant, scooped her into his arms and carried her inside.

"Dagny, what were you *doing* out there?" Alex said, taking her over to the fireplace. "*Daida*, this is Dagny Losh. Morgan's little sister," he said to the older man.

"Oh. Morgan. Yes... I'm very sorry to hear of your brother."

"Dagny, this is my grandfather," said Alex. "Are you feeling alright? We need to get you warm and dry."

Dagny didn't answer at first. She just stared at the ground. She felt strange, like she wasn't really here at all. And the heat from the fireplace was making her ill. Sweat began to bead and mix with the rainwater on her forehead. "Don't send me back there, please," she whispered.

"What's that?" Alex asked, kneeling down to her. "You mean back home?"

She looked at him. "Don't send me back. It took so much to get here. I'll run again if you do."

"I won't..." Alex brought her a change of clothes. Women's clothes. "These were my mother's. They'll do for now. Once this rain stops, I'll go get you something that fits, alright?"

"Okay..."

After changing, Dagny came back and sunk into a large, cushioned sofa that faced the fireplace. Alex's grandfather made tea, sweet with honey, and Dagny sipped it, staring up at a painting of jungle animals dressed like people, hanging above the mantel. "What's that?" she asked.

"Ah. That's the Lion's Court, dear," the grandfather said.

"Is he a king? The lion?"

"He sure is. He's the protector of all things good in this world."

There was something comforting about the way the lion looked. Peaceful, yet strong.

Alex came over and sat in the chair next to the sofa. "Are you alright, Dagny? Why were you out there? Did something happen?"

"I needed to leave. They were gonna send me to the vents. I heard 'em. Finkle said so. And then I bit a man. I think I hurt him real bad... but he was going to hurt me."

A look of concern spread over Alex's face and he glanced at his grandfather. "You'll be safe here. Morgan was a brother to me, and that means you're my family too, okay?"

Dagny watched the floor.

"Dag..." he put his hand on her shoulder. "I mean it. Don't worry about anything."

"Can I lay down here?" she asked.

"Yes, of course. You sleep here. It's the warmest place in the house."

Dagny curled up on the sofa, still gazing at the lion painting.

"Oh. I have something else for you, too." Alex left the room, and returned a short while later, carrying a dark bundle. "This is your brother's coat. He left it with me after... well... *here.* He woulda wanted you to have it." Alex draped the coat over her. "There you go. Tomorrow, after the rain. We'll get everything sorted out. I promise."

Sometime later, she fell asleep. Feeling, for once in her life, that everything would be okay.

18

Before she knew what she was doing, Dagny was halfway across the clearing, marching toward her sister in tears. Everything seemed slow-moving now, distorted. With each step forward, Dagny felt as though she might faint. Her heart pounding hard in her throat.

Grete's body jerked and tensed, as she noticed Dagny approach. She looked confused, her eyes wide with shock or fear, her mouth half-twisted in a snarl. She seemed on the verge of running.

"Wait!" Dagny threw her hands up and stopped a short distance away, not sure what to do. She was all too conscious of her own breathing, rapid and heavy. Did her sister recognize her? Grete looked so very different. A shade of the same girl from the Rakesmount, but growing into herself. She was taller than Dagny now, with long limbs and stooped shoulders.

The moment was brief. A split second, perhaps. Yet, it seemed to stretch far longer. Dagny gazed at her sister. Trying to recall the words she'd thought about for so long, but she was afraid.

Grete spoke first. A single word. "*Dag.*" Her eyes grew even wider, and they had life to them. Not the dead stare that Corlie described. They were vibrant and expressive.

What would she say? Dagny realized she was trembling. Her head felt dizzy and her knees began to buckle. *Say something.*

“I’m so sorry,” Dagny blurted out, her voice choking with emotion. “I’ve missed you so much.”

Grete reached out slowly, but suddenly pulled her hand back, as if recoiling from a hot stove. “I don’t understand,” she said. “How?”

“I’ve missed you, so much,” Dagny repeated. She felt eight years of grief and loneliness welling up, ready to pour out. It took everything she had not to collapse.

Grete reached toward Dagny again, hesitantly, and touched her arm. “I thought you died. I don’t understand.”

“I couldn’t let you go. I lived all this time thinking you were gone. But I couldn’t let you go.” Dagny began to sob. “Please forgive me for leaving you.”

“How are you here?” Grete asked, inching even closer.

“Can you forgive me?”

Grete took Dagny’s face in her hands. “Stop it,” she whispered. “I can't believe this. How did you find me?”

“I found your sketchbook in Limer’s Town.” Dagny sniffed and wiped her nose with the back of her hand. “I found Alice and the Wigmaker. Your drawings. They led me here, to you.”

“The sketchbook...” Grete mumbled under her breath.

“You drew this place,” Dagny began, then suddenly snorted and laughed wildly. “I knew it was important! I just knew it!”

“I thought of you all the time,” Grete said.

“You did?”

Grete nodded. “Every day since you left.”

"I should've found you sooner," Dagny said, shaking her head. Feeling very sad again. "I should have taken you with me all those years ago. I'm so sorry."

"We were both real young," Grete said, her voice easy and soft.

"I'm never leaving you again."

The sun spread over them, breaking through the remnants of last night's storm. It felt pure and comforting. Warming the coolness of autumn.

"I can't believe you found me. This all feels like a dream," Grete said, staring at Dagny's face, like she was trying to make sure it wasn't some kind of trick. "Where have you been? What happened to you?"

"I've been in Old Rork," Dagny said. "All this time."

A look of concern washed over Grete's face. "...And Limer's Town? You went there."

"I needed to find you."

"You didn't see Sliver, did you?"

"No. But I heard about him."

Grete stiffened. "He wants me dead."

Dead. Dagny knew as much from her talk with Alice, but still, hearing her sister say it...

"I had to leave that place," Grete continued.

"Of course you did."

"Are you here alone?" Grete asked.

"No. I'm with some people. Friends." Dagny grabbed her sister's hands. "It's okay. They're good ones."

"Who are they?" Grete seemed nervous.

"Two boys. One is from the city, Jauson Tasher, and the other is a child from... well, I'm not sure. We met him just the other day. In the underground. But he's sweet. There's nothing to worry about, alright?"

"Alright." Grete said, but still seemed tense.

Dagny spoke again, trying to calm Grete with her voice. "This is a beautiful place. How long have you been here?"

"Almost two weeks, I think. I ran out of food. I was getting ready to leave again, but the storm came." Grete looked behind Dagny, at the path she'd come down. "I knew there were others here. A child, you said?"

"Yes. Melwes. Do you want to meet him?"

Grete nodded, and grabbed a hand-stitched satchel hidden near a bush. They left the clearing, taking the path back through the gardens. "I have your sketchbook at home," Dagny said. "Your drawings are wonderful. I recognized them from Morgan's stories."

"It's one of the only things that kept me going," Grete said. "Those stories. Thinking that there was something else out there. Limer's Town was so dark. I wasn't okay there. But I felt different as soon as I left. Better, you know."

Dagny looked at her sister's beautiful face with all the promises of youth still remaining, and smiled.

"Thank you for saving my drawings," Grete continued. "I had to leave almost everything behind when I ran. Once I saw my chance, I had to go."

"Alice said you left with some musicians and went across the Shallow Sea. It's what everyone thinks. Sliver included."

"Good. That's what I hoped. I left on their boat, and made sure people saw me do it. Then, when they docked in the city, I snuck off."

"Why did you come here?" Dagny asked.

“I felt like it would be safe. Something inside me just knew it.”

“You hadn’t been here before?”

“No. Why?” Grete asked.

“Well, those sketches... How’d you know what it looked like? And how did you even find this place?”

Grete raised her eyebrows. “Don’t you remember? Morgan told us.”

“What do you mean?” Dagny said. “No he didn’t.”

“Sure he did. In those stories about the rat in the garden. I dreamt about it all the time in Limer’s Town. I figured out the rat was the Glitter Rat and the garden was the old palace. Those were my favorite stories, don’t you remember?”

Dagny didn’t remember any of that.

“There she is!” Tash shouted from a distance, standing on some rubble by the wall. He hopped down and ran to them.

“That’s Tash,” Dagny said. “He’s nice. You’ll like him.”

Before Grete could reply, Tash was upon them. “You’re Dagny’s sister, aren’t you? This is unbelievable. I mean, really. You're actually here!” The shape of Melwes appeared now too, peeking out from behind a flower bush.

Dagny squeezed her sister’s hand, then introduced them. “Grete, this is Tash, and that young one back there is Melwes.”

“Hi,” Tash said. “Nice to meet you. This is really incredible!” It was odd seeing him so excited. Almost like it was his own sister they’d just found. But it made Dagny happy, and comforted, to have someone else to share it with.

Grete just nodded and clutched her satchel, while keeping an eye on the young boy dressed in the dirty, soft sweater and metal headdress. “You’re an interesting one,” she said.

"I suppose," he replied, sniffing the flowers he had picked earlier. "You're the one that left me food, aren't you?"

"What's that?" Dagny asked. "Melwes, you brought her food?"

"She seemed hungry," the boy said.

"I was. Thanks." Grete knelt down and kissed his cheek.

"So, what now?" Tash asked. "You two probably have a lot to talk about."

"Yeah," Dagny said. Suddenly it dawned on her that Grete might not want to be so forthcoming around the boys. She stood in silence while the birds chirped.

"Hey, Melwes," Tash began, seeming to sense Dagny's discomfort. "Isn't there a solarium near here? I thought I saw it on my map. By the ruins, perhaps?"

"Yes," the boy said.

"Could you show me? I'd really like to see it."

"Fine," Melwes huffed, and began walking to the north.

"Wait," Dagny said. "What about the *bone crushers?* Will we be safe?"

"Probably," Melwes said. "They almost never get over the wall."

~

Dagny sat with her sister on the warm grass, and the two of them talked throughout the morning, into the early afternoon. Dagny told her everything she could remember. About her life with Alex and the Benzara family. And Grete told her how she'd sneak off to Water Street and listen to the sailors; about how she'd draw in the early morning, before anyone else woke up. She said nothing further about Limer's Town.

“I think you should come back with me. To Rork,” Dagny said after some time. She hoped she wasn’t being too forward, but she wanted to mention it before the boys returned.

“To Rork, huh?”

“Yeah. Why not? We could do whatever you want. Start a new life together. I know this is all a lot to take in. It’s a lot for me, too.”

Grete hesitated before speaking. “I don’t know. It’s so dangerous with Sliver and them out there. I couldn’t do that to you.”

“You know, Alice told me about the puzzle box. What if we figured out a way to get it back to him? Then Sliver’d have no reason to keep looking for you,” Dagny suggested.

“The puzzle box?” Grete said. A look of confusion on her face.

“Yeah.”

“This isn’t about that puzzle box. Sliver is obsessed *with me*. He wouldn’t let me go. People think I took that box?”

“Yeah. Everyone. Even Alice said you took it. She was sure of it. What about those dreams? Alice said you told her you were having weird dreams when you slept near the box, and that’s why you took it.”

“No. That’s... I had awful dreams when I slept near Sliver. Of course I would, anyone would. Especially me, and he always had that stupid box.”

“Why especially you?” Dagny asked.

“Really? Do you want me to go into it?”

“No. You don’t have to. I’m sorry. I was just trying to figure out what Alice told me. It’s confusing.”

“I have weird dreams. That’s true,” Grete said. “Ever since the flood, I think. I don’t know why. And they were even more intense when I was with him. Sliver told everyone that his special box beat, like a heart. And sometimes I think I heard it, too. You know, Alice *thinks* she was my friend, but I didn't have any friends. No one is a friend there. This is about Sliver controlling me. He told me he was in love with me, but I couldn't stand him. He's awful. I'm sure he wants me dead now. By running off, I embarrassed him, which is the worst thing you can do to someone like that."

"We could protect you," Dagny said. "You don't know Alex. He's so well established. Sliver wouldn't come to Rork."

"I'd like to think that's true."

"It *is* true." Dagny thought of Alex and some of the men he knew. Powerful people. They could stop some gang from Limer's Town.

Grete's face tightened. She was visibly distressed, her dark eyes taking on a haunted appearance.

"I'm sorry," Dagny said. "I should learn when to leave something alone. Whatever you wanna do, I'll support. But I'm not leaving you again. Wherever you wanna go, I'll go, too."

~

Later that day, the group returned to the underground, and Melwes retrieved some carrots from a hidden storeroom. He boiled them in a small fireplace near the Archives.

"I miss sweet things," Grete said, as the food cooked. "Do you ever get honey in Rork? You must, right?"

"Oh yeah. All the time," Dagny said. "Cate makes Jumtea. It's like a sweet, syrupy drink made with ginger and honey."

"Cate?"

"Alex's wife. Caternya Benzara."

"You mentioned that they have two kids, right?" Grete said.

"Yes. Lucas and Abrielle, soon to be a third. It might've already been born."

"Sounds like a big family," Grete said. "You really think there'd be enough space for me?"

Dagny locked eyes with her sister. "Absolutely. *Absolutely* there'd be. The house is huge. There's six bedrooms." Dagny hoped she wasn't making a false promise, but Alex would have to take her in. She'd make sure of it. This was Morgan's sister too, after all.

"Six bedrooms," Grete repeated. "That is big."

"It's about as far from Limer's Town as you could get," Dagny said. "And it's really safe. Children are always playing outside, even into the evening. Musicians come and play the plazas. There's always some event going on at the theatre or the Common Hall or library."

Grete pulled her knees into her chest. "I like music."

"I'm telling you, everyone wants to live there," Dagny said.

Tash agreed. "It's true."

"I'm still thinking about it, but my head hasn't been working right," Grete said. "I'm so confused about what to do."

"It's okay," Dagny said. "You've been through a lot. I just want to be with you now."

⁂

Tash grumbled about having to spend another cramped night in the storage room, and Grete agreed to return to the Station with them. Once the sun set, Melwes guided them back, taking a different route than before, far away from the girl in the wall. Grete said they could row back, using the small boat she had stolen two weeks prior, but it was docked near the hunting preserve, and no one felt like running from bone crushers. The passage Melwes took them down led to an old cellar below the Station's kitchen, and they quietly snuck down the hallway and back to the bedchambers.

"I guess Grete will stay with you," Tash said.

"Alright," Dagny replied. "And Melwes, what do you want?"

The boy ignored her and walked into her bedroom.

"You going to be okay?" Tash asked.

"Yeah. It's probably well past midnight, don't you think?"

"Definitely. Anyway, I'm right next door, if you need anything," he added.

"Thanks."

"Well, goodnight."

Dagny shut the door and retrieved a nightgown from her traveler's pack, handing it to Grete. Melwes curled up on the floor and shut his eyes.

"How did you get out of the Rakesmount?" Dagny asked, as Grete sat on the mattress and removed her boots. "How did you escape the flood?"

"I went into the rain after you."

"You came after me?"

"If you hadn't left that night... If you'd stayed, we'd both be drowned with the rest of them. You saved us both by leaving. So don't feel guilty about it, okay?" Melwes let out a powerful yawn, and Grete looked over and laughed before directing her attention back to Dagny. "Do you have many friends in Rork?" she asked, pulling the nightgown over her head.

"Not really," Dagny said. "I always felt out of place. But I've made some in the city recently."

"Who are they? Tell me about them."

"Well, you know Tash now. Then there's Sarna, she's a musician with her sister, Hanette. And there's a few boys. Rodolph and Kim and Max. They figure themselves adventurers. I joined their group a little while back. *The Naverung*."

"The Naverung, huh?"

"It's actually how I found you," Dagny said. "We rescued a child from a tower on Farrow Blood – he's one of the Marsh Rats – and when we went down to see them, I stumbled upon Corlie. It's a crazy story."

Grete fell onto the mattress and stared at the ceiling. "What do you do when you're not rescuing children from towers?"

"Oh, all sorts of things. There's this place called Stardust, *Of Stardust and Light*, and there's always music and drinking and storytelling going on there."

Grete smiled. "I like that."

"Will you please come? *Please*. I'm begging you," Dagny said, with a nervous laugh, joining her sister on the bed. "If you hate it, you can always do something else."

"The city *is* a big place."

"Really big."

"It'd be hard to try and find someone there," Grete said.

"Almost impossible," Dagny replied.

"—Especially if you thought that person went across the Shallow Sea."

"Yeah, no way."

Grete turned on her side, looking Dagny in the eyes. "I could cut and change my hair."

"Oh right. Good idea. What color, you think?"

"I've always liked blue."

"Like Morgan's hair."

"Yeah, like Morgan's."

Someone knocked quietly on the door, and cracked it open. Dagny had no sense of how long she'd been sleeping.

"*Dagny, are you awake?*" Tash whispered, carrying a small candle.

"Not really," she said wearily.

"Is it okay if I come in?"

Dagny rubbed her eyes, trying to force them open. "Alright."

"Thanks. You mind if I just sleep on the floor here?"

"That's fine. What's wrong?"

"Every time I close my eyes, I keep seeing that pale girl crawling after me, and my chest feels heavy and I can't breathe. I really thought she was here a moment ago, but it's just my mind."

"That's awful," Dagny said. "Of course you can stay. You can sleep with me and Grete. There's more than enough space on the bed."

"Thanks."

"I'm actually glad you came back," Dagny said. "This Station is a lonely place."

"Yeah." Tash paused before whispering again. He nodded at Melwes, asleep on the floor. "Where do you think he's from?"

"I don't know. Maybe an orphan or something. Those spirits are probably trying to help him, like they helped us."

"And those phrases '*takka shein*' he keeps using, like some other language. I think it's just gibberish. It doesn't sound like anything. He probably made it up."

"It's possible, I guess." Dagny lay on the mattress next to Grete.

Tash joined her, and spoke even quieter now. A faint whisper near her ear. "You know, I'd give back Ogden's set if it's really so important. I'd give it back to him."

Just then, another weight pushed down on the bed, and Dagny saw the pointy-eared shape of Melwes, illuminated by moonlight from her window. The boy didn't say a word. He simply crawled between the two of them and fell asleep.

"Goodnight Tash," Dagny whispered.

"Oh right, goodnight."

The next morning Dagny and Grete walked the grounds outside of the Station, talking about Rork and the city. Her sister would stay in the spare room next to hers, and Dagny would send Alex a letter explaining the situation. When they returned to the Station, Tash and Melwes were sitting on the floor of the bedchamber, eating a breakfast of blood eggs and cream.

"So, is she coming back with us?" Tash asked Dagny, his eyes wide with anticipation.

"Yes," Grete said. "I am."

"Oh, that's great. I'm really glad for you both."

"And what about you, Melwes?" Dagny asked. "Would you like to see the city?"

"I should get back to my duties." He had a serious expression on his face.

"You don't think the spirits would understand? It seems like they have a pretty good hold on things."

He hesitated. "I'm not sure."

Dagny thought of Galwed, still trapped in the wall, and wondered what would happen if she broke out. The thought of Melwes alone in the tunnels with those twins made her sick. "Don't you think the lights might've brought us together for a reason? Maybe they want us to stick together."

Melwes looked at her with hopeful, innocent eyes.

"Just think about it, okay?" Dagny reached down and ruffled his hair, like she would sometimes do to Lucas.

"Say, how do you think they get blood eggs and cream here?" Tash asked, eating his breakfast. "See any chickens or cows?"

"Maybe someone brings it to them," Dagny said.

"It's not bad. I've had worse, that's for sure... tastes a bit fishy... but in a good way."

"Sounds delicious," Dagny said with a laugh.

"You don't like fish?"

"Not in eggs mixed with blood and cream."

"Huh. That's weird," Tash said, taking another mouthful.

"*That's* weird?"

"Yeah. How can you live on the lagoon and not like fish?"

"I like fish, by itself."

"You *suuure* you don't want some?" Tash took another giant bite, chewed it up, and opened his mouth, exposing a mash of bloody red food. The juice that ran down his chin matched his hair perfectly.

Melwes snorted and burst out laughing. Dagny just shook her head. "You're disgusting."

"Suit yourself," Tash shrugged.

Later that day, as Tash grabbed his things and Grete napped, Melwes told Dagny he had to leave.

"Do you have to go so soon? How about you come to Rork with us, at least for a little while? I meant what I said about the size of our house. It could be a really nice life, if you're around the right people."

"I told you, I'm protecting the Under Road." He looked sad, but also doubtful. Balancing at the edge of an important decision.

"Yes, I know. But—"

"—I knew you'd try and stop me!" he said suddenly, recoiling from her.

"Melwes, wait, don't." She tried to talk gently, but Dagny could tell she was losing him.

"—No. I have to go... I have to... I told you!" The boy spun around and sprinted out of her room.

Dagny ran after him, but lost him near the atrium. She searched the hallways and the dining room, and rushed over to the cellar by the kitchens, but she couldn't find the secret entrance. She sprinted into the ballroom, and crawled back to the old well. Melwes was nowhere to be found. She stopped short of taking to route to the cistern, still fearful of the drowned twins.

"You can only do so much," Tash said, after she returned. "Melwes made a choice, long before we showed up. I didn't realize how serious he was about it. He wants to be here, whatever his reasons."

"I just wanted to protect him."

"I know, but you can only do so much."

∞

It was a strange feeling to be back in the city.

Their river boat pulled up to the Morca docks. Just beyond the warehouses and taverns of the quayside lay the city proper, and all the mundane trappings of that place.

"You know, I've never been on this side of the river," Grete said, as they exited the boat and crossed over to City Centre.

"It's like two completely different cities. The north and the south," Tash said.

"Are we going to that Stardust place tonight?" Grete asked Dagny.

"Ugh. You're taking her there?" Tash said, with a sneer of disgust.

"I don't know. Let's see how it goes after we get you settled in at home," Dagny said.

Grete nodded. "Okay."

"So are you both gonna be spending all your time there?" Tash asked.

"You can come, too," Dagny said.

"No thanks."

"Is something wrong with Stardust?" Grete asked him.

"Just not for me, is all."

"Tash doesn't get along well with a couple of the others who spend time there," Dagny said. "I told him it'd be fine, but he's got his reasons."

"They're pretty good reasons," Tash mumbled to himself. "Are you done coming to Sorn Rue?"

"No. Not at all," Dagny replied. "Am I done with you? Is that what you're asking me?"

Tash laughed. "I didn't mean it like that. I expect you'll have lots of things taking your time now. It's understandable."

"Do you ever play Talvarind?" Dagny asked her sister.

"No."

Dagny nudged Tash. "We can teach you, then."

They wandered into the sprawling Grand Plaza, which housed the Authority's governmental palace. Several posh cafes adorned the opposite end.

"Is that the Fountain Azure?" Grete asked, pointing at an enormous pool. Three giants of marble and stone spit clear water at each other.

"Yeah. The zoo's nearby, too. We can go sometime soon if, you'd like," Dagny said.

"Sliver played Talvarind all the time," Grete said suddenly. "I didn't wanna bring up his name on the river boat with the crew listening."

"Right. Good thinking," Dagny said.

"He was a master at it," Grete continued. "Sliver's a genius at most things. It's like he thinks different than everyone else. I wondered why he stayed in Limer's Town. He probably coulda done anything he wanted."

"Tash is a master, too," Dagny said. "He might be the best in the city."

"Oh yeah?" Grete asked. "Do you play Gambles?"

"Yes," Tash said.

"Sliver did, too. You gotta watch those. They can get you into real trouble," Grete said.

"Sliver? I thought only adventurers played for Gambles," Dagny said.

"Typically it was an adventuring thing," Tash said. "But others picked it up too, over time. Did you think *I* was an adventurer?"

Dagny cocked her head. "Tash, if you hadn't noticed, you *are* an adventurer."

The Odd Viddry Bell Tower chimed four o'clock as they exited the Grand Plaza and made their way to the oak-lined boulevard heading into Rork.

"Remember when I mentioned Corlie and the Marsh Rats?" Dagny asked Grete.

"Yeah."

"This is where I first saw her. She was stealing from people watching a theatre troupe perform right over there. I didn't realize it was her, but she recognized me and chased me all across City Centre."

"Why were you running from her?" Grete asked.

"I thought she was going to rob me."

"Corlie's not big. You coulda just busted her up," Grete said, nonchalantly. As if busting someone up in the alleys of City Centre was no big deal.

Dagny was exhausted by the time they reached the courtyard of the Benzara house.

"No!" Grete gasped in disbelief. "This can't be it... Not possible."

"Welcome home." Dagny opened her satchel and fumbled for the house key.

"You've been living *here* since you left the Mount?" Grete asked.

"Not the whole time. In the beginning, I lived with Alex and his grandfather. We moved here after Alex discovered the sunken treasure ship in Oulen and met Caternya."

"The Prize at Oulen? Wasn't that one of Morgan's stories, too?"

"Yeah. Alex actually found it."

"Coulda been Morgan, if he hadn't died," Grete said.

"Could've been..." And then they *could've been* together much sooner. Maybe Morgan wouldn't have gotten sick. What would their life have been like? The three of them, living in Old Rork together. Plotting their own expeditions, seeing far-off places, meeting men like Jesper the Oyster Knight on the Hard Road through Ostrotha. Maybe Morgan would've met someone like Cate and married her and had his own children, like Lucas and Abrielle, and Grete would've never had to deal with Sliver or Limer's Town. And Dagny wouldn't have lost all those years.

"You gonna open the door already?" Grete asked. "I need to see this place."

19

THAT NIGHT, DAGNY STAYED up late, sitting at the desk in her bedroom while Grete slept nearby. She wrote a message to Alex, trying to detail everything she'd been through since he left. And most importantly, to let Alex know that Grete needed to live with them now.

When she finished, Dagny rolled up the note carefully and placed it into a messenger tube. Tomorrow, she'd find someone down in City Centre to deliver it to Cate's family estate.

Grete's face was buried in one of Dagny's large feathered pillows. She snorted with each deep breath. It sounded... nice.

They had spent most of the day sitting in the garden out back, talking about simple things, like the types of flowers Cate had planted and what Lucas and Abrielle did for fun. Later, they took a brief stroll over to the last Scholar's Tower, watched the water, and then grabbed dinner before the cafes closed. Grete whined playfully about not getting any Jumtea and "broken promises." Dagny laughed, and told her she'd have to wait for Cate to return.

From outside came the melodic sounds of a fiddle player. The musicians would be stopping soon. They'd played much later tonight than usual. Dagny tiptoed onto the balcony and quietly closed the door behind her.

She was feeling nervous about the coming days. Soon she'd have to see Max, Sarna and the others. She hoped everything would work out okay. There was a heavy weight upon her, the responsibility of making sure Grete got along well here. If it turned out bad... if Grete didn't like it, or couldn't connect with Dagny's friends and life, would she leave?

The balcony door opened, and Gretchen stood there, rubbing her eyes. "How long was I sleeping?"

"Hours," Dagny said. "You passed out fast once we got home."

"I was more tired than I thought. What you doing out here?"

"Just listening... you like it so far?" Dagny asked.

"The music?"

"...The whole thing."

"Yeah, it's good." Grete sat on a metal chair next to her. "I'm excited about tomorrow. Will you cut my hair?"

"Sure, we can do it in the morning," Dagny said.

"It's been long and black forever — I won't even recognize myself. And then we're going to the shops, right? Get me some new clothes?"

"Right, anything you want."

"Okay." Grete gazed into the night sky. "Look, you can see the Trail of the Glitter Rat."

"Can you?" Dagny asked. "I could never figure that one out, there's too many stars to it. I always get lost."

Grete stretched her arm, pointing out the constellation. "You just need to find Azathur's head first, and then follow his gaze eastward, past the Bull, and *there...* that's the first marker, see?"

"Oh, right, okay. That's the Herald's Star."

"Good job. The whole Trail used to be part of the Night Road," Grete said. "The problem is, some of the stars are gone now. They used to all be up there, but that was a long time ago."

Dagny glanced at her sister. "How do you know all this?"

"What, 'cause I grew up in the Mount and Limer's Town?" Grete asked.

"Well, kinda... yeah," Dagny said.

"Limer's Town and Water Street are full of fortune tellers and star gazers and witches and spirit talkers. And sailors and scavengers of the lagoon are always coming through. The stars are like a religion over there. I know more than you think I do."

"I didn't mean to suggest anything," Dagny said.

"It's alright. I'm not gettin' mad at you. I just want you to know, I'm not dumb," Grete said. "It's important to me that you know that."

"I do know that." Dagny chewed her fingernail before speaking again. "Can I ask you some stuff? And then I'll never bring it up again."

"About Limer's Town, you mean."

"About... well, everything," Dagny said.

"That'd be alright."

"...What *happened?* After the Rakesmount and the flood?"

Grete took a deep breath before answering. "I don't remember it all. But I chased after you and got lost in the rain. I remember water rushing around buildings. And I remember wandering by the shore just outside the city. A man found me. He was one of them scavengers. He told me the Morca broke and a big chunk of the city flooded. He took me back to the Mount, but everything... was gone. I went with him for a time, scrounging wrecks in the lagoon. And then we came to Limer's Town, but the man got sick and died. I think he was probably poisoned. The way he went… it was terrible. Then I fell in with Sliver…"

"I don't know much about Sliver and his gang," Dagny said. "Is there anything you need to tell me? Anything you feel I *should* know?"

"I'm not sure where to start. I was there for years."

"Anything more about the box he says you stole?"

Grete crossed her arms and stared back into the night, a stern expression coming over her face.

"…I just wanna protect you, that's the only reason I'm asking," Dagny continued. "Otherwise, I could care less about him."

"I know all that Dag, and really, I wanna be here with you. But don't tell me you're gonna protect me. You couldn't do it before, and you can't do it now. So just stop."

"I just meant—"

"I know. But what do you think you're gonna do? *Really?* Look at you, growing up in this fancy place… It's okay, I'm glad you had it, but you can't protect anyone, and I just need you to stop with all that. If I ever see Sliver again, I'll kill him myself."

~

The next morning Dagny woke early, before Grete – or most of Rork, for that matter – and wandered outside into the predawn darkness to be alone with her thoughts. She headed down the main boulevard, in the direction of City Centre, taking the message she'd written to Alex.

The first time Dagny came to Rork, it had frightened her in a way. The large houses and broad streets and relaxed easiness of the place felt so bizarre back then. As a little girl, she knew she didn't belong here, and wondered how long it would take the residents of Rork to see her for what she really was: a fraudulent, dirty, spit-born, Rakesmount mutt. But the neighborhood was so beautiful. And she'd been with Alex and Cate, and they were so beautiful. Alex and Cate certainly belonged here, and they had taken *her* to this new life with them.

As it turned out, the people in Rork had been nice. Much nicer than the people at the Mount. No one tortured her here. No one smacked her face raw. No one made fun of her skinny legs, or the way she used to slur certain words or scratch long red marks into her skin just for fun. She'd gone to dances and birthday celebrations, and watched star showers while lying on soft grass. But something always gnawed at her, on the inside. That same feeling she had as a child. That all the goodness could be taken away, as soon as she became comfortable. That none of it really belonged to her. *Spit-born.*

No one was on the street at this hour. Dagny stopped and sat on the stairs of the library. She was in no real rush to get to City Centre or to get back home. Two large lamp posts framed the building's entrance, and Dagny stared down at her small hands and wrists in the light. They were delicate. They felt weak. Grete was right, she couldn't protect anyone from anything... especially not from a dangerous group out of Limer's Town.

Was she a delusional person? Had her mind turned everything into a fantasy? Did she really think she could travel with Alex, or be an adventurer like Morgan? Alex was too nice to say it. He'd just change the subject or come up with some excuse every time Dagny begged him to take her along. But he knew. He knew what she was. She must've sounded so foolish, talking about traveling the world. She felt humiliated, really. Everything that had happened this last month, from Farrow Blood and Limer's Town to the old palace and the underground... she was just lucky she wasn't killed.

Part of her wanted to run off now, away from the city, and find Lucas and Abrielle. Maybe they could play a game of *Hunters and the Hunted* out there at Cate's estate. She could tell Lucas all about the Oracle Tower, and he could look at her the way she used to look at Morgan. *I bet Cate's family has a feast prepared every single night.*

Dagny hopped off the library stairs and continued down the street. Why did she feel this way? None of it made any sense. She'd found Grete. She actually did it, and still she felt an emptiness. Why couldn't she just be *happy?* In the back of her mind, Dagny sensed the feeling would pass, like it always did... eventually... but that did little to ease the despair she felt now. For a moment... a brief moment... Dagny felt like walking to the Morca and jumping in.

~

The sun was dawning by the time she reached City Centre. Even at this early hour, people began flooding the market square. Sellers set up their stalls, and buyers scrounged for the best meats and choicest vegetables. Dagny found a couple of messenger boys sitting near the Odd Viddry Bell Tower, and paid one of them for the day trip out to Cate's place. *Maybe I'll head there soon, but not today,* she thought.

A couple coins poorer, Dagny took a mug of coffee, prepared in the Solevay fashion (dark and thick) and sat by the Morca, watching the ships pass. She felt no rush to get back. No rush for anything. Grete could take care of herself when she woke.

"Well, look who it is," a familiar voice said, startling her. Dagny jerked her head and saw the silhouette of Maris, standing against the rising sun.

"...Maris... you surprised me. I thought you had left the city."

"I returned the day before yesterday," he said, joining her on the riverside bench. "Thought I'd get out and stretch the legs. You're here awfully early."

"I didn't sleep good," Dagny said.

"Wait until you're my age. I never sleep good."

"You're not old."

"I still don't sleep good," he said.

"There's something you should know. Magu Ogden disappeared. Not long after you spoke with him."

"Huh." Maris considered it for a moment. "I'd like to say that's surprising, but he was always disappearing back in the day. He'd just vanish for long stretches. Sometimes he'd be gone for a year, or more."

"Really? Where would he go?"

"Who knows? He didn't tell me. Your brother, now, he might've known."

"Morgan? Why would he know?"

"Well, he went with Ogden sometimes. I'm not sure even Alex knew what they did."

"They were that close?" Dagny asked. "Morgan and Ogden?"

"Oh yeah. Much closer than Alex or me were with the old man."

"Wow. I had no idea."

"Actually... never mind, I'm not sure I should say it..."

"What?" Dagny suddenly felt nervous.

"When Morgan caught that fever, he was with Ogden."

"Wait... what? No. He was with Alex."

Maris shook his head. "No. Ogden took Morgan to Alex's house after they returned from who-knows-where."

Dagny tried to process what Maris just said, in silence.

"I didn't make you sad, did I?" he asked. "I'm no good at keeping things like that secret."

"I'm not sad. Was it supposed to be a secret?"

Maris shrugged. "Probably."

"Hey, you remember those boys you saw at Ogden's that day?" Dagny asked.

"Vaguely. Those little piglets haven't given you a hard time, have they?"

"No, no. They're friends of mine now... it's just," she considered telling him what Max had said, about Ogden's mind slipping and it becoming worse, then thought against it. "A lot's happened since I saw you... You're not leaving again, are you?"

Maris stretched his arms and put his hands behind his head. "There's nowhere I need to be, at the moment."

"I found my sister," Dagny blurted out.

"Your sister? You have a sister?"

"Yes. Gretchen. You don't remember her?"

"No. I don't think I ever knew."

"She'd been living in Limer's Town," Dagny said. "And some bad people are after her."

"Where is she now?"

"At Alex's place."

"That's good... Limer's Town is full of degenerates. Less than human. Wasn't always that way. The refineries over there used to supply the brick and iron for the whole region. Limer's Town metal can be found in just about every old gate around here."

"It must've been a long time ago," Dagny said, thinking about how decayed the area had become. *A long, long time ago.*

"It was."

"What happened?"

"A curse came down from the mountains. The people of that place stirred something up, and a cold presence emerged from the underground and ate away all the goodness kept in their hearts."

"That doesn't sound real."

"Eh. What do you know?"

"...I found Grete near the old palace."

"Who?" Maris asked.

"Gretchen. My sister. Pay attention."

"—The old palace?" Maris thought for a moment. "The one at Deep Lake?"

"That's right. We found our way into the underground beneath it. Through a secret passage near the cistern."

"There's an entrance there?" Maris asked, raising his eyebrow.

"Yes, but there's some terrible things down that way. Have you ever been?"

Maris shook his head. "No, but I know about it... the old palace... People used to say it was an entrance to the Great Below."

"Were you listening to me? I said there were terrible things there."

"I've seen terrible things before, girl. But I'll play along. What did you see?" he asked.

"First there were the bone crushers—"

Maris scoffed. "They don't concern me."

"And the twins. They were the worst."

"Huh?"

"The Drowned Twins of Gort. You know about *them*?"

"No..."

"They're still there. By the kitchens. Trapped in a wall. They were awful Maris, awful."

"Oh, okay... good to know," he said.

"Hey. I'm scared about what'll happen if those people from Limer's Town come after Grete. Would you help us? Until Alex gets back, anyway."

"You have any reason to think they're coming here?"

"No. In fact, they think Grete went across the Shallow Sea."

"Oh, then I'm sure you're fine. But look, if you're that worried, I'm staying at the *Ground Goose*, by River's End. I'll come check on you, alright?"

"Alright. Thanks. I'd really appreciate it," Dagny said, just as the Bell Tower chimed seven o'clock. "I better get back to Grete."

"Sure, sure... Hey, the old palace, how deep did it go?"

"Why?" Dagny asked, but he just smiled. "...Maris, don't go there... I mean it... those twins are dangerous."

"Yeah, I heard you."

~

Gretchen was sitting in the dining room, staring out the window, when Dagny walked in.

"You left me."

"Sorry. I had to take care of a few things," Dagny said, handing her a wrapped loaf. "Here, I brought you some sweet bread."

"Okay, you're forgiven," Grete said with a sudden grin. She wore one of Cate's long-sleeved nightshirts.

"You sleep alright?" Dagny asked, noticing that Grete's sketchbook was on the dining table.

"You mean, did I have any bad dreams?"

"I guess..." Dagny pointed at the book. "I saw you drew Drey Garders in there."

"I don't know what those are."

"The long-eared cats."

"Right," Grete said. "From Morgan's stories."

"Are you sure?" Dagny asked.

"Of course I am. Why?"

"I don't know... those cats, and that room with the toads... those aren't stories I remember."

Grete shrugged. "I don't know what to tell you."

"Alice mentioned that you had dreams of the underground, and of a shifting city and a cauldron of black iron. But none of those were Morgan's stories, either."

"I thought we weren't gonna talk about that anymore, after last night... Didn't you promise that?"

"You're right," Dagny said. "I was just curious."

Suddenly Grete slammed her hands on the table. "*I don't want to think about that place anymore!*" she screamed.

The sound sent a jolt of fear through Dagny. "I... I'm sorry..." she said. "I shouldn't have mentioned it... I'm done."

Grete scowled at her. "Are you sure?"

"Yes... I love you," Dagny said. That one remark softened Grete instantly.

"...You do?"

"Of course I do."

Grete smiled. "I love you, too."

∾

They set up in the garden, where the sun was brightest, and Dagny drew the shears close to Grete's shoulders.

"How short do you want me to go?" Dagny asked. She hadn't cut anyone's hair since living at the Rakesmount, and, come to think of it, the last person's hair she'd ever cut was Gretchen's.

"Go real short. Higher than my shoulders."

"Alright, here goes nothing. Don't get mad."

Grete tried to stifle a laugh, but snorted. "You better not butcher me."

It actually didn't turn out half-bad. Dagny had cropped it a bit shorter than she would've liked, but Grete looked... cute.

They wandered into Cate's enormous vanity room and raided her cabinets. It was surprising – Cate almost never changed her hair color, but she had chalks and pastes and dyes for almost every shade imaginable.

"Let's do the darker blue," Dagny suggested. "It's a stark-enough change, but not so noticeable as to draw attention."

"Okay. I trust you," Grete said, and Dagny flashed her a sly smile.

Back in the garden, as Dagny ran the pasty substance through Grete's hair, she wondered if she should change her own appearance. She'd never really given it much thought until now. Her mind had usually been consumed with other things: adventures and far-off lands, combing through Vittendorf's descriptions of stilted-men or blood forests.

"Have you ever been in love?" Grete asked.

"Not really."

"What's that mean?"

"It means, no. I haven't."

"Have you ever been with a boy?" Grete asked.

Dagny felt blood rush to her face. "No. Not like that, anyway."

"Dag! You should've taken advantage of being here... stealing Rork boys' hearts."

"I never had much interest in it, I guess. Never met anyone I really liked, or that liked me." Although the first part probably wasn't true. She just never got that kind of attention here in Rork.

"I want to be in love," Grete said with a sigh. "Be with someone who could really care for me. Someone to have fun with. Someone more pure than I am."

"I'm sure you'll have no problem with that. You're adorable."

"You think?" Grete asked, touching her newly cropped hair. But Dagny figured she already knew that.

After lunch, they took a ferry boat over to Barchpool, where the finest clothiers in the city were based. Alex and Cate always left Dagny with plenty of money. That was one thing, at least, she never had to worry about. She'd easily be able to buy Grete a whole new wardrobe.

"They'll need to measure you, and we'll have to come back in a month for most of it, but there should be a few nice things we can get today," Dagny told her.

"I'm thinking at least a couple of those skirts, like the ones I seen in Cate's closet. Something real pretty."

"Don't worry, we'll get you looking fashionable."

"—What do you think *they're* doing?" Grete asked, pointing to a group of men and women in a field by the playhouse.

"Actors. Looks like they're rehearsing for something."

"A show?" Grete almost yelped with excitement. "A theatre show? Have you ever seen one?"

"Plenty of times. Every year, they do *The Winter's Comet*. I saw it last season."

"What's that about?" Grete asked.

"A poor girl, who turns out to be the daughter of an exiled empress. It's a simple story. But there's beautiful costumes, and lots of singing and dancing."

"It sounds *amazing*. Can we go?"

"They're not doing it now, just getting ready for it later. It'll probably be a couple months. We can come back then."

"It's all so incredible. I feel like my heart is going to explode. I never want to leave. Okay, Dag? Promise me that. Promise me I'll never have to leave all of this. That this is gonna be my life now."

"I promise."

20

It was a light crowd at Stardust tonight. A handful of regulars Dagny'd seen, but didn't know, milled around the fireplace. The room was warm, a welcome reprieve from the hard autumn chill that had descended on the city. Grete removed her long coat when they entered, exposing a suit of brushed suede, the color of a lion's hide, which hugged her like a second skin. Several young men turned and gawked, as they made their way to the bar. It bothered Dagny, the way they were eyeing her, but Grete didn't seem to mind.

For the last week, Grete had mentioned Stardust every day, asking if they could go, and Dagny kept coming up with excuses to avoid it. Tonight, however, there was no more putting it off. Grete asked if Dagny was embarrassed by her, if that was the real reason she hadn't met any of Dagny's friends. It felt terrible.

As she looked around for a familiar face, Dagny heard Rodolph's distinct laugh coming from somewhere further back. She took Grete around the edge of the bar and spotted the broad-shouldered boy sitting with Hanette and Sarna in the corner, between the stage and wall.

"—It's not that funny," Sarna said from the table.

"Yeah, calm down," said Hanette.

"I'm sorry, it's just *so stupid,"* Rodolph howled. They were so engrossed in their discussion that none of them noticed the girls approach.

"Did I miss something?" Dagny asked, from behind Rodolph.

"*Dag!*" Rodolph yelled, jumping out of his chair. He lifted her into the air and spun around. "It's so good to see you!" He was glassy-eyed, and smelled both sour and sweet.

"Put me down," Dagny said playfully. "You're drunk."

"Maybe a little bit..."

"I'd come give you a hug too, but I hurt my knee," Sarna said.

"What happened?" Dagny asked.

Rodolph answered, "She fell off the stage, trying to flirt with Feruda."

"No." Sarna glared at the boy. "Not flirting."

"Whatever you say. Feruda was nice enough about it, and left to go get..." Rodolph looked around. "Well, where *did* she go? I guess you've been abandoned, Sarna."

"Who's Feruda?" Dagny asked.

"She plays strings with Marfisi," Rodolph said, still scanning the crowd. "Where'd she go?"

Dagny turned and opened her arm, inviting Grete forward. "Everyone, this is my sister, Gretchen."

For a moment, the table was silent. All three of them gawking, like the young men by the fireplace.

"...What?" Sarna finally said.

"The same sister from *across the water*?" Rodolph asked. "Or... another one?"

Dagny shook her head. "I only have one sister."

Sarna struggled to her feet and limped over. "I can't believe it. How?"

"It's a long story," Dagny said.

"Can I give you a hug?" Sarna asked Grete.

"Umm..." Grete looked nervously at Dagny. "...I guess..."

"—Knee is feeling better already!" Rodolph shouted.

Sarna pulled Grete close. "Welcome, Gretchen. We're so glad you're here."

It was an odd collision of her two lives here in Stardust. That past life, before everything drowned in the Rakesmount, and the promise of her new one, caught in the smile of Sarna and the drunken gaze of Rodolph.

Dagny and her sister joined the group at the table, while Rodolph poured himself another drink.

"So, Limer's Town?" he asked.

"Shh. Don't talk about that," Dagny said, quickly. She glanced over her shoulder to see if anyone had heard.

Hanette huffed and crossed her arms, scrunching her freckled nose.

"She still doesn't forgive us," Sarna said. "For bringing me over there."

"How could I? You coulda disappeared forever, and then what?" Hanette said.

"Anyway..." Sarna leaned forward, her eyes active and wide. "How did you do it? How did you find her?"

"I'll tell you the details when we're somewhere more private, but I went to the old palace, the one at Deep Lake, and into the underground – and you know who helped me? *Jauson Tasher.*"

"What?" Sarna said. "Are you serious?"

"I couldn't have done it without him. He's actually pretty great."

Sarna shook her head in disbelief. "Jauson Tasher. No kidding. Why didn't you tell us you were going there?"

"I wish I had a good answer for you," Dagny said. "I was torn about it. First, Max and me got into that fight..."

"—Yeah, he's real heartbroken about that," Rodolph said.

Dagny glanced at him—she couldn't tell if he was being sarcastic—and continued, "...Second, I didn't wanna put you all in any more danger, after what happened across the water."

"Good decision," Hanette said. "For once."

"But you put Tash in danger, right? You trusted him," Sarna said.

"I just asked him to tell me where to go, but he insisted on coming. And, truthfully, if he hadn't, I wouldn't've made it."

Sarna smiled. "I'm glad he was there for you, then."

"I didn't offend you, did I?" Dagny asked. "Please don't be hurt. It's been a lot for me to handle. I tried to do the right thing."

Sarna reached out and grabbed her hand. "No, no. You did the right thing. I just wanted to help, if you needed it. And I'm sure Rodolph feels the same. I'm so happy for you."

Rodolph nodded along, and watched them. Dagny thought about asking where Max was, but just said, "Anything new here?"

"Eh... there's a rumor that Griff Majestic is close to finding a treasure horde from the Regime of Man," Rodolph said. "Apparently he has some big lead. No one knows what it is. I'm not sure what to believe."

"Huh. That's interesting," Dagny said, but she didn't really care.

"Max always thought there was some treasure buried in Glimmer Ghost. We looked awhile back, but didn't find anything. There's lots of tunnels inside. Easy to get lost in those caves."

"Why did he think it was there?" Dagny asked.

"You'd have to ask him. I don't remember. He's up on the roof, if you're interested."

"Why would I be interested?" Dagny said.

"Oh, don't be like that. He didn't mean anything before. Max just gets that way sometimes, right Sarna?"

Sarna rolled her eyes. "Yeah, but so what? Doesn't mean Dag should have to deal with his mood swings."

Rodolph looked back at Dagny. "I'm just saying he cares about you is all, and he's a good person."

"Max, Max, Max, Max, Max," Hanette said, clearly agitated. "*Enough already*."

"You're really in a foul mood," Rodolph said.

"Ugh! I'm getting another drink." Hanette grabbed the pitcher and stormed away.

Rodolph smiled at Grete. "Welcome to Stardust!"

∾

Sarna and Rodo took turns questioning Grete. What did she like to do for fun? Does she play any instruments? Is she into adventuring? How did she survive the Rakesmount flood? Does she enjoy stargazing?

"If you do, the stargazers are on the roof tonight with their scopes," Rodolph told her. "Supposed to be able to see some comet or something."

Grete asked if they could go, and Dagny took her up top. People crowded in the dark on the flat, concrete roof. Several large telescopes were set near the edge, and groups whispered and pointed at the stars. Someone nearby complained of too many clouds tonight.

"You probably know more than anyone else here," Dagny said. "Do you know what comet it is?"

"Dreg's Protector. It'll pass through the constellation Gylathrik. Anyone who sees it is supposed to have good luck." *When you talk of the stars, you sound like a scholar*, Dagny thought.

It didn't take long for her to notice Max standing alone, staring up. He looked easygoing and comfortable, with his hands stuffed deep in his pockets. Despite how he made her feel the last time they spoke, Dagny felt a warm rush of excitement. Had he really been jealous over Tash? Was that it? Or had he just been trying to protect her? She wondered if she should say something.

Suddenly, Max looked straight at her. He blinked rapidly, and opened and shut his mouth, clearly caught off guard. He raised his hand slowly and waved.

Grete nudged her. "Go on. I'm gonna see if I can get a look at one of these sky scopes."

Before Dagny could respond, Grete walked off toward a crowd, near the edge. When she turned back around, Max was standing in front of her.

"Hi..." he said.

"Hello..."

"Is that your sister?"

"Yeah... good guess."

"She's pretty. She looks like you."

"No, she doesn't."

"Hey, I want to apologize—"

"It's fine. I'm over it."

"I'm really upset at myself. I'll never treat you like that again. I'm just... really, really sorry."

"It's fine, but thanks."

"I'd ask if we can go back to before," Max said. "But I'm afraid of what the answer will be."

Dagny sighed. "I don't know what you want me to say."

"Right. I get that." He thought for a second. "I want you to say that you forgive me for being so stupid."

"I forgive you."

They stood there, awkwardly, not sure what to do, before Max spoke again. "How did you find your sister?"

"Tash and I found her over in the old palace, near Lomenthal Station."

"The old palace, huh? He helped you?"

"Yeah."

"That's good..."

"Max..." she whispered.

"You don't need to tell me anything else." He shifted his weight, uncomfortably, between both feet. "Think we'll be able to see the comet through these clouds?"

Dagny looked up. "I'm not sure. I guess you get good luck if you see it."

"Yep. Not like you need it, though."

"I'll take all the luck I can get," Dagny said. "I'm afraid I might've used all of mine recently."

"You're either lucky or you're not. I don't think it's something you run out of."

"I think I'm gonna go see my sister. It's her first time here."

"Oh sure. Of course. See you around."

When Dagny found Gretchen, she was looking through the lens of the biggest telescope on the roof, and pointing at the sky. "It'll pass to the left of the Endahl before approaching the Black Star. You'll be able to see it soon," she said to a group of observers who had gathered around.

Dagny didn't know why she had worried about Grete making friends. She seemed to have a natural talent for it. Dagny allowed herself to relax somewhat, and gazed up with the rest of them. She wondered when the clouds would part and reveal the comet, but they never did.

~

Back downstairs, Rodolph had his head on the table, eyes closed with a peaceful smile.

"Are you gonna stay for a while?" Sarna asked Dagny. "We'll be going on stage again shortly."

"—Yes," Grete said, before Dagny could answer.

"Good." Sarna checked the tuning on her fiddle by plucking its strings. "Hanette and me will be leaving for a few weeks."

"What? Leaving? Where?" Dagny asked in quick succession.

"Traveling with Marfisi and Feruda, up river and into southern Vahnland. We'll be playing the towns all the way to Vahnes itself, and finishing at their Harvest Fest."

"Oh, that's great..." Dagny said, but it didn't feel great. Not to her. It felt sad.

"Don't worry, we'll be back." Sarna gave her a wink.

"I know. It's just, I feel like I haven't seen you that much, and now you're leaving."

"Don't *worry,* silly," Sarna said. Hanette kept eyeing them. It was clear she didn't like Sarna having to explain anything.

"It'll give you plenty of time to go exploring," Hanette said, coldly, "with people who actually want to go."

"I think I'm all done with that," Dagny said. She tried to soften her voice, to let Hanette know she wasn't a threat.

"All done, huh? Does *he* know?" Hanette pointed at Rodolph.

"I don't know, maybe."

"I don't think he does. He was already making plans about you all searching Glimmer Ghost. Looking for some stupid, fake treasure."

"I didn't say I wanted to go," Dagny said.

"It doesn't matter. That just seems to be how you operate — make people think *they* came up with an idea, when it was you all along. You're a manipulative liar."

"What are you talking about?"

"When we first met, you said you were from the Rakesmount, when you're really from Rork, and then you manipulated Sarna into risking her life in Limer's Town. You don't even know us, or Max or Rodolph, yet everyone keeps putting themselves in danger for you."

"...She didn't manipulate me," Sarna said.

Hanette gestured at her to keep quiet. "You're nothing but trouble, Dagny. Why don't you do us a favor and keep Sarna out your plans. Just go away."

"Why don't you shut your ugly freckled face," Grete said, calmly, "before I smash your teeth onto the floor."

The table turned quiet. Hanette smiled awkwardly, unsure of what to do. She glanced at her sister and then at Dagny.

"Don't look at her," Grete snapped. "No one's gonna help you." In the glow of the lamplight, her eyes were black and merciless. She seemed like a feral creature about to attack.

Hanette sat there in shock, with her mouth open. The girl looked terrified. It was apparent she had never been spoken to like that before.

"*Grete...*" Dagny whispered.

"What?"

Hanette stood and grabbed her mandolin. "I think we're going to take the stage now," she said, quietly. Sarna gathered her things, keeping her eyes down, and hobbled to her feet.

Dagny reached for her. "Wait. She didn't mean it."

"I didn't?" Grete said.

"I'll... umm... see you later," Sarna said and left.

"That freckled girl is a shit. I don't like her," Grete said, loudly, almost challenging the sisters to hear.

"Your feelings are obvious. Sarna's been a good friend, though. I need to apologize."

"You didn't do nothin' wrong."

"I brought you here, and you threatened to beat her sister."

"She was being rude to you."

"Don't you think that was an overreaction?" Dagny asked.

"You want me to apologize?"

"Kinda."

Grete shrugged. Then she took Hanette's mug and downed the rest of the drink.

Behind them, the crowd cheered as Sarna and Hanette took the stage. It took the girls awhile to get going, and when they started into *Mergle's Gurgle,* Sarna's voice was much more subdued than usual.

"They sound good," Grete said sarcastically.

"You scared her. People don't act like that around here."

Grete looked past her, ignoring the comment. "Isn't that your friend Tash?"

Dagny turned around and saw him standing near the bar, scanning the room. *Tash actually came*. This certainly was a night of firsts. And, *of course*, Tash would show up right in the middle of so much tension. But, she was glad he showed. Maybe it would actually help defuse the situation. Rodolph, asleep at the table, certainly wasn't helping. Dagny stood and waved her arms, trying to get his attention.

"So, you and him... are you... together?" Grete asked from the table.

"Huh?" Dagny glanced down at her. "You mean..."

"—*Together,*" Grete said with a wink.

"No. Not at all."

"Good to know."

Before Dagny could ask what she meant by that, Tash appeared at the table and spoke, "Wasn't sure if you'd be here. I almost left. Crowds like this always make me uncomfortable. Especially here."

"Why don't you sit, Tash?" Grete gestured to the chair next to her and poured him a drink in the mug Sarna left behind.

"I missed you today at Sorn Rue," he told Dagny.

"We'll come by soon. Are you ready for the next tournament? You're playing in two days, right?"

"Yep. And I'm ready. It don't matter who shows, I already got 'em beat."

"Be right back," Grete said, turning the pitcher over. "All empty."

They watched her walk off, before Tash leaned over and whispered, "How's *she* doing?"

"I don't know. I thought it was fine, but tonight's been weird." Dagny wasn't sure how much to reveal to Tash right now.

"It'll probably take some getting used to. New place and all."

From the corner of her eye, Dagny saw a form approach. At first she assumed it was Grete, returning for some money, and reached toward her belt-purse. But it was Max who spoke.

"Jauson..." he said. Dagny's heartbeat quickened. She couldn't take any more confrontation tonight.

"Hi Max," Tash said.

Dagny opened her mouth, about to cut off the conversation before it turned mean. She could just leave. Take Grete and run back to Rork. Coming here had been a mistake.

"—I want to apologize," Max said to Tash. "I didn't say the greatest things about you before. But Dag here mentioned how you helped her, and that you took her to the old palace. I misjudged you, and I'm sorry about that."

"Don't worry yourself about it," Tash said.

"Well, that's all I wanted to say. I'll leave you two alone." He grabbed Rodolph around the chest and hoisted him up. "C'mon, time to go home."

Rodolph stumbled, his head wobbling, and looked at Tash. "Oh... it's you... the Talvarind guy... Did I miss anything?"

"No. I don't think so," Max said, leading him to the door. "Just another boring night."

Dagny watched them go, too surprised to say anything. Maybe she had misjudged Max. There seemed to be a lot of misjudging going around.

"That was unexpected," Tash said. She could barely hear him over the music and the singing crowd, which erupted as Sarna started into the lyrics of *Freshing's Kiss*.

"I should talk to him. You gonna be alright?" Dagny shouted.

"I'm not a child. Go."

Dagny headed to the door, squeezing through the mass of people and bumping into sweaty bodies as she went. She caught a glimpse of Max and Rodolph, but they disappeared again. The front door opened and shut, and Dagny was almost running as she broke free from the crowd and rushed out of the building.

"Max!" she called. The two boys were standing across the gravel yard by the rusted gate. A misty rain had started to fall, and from far off Dagny could hear the night-song of the city. "Hey..." she continued, panting shallow breaths as she approached. "...Thanks for that."

"Oh, sure. I meant it, though," Max said. "I'm not sure what happened with Ogden and him, but it doesn't matter. He helped you out, and he's a friend of yours. That means more than anything else."

"If you wanna start over... go back to before that night... I'm okay with it."

"I'd like that. I'd like that a lot," Max said. Rodolph had stepped away and was supporting himself on the fence, gazing out across the street.

"Is he gonna be alright?" Dagny asked.

"Yeah, don't worry. He's been ten times worse. You'll have to tell me about the old palace and your adventure soon."

"I will. Those old ruins are special. Really unbelievable."

Max nodded, like he knew. "Hey. There's something I wanna show you. If you're up for it."

"What is it?"

"Ha. It's a secret, of course. I'll come by your place tomorrow morning, if you want."

Dagny hesitated. There was so much to worry about right now, and only so much time in the day. It seemed like everyone needed her attention. Still, there was no denying the way she felt about the person in front of her. He was handsome and looked kind of dashing in the rain. With his dark hair catching water, he didn't look like a rat — he looked like one of those sailors she'd pictured in her mind, like Dreel of Bluestone sailing the Shallow Sea. He excited her. And Dagny felt something else inside, something unexplainable when he was close. She wanted to give in and trust him.

"Well?" Max asked.

"I gotta get out of this rain." Dagny turned and walked back to Stardust. "See you tomorrow. Don't keep me waiting."

21

Dagny didn't sleep well. She kept having dreams of Farrow Blood Island and the Tower, but in her dreams the Island was full of life. Animals talked like people, and the Oracle wandered among them – a young girl with ears like a fox and a long monkey tail. The giant crow came in the night, and the Oracle welcomed it as an old friend. They talked of the stars, and the crow warned her of the city-folk. It was trying to convince the Oracle to abandon the Island and return home.

When Dagny awoke, she was convinced the dream was real. She'd never had a dream she remembered so vividly before. She lay in bed for a long time, tossing around, until dawn came several hours later and with it a knock on her bedroom door.

"Dagny..." Grete whispered from the hall. "Are you awake?" Her voice was soft and sweet, like a child's.

"Yes. I've been up for hours."

"I couldn't sleep either," Grete said, crawling into bed with her. "I'm not proud of myself last night. The way I acted around your friends."

Dagny didn't respond. She just listened.

"Sometimes I feel like I'm two different people. Does that make sense? The things I want, and the way I am. I don't know what's wrong with me."

Dagny rolled over and looked Grete in the eye. "Nothing's wrong with you. We'll just apologize. Everything will be alright."

"I don't want to create trouble for you." It sounded like Grete was about to cry. "It's more than just last night. It's something bigger."

"Like what?"

"I'm just messed up, in my head. I'm not right. I can feel it," Grete sobbed.

"No, you're fine." Dagny reached out and touched her shoulder. "And I'm here. We'll get through it together, okay?"

By breakfast, Grete had retreated into herself. She sat near the window in the dining room and furiously sketched in her notebook. Dagny would've asked questions, but she sensed now wasn't the time. Instead, she brought Grete boiled eggs, bread and jam, and stepped into the garden.

It was a good thing Max was coming over today. Dagny felt like they both needed a distraction. And her curiosity was overwhelming. What did Max want to show her? Was it a thing or a place? The last time Max offered up a secret, it took them to Farrow Blood and Jorgie, and then to the Marsh Rats and Limer's Town. What would this one bring?

He entered the garden by mid-morning, coming through the side gate. Dagny had already been dressed for hours.

"I was knocking, but no one answered," Max said. He wore thick boots, the same black jacket he'd worn to Farrow Blood, and carried a backpack with two canteens strapped to either side. Dagny was dressed for traveling as well, in her riding slacks and a bulky, waxed mountaineer's coat she'd picked up in Barchpool.

"I figured you were gonna take me somewhere adventurous," she said, standing up to greet him.

"You did, huh? Maybe, I just wanted to show off my new backpack."

"That thing isn't new. Where are we going?"

"It's a surprise."

"Can I bring Grete?" she asked.

"Yeah. Sure," Max said. But Dagny could tell he was disappointed by the prospect.

It turned out that Gretchen didn't want to come anyway. So Dagny showed her the money chest, and asked her not to go too far, until she learned her way around. Then Max and Dagny left.

They walked to City Centre and boarded a canal ferry. A slight panic began to set in once Dagny realized they were headed south, further and further into the city. "I don't want to go anywhere near the Rakesmount, Max," she told him.

"Don't worry, we're not. I didn't wanna give away too much, but it's in Southend. Past where the maps end. It's nothing dangerous. It's quite peaceful, actually. You hate it that much, huh? The Rakesmount."

She glanced over her shoulder at the boatsman. He was focused on the waterways and could probably have cared less about their conversation. "I just have a lot of bad memories buried there," Dagny said. She realized she was hunched over and rolled her shoulders back. "They should've left that place in ruins. The new tenements are built on top of corpses."

"That's twisted," Max said.

The ferry took them to the edge of Southend, and they disembarked in front of a dusty sycamore tree that clung to the embankment. It was set to be a gloomy day, with the morning chill lasting longer than it should have. They stood for a moment, watching the boat slip off into the fog, before crossing the Grand South Canal. Southend was by far the largest district in the city. It spread deep into the peninsula and even trickled down to the marsh. No one really knew where it ended or where the original city boundary had once been. The whole thing was swallowed up by a string of shanty towns that grew, and died, and grew again, over the course of millennia.

There were few people on the streets today. A burly man pushed a sausage cart and disappeared around a bend. A woman in a stained coat slept on the ground, while two toddlers stood guard like a couple of rat terriers, glaring at Dagny when they passed.

Max took her to a square, brick building surrounded by scaffolding at the edge of a deep ditch. Several men worked on repairing the roof, and the building flew the black flag of the Southend Authority. The ditch marked the unofficial end of the Authority's jurisdiction. This is where most of the city maps stopped. On the other side of the ditch was simply "After Southend." The men on the roof watched as Dagny and Max crossed a small wooden bridge. Max nodded and waved, but the men only stared.

He led the way as they wandered deeper and deeper into the district. This part of Southend wasn't exactly a labyrinth, but it was close. Without Max, Dagny doubted she'd be able to find her way in, or out. Near the main throughway, the buildings were brick, old and unmaintained, but appeared sturdy. However, the further they got, the more decayed and rotten things became. The dwellings here were wood, built upon generations of toppled scrap. Yet, there were hints of something *older*, just under the surface. Something formidable. Spots where the road turned, momentarily, from dirt and mud into heavy grey stone; or when they walked by the head of an enormous statue, the size of a cart, rolled onto its side, staring blankly at the earth.

"The old palace sounds like a magical place," Max said, as they neared a crossroad. Opposite the path were a mausoleum and headstones overgrown with moss and vine. "I can't believe you went there. I'm jealous you got to see so much."

"It was surreal," Dagny said. "I wish you had come with us. It's almost impossible to explain."

"And Tash took you... that's great." Dagny couldn't tell if that's how Max really felt, but she doubted it. "How did you know your sister was there?" he asked.

"I didn't," Dagny said. "I was just hoping I would find something that could lead me to her. She had filled that sketchbook of hers with drawings of the place."

"Oh. Why?"

"Probably for comfort. Half of her book was drawings of stories that Morgan told us, and the rest were things from the old palace. Grete said those were from Morgan's stories, too. I don't remember them, but I feel like I've forgotten so much. Like there's a wall blocking me from remembering things." She looked at Max, who ran his hand along the black, piked fence bordering the graveyard. "Morgan probably told us hundreds of stories when we were little. I think he wanted to distract us from the misery of the Mount."

They walked along the fence until they reached a gaping hole of twisted iron. Max stepped through and took Dagny's hand, helping her over a jagged portion and onto the packed earth beyond.

In the middle of the graveyard, Max stopped and pointed to a small hilltop that rose in the distance over a line of buildings. It was covered in vegetation, like the wet jungle of the marsh had taken over the urban landscape in the middle of Southend. On top of the hill, Dagny could barely make out crumbled shapes and broken spires sticking through the canopy.

"Is that where we're headed?" Dagny asked, somewhat hesitantly.

"Yep."

They cut between two massive gravestones depicting twin harpies, and rested on a stone wall, where Max opened a tin of cheese and biscuits and offered some to her.

"Thanks," Dagny said. The biscuits tasted sweetly of honey. "You always come prepared, don't you?"

"I've gotten better at it. When me and Rodolph went to Glimmer Ghost, we ran out of food and spent an entire day hungry before getting back to the city. So now, even on day trips, I make sure to eat... a lot."

"I missed you," Dagny said, abruptly. "But I really hated how you talked to me."

Max nodded. His brow furrowed, his face was sad. "I know. I acted like a child. Sometimes I shut off. Especially when I feel like people I care about are pushing me away. But I'm not going to do that anymore. I'll prove it to you."

"I'm only saying this because I like you. What we have is really important to me. And you hurt me."

"I'm sorry. I really am. I want you to know how serious I am about that. You're important to me, too."

Dagny reached into the tin and took another biscuit. "These are good. Did you bake them?"

"No." Max stood and stretched, then reached for her hand. "C'mon."

Dagny followed him off the path and over a wild hedge of bramble weeds. They spent what seemed like an hour walking through the maze of Southend.

"What time is it?" she asked after awhile. "My legs are sore. I didn't think it'd be so far."

"We're getting close. Just through the hill coming up."

"Through?"

Max led her around a vacant building, and almost immediately they entered an area of wild jungle. Dagny heard what sounded like squeaking in distance.

"What is that?" she asked.

"Monkeys. They're harmless, but will steal anything you set down." Max pushed and swatted his way past branches and vines. If he was following a trail, it wasn't clear to her. She had no idea how he knew where to go.

Just then, a moss-mouthed cave opened in front of them.

"I didn't think we'd be going in caves today," Dagny said.

"Not a cave. It's a gate," he said, pointing out stacked stone under the foliage. "It's not far. This is just a passage to the other side, look."

Dagny crawled up to the entrance and peeked into the tunnel.

She was greeted by the sweet-rot scent of wet earth. Roots from trees above broke through a tile ceiling and twisted around stone pillars. A short distance away, the passage ended at a waterfall. Sunlight from the other side reflected against the water in shimmering rainbow waves.

"That's beautiful," Dagny said.

"Yeah, it's actually part of an old, broken aqueduct. But that's not what I want you to see. C'mon." Max hopped past her, rushed to the opposite side, and disappeared.

"Hey!" Dagny called, chasing after him; the spray from the waterfall wetting her face.

Max had wandered outside, onto a ledge, and stood there pointing. "Come here and look."

She skirted the waterfall and stepped into the sunlight, joining him on the ledge. Below was a pond, peaceful and serene. Its basin full of colorful stones. Slowly, Dagny began to make out man-made shapes carved into the high walls that surrounded them: stone steps leading into the pond; alcoves in the rock containing the blotchy and weathered forms of statues. Above them were more ruins, the remnants of an old temple, perhaps. She had a sense that they were intruding on something sacred.

"What is this place?" Dagny asked.

"Take a guess," Max said.

"I have no idea. Something religious?"

"You're not far off. This was an artisan glass factory. An ancient one. Probably the first in the city."

"Really?" Dagny looked down at the water. "So those colorful stones..."

"—It's all glass. Leftovers from a thousand years ago."

"And those statues?"

"I think those would've been former masters, or famous artists of the time. They've been molding glass in this city since the beginning. I don't think anyone else knows about this place, though. I spent some time pulling maps in the libraries and nothing marks it. I haven't seen anyone else here, either. No one except the monkeys, that is."

"How did *you* find it?"

"The day after our fight, I was helping my brothers collect stones from old buildings in Southend, and I just stumbled upon it. You said you liked ancient things, right?"

Dagny laughed. "Yeah."

"I haven't shown anyone else," Max said.

"Really? Not Rodolph?"

"Nah. No one knows about it except me, and now you. Wanna go down to the water?" Max asked, and started down a narrow path before she could respond.

"...An ancient glass factory, hidden by the jungle in the middle of Southend," Dagny said, following behind him. "I'm afraid I don't know that story."

"Maybe it hasn't been told yet," Max replied. "The jungle, the forests, all of the old world... it's just waiting to take everything back. We don't really belong here. None of us. We're just intruding for a time."

A small pebble beach had formed around the base of the pond. Max picked up one of the stones and skipped it across the water.

"Why didn't you tell Rodo and Kim about it?" Dagny asked.

"I'm not sure. It felt kind of special to me." He shrugged. "Maybe I just didn't want anyone else to know."

"Until now?"

Max laughed. "Yeah..." It felt like he was about to say something else, but stopped himself.

Dagny walked close to him. She wanted to feel the energy of his body. There was no thought to it, it was all instinct.

"I've never been good at skipping rocks," she said, picking up a random one off the ground.

"Here... just, umm, hold it like this." Max made a gesture with his hand, like he was holding an invisible bird. "And then you just... fling it."

Dagny backed herself into his chest, and looked out toward the water. "Show me..." She could feel his stomach rise and fall with each breath, and pressed closer to him, almost knocking him off balance.

"Yeah, alright." He took her hand and slowly swept through the motion of flinging the rock.

"Max..." she said.

"Yeah?"

"I don't really care about throwing rocks."

Before he could respond, she turned around and kissed him. She didn't have much practice, but found his lips on the first try, breathing in deep and closing her eyes. Max's pulse quickened against her body; she felt a quiver, and for a moment thought he might reject her. But then his hands were on her waist, and when she risked peeking at him, his eyes were closed as well.

Dagny wasn't quite sure how long it should last. She wanted to keep going, but was afraid of being weird. She pulled away, and he pulled her back into him, kissing Dagny deeper than before.

Her breath caught in her chest, like she was on top of a mountain taking in the frigid air. She touched his face. It was smooth, free from any trace of stubble. At the same time, his fingers found the back of her neck. It felt like he had reached inside and spread his hands over her heart.

"You're beautiful," Max whispered. It felt awkward, hearing him say it. No one had ever told her that before. She no longer wanted to just kiss him, she wanted to give herself over completely. Taking his hand, Dagny placed it on her breast.

"Can you feel my heart beat?" she asked. He answered by kissing her neck, and reaching down her back with his free hand.

"You tell me when to stop," he said.

"It's okay, you can touch me. I want you to." She was outside of herself, a flurry of surreal emotions. Foreign, but welcomed. His fingers were on her bare skin. They slipped into her pants and rested below her waist. She was suddenly conscious of her skinny body as Max traced the edge of her hip. His hand felt strong and warm.

"Am I enough for you?" she asked, feeling incredibly vulnerable.

Max pulled back and looked at her. He had a concerned expression on his face, almost sad. "Why would you ask that?"

"I... don't know."

"I think I'm in love with you."

"Touch me again," she said, and he did.

∞

Dagny lay next to him for a long time after, on top of their coats, on top of the pebbled beach. Resting naked in the sun.

Max had fallen asleep, and Dagny watched his chest rise and fall. A pale, horseshoe scar rested just below his collarbone. Otherwise his body was tanned brown, like he'd spent every day since birth on the lagoon.

She didn't know if what they had done meant anything, or even if it needed to. She just wanted to feel him again, and almost touched his lips to wake him and insist they do just that. But instead, she sat up and gazed across the water.

The shadows from the surrounding hill covered most of the pond now, stretching almost to the shore. What types of people worked here in the distant past? Quietly, Dagny slipped away from Max, walked to the edge of the water, and gazed at the ruins above. *What kind of mysteries are you hiding inside?*

She had company: a small brown monkey moved off to her left, climbing into an alcove above her. Dagny watched it for a moment, then crept close. The animal locked eyes with her and cocked its head.

"Hello, there," she whispered. "I'm not going to hurt you." Its fur was the color of honey and cream, and it had the most incredible, light-blue eyes.

"You found one of the resident watchmen," Max said, still lying on the beach, his voice soft and sleepy.

"Yeah. It's beautiful. I've never seen one like it. Do they all have blue eyes?"

"Most of them, yeah." He studied her for a moment. "I like looking at you," he added.

Instinctively, Dagny covered herself. "I'm starting to get cold."

Max looked away, and started to dress. "We should probably head back, or it's going to be dark before we get out of Southend."

"Okay," she sighed. "If we have to." She probably should check on Grete. It had been rough for her this morning. But Dagny wanted to stay here with Max, and everything else felt like a burden.

"We don't *have* to do anything, I suppose. We could stay as long as you want."

"I wish we could just stay," she said, pulling her shirt over her head. "Thanks, by the way."

Max gave her an odd look. "For what?"

"Everything."

They left the hidden pond, and began the trek back to Rork.

"Why is everyone saying there's a treasure in Glimmer Ghost?" Dagny asked, as the sun began to set behind them.

"A king used to live under that mountain. So it just makes sense that there'd be something there, but who really knows," Max said, with a shrug.

"You have any interest in going back?"

"Who knows."

"Rodolph was practically planning an expedition last night," Dagny said, gazing up at him as they walked back through the graveyard.

"He was drunk. Besides, there's other things I'm focused on at the moment."

"Like what?"

He shrugged again and buried his hands in his jacket. "Like you, I guess."

"Aww... you're sweet."

Darkness had descended well before they reached the nearest ferry station. By the time they crossed City Centre and entered Rork, all the shops and cafes had been closed for hours, and no one else wandered the streets.

"You're probably starving," Dagny said. "I know I am. Come in and I'll make you something." She wanted Max to stay in her room tonight. She wanted to watch him sleep, in case she couldn't.

He didn't respond, and started to whistle a tune.

Despite the late hour, there were lights on inside the Benzara house, and Dagny heard talking when she opened the front door.

"Hello?" she called.

It was Grete who answered. Her voice sounded light and energetic. "We're in here."

Dagny rounded the corner into the study and saw Grete sitting with Tash, opposite a Talvarind board.

"I already beat him once," Grete said, grinning.

Tash just shook his head. "I came over looking for you, and she asked me to teach her the game... Hi Max."

"—Hey."

It was strange seeing Tash with her sister, in the same place she often played with Lucas. Grete seemed happy. Her eyes were alive, and she chewed her lip as she advanced her Red Guard. There was no way she beat Tash, however, unless he let her. And Tash had never let Dagny win.

"Did you go anywhere today?" Dagny asked.

Grete answered while still focused on the game board. "No. I got worried about you, though."

"Oh, I'm fine."

Grete glanced up and gave her a sly, knowing look. "I see that."

Dagny felt her face flush. "I'm going to warm the fisher's stew," she said quickly, and walked off to the kitchen.

Max was behind her at the icebox. "I'm not really hungry," he said.

"Oh. Okay. Did you wanna see my room?"

"I already seen it, remember?"

"Right... wanna see it again?"

Dagny's heart raced as they walked up the stairs, and the instant they reached the top, Max lifted her into the air and Dagny wrapped her legs around his torso, kissing him passionately. Their mouths were so much wetter than before, and Dagny had to laugh and wipe her chin.

He dropped her on the bed and flung his shirt onto the floor, then suddenly stopped and looked around, slowly. "This really is a nice room... Is this where you spend most of your time?"

Dagny smiled and shook her head. "...I guess."

"What do you do? Read books?"

"Get over here before I change my mind and fall asleep."

Max laughed and jumped on the bed next to her. "Do you think your sister will care? I don't want her thinking bad of me."

"No. She'd care if you didn't do anything. Besides, I think she's working on something of her own, downstairs."

"With Tash? Really?"

"I don't wanna talk about that right now." She kicked her boots off and slid out of her pants. "Kiss me."

His tongue was in her mouth when he pushed himself inside her. Dagny caught her breath, then sighed and grabbed his hair. "Tell me if I'm doing this right, okay," she said.

Max just nodded. She could feel his eyes on her neck and chest. The first time had been so rushed and crazy and unexpectedly out of control. She'd been more concerned about getting through it without making a fool of herself.

This time was more focused. She concentrated on his movements and the enjoyment of feeling his body. When it was over, Dagny turned to the side and closed her eyes. Feeling strangely complete.

She didn't want him to leave and was glad when she heard his breathing become slow and heavy. A long time passed before she was able to fall asleep herself, but when she did, she slept til morning. And without dreaming.

22

Weeks later, Dagny found herself walking through the Viddry Park Zoo with Max and Grete. Her sister was almost unrecognizable from the girl in the grove, with her chopped, blue hair and newly tailored clothes. No one would think this was a Limer's Town exile.

Max stopped in front of the captured wolf enclosure and watched. Four of the creatures lounged about on rocks and dirt, staring back at them.

"It's sad, don't you think," Max said. "Imprisoned like that."

Dagny took his hand, and pulled him toward the aviary. "I don't disagree, but there's only so much someone can do. At least they won't starve here."

"Personally, I'd rather starve."

"When you become governor, you can offer them freedom," she said.

Max nodded. "Maybe I will be. You never know."

For the past few weeks, Dagny had spent every day with Max and Grete. Tash came by on occasion to play Talvarind, or to share lunch outside in the courtyard. He stayed over last night, falling asleep in Alex's study, while reading Kofric's *Ruminations.*

Grete had been adjusting surprisingly well, ever since that day after Stardust. It was like the swish of a match. A light was lit and a different person began to emerge. It helped that Alex had replied to Dagny's letter. *Of course she can live with us*, Alex wrote. *Gretchen is welcome to stay for as long as needed.* The child was born, too. A son. Named Morgan. *I hope that's alright with you. He was the closest friend I ever had. It was Cate's idea actually. We wanted to wait to tell you, to make certain we had a boy.*

Grete took the vacant room next to Dagny, on the second floor. They spent two full days scouring the market and craftsmen shops, picking out furnishings that would suit Grete's new life. She also picked out a small flute. Alice had begun to teach her the basics of melody. "I miss her," Grete said. "I hope she's alright. I didn't mean what I told you before. Alice *was* a friend. She was kind to me."

They heard that Sarna and Hanette had returned from Vahnes. Rodolph spotted them the other night at Stardust. Dagny hadn't been there since the argument.

"I'd like to apologize to them," Grete said this morning, before heading to the zoo. "You know where they live? Think we can go to their house later?"

After the aviary, they took a short walk through the City Centre Park, and back to Rork.

"I'll let you two go to Sarna's without me," Max said. "I think I'd just complicate matters. She kind of closes off when I'm around."

"Thanks," Dagny said, and kissed his cheek. "Come over tonight though, okay?"

They found Sarna in front of her home, watering potted flowers. Dagny waited for a moment, nervous about how to approach. It had been almost a month since they'd seen each other.

"Excuse me," Grete said from behind, softly.

Sarna spun around. "Oh. You scared me," she said. Her voice didn't carry the same joyful resonance that it typically did. She seemed guarded and cold. "What are you doing here?"

Dagny felt like crying.

"I was hoping to talk with you and your sister," Grete said.

"She's not here. And why would you wanna do that?" Sarna held the watering can in front of her, ready to block them from moving forward.

"I want to apologize to her... and you."

"Alright. I'll let her know. Is that all?"

"Sarna..." Dagny said. "Please don't."

"Don't what?"

"Throw me away like that."

Sarna's face softened somewhat. "Throw *you* away? You threw *me* away. You really hurt me, you know."

"I'm really sorry. I'm just so confused. I don't know what to do."

"—It's my fault," Grete said. "Don't put this on Dag. She cares about you. My anger gets the best of me sometimes. I'm still trying to figure this all out... But your sister was kind of asking for it."

Dagny slowly turned her head to Grete, then looked back at Sarna. The girl's brow furrowed, and her purple hair hung messy over her soft, round face. Then, suddenly, Sarna began to smile.

"Yeah. I suppose she kinda was. But still, you can't say things like that, alright?"

Grete nodded. "I know."

Sarna glanced between them, still guarded. "I'll forgive you, and maybe Hanette will too, in time." She took a moment before speaking again. "You want to come inside? I have a lot to tell you, about Vahnes and everything. The Harvest Fest was *incredible*."

Sarna poured them tea and described her recent travels up the Morca, through the river towns of Satchels and Iverry. She alluded to drunken nights with *Marfisi and the Mirage.* So many troupes and artists and joyful vagabonds had poured into Vahnes for the festival. "It was like the city had been conquered by the freest of spirits. It was almost life-changing."

"It sounds like you and *The Mirage* have been getting along well," Dagny began, when Sarna cut her off.

"—I'm actually going to see them soon." Then Sarna's eyes widened. "You two should come with me! There's no reason we shouldn't all be friends. Don't worry, Hanette isn't there. She's with Telga. What do you say?"

Dagny looked at Grete. "Sure, why not."

They were staying outside of the city, on the long road to Sternhome. *The Mirage* consisted of Marfisi (its singer), Feruda on strings, and two brothers: Vega and Vex. Sarna tried to act nonchalant when mentioning Feruda.

They left the city via the River Gate. The land out there seemed immense. Stretching on forever. It was a kind of lazy day, with cool autumn air and a warm sun, and none of the restrictions of time or space that the city demanded. They turned away from the river and entered high, open fields, traveling southward under gigantic clouds. In the distance, small villages sprang from the land, set along roads birthed by the city. Even further still was the forest and the jagged grey outline of Glimmer Ghost Peak.

Finally, just after noon, they stopped at a simple crossroads with an inn and several buildings. *The Mirage* were all staying together in the attic of an old stable here, converted into living quarters. As they approached the open stable doors, Dagny could hear music coming from inside.

"It sounds like they're working on a new song," Sarna whispered. "I haven't heard this one before, and I was sure I'd heard them all."

Vega, a boy younger than Grete, met them at the entrance. He wore a baggy coat made from something coarse, like burlap. "There's no drums in this one," he said, softly. "So I gotta sit out."

Grete slowly approached the small circle of musicians. Feruda sat cross-legged plucking a guitar, next to Vex. She was very pretty, with jet black hair and fair skin. Her thin eyebrows connected into a single wispy line. She seemed talented. Dagny could see why Sarna was drawn to her. Marfisi sat nearby, humming a melody.

The musicians wore an assortment of mismatched clothes that all blended together in an odd way: loose wool socks bunched around ankles; split stockings and pleated skirts; patched vests; greys and browns with a streak of red from a tattered scarf; a hint of green. The boys had sooty circles under their eyes, resembling a pair of badgers. The whole group looked like someone constructed them after rummaging the junk piles.

Grete stared at Marfisi, as if in a trance. Suddenly, Feruda stopped playing and grinned. "Sarna!"

The girl jumped up and ran to them. Before Sarna could say anything, Feruda stepped into her arms and embraced her.

Marfisi smiled politely and bowed her head. "Welcome."

"Hello," Dagny said. "I saw you once before at the Ironhead. It was really great."

"—Was that a new song?" Sarna asked Feruda.

But it was Grete who spoke. "Not new. I've heard it before."

The musicians all looked at her. "You're mistaken," Marfisi said. "We've never played it for people."

"It's an old one, isn't it?" Grete said.

Marfisi shook her head, keeping her polite smile. "You're mistaken."

"No. No. I know it." Grete reached in her bag and pulled out the small flute she'd purchased from the market. "I'm not very good..." she said, pressing her lips to the instrument.

The musicians patiently watched her, as Grete blew out the melody, slow but clear. When she had made her way through several bars, Grete lowered the flute and said, "That's it, right?"

Dagny noticed the boys and Feruda looking at Marfisi, who offered another smile, somewhat forced, before speaking. "How do you know that song?"

"I don't really remember," Grete said. "I think, maybe, I heard it..." She stopped herself. "I'm not really sure."

"Are you hungry?" Marfisi asked the group. "We have yet to eat, today."

Sarna nodded. "I'm starving."

They left the stables for the inn. When Dagny glanced back, she noticed Feruda quietly speaking with Marfisi.

Other than several farmhands, there was no one else inside the common room. Dagny quietly ate, listening to the group talk of Vahnes and a future trip to Caltra Island. Sarna held Feruda's hand under the table and didn't look at Dagny once.

Dagny felt like an outcast and wondered what Max was doing. She wanted to be with him right now. She should've just apologized to Sarna and returned home. Grete gave her a look, like she knew what Dagny was thinking, and nodded.

Just then, Marfisi touched Grete's shoulder, and asked to speak with her outside. "It'll just be a moment, nothing to worry about."

Nothing to worry about? Dagny thought that was an odd comment. Grete agreed, and Dagny followed them into the courtyard, half expecting Marfisi to stop her.

"I'd like you to tell me where you learned that melody," Marfisi said.

Grete cocked her head, confused. "Like I said, I don't really remember."

"Is that the truth?" Marfisi wasn't confronting her, but spoke out of genuine curiosity and concern.

Grete opened her mouth, ready to repeat the same line, then shook her head. "It's going to sound strange."

"That melody is of ancient Jud," Marfisi said. "You couldn't have heard it before. We are the only ones who've taken it from the woods. Do you understand? It's not possible."

"But... I did hear it before," Grete said.

"But, you did." Marfisi pursed her lips, considering something. "Will you take a walk with us, into the trees?" She pointed to the western forest. "I don't want to reveal anything yet. I'm just curious."

The road skirted the great woods, before cutting back toward the open fields. The trees here were massive things, blocking out the sun and casting long shadows across the grass. There was no one within eyesight when Marfisi stepped off the road and into the forest.

The singer and her companions seemed natural walking through here, across the roots and stones, and pushing into the brush. Dagny walked next to Grete but checked in occasionally on Sarna, who seemed just as confused as she was.

Further and further they went, until the farmland was nothing more than a forgotten thought. As though it never existed. They traveled down a sloping hill, deep within the forest, when Marfisi finally stopped, at a boulder the size of a house.

"Do you recognize this place?" she asked. It took Dagny a moment to realize she was speaking to her sister.

"I don't think so," Grete said.

"Just take your time. What do you *think* is beyond the way?"

Vega and Vex watched Grete like excited children, chewing their lips, trying not to blurt out the answer.

Grete closed her eyes. "I... it's a tower, isn't it? I see a slender spire, dark blue... almost black, like the night. And a trail through the brush. An animal's trail."

"Yes," Marfisi whispered. "That is how it *used* to look. The spire is broken now but still stretches into the sky."

"What is going on?" Dagny asked, nervously. "What is this place?"

Marfisi continued to look at Grete as she spoke. "This marks the farthest reaches of Lazim, The Eternal Forest. And the tower you envision is the Nedgling Tower. The tallest one ever made. Although it is only a ruin of its former self."

Dagny felt a panic building within her. "Why did you bring us here?" she demanded. "What do you want from my sister?"

"Before the city was built. Before the withering. This marked a passage into the Great Below." Marfisi gently took hold of Grete's wrist. "You know who we are searching for, don't you?"

"Who?" Grete asked. "I *don't* know."

"Come with us. We'll show you the way home."

Dagny grabbed Marfisi's hand and flung it off of her sister. "No!" she shouted. "She's not going anywhere with you! Leave us alone!"

Marfisi was unfazed. She stood there calmly. "It is not your decision to make, Dagny. It is *hers*."

Grete looked nervously at the group. "No. I don't wanna go. I wanna go home. To *my* home. Not yours." Then she turned around and started back up the hill.

23

DAGNY SAT ALONE BY the Morca docks, watching the boats come into the city from the west. Max had been gone for three days, on a trip upriver with his father. She didn't plan to meet him here; he wasn't returning until this evening and said he'd come over as soon as they docked. She just didn't have anything better to do right now, or so she told herself. Truth was, Max had been on her mind constantly. When he wasn't around, her stomach turned in knots. But when she was with him, everything calmed down and she could just exist. Nothing else mattered.

For his part, Max seemed to be particularly upset about leaving. "Don't worry," Dagny had told him. "This'll give me more time to spend with Grete. I feel like I've been ignoring her." The comment frustrated Max, and he told her he didn't want to be the reason for that. But there was more to it. Ever since the forest, Grete had retreated into herself again. The experience with Marfisi had upset her deeply. Dagny didn't know what to do, or how to be there for her sister, so she just left her alone, thinking Grete needed some space.

The boats continued to come into the city as evening approached, but there was no sign of Max and his father yet. Watching the river, Dagny thought about how little she really knew of her surroundings. As much as she studied and had learned about the countryside from books and stories, she'd hardly been anywhere. All the towns upriver: Satchels, Iverry, Aladare and Sternhome, and eventually Vahnes; Dagny'd never been to any of them.

Two months ago, Dagny would've given anything to travel upriver and escape the boring, peaceful privilege of Old Rork, but now things just felt different.

One of the long, flat barges pulled against the dockside and moored. Half a dozen laborers rushed over to begin the slow process of unloading, and a stream of passengers trickled out along a narrow plank. They were all men of a similar age.

The night before Max left, he mentioned that some of the Marsh Rats had disappeared. He didn't know if Corlie or Jorgie were among them. "Rodolph would know more about it," he told Dagny. "I'll go with you when I get back, if you want." But Dagny couldn't wait that long, and she wandered over to Rodolph's house the next day with Tash.

It took Rodolph a while to open the door. When he did, he was glistening with sweat and had an awkward smile on his face.

"Hi Dagny, need something?" he asked, paying no attention to Tash, who stood just behind her.

"Hello," she said. "Didn't want to bother you."

"No. You're good." But his eyes looked rushed.

Dagny got right to the point. "I wanted to ask you about the Marsh Rats. Max mentioned something happened."

"Yeah. Some of them went out to one of the islands, I heard, and never came back."

"Do you know if Corlie or Jorgie was with them?"

"That girl from the stilt houses? I doubt it. And not Jorgie. It was a bunch of men and a couple of the higher-ups. You remember that guy Ferko?"

"He was the older one, right?" she answered. "The man in the blue greatcoat who was yelling at me about the Oracle Tower."

"Yeah. A real treat, that one. He's one of the people that vanished."

"Do you think they went to Farrow Blood?"

"I couldn't tell you."

Telga stepped into the light behind him. She wore Rodolph's black jacket and nothing else. She didn't say anything, but stared at Dagny impatiently.

"Oh, sorry," Dagny said. "I didn't mean to disturb you."

Rodolph smiled awkwardly. "Don't worry. I'll see you around." He closed the door before she could say anything else.

Dagny nervously turned and looked at Tash. "I'm sorry… I didn't know she was here."

Tash seemed surprisingly unconcerned. "That's alright. I don't care."

"You don't? Is that true?"

"Yeah, it's true. Come on, let's go to City Centre. I promised Grete I'd pick up some sweet bread on the way back."

Jauson Tasher had seemed unconcerned with lots of things recently. He ended up losing his second tournament in a row to Lana Dusk – and didn't care. "It's only a game," he had said. It was certainly odd, but Tash was still himself. He just seemed much more carefree.

A ship's bell rang and Dagny anxiously scanned the river. There was still no sign of Max. She was beginning to wonder if she should just get something to eat and head home, when a man approached.

"Excuse me, do you know where I can find a coach to take me north?" he asked her. The man had a rough-cut face and carried a large canvas traveler's bag. He looked to be about Alex's age.

Dagny glanced over her shoulder, back toward the warehouses and market square. "If you head that way, there's a coach house on the opposite end of the plaza."

"Okay, thanks. Think they'd still be running in an hour? I was hoping to get a meal before heading out." He set the canvas bag down at his feet and rubbed his shoulder.

"I don't know. I think so."

"Good. It's been a long trip."

Dagny didn't really care to have this conversation, but the politeness of her Rork upbringing took over. "*Arlen's Roasted Hen* is nearby and real good."

"Thanks again." He smiled and sat down next to her, letting out a long sigh. "I should get a better pair of boots. Once they turn on you, that's it."

"Are you traveling far?" she asked.

"Yeah. Afraid so. I'd like to spend more time in the city, but adventure calls."

"Oh, are you an adventurer?"

"I suppose so. I suppose most of us are, in our own way, don't you think?"

"Some of us... not most," Dagny answered. She continued to watch the water, but was also keeping an eye on the man.

"I'll be heading north toward Ostrotha, and then, who knows? I've spent way too much time stationary in my life. Long as it's been. I owe it to myself to carve another path, if that makes sense."

"It does."

He nodded. "You don't mind if I just rest here a bit, do you? I don't wanna make you uncomfortable."

Dagny appreciated him asking. "It's fine. I don't mind the company."

"Thanks. You waiting for someone?"

"Yes. He'll be here soon."

"That's good. It's important to have people in your life. The right ones, anyway."

"It is," she agreed.

"I'm all out of friends and family. I hope it'll change. Who knows what'll happen, but I'm looking forward to it. I feel like everyone has a family except me."

"That's not true. A lot of people are alone."

"Yeah? And what about you?" the man asked.

"No, I'm lucky that way."

He pushed his eyebrows together, in a sort of half-frown. "Yeah. I suppose you would be."

"It wasn't always like that, though," she said. "In fact, it was pretty recent that I found them."

"Found 'em?"

"Yeah. My sister. She just came into my life recently. I thought she was dead."

"That's rough," he said, nodding with sympathy. "A dead sister, and you're so young. I'm glad it turned out better for you."

"Yeah..." Where was Max? The frequency of ships coming down river had slowed considerably. "...Did you see lots of boats on the river when you came in?"

"I didn't come down river," the man said.

"Oh, you didn't? I figured you stepped off that barge."

"No."

"Where did you come from, then?" Dagny asked.

The man laughed. "You haven't figured it out, girl?"

Dagny scrunched her face and looked at him, confused. "...No... how would I know that?"

"Just thought you were smart."

She studied him more closely now. He had thin lips and sharp features, but charming eyes. And although he wasn't that old, there was a hardness to him. "Who are you?" she asked.

"Oh... I think you know who I am, Dagny Losh."

"How do you know my name? Who *are* you?" she repeated. But before he answered, she realized it.

Sliver. She gasped, and started to recoil from him.

"Don't worry. I'm not gonna hurt you. But don't run away," he said. "Got it?"

She nodded and had to force herself to remain seated. She looked over her shoulder and scanned the area for other people.

"There's no one else," Sliver continued. "I'm alone."

"Why are you here? Grete isn't with me. She's far away, you'll never find her," Dagny blurted out.

"Calm down. I don't know what she told you, but I'm not after her."

"Of course you are."

"No." He crossed his arms and stretched out his long legs. "I was upset when she left and, I admit, I didn't handle it well. But I'm all better now."

"So why are you here, then?"

"I came to warn her, but I figured I could never get close enough for her to listen. She was one of my favorites, that girl."

"Warn her? About what? You're the only one who's a threat."

Sliver shook his head. "Dead Girl never really *knew* me. Limer's Town corrupts everything. It's not an easy place to live, and an even tougher place to thrive. And me? I'm a thriver."

"I'm not gonna tell you where she is," Dagny said forcefully.

"I wouldn't expect you to." His face was relaxed, and Sliver took a deep breath as he stared out at the river.

"So what do you need to warn her about?"

"My old *friends*. They're coming for her."

"What do you mean, your old friends? Your gang?" Dagny asked. "You left them?"

"I didn't have much of a choice. You can feel when people start to turn on you. It's a gift I have. So I cleaned everything out before Jago and them could slit my throat, and I'm following my own path now. Anyway, they're after that box themselves now. Or what was in it."

"This doesn't make sense. Why are you telling me this? And why would you waste time finding me, just to warn Grete, when you wanted to kill her?"

Sliver glared at her, sending a chill through Dagny. "I never wanted to kill her, got it? She never understood me. She just saw me as a product of that place. I actually liked her. I brought her close to me, and she just couldn't appreciate it. I mean, Jago? He wouldn't have been as kind as me, if he'd taken possession first."

"If you really cared, you wouldn't have told everyone that Grete stole that box of yours. If you really cared, you'd tell Jago and those men the *truth*." Dagny was almost yelling.

"You need to learn how to control your emotions," Sliver said, calmly. "Shit like that will get you killed."

"...You should've told them the truth," Dagny repeated, quietly.

"What are you talking about?" Sliver said. "I did tell them the truth."

"No. You lied and said Grete took the box. She didn't."

"She may not have taken the box itself, but she took what was inside, and that's close enough."

"What? Took what was inside? You're lying again," Dagny said.

"I found the empty box the night she left. Stuffed under my mattress. Dead Girl had solved it... solved the puzzle... Smart girl, that one."

Dagny studied his face, trying to determine if Sliver was lying, before muttering, "If you didn't see her do it, you don't know it was her. You can't be certain."

"You think I allow lots of people in my private rooms? Dead Girl was the only one."

"How can I believe you? How do I know you're not tricking me?" Dagny felt foolish asking such childish questions, but she didn't know what else to say.

"Think whatever you want... I'm leaving shortly, and you'll never see me again. I just didn't want to leave without telling her. Must be my good nature." He stood up and lifted his bag. "I'm redefining myself. I'm leaving my old life behind. Truthfully, I'm glad to be rid of that awful burden."

"The box, you mean?"

"It drew all sorts of bad things to it. Weird, strange things."

Dagny thought of the pale, bloated face in the dark, and the naked woman. "That dark place, near the church. Your men chased me there. They were afraid to enter."

"Yeah. *Things* had been showing up. They were coming for the box, I'm sure of it. One of them caught and dragged poor Landry by the old church there. Heard him screaming for days. Well. Goodbye."

Dagny jumped to her feet. "One more question. How did you find me?" Then realized it. "Alice... What did you do to her?"

"Not me. Jago went to work on her. And after she spilled her secrets, it wasn't tough for me to find you. I'm smarter and quicker than they are, though. Still, it won't be long before they find you, too."

"Is she okay? Alice?"

"Alice is gone, girl. You shoulda figured that one out, at least." With nothing left to say, Sliver turned and walked off.

Dagny didn't know what to do. She almost expected Sliver's men to come running out of the shadows. Jago's wolf-eyes and orange mustache were still sharp in her mind. And the way he had grabbed her... hurt her, like she was nothing, less than human. The fat man with the tattooed head still laughed in her mind. She could even remember their smell. The spice and the smoke. What had they done to Alice? That sweet lady who'd helped her, and helped Grete... Alice had said she was twisted like everything in Limer's Town, but Dagny knew she had a kind heart, and was unbelonging of that place.

She instinctively moved into an alley between two warehouses and tried to get her head straight. Max still wasn't here... *Where are you?* she thought. *I need you now.* She couldn't wait any longer. She needed to get back to Rork and warn Grete, but then what? What could they do?

Maris.

Maris was staying at the... where did he say, again? Somewhere in River's End. The something Goose... *Think damnit.*

Dagny took the backroads to City Centre and rushed down the pathways that split the Rork gardens to reach the Benzara house. It was possible Jago and the others had followed Sliver here. She couldn't take any chances.

The kitchen windows were open, and Dagny locked the back door behind her before slamming them shut. She ran to the front, past the study where Grete and Tash sat, and locked it, too.

"Dag?" Grete called. "...What are you doing?"

"Check those windows! Make sure everything is shut tight." Dagny grabbed two chairs from the dining room and barred the front door.

"You're scaring me," Grete said, standing in the hall. Tash, however, sensed her urgency and rushed to the windows.

After the house was locked up, Dagny continued to go through the place like a mad person, drawing every curtain and turning out the lights. Finally, she opened Alex's weapon armoire and removed the rifle and sabres.

Grete grabbed her. "Stop it. Tell me now. Is it Sliver?"

"Yes. He's not here, but I saw him."

Grete gasped, fear spreading across her face. "Where?"

"At the river docks... he found me... said he wanted to warn you."

"He followed you! I know it!" Grete spun around and stared at the front door.

"No. He didn't. I watched him leave. He told me he fled Limer's Town... that Jago and the others turned on him, and that he was leaving the area forever."

"What did he want to warn me of?" Grete looked skeptical.

"The other men. They're after the box. Whatever was in it."

"I told you—"

"I know... you didn't take it. I told Sliver that, but he said he found the box after you left. It was open, and empty."

"I don't know nothing about that," Grete said.

"It doesn't matter. They think you took it, and they know about me. Know I live in the city."

"How?"

Dagny almost didn't tell her, but felt her sister needed to know. "...Alice."

"What did they do?" Grete asked, and when Dagny shook her head, she started to cry.

"What are we gonna do?" Tash asked, quietly.

"Maris might still be in the city," Dagny said. "I think we need to try and find him first."

"Who?" Grete asked.

"Maris Troipel. A friend of Alex. He'll keep us safe."

Grete nodded. "Okay."

On the way home from the river docks, Dagny had thought about going to Cate's estate and directly to Alex, then thought against it. What if they were caught in the open fields? There would be no one to help. And besides, as much as she needed to protect Grete, she couldn't lead these men to Lucas and Abrielle and the new baby.

"I can go find Maris on my own," Dagny said. "You and Tash hide here. Take the rifle."

"No. We'll go together," Grete said. There was something in her eyes that told Dagny not to argue.

The Ground Goose... that was it. Tash and Grete followed closely behind Dagny, through the alleys and across the Central Bridge. She wrapped the rifle in a blanket and carried it under her arm. Hopefully there would be no need for it tonight. Dagny had never fired the gun before, and wasn't sure she could, even against men like Jago. But if she saw them, she would find out.

They reached River's End and stuck close to the Morca. Most of the inns would be hugging the waterline. Still, they didn't know where it was, and sent Tash into a late-night drinking hole to ask. The *Goose* turned out to be an old water-stained building at the end of the road, built right at the edge of the city, overlooking the lagoon. It seemed deserted.

Dagny handed the rifle to Grete. "I'll go inside, by myself. You two stay out here and hide. Have you ever used a gun before?"

Grete shook her head.

"Tash?" Dagny asked.

"No, but I have an idea."

"Just point and pull the trigger," she said, trying to sound confident. "Hopefully, just the sight of it will send trouble away. You probably won't even need it, though."

∞

A small fire slowly burned out in the empty common room, casting a glow over warped wooden tables and floorboards. Dagny approached the bar. No one was here, but she heard the sound of clanging metal from beyond, and tried to get a glimpse into the kitchen.

"Hello?" she called out.

An older woman appeared and coughed. Dagny didn't wait for the woman to talk. “Can you tell me where Maris Troipel is?”

“Don’t know who that is?” the woman said.

“Are you the proprietor here?”

“The what, now?”

“The owner. The innkeeper,” Dagny explained.

“Don’t I wish? The owner lives way over in Barchpool, but he don’t come around.”

Dagny nodded and tried her best to describe Maris. The woman just frowned and shook her head. “No one here like that.”

“Maybe he slipped in when someone else was working and you didn’t see him. Can you tell me which rooms are occupied?”

“Won’t do you any good. If I didn’t see him, he didn’t come in,” the woman said, pointing to her milky eyeball.

“Can you just tell me?” Dagny repeated, impatiently. "I'll check myself."

The woman shook her head again. “There ain’t no one here. Just you and me. No one’s stayed here for months...”

Months?

The word echoed in Dagny’s head, as she made her way back to Rork with Tash and Grete. When she had walked out of the *Goose*, she stared up at the sign for a long while, thinking she’d made a mistake... but it was the *Ground Goose* alright, and there wasn’t a single light on upstairs. Did Maris lie to her? Why would he do that? He just didn’t wanna help her, that’s why... and *lied* about it. She felt abandoned and helpless.

With nowhere else to go, they snuck back into the Benzara house through the kitchen door. Dagny locked it, barred it with a chair and scanned the room for any sign of a disturbance.

"We should all stay together tonight. We can figure something out in the morning," Dagny said. "Let's sleep in my room. If we need to, we can escape out the trellis."

Grete grabbed her hand. "I'm so sorry... I didn't wanna do this to you."

"It'll be alright," Dagny said. "We just gotta be careful. I'll get a note out to Alex tomorrow morning."

They pushed one of Dagny's dressers against the bedroom door, and as Tash and Grete sat on the mattress, Dagny stepped onto her balcony to get a look around. The streets were empty and the grand oaks rustled in the wind. Just when she was about to go back inside, Dagny spotted something at her front door. A shape on the ground. She stared at it for a while, straining her eyes. It didn't move, but she began to recognize features, and clothing, and a braid of dark hair.

24

A SENSE OF DREAD overtook Dagny as she raced down the trellis to the courtyard below. She landed hard and rushed to the side gate. *Max... please... please be okay.* Her foot caught a raised brick, and she stumbled, almost falling. Dizzy from panic.

"*Max...*" His name caught in her throat. He lay curled on his side, not moving, but then, slowly, he opened his sleepy eyes and smiled.

A wave of emotion forced Dagny to her knees, sobbing.

Max sprung up and embraced her. "Dag, what is it? What's wrong?"

She shook her head, and touched his face. She tried to talk, but couldn't stop crying.

Grete called down to them from the balcony. Max asked her to unlock the front door, then picked Dagny up, and carried her inside. He brought her upstairs, to the bedroom, and laid her down. Dagny could feel Grete and Tash's eyes on her. "Lock the door," she managed to say.

"What happened?" Max asked.

"She thought you were hurt," Grete said.

Dagny felt Max touch her head. "I'm fine, Dag. Just got back late and fell asleep waiting for you."

"There's good reason for her to worry," Tash told him. "Those men from Limer's Town are coming."

"Coming? What?" Max turned to Grete. "They know you're here?"

"Sliver found Dag," Grete said, and began to explain what had happened.

Dagny didn't want to open her eyes. She just wanted to stay here, curled up in bed with Max and her sister and Tash, and never leave. The group continued to talk, but Dagny just focused on Max's hand on her shoulder. She pictured that they were lying by the fireplace in Alex's old house, gazing up at the painting of the Lion's Court. She imagined Grete asleep on the couch, a peaceful look on her face. And she saw Morgan and Alex there, sitting at the table by the window, drinking tea and laughing.

"We need to get Rodolph," Max said. "I'll feel better with him at our side."

"Should we leave the city?" Tash asked.

"They don't even know about you," Grete said. "You need to go back home."

"—I'm not going anywhere."

"The guards... we could go to the Authority," Max suggested.

"Would they help us?" Tash asked.

"No one can help us," Grete said. "They'll find me eventually."

Max moved off the bed. "Gimme that rifle. I'll stay awake. Everyone try and rest. I need to think."

"You know how to use it?" Grete asked.

"Yes."

∞

In the morning, Dagny wrote a note to Alex, telling him about Sliver and the others from Limer's Town. *"I need your help, but please be careful."*

Tash would be the least recognizable, so he volunteered to take the letter to City Centre and then get Rodolph.

Grete snuck around the house with Alex's sabre, looking through windows and double-checking locks. She was convinced it wouldn't be long. Dagny sat with Max outside on the balcony.

The residents of Rork were unaware of what was coming. Privileged men of affluence strolled down the Main Boulevard while their children played in gardens, like any other day. Girls, several years younger than Dagny, walked in front of the Benzara house on their way to school, carrying books and giggling.

"I was thinking all night, but still haven't come up with anything," Max admitted. "We need to do *something*, can't just sit here waiting for them. Do they know you live in Rork?"

Dagny shrugged. "Sliver didn't tell me. Not sure how they would, though. I'm not even sure how Sliver found me."

"Let's see..." Max began, "Alice knew your name, and that we were from the city... and Sliver would've known you were from the Rakesmount originally, because that's where Grete is from. I suppose with some investigation and time, he coulda found out about the Rakesmount girl living with Alex Benzara... *one of the most famous explorers ever.*"

"But he found me at the river docks, not here."

"He probably just followed you there."

"Yeah..." Dagny shook her head. Max was right. It was so easy, and she was so naive and stupid to think they could forget Limer's Town and live in peace.

"You didn't have a choice," Max said. "What were you going to do? Leave your own sister to those freaks? You had to get her. I love you for that. You're brave and you care about others." His hand was on her knee.

"I love you Max. Whatever happens, I want you to know that."

"Nothing is gonna happen to you. And nothing is gonna happen to me. Or Grete. Okay?"

"Okay."

"Now Tash..." Max smiled, "I'm not so sure about..."

Dagny started to laugh. "Stop it."

"I'm just kidding. Tash is gonna be fine, too. He's quick, that one," Max said, tapping his head.

Dagny scooted onto Max's lap, draping her legs over the side of his, hugging him close. "When I thought something had happened to you... it was one of the worst feelings of my life. I can't handle any more loss. There's been too much for me. I can't handle it."

"I'm sorry Dag, I wish I knew what to say."

Dagny grabbed Max's face and looked hard into his eyes. "Don't ruin me, okay? Don't risk yourself. Don't make me happy and then... disappear. Just stay safe."

Max stared at her, wide-eyed, and nodded. She cuddled into him and they sat there for a long while, until Tash returned with Rodolph.

~

They made the decision to try to sneak over to Tash's house. No one from Limer's Town knew about him, and no one but Dagny even knew where he lived. If they could make it there unseen, it would probably be the safest place around. They just needed to hide out until Alex got the letter and returned.

Tash lived north of the Morca, just outside the city walls, in his grandfather's old house. They would leave under the cover of night. Each of them filled packs with everything from hard bread and cheese to jars of pickled fish, cookie tins, candles, blankets, and extra socks. It was best to stock up, so they wouldn't have to leave Tash's house after they arrived. The boys took some shirts from Alex's closet, and Rodolph grabbed a fishing pole.

Once everyone was ready to depart, Dagny led them out the kitchen door and down the back pathway, between the gardens. Max followed directly behind her, with the blanket-wrapped rifle. Everyone watched for any sign of being followed. None of them spoke.

They crossed the canal by the last Scholar's Tower, and worked their way over to the field behind the Rork library, taking care to move in the darkness, avoiding the paved streets.

The River Gate was the busiest route out of the city. It presented the greatest risk they'd be spotted if someone from Sliver's old gang was watching the road. Max took the lead near City Centre, and guided them to a seldom-used postern door, set into the city wall.

"This'll go straight into the fields," he said, pushing open the old wooden door. "It was originally for traders from Satchels. There used to be keys and everything. Now it just sits unlocked all the time."

The stars stretched from horizon to horizon. *The Night Road*, Dagny thought. It seemed fitting that a sky like this would take them to safety. Everyone stayed vigilant and quiet, but she could feel the mood becoming more relaxed.

They followed the city wall north, walking into grass that stood undisturbed and as high as Dagny's waist. She ran her hands over the tops of it, part of her wishing they could just lie down and hide here.

Eventually, a small settlement appeared in the shadow of the wall, containing a dozen or so buildings. Tash led them around the outer edge, and into the back yard of his grandfather's house. It was a formidable structure, with a peaked roof and stone columns. A low, brick wall surrounded the yard, although more for carving out its boundary than defense.

"Was your grandad the mayor or something?" Rodolph asked.

"No. The Archivist, why?"

"This is the biggest house here. That's why."

Inside, the place was stacked with books and maps, pamphlets, hand-written scrolls, thick sheets of woven paper, and every other sort of material used as a writing surface at one time. There were even clay tablets piled under a desk.

"*The Archivist*, right..." Rodolph said. "He sure liked to take his work home with him."

There were three bedrooms on the first floor, and a loft overhead. Tash drew the curtains closed and lit a single lamp, placing it in the middle of the main room.

"We should do watches," Max said. "Just until we know for sure nobody followed us."

"We should do watches for as long as we're here," Tash said.

"Yeah," Max agreed. "You're right."

Tash took the loft. It was where he always slept, anyway. The three remaining bedrooms were split between Dagny, Grete and Rodolph. Max decided to sleep in his bedroll by the front door.

"Think we'll need to stay inside the whole time?" Rodolph asked, as he unpacked his bag. "I can see us getting bored real quick."

"We'd only be so lucky," Dagny said. "If you played Talvarind, you could keep busy. Tash has got every set."

"Oh, great," Rodolph added, sarcastically.

Max took the first watch, positioning himself in front of the side window, facing the street, and peeking from behind the curtain. Dagny joined him, after everyone else had gone to their rooms.

"I was thinking..." Max began to say, "When this is all behind us... if you want... we could take a trip into the Vahnland, or go see the Winter's Palace at the Edge of the World, things like that."

"I don't know," Dagny said. "I'd like to, but I can't think about leaving Grete right now."

"Oh, I meant both of you," Max said.

"It's hard for me to think about stuff like that."

"I understand."

Max continued to stare out the window. He held the rifle on his lap and yawned.

"I'm glad you're back," Dagny said. "I missed you." She couldn't see his face, but it felt to her like he was smiling.

"I missed you so much," he replied. "You have no idea."

"Really?"

"Yeah... you have no idea."

If they didn't have to keep watch, Dagny would've climbed on top of him; kissed his neck, his mouth; would've lifted his shirt off... she desperately wanted to be naked with him right now. It was such a weird feeling. The desire to be close, mixed with the sense of approaching danger. But she couldn't help it.

"What you thinking about?" Max asked.

"...Nothing..."

He laughed. "Sure," and gave her a quick kiss on the cheek.

"You missed," Dagny said. She took his face in her hands, kissing him properly in the darkness. It took a moment, but soon his tongue was playing with her own, tracing her teeth. Dagny sensed him moving the rifle off to the side, and suddenly his hands were on her legs. *Maybe we should stop,* she almost said. They needed to watch the yard. But, instead, Dagny adjusted her position and Max moved his hand high on the inside of her thigh.

She slid onto his lap, and tried to muffle her sounds. The last thing she wanted was to wake the whole house. Max took her around the waist, helping control her movements, then reached into her shirt with one hand, feeling her skin, rubbing his thumb across her breast. They made quick work of it, and soon after that familiar rush of euphoria shuddered through her body, she felt Max jerk underneath. She stayed there for a while, breathing into him and touching his hair, then kissed him goodnight and crept into bed.

∾

Hours later, just before dawn, someone walked past her room, stopped and walked past again.

Dagny slipped out of bed and cracked the door. "Hello?" she whispered.

"Dag..." Grete said, appearing in front of her.

"Are you alright?" Dagny asked, wearily. "Your eyes... you look frightened."

"I had a bad dream. Of that tower in the woods. It was plunged deep into the ground, like a spear, and the earth itself cried in pain. An ocean of blood came pouring out and drowned us..."

"Here, come inside," Dagny whispered, and sat her sister down on the mattress.

"There's another dream too... one I meant to tell you, but didn't..." Grete's voice trembled, filling Dagny with apprehension.

"What was it?" she asked, chewing on her thumbnail.

"I dreamed it just before I left Limer's Town. It stayed with me. Unlike any normal dream that you forget..." Grete stopped and took a deep breath.

"Go on. You can tell me."

"I was in some kinda building, and I couldn't get out. Each door was a puzzle. There were no locks or handles, just symbols and switches, pieces of wood you could turn. Things like that. Something was coming for me, and I had to move quick. All around me were dead animals, I could smell them... it was so terrible. It was like I could feel how they felt just before death. And as I worked my way past puzzle after puzzle, I came to a dark chamber and in the center was a woman. Naked, with antlers coming out of her head. She was sprawled on the floor and her chest was torn open... but inside... beat a heart."

"That's... *horrible...*" Dagny said.

"I knew there was only one way to get free from the prison... I approached the body, and reached inside, grabbing her heart with both hands. It was a black thing and still beat, even after I removed it..." Grete tried to steady herself.

Dagny almost didn't speak, but then heard herself ask, "What happened?"

"*...I ate it... I ate the heart...*" Grete started to clear her throat, like something was lodged inside. "And I could *feel it...* enter me."

Dagny embraced her. "It was just a dream. It's okay."

"I don't think so, Dag, I don't think it was."

"What do you mean? How could it not be?"

"What if Sliver wasn't lying? What if it really was me who opened that box? And I ate what was inside?"

Dagny shook her head. "No, no, that's not possible. He's a liar. You can't believe what he says."

Grete put her face into Dagny's shoulder, and wept.

25

Dagny needed to take her mind off things, for her own sake as much as Grete's.

They sat across from each other on the floor, as Tash made tea, and Max and Rodolph quietly talked. Grete placed the great bear guardian in the center of the board, and carefully withdrew her hand. "Okay... your turn..." she said.

Dagny considered her options. She'd never played the Night Princes before, but thought it fitting that she should play Lucas' favorite, while Grete handled the Wild Court. Dagny finally decided on advancing the Moon Child up to the fourth column, threatening Grete's weak side.

"Did you really beat Tash?" Dagny asked.

"Yep. More than once, too." Grete concentrated on the board, placing her hand over one of the meerkats. She spotted something with Dagny's line, then withdrew it.

"And you never played before coming back to the city?"

"Nope. But I did watch Sliver a bunch, and Tash has been teaching me." Grete went back to the meerkat and moved it behind the bear. "We played pretty much every day."

"Really? I didn't know that."

"You've been busy." Grete looked up at her and flashed a quick smile. Whatever its intended effect, it made Dagny sad. She should've been spending more time with her.

"I always used to imagine what games Morgan must've played with his set," Dagny said, gesturing at the Wild Court. "What types of people he must've met and challenged."

"Talvarind was more of a thing between you two. Maybe he thought I was too young for it back then."

"You're a natural," Dagny said. "You've learned it much quicker than I did."

Max's voice rose abruptly near the back corner of the room: "—No, we need to stay here," he said to Rodolph, then lowered his voice again.

Grete retreated her knight to the back column, but Dagny could tell she was paying more attention to the boys talking than to the Talvarind game.

"...I've never played the Night Princes before," Dagny said, trying to distract her. "Lucas has a set just like this one. He's really sweet. You'll like him."

"Sure."

Dagny advanced the Wizard of Luxdar two extra spaces.

"Hey, you can't move that far," Grete said, her attention suddenly back on the game board.

"Actually the Wizard can move like the Queen from the original Red Guard, but only when threatened with capture, and your rabbit whistler has a clear shot."

"That's tricky..." Grete took a deep breath and stretched her arms. "Okay, now I'm refocused, so you better watch it."

Tash slipped into the room, poured the girls some tea, and fell into one of the armchairs. He watched the Talvarind game as he spoke. "Rodolph wants to head out to the lagoon, to one of the islands, saying we should hide there instead."

"And how long could we really last out there?" Grete said. It seemed like she'd already thought it through. "A whistler can move double once it crosses the river, right?" she asked.

"Yeah," Dagny and Tash said simultaneously.

After Grete played her piece, Dagny picked up the golden cat figurine. "I got this piece and the Wizard for Lucas, on the same day Corlie chased us in City Centre."

"You really care about him, don't you?" Grete asked.

"Lucas? Yes. Of course."

"And that little girl, Abrielle, and Alex and Cate." Grete was smiling.

"Of course. And you will, too." Dagny placed the cat figure behind the Wizard. "When Alex comes back, he'll make all of this right. You'll see. You don't know him like I do. We'll all be safe then." She tried her best to sound convincing, but somehow her words felt hollow. "You better watch your weak side. Your guardian is exposed."

Grete looked at her sister for a long time. "That's alright."

The next morning, she was gone.

"Where is she?!" Dagny yelled, throwing open the front door and rushing into the yard. She scanned the road, then turned back to the house. The three boys stumbled behind her in the doorway. They were moving too slowly.

Dagny ran back at them. "Where is she?!? You were on watch, weren't you?" She poked her finger at Rodolph, who stood there awkwardly. "How did you not see her leave? Were you *sleeping*?"

"No," he said, defensively. "She musta snuck out the window or something."

Dagny pushed past them and pulled on her boots.

"Where are you going?" Max asked.

"I need to find her, before she disappears again. We need to get Sarna and Marfisi."

"Who? The singer?" Max asked. But Dagny was already heading for the street.

"Wait!" Max called, fumbling with his own boots. "I'm coming, but we need to be smart about this. Sliver's men could be watching the road and gates. We need to move slow."

"There's no time!" she shouted.

The boys sprinted after her, catching up in the high grass outside of the settlement. Rodolph had enough sense to grab the rifle, covering it with his jacket.

"Can you talk to me, please?" Max huffed. "Why do we need Sarna or that singer? You think Grete went to them?"

"I don't know," Dagny shot back. "It's the only thing I can think of. There was something between Marfisi and Grete."

"Like what?"

"Something in the woods. I can't explain it right now." Dagny picked up her pace again, jogging along the city's outer wall.

"But why would she leave?" Max asked, matching her speed.

"I don't know!"

"I may have an idea," Tash said, from behind. They all stopped and turned.

"What do you know?" Dagny asked.

"I kind of mentioned the twins."

"What?!" she snapped. "Why would you do that?"

"—Twins?" Rodolph asked.

Tash stiffened. "She asked me what happened in the palace before we found her. I wanted to be honest. I didn't think it was a huge deal."

"You didn't, huh?"

"No, not at first. But then Grete got sorta spooked about it. Thought they might be after her. I told her that was ridiculous."

"Who are the twins?" Rodolph repeated.

"—The Drowned Twins of Gort," Dagny said. "I can't believe you did that, Tash. I really can't."

Max cut in, as they started to walk again. "Can someone explain this?"

"Don't you remember Limer's Town?" Dagny said. "Those strange *people* beyond the church. The bloated man, that naked woman... Sliver told me they started showing up after he found the box. He swore they were after it. Grete probably thinks the twins are after it, too."

"But I thought she didn't take it," Max said.

Dagny just shook her head and started to run.

∞

The market outside of Sarna and Hanette's place was thick with bodies. Dagny pushed her way through, the boys following behind her in a line.

"—All I'm saying is, we gotta be smart about this," Max said. "You're too emotional. You're not thinking straight."

Dagny ignored his comments until she reached the small courtyard in front of Sarna's door, then turned and faced him. "You can leave if you want. Nothing's forcing you to be here. But don't get in the way."

Max was stunned. "I'm not going anywhere. I'm just trying to help you. We were trying to stay hidden, and now we just marched through the River Gate and the market, like it was nothing."

Dagny pounded on the door. Tash must've been thinking the same thing as Max, as he nervously looked over his shoulder and scanned the crowded plaza.

"Hey Dag," Max said, touching her arm. "We're not gonna be able to find your sister if those men find us first." But Dagny shrugged him off.

Sarna answered the door, rubbing her eyes and wearing nothing but a nightshirt. "Umm. Hello? What time is it?" she asked.

"It's Grete..." Dagny responded. "She's gone. I need to find Marfisi. Do you know where she is?

"Umm. Did you check the crossroads?"

"No. Your place was closer, and I thought Feruda might be with you."

"She's not. She was supposed to come over last night, but didn't get around to it, I guess. What's this about?"

"Please, I need to find her."

Sarna threw on some clothes and joined them outside. Dagny told her what happened as they made their way back out the River Gate, following the path toward the crossroads and great forest.

It was late morning when they arrived. The day had gotten colder, even as the sun emerged in the sky. Dagny's feet ached, but she sprinted to the old stables once it appeared in the distance. The place was vacant. Dagny knew it even before she threw the doors open, panting so hard her throat hurt.

Still, she called out. "Grete! Marfisi! Anyone!... Hello?!" Nothing. She rushed up the ladder into the loft. Everything was gone. There were no bedrolls. No piles of clothes or cooking pots. No instruments. The group had left, taking everything with them.

Dagny was coming down the ladder when Sarna and Max entered the building.

"Anything?" Max asked.

"No."

Sarna ran back outside and across the yard to the inn. When she emerged several minutes later, she looked despondent.

"The innkeeper says he saw them leave before dawn," Sarna said. "Heading west. I can't believe they'd just leave like that. You'd think they'd've told me, at least."

Dagny chewed at her thumb. "Do you remember the place in the woods, where Marfisi took us? Think we could find it again?"

Sarna considered it. "We could try."

The five of them continued along, into the sprawling farmlands and toward the forest, looming on the horizon. Up ahead, in the distance, several farmhands could be seen working the land. And on the road leading back to the city, they saw a small group of travelers approaching.

"I take it none of you have a spyglass," Rodolph said, shielding his eyes from the sun.

"Think it could be them?" Max asked.

"Them who?" Sarna replied.

"Sliver's gang."

Tash rushed ahead. "C'mon, let's just get to the woods."

They lost sight of the travelers in the high grass, after cresting and descending a small hill. Who knew if the strangers had anything to do with Limer's Town. Plenty of people used the road to Sternhome. Maybe they were paranoid, but there was good reason to be. Dagny was glad her friends were here, and that Rodolph had taken the rifle. She felt awful for how she treated him earlier.

As they neared the tree line, Sarna walked next to Dagny and took her hand. "I'm sorry, I don't think I'll be able to find the place. I can't even remember where we entered the forest. It all looks the same to me."

But Dagny remembered. One particular gnarled branch, high above their heads, seemed to reach out, gesturing toward the sky. Something about the way it twisted reminded her of the walnut tree back in Rork. She thought it peculiar when she came here the first time with Marfisi.

"Let me know if you see anything," Dagny said to the group, before stepping into the shadowy green. "Otherwise, just let me think."

Somehow, it all came together so easily. She recognized a tangle of moss-covered roots and a pile of stones. Even the brush seemed to rustle the same way as before. They moved slowly. Dagny listened to the wind and birdsong high above. Part of her felt that if she rushed it, she could lose the path, and they'd be lost. She needed to let the woods guide her.

After some time, she found the gully, and the boulder as big as a house, where Marfisi had asked Grete about what lay beyond.

Grete had seen it in her mind. An ancient, broken thing...

"Is that a tower?" Tash asked. He had walked around the boulder, and pointed through a thin break in the trees.

Max and Rodolph wandered over to him, and Sarna glanced at Dagny, a look of concern on her face. "Do you smell that?" Sarna asked. "It smells like blood."

Or rust.

"Hey, I think this tower is metal," Tash called out. "Should we take a closer look?"

Dagny walked forward and breached the tree line, stepping into a clearing. A short distance away rose a slender spire. Just like Grete had described. It was dark as night, almost black, and the top of it was broken and flat – like a giant hand had descended from the heavens and lopped it off. Still, the tower was almost as high as the surrounding canopy. At one time, it must've been *very* tall indeed.

"Alright, what's the plan?" Max asked. His voice was muffled by the wind and rustling branches. "Think Grete and them went inside?"

"—We should take a look around," Rodolph said.

Dagny was in a daze. She moved cautiously around piles of jagged debris and grass-covered stone, walking toward the tower. Something angular and sharp jutted up from the earth, casting shadows that looked like bear teeth over the field.

"Dag, are you going inside?" she heard Max shout. "Hold on, wait for us."

She wandered around the back of the tower and found a gap in the blue metal, where the walls overlapped and separated. An opening.

"That's interesting..." Max said. "I'll go first."

Dagny followed right behind, and one by one, they entered.

She skirted around a curved, inner sheet of metal, like she was walking through a seashell, and stepped into an open, barren chamber. Sunlight seeped in through thin gaps in the wall where the metal had buckled. At the far end of her vision, a set of steps led into the ceiling.

"Grete!" Dagny yelled. Her voice echoed around the room.

They took the stairs to the level above, and entered the heart of the tower. A single staircase continued upward. There must've been rooms here at one time, but all the doors were gone.

"I don't know if we should continue on," Tash said, as Dagny approached the second staircase. "These steps are really old. They could collapse at any time. Besides, Grete isn't here."

"You don't know that," Dagny said, softly. "I'm going up. I'm the lightest anyway." Before anyone could stop her, she cut the corner and began to ascend.

Rusted metal steps funneled her through a rusted metal shaft, and thin slits in the wall looked down on the clearing outside. She ran her hand over rivets as she went, wondering if this whole tower was made of Limer's Town iron, harvested from the mountains of that awful place. The curved passage created the impression that the staircase was closing in on her; that the steps themselves were narrowing. But Dagny trudged on nonetheless, climbing higher, until she finally reached the top and arrived at open sky.

Stretching in front of her was a flat, borderless landing littered with debris. Its edge dropping off into the field below. There was no sign of Grete.

Without moving, Dagny gazed over the forested tree tops surrounding her. A solid block of green. She shouted again for her sister, already knowing it was hopeless.

What was it Marfisi had said? That before the city was built, this tower marked some kind of a passage? Had there been a path here at one time through the forest? Whatever she meant, Dagny saw nothing down there now.

She stepped back into the shadows. This place didn't feel right. Descending the staircase, she paid close attention to her footing. The curved passage was hypnotizing and a long way to tumble if she fell. This was not a good place to get hurt.

When she came back to the main chamber, everyone was gone except for Sarna.

"The boys wanted to have a look outside," she said. "To see if there's any sign of Grete. I told them not to go far. But you know how they are."

"She's not here," Dagny said. "Not anymore, anyway."

"Why do you think Marfisi has something to do with this? What could she possibly have wanted?"

The same thing that the twins want, and the bloated man, and others, most likely.

"It doesn't matter," Dagny said. "Grete is my sister. Not theirs. They had no right to take her away."

"Didn't Grete go looking for them? I mean, is it really Marfisi's fault? Sounds kinda like Gretchen knew what she was doing."

Dagny felt her blood rise. "No. It's Marfisi and them. It's all their fault, including your precious Feruda. They brought her here. They took advantage of her. My sister isn't well. She doesn't think clearly. You have no idea what she's been through."

"You don't have to be mean about it," Sarna said, calmly. "You and Gretchen have something sharp inside, you know that?"

"What are you talking about?" Dagny glared at her.

"See, even now... the way you're looking at me. Like you hate me, just because I say something you don't agree with."

Dagny shook her head. "I can't talk about this now."

"You know, I came all this way, into the forest, just for you," Sarna said, then she walked away, down the stairs and toward the exit.

Dagny was so angry. She shouted, "Just go back! I don't need you here!" But Sarna didn't respond.

When Dagny finally emerged from the tower, Sarna was standing far off at the edge of the clearing with Max. Probably warning him about her. Neither Tash nor Rodolph were in sight. Dagny sat on the ground and stared at the sky. Everyone was leaving her, but what did any of it matter? She'd been alone before. She could just wither away again. No one would care.

On the other side of the clearing, a rifle fired.

26

DAGNY LEAPT TO HER feet and scanned the tree line. She looked over at Max and Sarna, who were doing the same. Where had the blast come from? Somewhere beyond the trees. The echo from the rifle shot faded too quickly for her to determine its exact location.

Rodolph.

She almost shouted for him, then crouched behind a heap of stone near the tower, keeping her eyes on the woods. She hoped the shot had been accidental, but feared the worst.

Max took several steps into the clearing. *What are you doing?* Dagny thought, trying to wave him down. *Go back. Hide.* He hunched over and watched, trying to decide on a course of action.

Again, she concentrated on the tree line, trying to will Rodolph to appear. Envisioning the broad-shouldered boy bashfully apologizing for scaring them. Max would shake his head, and take back the rifle. And Dagny would laugh and hug him. Then they could leave. It was possible Grete never came here to begin with. She just as easily could be hiding somewhere else.

Rodolph. Where was he? And where was Tash?

Max locked eyes with her from across the field, pressing a finger to his lips. Then he moved back into the bushes with Sarna.

Dagny considered working her way around the tower, getting into the trees, and sneaking over to them.

A broad-shaped figure appeared in the shadow of the canopy. Dagny strained her eyes but couldn't make out any features. Then another shape appeared next to it. *Tash?* she briefly thought, ready to step out and greet them, but something held her back. Something was off. She continued to focus on the shapes, when a third figure appeared. And another.

She ducked behind the heap of stone and pressed her face into the grass, her heart pounding in her throat. Jago and the men from Limer's Town. They'd found her. She tried to listen for any sound or movement. There was only a rustling wind. The birdsong had been extinguished in the crash of rifle-shot.

For a few moments nothing happened, but Dagny knew the men were watching the field. They had seen them in the city, most likely, and followed them to the forest. And they'd found Rodolph.

She could run. Crawl to the edge of her hiding place, and then sprint off into the woods. She'd run from the men before. But then what would she do? Leave her friends? Leave Max? They were only here because of her. She hoped Max had already fled, but she knew he hadn't.

Someone stepped through the clearing. They had to be close. Dagny could hear the crunching of dry grass over the wind. She continued to lie flat, too frightened to move.

A hulking, fat-bellied man walked past. Dagny saw the back of his head, tattooed in the shape of a giant beast. He stopped near the tower, and for a brief moment, Dagny thought he would go inside.

Yes. Go inside, all of you. That would be perfect. Then they could escape.

But the man didn't go inside. He scanned the edge of the forest, then walked away from her. Instinctively, Dagny felt a sense of relief, until she realized where the man was headed. Straight toward Max and Sarna.

Another man followed behind him, thinner and carrying a sack that clanked with metal. Dagny didn't recognize him from Limer's Town. How many of them were there?

She held her breath for as long as possible, then slowly exhaled, inhaled, and held it again. She felt exposed, even behind the stone heap, thinking at any moment someone would spot her. She waited for Jago to appear. She knew he was here – looming on the other side of her hiding place, perhaps? Playing a game with her? But he didn't appear, and the other men were getting closer to the forest with Max and Sarna. She couldn't let her friends be caught.

Dagny reached out and grabbed a piece of stone that had broken off from the larger one. Slowly, she pushed onto her knees, took one more deep breath and flung it at the tattooed head.

Before it landed, Dagny turned and began to run toward the opposite end of the clearing, away from Max and Sarna. She'd taken only two steps when a thundering boom exploded nearby, sending bits of stone onto her face. The shot jolted her to the ground. She glanced around in a daze, looking for its source. Across the clearing, near the tree line, stood Jago. He had stepped into the sunlight. Dagny could see his orange mustache, hanging past his chin, as he cocked the rifle and raised it for another shot.

She moved before it fired again. If the men were shouting at her, she couldn't hear it. She couldn't hear anything but a pounding in her ears. The fat-bellied man was running at her now. Jago meant to kill or maim her in the field. Without a second thought, Dagny sprinted into the tower.

Her eyes had no time to adjust to the dim light. She ran blindly through the barren chamber and smelled the scent of old blood when she crossed the rust-stained floor. Dagny raced up the first set of stairs and stopped. Part of her wanted the men to follow, away from Max and the others. What were they doing? She still couldn't hear anything. Maybe the men had already seen her friends and decided to chase them into the forest.

There was no place to hide in the tower. Nowhere to go, but up. She'd be trapped now. Maybe this was where her story ended. Maybe she was supposed to have died in the flood along with her family, or inside the Oracle Tower. Trapped in that awful chimney, and she'd just been playing with borrowed time ever since.

She reached into her jacket, hoping to feel the polished stone that Max had given her, but she'd left it at the Benzara house. Had she really been lucky? Did the Blackstar really watch over her? The eye of Gylathrik, torn out and tossed across the sky. *That's romantic*, she told Max under the stars. He had looked at her and laughed. She might've loved him then. Right at that moment.

From the room below, footsteps thundered on metal. The men were coming for her. Dagny started to run again, rushing up the spiraling staircase. Eventually she would run out of space, but at least she could buy Max some time.

It didn't take long for the men to reach the base of the stairs. Their steps were heavy and furious. Dagny felt the vibration in the walls. She wouldn't survive if they caught her. There was no doubt about that.

She ran as fast as she could, her legs burning as she hurdled over the steps two at a time. Finally, Dagny reached the top of the tower and stumbled into the sunlight, struggling for breath. Pieces of odd junk and old clothing littered the area. There was a strange, peaceful calmness up here. The late autumn wind blew across her face. As she inhaled it, her lungs burned and she began to cough violently.

Dagny moved toward the far edge, but halfway across the landing, she had to stop and grab her knees, her heart thundering in her chest. The run up the tower had taken too much energy. Even with all the adrenaline coursing through her veins, Dagny's body began to revolt.

The men stepped onto the landing behind her. They had slowed, too. Dagny glanced over and saw Jago, holding Alex's silver-plated rifle, but he didn't aim it at her. Instead he held it like a club. Dagny pushed up, off her knees, and moved again, closer to the edge. Unsure of what to do.

Jago said something, then laughed. A sick laugh. The sound of a sadist.

"There's no place for you to go, stupid bird!" he yelled, marching forward.

"*Just go away...*" Dagny pleaded. "*Please! Leave me alone!*"

The man moved closer and grinned.

"What do you want?" she asked.

"I want to have fun with you." Jago closed the gap.

"What do you mean?"

"Stop moving now." In a single motion, Jago sprung toward her and swung the rifle. Dagny didn't see it land. Grim anticipation forced her eyes shut. But she heard the crack of wood on bone, and felt the blinding pain shoot across her hip. The rifle butt found the same spot where Jago had hurt her in Limer's Town. The force of the blow spun Dagny in a circle, spilling her onto the ground. She didn't scream. Instead she spread her hands across the floor and tried to crawl away.

Jago's free hand grabbed her leg and he pulled her back, closer to the middle of the landing. He wouldn't risk her going over the edge; he was planning to do the work himself.

Dagny turned toward him as he dragged her. "Just stop it... Stop it, okay." Her voice quivered, but she tried to speak calmly, like she was talking to one of the children back home. "You don't need to do this." For a moment, Jago hesitated. A look of confusion washed over his face. He was considering something. But the moment was fleeting. His eyes became aggressive once again. Jago yanked her so hard her boot flew off. *He's going to do it. He's going to kill me.*

Dagny sat up and grabbed the rifle before Jago had a chance to bring it down on her chest. Her effort surprised him. He fumbled at it awkwardly, as the gun started to slip. Her heart raced. This was her chance. She pulled and twisted and grasped the thing so hard it felt like the bones in her hands would crack. She screamed with everything she had. Screamed so loud it must've echoed across the entire forest. But she couldn't do it, she couldn't get it away. Jago grunted, stomped at her face and yanked the gun out of her hands. He cocked his fist back and pummeled it into her head. "Don't.. you... do that," he said in short, panting breaths. She tried to cover herself, but one of his fists caught her ear, forcing out another scream.

Finally Jago stopped, gasping for air himself. He gave her a half-hearted kick and took a step back. In that brief instant, an opening appeared. Dagny rolled away, hobbled to her feet, and broke for the stairs. Adrenaline smothered her pain, but her leg wasn't working right. The fat man lumbered over, attempting to cut her off. She knew she could beat him. It was just... the staircase seemed so far away. Jago chased after her. His breathing heavy and strained. She could almost feel it on her neck.

Something popped up from the floor, catching her foot. She stumbled, tried to regain her footing, then tumbled onto her side, smacking her elbow on the hard metal. A numbing jolt shot down to her hand.

Still, she tried to crawl away. Stretching toward the stairs, until a thick-soled boot stepped in front of her face. She would've rolled again, or jumped up and clawed at the man. But there was just nothing left. No strength left to fight.

Dagny turned onto her back, her chest heaving rapidly. She could feel her lips drawn back in a painful snarl. That was it. It was over. Jago mumbled something. She heard the word *kill.*

Dagny looked away from him, trying not to listen. She was crying now. Staggered, aching sobs. Jago's shadow spread over her, blocking the sunlight. She curled into herself, and focused on the glistening metal floor. She wouldn't look at the man, wouldn't give him the satisfaction of seeing the fear on her face.

There was nothing left to do. Dagny gazed across the landing, trying to take her mind away from what was about to happen. Objects littered the floor nearby. A pile of branches, and a boot. A glove, trapped under some rubble. A heavy coat flapping in the wind. She'd had a nice coat once, but she lost it in Limer's Town. These same awful men had snatched it from her. This one was different though. It was a pretty blue, almost matching the landing itself. It looked familiar. Perhaps she'd seen it in another life, perhaps she would see it again in a future one... a greatcoat, with brass buttons... and stained with blood. She caught her breath. It didn't just look familiar. She had actually seen this coat before. *Ferko. That man from the Marsh Rats.*

Dagny looked into the clouds. Jago stood over her. His face was hard, but Dagny didn't focus on it. Instead she focused on something else. A shape. A dark, massive shape in the sky that was bearing down on them.

The fat-bellied man had seen it. He watched, frozen in place; his mouth gaping like a stupid child. But Jago stared at her. And as the giant crow descended, Dagny closed her eyes and covered her head.

Jago laughed again. He must've thought she was hiding from him. His scream was unlike anything she'd ever heard before. Dagny jammed her palms over her ears, trying to block out the sound. Something wet hit her face, and then she heard the fat man scream. It was high-pitched and pleading, like the butchering of a small animal.

She heard soft things hit the landing hard, and something thudded onto the ground far below. A ripping sound, like the shredding of cloth, cut through the other noise, and for a brief moment, one of the men gurgled nearby. Dagny couldn't tell which one. She flattened her body onto the landing, trying to hold on, as the gust from the creature's wings threatened to blow her across the floor. And then, suddenly, it stopped.

Everything stopped. There was no more screaming. No sound but the distant rustling of trees, and the breeze swishing through her hair.

Slowly, Dagny opened her eyes. A mass of misshapen flesh, unrecognizable, curled awkwardly on the floor in front of her, and a tattooed arm, torn from its socket, rested inches from her face. Standing up, she tried to divert her attention away from the mess, focusing on her own footsteps, as she made her way back to the stairs. Just before stepping inside, Dagny turned and looked to the skies, but the crow was gone.

She worked her way down the staircase, in a daze. There was blood on her hands and shirt. She could feel it in her hair. Her head throbbed and her face felt numb. It had all happened so fast. The violence had probably lasted no more than a few seconds. And then, nothing. Was it really over?

She heard someone approaching on the stairs. Boots on metal. Dagny braced herself. One hand on the wall, and her other clinched into a fist. Ready for whatever was coming. She couldn't run anymore.

Max turned the corner, almost stepping straight into her. Dagny reached out and grabbed his shirt, just as he gasped and stumbled backward.

"Dag," he whispered, putting his hands on her face. "You're hurt." He was trying to wipe the blood off, but only succeeded in smearing it across her cheeks.

"It's Jago's... not mine..." she said, calmly. Deep inside, Dagny was surprised at how steady she felt.

"He's dead?" Max asked.

"Two of them are. What about the other men?"

"They ran when that creature went to work and the screaming started. I've never seen anything like that." He was staring at her face. "Are you alright?"

Before she could respond, Max took her bloodied hands and placed them on his chest. He opened his mouth, as if to say something else, then stopped and embraced her.

Outside of the tower, Sarna stood next to Tash, and Rodolph rested by the heap of stone with glazed eyes. His forehead was split and streaks of blood covered his face.

"Dagny..." Tash called out with concern.

"I'll be okay," she said, limping forward. "Is he?"

Max rushed to Rodolph's side. It was clear he hadn't seen his friend before entering the tower. Dagny felt like she should go to him also, but didn't move.

"—We need to get back," Sarna said. "Rodolph needs a physician. He's not well."

"I tried to shoot them," he said, softly. "They just appeared."

Sarna knelt down, trying to reassure him. "Quiet, now. It's okay."

"How did you get away?" Dagny asked. She was surprised by the coolness in her voice.

"I fell... in the brush."

They were still concerned about the other men who had fled, but found their bodies shortly after entering the forest. Something had slaughtered them in the gully, near the giant boulder, leaving nothing but a mound of mangled flesh. For a moment, none of them could believe that the carcasses were human, but then Dagny noticed the thin man's sack of metal, and Max pointed out a scabbed leg and boot.

They stood there for a time, studying the pile from a distance. Strangely enough, it didn't seem as horrifying as Dagny thought it should. She felt relieved. Yet, the rest of them were afraid to cross. "What do you think it was? A bear?" Max whispered, but before anyone could answer, a powerful rustle in the woods nearby sent them hurrying across the gully. They didn't stop until reaching the farmland.

At the crossroads, a local farmer offered transportation back to the city, and left to get a cart. They entered the inn and sat Rodolph down in front of the fireplace. He told them he'd be alright, but his eyes were glassy and distorted.

"He almost got killed because of me," Dagny said softly to Max. "I don't know if I can forgive myself for that."

"It's not your fault," Sarna whispered from behind, but it wasn't clear if she really believed it.

Max touched Dagny's shoulder. "We need to take care of you now. Clean you off. I'm sure there's a bath upstairs."

Once the tub had been filled with steaming hot water, Dagny stripped off her clothes and gingerly lowered herself in. Sarna, Rodolph and Tash were resting in the great room, with plans to leave as soon as the farmer returned. Max stood close by, trying not to stare, but Dagny could tell he was eyeing the bruised marks on her body.

"I don't know what to do now," she said. "About anything."

"Maybe there's nothing you need to be doing," Max replied, as he began to ladle water out and pour it over her head. "You know what happened today, with all the violence?"

"What?"

"Jago and the ones who were after Grete... they're all gone. Your sister won't have to worry anymore."

"There are others, though, still out there. Things like that bloated man we saw, and the twins... and the rest of Sliver's men." She felt defeated. Like all the energy had been sapped from her heart. "There are so many more."

Max took a cloth and began to gently wash Dagny's skin. "Maybe. But we don't even know for sure if they're after her. It's just a lot of guessing."

"I wish I could kill all of them," Dagny said, staring at the dirty water. "Then she'd be safe. Then she'd come back to me."

Max paused before speaking. “I understand what you’re saying, but you’re not a killer, Dag. Don’t let them turn you into something different.”

She looked down at the grit underneath her fingernails, wondering if it would ever come out.

27

THEY LEFT THE CROSSROADS and the great forest behind.

The ride back to the city seemed to take hours, with most of it occurring in silence. The farmer's cart set a slow pace, and Dagny's hip ached with every bump in the road. After her bath, she had to dress in the same shirt and trousers, crisp with dried blood, but left her ruined jacket by the old stables. She would burn her clothes in the garden back home.

The late afternoon slipped by slowly. There was a calming breeze over the grass as they traveled, and the finches came out to dart and play in the field. Dagny knew the children of Rork would be out now too, laughing as they hunted each other in the cobbled courtyards and quiet alleyways. She felt the sun, low in the sky, warm her neck, and watched the land turn from warm brown into rich gold. Max sat next to her, seemingly unsure of what he should do. At one point, he briefly tried to take her hand, but when she didn't give it, he let it go and didn't try again.

They arrived at the River Gate just before dusk, where Rodolph, Tash and Sarna parted ways.

"We need to get him to a physician," Sarna said. "Just to be safe."

"Do you need anything?" Tash asked Dagny before departing.

"Thank you, but I'm fine," she responded.

Tash eyed Max. "Take care of her please."

"I'll try, but she's not that good at being taken care of," Max said, trying to lighten the mood.

"This is true," Tash said with a laugh.

A part of her wanted to smile and laugh with him, but then Sarna tugged Tash's sleeve and told him to "come along."

It hurt seeing Sarna become so distant. In a way, it hurt more than Dagny's throbbing hip and head. She'd almost died at the tower, and Sarna had barely said a word to her. She wondered how everything had changed so quickly.

Max and Dagny took the main road through City Centre, passing several cafes by the Rork Library. Max asked if she wanted some food, as they hadn't eaten since last night. Dagny just shook her head. She didn't know if she'd ever be hungry again.

"I'd like to stay with you tonight, if you don't mind," Max said once they reached the Benzara house.

"I don't mind."

"Tomorrow, I'll need to check on Rodolph. I feel like I shoulda left when he did. I thought maybe you needed me more." Max waited for a response, and when it didn't come, he continued, "Dag?"

"Yes."

"I don't really know what to say. I don't want to say the wrong thing." He nervously rubbed his arm as she unlocked the front door. "I'm not that good with words."

"That's alright. You don't need to be."

They walked through the house and into the back garden. The sun had completed its journey, and the yard was lit only by the stars. Dagny gathered some tinder and started a small fire in the open hearth, where

Alex and Cate would sometimes sit with the children to tell stories and watch the sky.

She stood there, watching the fire for a while, before removing her clothes and tossing them to the flames. Her mind was blank. She felt no panic or relief, no fear or sadness. It was as if the entire world had faded away and was replaced by a nothingness. She glanced down at her body, and the bruises that had taken shape on her thighs and hip. She had no idea how long she'd been standing there, but when she finally turned around, Max was sleeping on the ground.

Dagny lay next to him, looking up at the stars. She found Azathur's head and followed its gaze eastward to the Herald's Star, just like Grete had shown her. For a long time, she traced the Glitter Rat's Trail, until she finally lost it, and closed her eyes.

Max left in the morning to find Sarna and visit Rodolph. Dagny gave him a stack of treasury notes to pay the physician and for whatever else might be needed. Although Max didn't ask, he lingered at the door, waiting to see if she would come along. But Dagny felt too guilty about everything to go. She could tell that Max was disappointed as he left, glancing back at her when he reached the main road.

The emptiness of the Benzara home seemed overwhelming. Dagny took her time, wandering though the quiet halls in a half-daze, stopping just outside of Grete's bedroom. It felt emptier than all the others. Her sister's sweater, rescued from Limer's Town, was neatly folded on the dresser. But there was something else there, too. Glinting in the light. Dagny entered the room and walked over to the dresser. Protruding from underneath the old sweater was a tin bracelet carved with flower petals. Dagny almost choked when she saw it. The bracelet from Gretchen's father, the one Finkel had forced Dagny to sell in the market, then slapped her raw when she refused. She put her hand to her face, rubbing the cheek where she'd been hit all those years ago. Was that the first time she felt real pain or fear? She had thought the ogre meant to kill her then.

She must've told Grete about the bracelet's hiding place, although Dagny couldn't remember doing so, or where she had even hid it. *Somewhere under rotting floorboards.*

She pulled the sweater over her head and clasped the bracelet on her wrist. The fit on both was tight, but Dagny didn't mind. It felt to her like she was being embraced.

The men arrived at the front door while Dagny sat on her balcony overhead. Three men, all dressed in dark brown capes that glistened with an oily shine. Each held pistols at their sides.

"You there, girl," one of the men called to her. "Are you the Benzara ward?"

"I am. Who are you?"

"Come down here then, unlock this door." The man stood erect, with a trimmed black beard.

"That's quite alright," Dagny said. "I think I'll just say up here, if you don't mind."

The bearded man huffed his displeasure with her response, but quickly regained himself. "Are you alright? Is anyone up there with you? Anyone... *dangerous* around?"

"You're late," she said.

"What's that, then?"

"Nothing. I'm fine. There's no one else here. You're from the Authority? I don't recognize your uniforms."

"We are. We're here to help you. Alexander Benzara is approaching. He should arrive this afternoon. We are going to have a look around... secure the area."

"Suit yourself." Dagny watched as two of the men split off, disappearing around the house. The man with the black beard entered the courtyard below and began looking through the bushes.

"You can never be too sure," the man called up to her. "You'd be surprised where scoundrels can hide."

"I suppose. Although I really don't think they're around anymore."

"Well, if they are, we'll find them," he shouted back, almost comically, from underneath a hedgerow.

Alex was arriving today. Dagny almost couldn't believe it. He'd received her letter, and sent these soldiers ahead to protect her and Grete. Only too late.

"Do you *know* Alex?" Dagny asked the man below.

"Not personally, no. But I'm familiar." He stood and dusted off his leggings. "The men we're looking for, they're from Limer's Town?"

"Yes," she answered.

"Full of degenerates, that place." The man sounded like Maris.

"Not everyone," Dagny said, almost to herself.

"What's that?"

"I said, *not everyone!*"

"It's still best to be avoided." The man walked into the middle of the courtyard, facing the road. He had the straightest back Dagny'd ever seen. "The message we received mentioned two girls," the man added. "Is there another?"

"There was. But she's gone."

"I see. Well, we are here to protect you now. There's nothing to worry over. And if there's anyone looking to do you harm, hiding out in Limer's Town, we will root them out as well. There will be no more clemency. Not from the Authority." The man seemed to be speaking as much to himself, as to her.

Without another word, Dagny stepped into her bedroom and closed the balcony door. She'd just wait inside until Alex returned. She didn't want to hear about Limer's Town, or the promises of hardened men to protect her. Even Alex had been a disappointment, although she really couldn't think of what he did wrong. Still, he had let her down just the same.

When Alex did arrive, he threw the front door open and shouted for her. There was panic in his voice and his breathing was heavy, as if he'd run the entire way from Cate's estate. He rushed into her bedroom and lifted her with strong, powerful arms. Dagny could sense the desire to let her emotions pour out and give in, allow Alex to comfort her. But nothing happened.

"I'm fine. You can put me down," was all she said. Alex nodded and returned to the soldiers outside. An hour later, three more men appeared, and by nightfall the house was surrounded by a dozen.

It would be six more days before Alex sent an escort to fetch Cate and the children. By then, Sliver's Crescent Lounge had been raided by the Authority. Alex wouldn't discuss the details, but told Dagny she'd never have to worry about those men, *ever again*. The tone in his voice had a confident finality to it.

Dagny spent the winter locked in her room, or in Alex's study reading, or wandering the gravel pathways that split the Old Rork gardens. Max continued to come by regularly, but most of the time they would just end up sitting awkwardly in the parlor or going on short walks. She didn't understand what had happened, or why there seemed to be a difficulty connecting. He would invite her to Stardust, or to visit Rodolph, but she couldn't bring herself to do either one.

The only other thing to happen that winter was the discovery of Magu Ogden. It was the day before the Winter Festival, as Old Rork was busy decorating for the parades and celebration, when a man from the Authority unlocked the last Scholar's Tower. The district mayor had an idea to drape the structure in colorful banners, flowing down from the rooftop. Ogden was found in the meditation chamber, in a dark, windowless room, frozen in the cold. The Mayor's men thought he was dead, at first — motionless as he was. But Ogden was still very much alive. Alex was one of the first to arrive, and brought the old man home. Fashioning a room for him, in the place where Grete used to sleep.

Two days later, a striped, orange cat began to appear in their gardens out back. It made her think of the Wizard of Luxdar tale, told all those months ago by the shopkeeper's assistant in City Centre. Dagny thought it more than a coincidence. Maybe the cat was seeking out Ogden, the Wizard of Luxdar, wondering when they would return to the stars. Ready to keep the darkness at bay.

"I think you should come with me to Satchels and Iverry this spring," Max said one day, as they stood by the icy canal. "It won't take long, maybe just a day or two. My father will be dropping off some goods to a couple trader friends up there. I think you'll like the river... and if I'm right, we could go to Vahnes after."

"I'm not sure," she said.

"Come on now, Dag. I'm really trying here. This isn't good for you, giving up on everything."

"What am I giving up on?"

"I don't know, life?"

"That's not fair," she said, shivering from the cold.

"You said before that you couldn't bear to lose me, you remember that? Well, I'm still here, but you're losing me all the same. I need something more from you."

"Or what, you'll leave?" Dagny asked, challenging him.

Max stared at her. "Is that what you think? No. I'm just telling you how I feel. I'm not going anywhere. I'm just upset."

Dagny stepped to the edge of the canal, being careful not to slip. "Isn't it odd to think about how this same water can take you anywhere in the world? Across the lagoon and into the Shallow Sea. It'll even connect to the Ilvar, eventually, and take you to Ostrotha."

"Really? That's your response?"

"Where do you think she went, Max?"

He hesitated, before speaking again. "If I knew, I'd go get her for you."

"To Jud? That's where I think Marfisi wanted to take her."

"I don't know much about those stories," Max said.

Dagny nodded, still gazing at the frozen water. "Me neither... I'll go with you. I'll go to Satchels and Iverry, okay?"

"You will? Seriously?" Max asked, his face hopeful and pure.

Dagny touched his hand. "Just know that I'm trying my best."

⁂

Come spring, as the ice began to melt, they discussed their plans to travel to Vahnes. Max's father would leave them at the Water Inn by Iverry. They'd take one of the fancy Vahnland carriages into the heartland, going the long way round, and stop to visit the glass blowers near Storie Lake.

The days grew longer again, and Dagny felt more herself, shedding the bleakness that accompanied winter. She looked forward to being alone with Max, lying in bed and feeling his body. With both of their houses so full now, the opportunities to be close were almost nonexistent.

Although the nights stayed cool, it was pleasant enough for the Benzara family to gather outdoors, over the open hearth where Dagny burned her clothes months before. She never told Alex what really happened that day, just that they ran from Jago and hid. She would keep the crow a secret. Even from Alex. Who knew what harm could come from revealing her savior? The Marsh Rats had wanted to trap and destroy it, for no reason other than Man's desire to control and possess. She trusted Alex, but still...

Alex did ask about Grete, of course. She told him the truth about that. Grete didn't want to endanger them, so she left in the night.

⁂

"Tell us a story, Dag," Lucas said, facing her with his back to the fire.

"What kind of story do you want to hear?"

Caternya held the baby, Morgan, while Alex worked the hearth. Abrielle had bundled herself so tightly that nothing showed except her eyes.

Lucas chewed his lip, carefully considering her question. He was holding one of his Night Prince figures, the Moon Child, and held it up. "Do you know one about him?"

"Hmm... let me think..." Dagny said. Cate smiled at her and Abrielle watched intently. Her wide eyes peeking out over the blanket. "Yes, I remember now," Dagny continued, making it up as she went. "The Moon Child... he was born a long time ago, in the underground, and always dreamt of reaching the stars. But he was so far away from them, and it was so lonely down below. He would travel the ancient roads and passageways, seeking out the hidden, forgotten creatures and beasts that knew the old secrets, and begged them to share their knowledge."

"There's roads underground?" Lucas asked.

"Oh yeah. They're all over the place," Dagny said.

"Why? Where do they go?"

"No one really knows. They were built long ago, and people forgot."

"Ah, the Under Road," Alex said absently, as he prodded the fire.

"You know about the Under Road?" Dagny asked.

"—Dad thinks he knows everything!" Lucas shouted.

Alex laughed. "I know enough. The Under Road was carved out before any of the great cities were built."

Lucas was skeptical. "Who did it then? If there were no people?"

"A giant rat!" Alex responded, making a silly face in the firelight.

Both children screeched and giggled.

"No way," Lucas said.

"Oh yes. He came down from the heavens. You see, the rat used to be up there," Alex said, pointing to the sky. "Thousands and thousands of years ago. The creature had followed the Night Road for so long, he'd memorized it, and when the rat finally visited the earth, he created it again in the deep below."

Dagny's mind began to turn.

"You're messing up Dag's story," Lucas said. "Go on, please."

She thought for a moment before continuing, keeping her eyes on Alex. Looking for the slightest reaction. "The Moon Child had heard of a great shifting city, and of a giant king soaked in blood... Do you know that one, Alex?"

"I don't think so. Should I?"

Dagny could tell he was paying more attention to the fire than to her. "Just wondering if you'd heard it," she said.

Caternya gave a polite cough, intended to grab Dagny's attention. "I hope this story is appropriate for children."

Lucas shook his head. "Of course it is, mother. Please go on..."

Dagny did her best to try and finish the tale. Telling Lucas about how the Moon Child encountered an immortal engineer, who built an enormous metal tower to the sky, and allowed the Child to use it so he could reach the stars. Lucas seemed satisfied enough with the ending, and spent the rest of the evening holding his Night Prince close to his face.

Alex abandoned the fire, content with letting it slowly burn out, and sat down to hold Cate and the baby. Dagny didn't know what to make of Alex's mention of the Under Road, and when she tried to ask him more about it, he just said he'd tell her later.

28

"Do you see it yet?" Jauson Tasher asked.

Magu Ogden lifted one of his glass knights, then scratched his chin, studying the board.

"Don't rush him," Dagny whispered.

"I'm not rushing," Tash replied. "Just asking."

They had spent the entire morning playing Talvarind under the walnut tree. Tash had won every game so far. Beating Max twice, Lucas once and even Alex. Only now, Dagny could sense the match starting to shift. Tash continued to act confident, almost cocky, but Dagny knew his game all too well. Ogden actually stood a chance.

Tash was at a disadvantage, of course. He played the Caltra Teamen, having returned Ogden's famed Court of Jud. "I enjoyed it, but it belongs to you," Tash had said. "Besides, it'll give me a reason to practice something else."

At first the old man didn't seem to recognize the set, but as the weeks passed, Ogden became more and more animated. He began to study the figures and would orchestrate moves by himself. He started to leave the house with Alex or Dagny, and they would walk the oak-lined streets to the Rork library and back.

Dagny would have to reintroduce herself to Ogden every day, as fragile as his mind was. Every morning he would watch her with distrustful eyes, until she mentioned she was the sister of Morgan Losh. Ogden seemed to remember her bother vividly. Recalling details even she had forgotten. The toughest part was when Ogden would ask if Morgan would be stopping by. Dagny found it easier to lie, telling the old man that Morgan was off on an adventure, but would be back soon enough. By the next day, Ogden had forgotten everything once again.

"Ahh..." Ogden said under his breath. "I see what you've done there, boy."

Tash smiled, but Dagny could tell he was nervous.

"And what do you think I've done?" Tash asked.

"Drawing me into your trap... Maybe that trick would work on lesser minds, but you've found yourself challenging another master, don't you know." Ogden placed his knight behind his queen, Odestinas. "Your go, boy."

Tash swept his hair back and leaned close to the board. "I'm not gonna go easy on you. I don't care that you're friends with Alex."

"I'd expect nothing less," Ogden replied.

Tash never went easy on anyone. Even when he played Lucas earlier today, he demolished the boy in five moves. If Grete beat him, she did it fair.

The two masters continued to exchange moves. Dagny found their positions confusing and had no clue what either of them had planned, yet she watched intently, trying to follow along. Maybe she was slipping, herself. Dagny hadn't played Talvarind since that last night with Grete. She just couldn't bring herself to look at the pieces. But with the passing of winter, and the renewal of spring, Dagny felt like a change was in order. She had brought down her brother's set, the Wild Court, and sat patiently with it on her lap.

Tash created a defensive line in front of his king, while trying to create an opportunity to advance his magistrate, but Ogden broke through with his glass knights. "I saw it coming, you know," Tash said, when it was over. "You just got lucky with the initiative."

"Ah. Luck," Ogden said. "Yes. Maybe."

Max wandered over, clearly impressed. "Nice job. I've never seen anyone beat him."

"It happens," Tash replied. "Anyway, who's next? Who wants to take on the great Magu?"

"It's Dag's turn," Lucas said, causing everyone to look her way.

"You're playing?" Tash asked.

"I was thinking about it."

"Okay then, let's see what you got." Tash scooted over to let her take a place at the table.

"Is everyone gonna watch me?" Dagny asked the group.

Max just laughed and then turned his gaze up to the clouds.

"Dad!" Lucas called. "Dagny's gonna play, come see! She's really good!"

"I'm a bit rusty, so be forgiving," she said, while opening her case. She noticed Ogden staring vacantly at the ground.

"*Ogden...* are you alright?" she whispered.

The man broke his gaze and looked at her. A flash of fear across his eyes. "Huh? What now?"

"We don't have to play, if you don't want."

Max put his hand on Ogden's shoulder. "Wanna sit this one out? Dag can play Tash."

"Sure," Tash said. "You just watch."

Alex came over and helped Ogden into the shade, while Tash began to set up his own figures. "I missed playing you," he said with a smile.

"Me too." Dagny reached into her case and started to remove her rabbit whistlers. "It's been hard..."

"You don't have to explain it. I understand. It's been hard for me, too."

"You really liked her," Dagny said.

"Yeah, I really did."

She made a line on both columns with the pieces she would play. Plucking them out one at a time until there was only one spot left. Then stopped.

"What's wrong?" Tash asked.

"It's..." Dagny looked around her feet and under the table. "That's weird."

"What?"

"My bear. It's not here."

Tash stood and scanned the ground. "Really? Did you drop it?"

"No. I don't think so."

Max came over and joined the search. "When did you see it last?" he asked.

Suddenly, Dagny stopped looking and started to cry.

"Dag..." Max said, sitting next to her.

"I'm alright... I was just thinking about her."

"Yeah." Max hung his head and nodded.

"The bear's not missing," she sniffled. "Grete took it."

"Why would she do that?" he asked.

"I don't know."

"Maybe she wanted something to remember you by."

"Maybe."

Just then Magu Ogden muttered something under his breath. Dagny turned and saw him observing the Talvarind board.

"You say something?" Tash asked him.

But it was Alex who spoke. "*Calregale Untroth.* It's the old name for your guardian. The missing bear."

"I've... never heard that," Dagny said, wiping the last tears from her cheek.

"The whole set is based on myth," Alex explained. "Actually, a lot of them are. Take the Court of Jud, for example."

"Yeah. I know the history," Tash said. "There's Odestinas, the first queen..."

"Did you know she was supposedly buried somewhere around here?" Alex asked.

"No."

"Yes. Somewhere far below. People have been looking for her for a thousand years. That's a puzzle that will never get solved."

Dagny cleared her throat. "And *Calregale Untroth*? What's that mean? You said it's the bear?"

"That's right," Alex answered. "The sets are actually connected, in a way. The Court of Jud represents the first part of the Odestinas saga, and the Wild Court, the second. You see she was exiled from that place, Jud."

"—By the Imposter!" Tash said.

Alex nodded. "The great bear guardian was her protector, and followed her into the Great Below."

"The Great Below, huh? That's interesting," Tash said. "Isn't that *interesting* Dag?" The way he was looking at her... Was Tash thinking about the old palace as well?

“Yes that is interesting,” Dagny said, then shrugged. “It’s just a piece though. Grete knew I carved it, that’s all there is. I’m glad she has it.”

So instead of playing the bear, Dagny fielded an extra lion, and tried to calmly play through the next game. Tash could’ve been done with her quickly but dragged it out, which frustrated Dagny greatly. When they were done, she told everyone that her head hurt and wandered up to her bedroom.

Deep inside, Dagny knew she’d return to the underground one day. She just didn’t expect it to be so soon. She knew that Grete had gone somewhere with Marfisi, and she knew the singer was connected to Jud. Were they looking for this Odestinas queen, too? Like so many others?

Grete had taken the bear, but why? She recalled Tash talking about the bear so many months ago. He said it was the protector of the Court, but destined to sacrifice itself. And now Alex mentioned something similar. Did Grete know she was heading into the underground the night she left, and did she need a protector? Or was Grete sacrificing herself for Dagny and the others? Whatever it was, Dagny felt like Grete was trying to send her a message... She didn’t have all the answers, but knew someone who might help.

Dagny also knew there was danger in the Great Below, and thought of the Drowned Twins of Gort. She wouldn’t risk anyone else’s life this time. She loved all of them, really. Rodolph and Tash, and Sarna — even though they hadn’t spoken since the forest. And Max. Especially Max. She knew that if she mentioned her plans, he would come. There’d be no stopping it.

So early in the morning, before dawn, Dagny wrote a letter to him. He’d be there soon, expecting to take her to Vahnes. She apologized for leaving him now, and hoped he’d forgive her if she vanished forever.

Then she snuck down the trellis with her adventuring pack, and stuck the letter in her front door.

At City Centre, she boarded a river ferry to Lomenthal, and watched the city disappear around a bend. She arrived at the Station in the early evening; had dinner with the Steward; and, once night fell, she left her bedchamber and wandered to the ballroom. She was hoping to see the lights again, but she found nothing.

She stepped outside and walked around the pathway bordering Deep Lake, then crawled over to the old well. She tried to empty her mind as she made her way down and into the cistern. Fear wouldn't do her any good.

She stripped naked and shivered across the underground lake. She found the old palace kitchens, and when she nervously entered the dining room where she'd seen the spirit lights, she found the broken wall. It was no longer the jagged crack that had trapped the twins. It was now a gaping hole, where Galwed had dug her way out.

She passed over the crumbled stone and found the copper door: busted and bent, laying flat on the ground. The star prism was there. The same ancient thing that had brought Maris to Alex all those months ago. It was tossed carelessly on the ground. Abandoned. Maris hadn't listened to her. She wondered if the twins had him now.

She sucked in breath, and steadied herself. She wandered into the Archives, her lantern reflecting rich tones of amber and gold. She wanted to shout for Melwes, but despite the courage that had brought her here, she was afraid. She scanned the walls for his cramped space, where they'd spent that first night, but there was only solid stone. Like it had vanished completely.

The boy had come from somewhere beyond. He was not an orphan of the city as she first thought. He'd come from the same place as Marfisi, Feruda and the others. Dagny just knew he had. And the boy knew the Under Road... if she could just find him.

Onward she went. Into the darkness. A wanderer in a land of endless night.

She stumbled upon old, unfamiliar passages, with carvings of beasts on the wall. Beasts she didn't recognize: an enormous bull with four horns, a sleeping bear covered in thorns. She was lost now, but hopeful that she was on the right path. Hopeful she would see the boy again, and that he could lead her into the Great Below. Dagny touched the tin bracelet on her wrist. She would find her sister. She refused to let her go.

Something twinkled in the distance. Floating in the air.

Dagny turned her lantern out, and stepped into the light.

About the Author

Michael Breen grew up in Florida and has a background in theatre (favorite playwrights tend to be a bit dark and Irish). He used to write simple songs with good friends and still listens to the same punk bands that he did in high school. Michael likes truthful fantasy, books that are fearless, and British TV shows. When not writing, he is usually thinking about writing or trying to figure out how a mandolin works.

Ever the Night Road is Michael's debut fantasy novel. It won the gold medal for fantasy in the 2023 Independent Publisher "IPPY" Book Awards, the gold medal for young adult fantasy in the 2023 Readers' Favorite International Book Awards, and a bronze medal in the U.K.'s Wishing Shelf Book Awards. The sequel, Jud, was released in January 2024.

For more content and info on new releases, please visit:

MichaelBreenBooks.com.

Customer reviews allow independent authors to continue sharing their stories. Please consider leaving a review on your chosen platform.

The adventure continues...

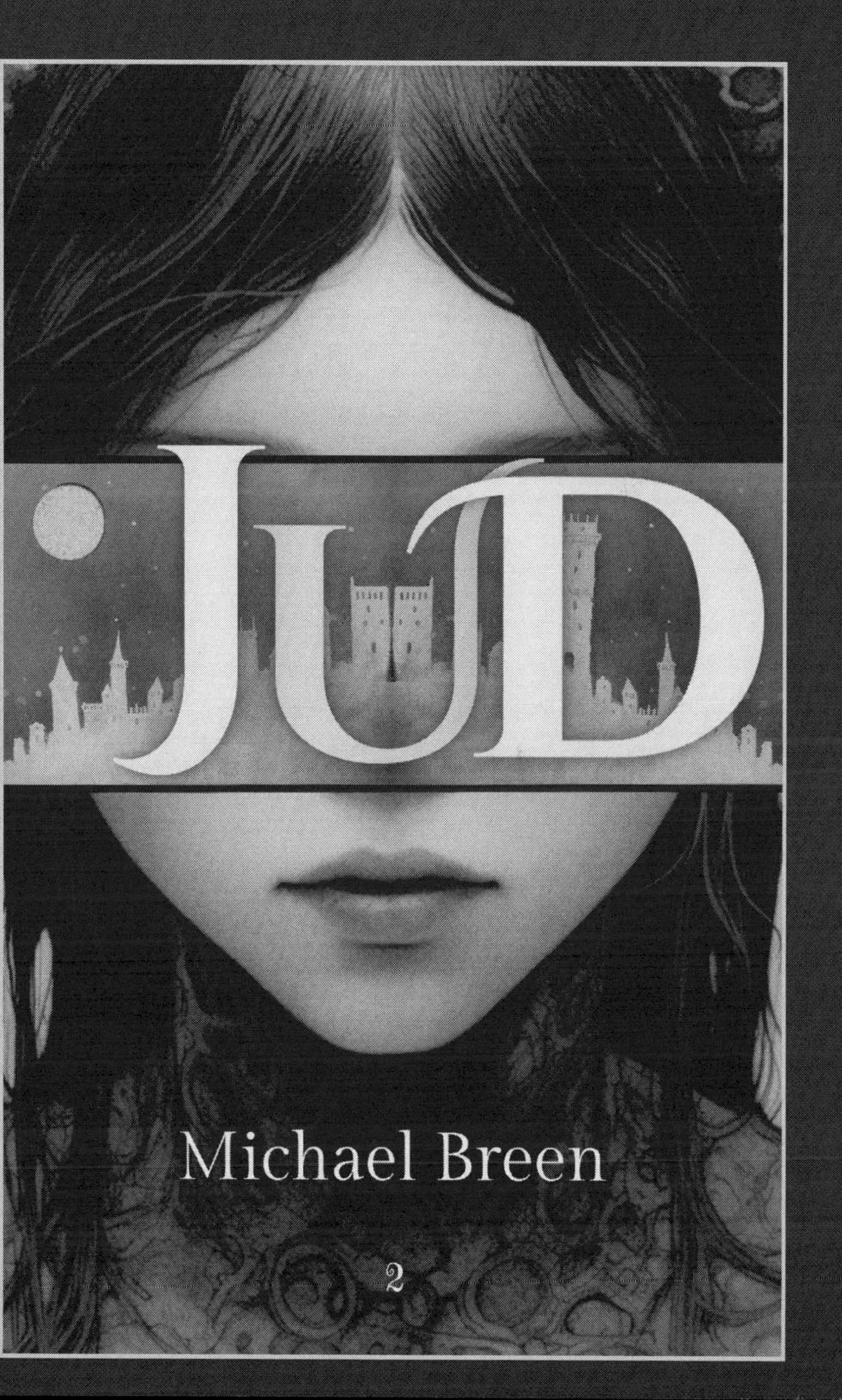

Made in the USA
Columbia, SC
25 June 2024

0df31b15-ab1c-4d6a-a545-61a68f6d8e70R03